Peter Wicked

The Matty Graves Novels
by Broos Campbell

No Quarter

The War of Knives

Peter Wicked

Peter Wicked

a Matty Graves novel

Broos Campbell

McBooks Press, Inc.
www.mcbooks.com
Ithaca, NY

Published by McBooks Press, Inc. 2008

Dust jacket and book design by Panda Musgrove.

Dust jacket illustration composited by Panda Musgrove.

Cover composite created from the following images:
Map: "A map of the most inhabited part of Virginia containing the whole province of Maryland with part of Pensilvania, New Jersey and North Carolina." Drawn by Joshua Fry & Peter Jefferson in 1751, courtesy of American Memory, Library of Congress.
Pistol: used under licensed from Shutterstock.com: copyright © 2007, Lagui.
Blood spatter: licensed from iStockphoto.com: copyright © 2008, nicolecioe.

Library of Congress Cataloging-in-Publication Data

Campbell, Broos, 1957-

Peter Wicked : a Matty Graves novel / by Broos Campbell.

p. cm.

ISBN 978-1-59013-152-7 (alk. paper)

1. Graves, Matty (Fictitious character)—Fiction. 2. United States. Navy—Fiction. I. Title.

PS3603.A464P48 2008

813'.6—dc22

2008012149

All McBooks Press publications can be ordered by calling toll-free 1-888-BOOKS11 (1-888-266-5711). Please call to request a free catalog.

Visit the McBooks Press website at www.mcbooks.com

Printed in the United States of America

9 8 7 6 5 4 3 2 1

To Mo

Dramatis personae

Matty Graves, recuperating from a brain fever.
Lieutenant William Trimble ("Cousin Billy"),
former commander of the *Rattle-Snake,* deceased.
Lieutenant Peter Wickett, commander in the *Breeze.*
Humbert Quilty, naval surgeon at Le Cap.
Greybar, a cat.
Corbeau, a captivated Frenchman.
Cyrus Gaswell, commodore of the San Domingo squadron.
Dick Towson, a planter's son.
Ben Crouch, acting bosun in the *Breeze.*
Freddy Billings, ship's boy in the *Breeze.*
Jubal, Dick's slave.
Gypsy, ship's cat in the *Breeze.*
Plank, master of a log canoe.
Zeus, Plank's crew.
Captain Tingey, superintendent of the Washington Navy Yard.
Lieutenant Crawley, Tingey's adjutant.
Whitlow, Tingey's clerk.
P. Hoyden Blair, assistant U.S. consul in San Domingo.
Arabella Towson, Dick's sister.
Uncle Jupe, Jubal's father.
Elver Towson, a planter.
Lily Towson, his lady.
Phillip Graves, Matty's half-brother.
Geordie Graves, Matty's brother, deceased.
Constance Graves, Phillip's wife.
Mèche, a pirate.
Asa Malloy, captain of the *Constellation.*
Fugwhit, barman at the Quid Nunc Club.
Pratt, a privateersman.
Patrick Fletcher, captain of the *Insurgent.*
Old Man Graves, Matty's father.

Peebles, midshipman in the *Tomahawk.*
Fred Horne, acting-bosun in the *Tomahawk.*
Gundy, a West Countryman
rumored to know summat about smuggling.
Erne Eriksson, seaman in the *Tomahawk.*
Liam O'Lynn, ditto.
Bob Wilson, ditto also, plus his mate.
Benjamin Hillar, captain of the *Pickering.*
John Rogers, sailing master in the *Pickering.*
Zamora, captain of a Spanish *guarda-costa.*
Simpson, waister in the *Tomahawk.*
Hawkins, ditto.
Yancy, acting sailmaker in the *Tomahawk.*
Browbury, master of the *Horseneck.*
Martha, his daughter.
Oxford, captain of the *Choptank.*
Brownstone, his first lieutenant.
Halliwell, a lieutenant in the *Choptank.*
Smiley, a midshipman in the *Choptank.*
Doc, ship's cook.
Agnell, an English renegado.
Kennedy, a wild Irishman.
Martin, late captain of the *Shearwater.*
Isaiah B. Harrison, a bellyacher.
Manson, a British mutineer.
Morris, ditto.
Jakes, ditto also.
Jeffers, a man with a broken head.
Cocro, a man at Charlotte Amalie.
Kakerlak, his pal.
Lamb, skipper of a Yankee bark.
Mrs. Ebeneezer Bunce, a George Town matron.
Mr. Adams, president of the United States.
Mrs. Adams, his lady.

Peter Wicked

ONE

Grenadiers, à l'asso!
Se ki mouri zaffaire à yo.
Ki a pwon papa,
Ki a pwon maman.
Grenadiers, à l'asso!
Se ki mouri zaffaire à yo!

I turned out of my hammock to watch a couple of Toussaint's battalions march up the road that morning. The heavy companies sang the song of the grenadiers as they stepped along, the one about how they have no papa and mama, and them that dies, that's their own affair, with the fusiliers joining in on the chorus. It sounds fiercer than lions in French, and doubly so when it's roared out by sixteen hundred ex-slaves stomping past in new boots and the drums all rattling like sixty. The men were decked out in smart blue coats with white facings and red piping, and snug white britches and black gaiters instead of the usual loose brown trousers, but they'd pulled down the brims of their bicorns and made them comfortable and shady, like old campaigners always do. The war between Toussaint's blacks and Rigaud's mulattoes was pretty much over. The troops were on their way to do the Spanish a mischief over on their side of the mountains in Santo Domingo, which we called it that to distinguish it from the French side, which we called San Domingo.

That's where I was, in San Domingo on the island of Hispaniola. I kept telling myself that. Sometimes I forgot.

The dust still hung in the air, drifting in the pillars of light among the paw-paw trees.

Mr. Quilty's patient was taking God's own time in dying. I distracted myself with a few turns up and down the road in the shade of a paw-paw tree, tallying up all I'd accomplished in our quasi-war with France. I'd gotten Cousin Billy shot dead in a duel, and then I'd sunk the *Rattle-Snake* schooner out from under Peter Wickett during a brawl with *L'Heureuse Rencontre* and the *Faucon,* a privateer corvette and an old frigate with two hundred infantrymen aboard. We'd stopped them from raising an empire in the Spanish lands across the Mississippi, but things had gotten tarnal damp for a while. Between times I'd let a man be hanged as a pirate, slit some throats on Toussaint's behalf, and fed a traitor to the sharks. And I'd packed it all into five months, which I guessed must be some kind of a record for a seventeen-year-old. It weren't my fault entire, but the memories followed me around like a turnip-fart. You know the kind I mean: you dasn't fan it for fear of calling attention to who done it, but if you *don't* fan it, you're like to go blind from the smoke.

I valued four things and kept them with me always. The first was a miniature of my dead mother in a heartshaped pewter locket, dented on one side and grimy all over, which I wore on a chain around my neck. The second was an old epaulet that Peter Wickett give me when I made acting lieutenant; the embroidery was tattered and the brass shone through the gilt, but I wouldn't have traded it for one of solid gold. The third was a beat-up old hat, flat-crowned with a flaring brim and a red and white plume, that'd belonged to my friend Juge; I wore it low on my brow the way he had and hoped it made me look a little like him. The fourth was a steel-hilted sword that I had picked up during the siege of Jacmel, down on the south coast of the island, where Toussaint had broke the mulatto rebels at last. I didn't wear it because I liked it; I wore it because its superb blade was made of tiger-striped

Damascus steel and I couldn't afford another of its quality. It was a tool of my trade, like a mechanic's saw. It had once belonged to a man who killed Negroes for a living, and was decorated with a death's-head on the pommel and arcane mottoes engraved along either side of the blood-gutter.

It had recently come to my attention that I was a bastard and a Negro. One minute the world was my oyster and the navy was my pearl; the next I was the keeper of a pair of secrets that oughtn't to be secrets at all. It poisons a man to deny that he is what God made him.

I walked up and down the road, breathing dust and feeling the sun and shade pressing on my shoulders. The paw-paw is an indifferent tree for shade, I thought, looking up. The tropical variety, what your Spaniard calls a *papaya,* grows taller and straighter than ours, and not so bushy. It's got leaves like wide-stretched hands at the ends of skinny arms, and they wave around in any kind of a breeze. They let the daylight through, which ain't what you want for keeping cool in the Fever Islands.

Quilty had set up the sailcloth shelters and grass lean-tos that made up his hospital at the edge of a wide grove of paw-paws; the tree that Toussaint had give him for his own use, the one I now stopped next to, consisted of a straight shaft about ten feet high, heavily scarred along its stem where previous growths of leaves had sprouted and fallen away. The fruits that clustered at the base of its wide leafy crown had mellowed in the past few weeks from dark green to canary yellow. I could smell the gooey orange flesh ripening inside them.

Which was making me thirsty, and I commenced to moving again, stepping in and out of the flickering sunlight as I paced. I wasn't above stealing fruit, but I guessed Quilty knew exactly how many paw-paws he had on his paw-paw tree, and it don't do to steal from a man that can take your leg off and get you to thank him for it after.

The sick-list men in the tents and palm-frond lean-tos moaned and thrashed with the black vomit. There was some, too, that looked like they had slipped their hawsers but hadn't been hauled away yet. One of the livelier ones was a French lieutenant of my age, or near enough as makes no difference. For several days he'd puked out stuff that looked like old coffee grounds and stank like the seat of Satan's britches, but today he squatted under a palmetto across the road and watched me walk up and down.

He was looking at my feet. Leastways that's what I hoped he was looking at. He had the dark, deep, liquidy sort of eyes that lady novelists call "brooding," a mass of jet curls that cascaded down his forehead, full moist lips, and a pudgy but sturdy cleft chin. He was dressed in a blue coat, red vest, red pantaloons, and a red sash, all of which he had managed to keep clean somehow. The mademoiselles would swoon over him, though I calculated it might escape his notice.

"Oui, qu'est-ce qu'il y a?" I said, just to let him know I knew he was watching me. "What's the matter?"

He shrugged.

"Why don't you shove off, then?"

"I dare not, *monsieur.* The *nègres,* they might send me back to France, or they might execute me. There is no telling."

Nègre was French for nigger or Negro, depending. I didn't know him well enough to know which he meant, or even if he knew the difference.

"Without a doubt," I said. "You've given them a hard time of it. Why don't you fellows go home?"

"What, and leave the most valuable colony in the world to you rustics?"

"We don't want the blame thing. We're willing to pay for sugar and coffee."

"Yes, just as you do with harvesting your wheat and Indian corn, and lading your ships, and polishing the silver, and everything else your slaves do for you."

I came abreast of him and made my turn, prepared to ignore him all day if I had to.

As I turned, I saw a man away down the road striding up from Le Cap. He was made small by distance, diminished by the billowing green mountains to the left and dwarfed by the wrinkled expanse of the blue Atlantic to the right, but he wasn't an inconsiderable man all the same; and though his image stretched and jumped in the heat waves that shimmered on the dusty road, I could tell as much about him as I wanted to know. He wore a black cocked hat, a blue frock coat with the tails turned back and a gold epaulet on the right shoulder, and a white vest and britches. That made him a navy lieutenant, same as myself, and there weren't but one lieutenant in the squadron as tall and skinny as that bird.

Shit and perdition! I hadn't even knowed he was back in the islands. I reached out and shook the fly of the tent beside me. "Ahoy! Mr. Quilty, there! Ain't you done yet?"

"No, Mr. Graves, I am not." The surgeon didn't bother to stick his head out, and the canvas wall muffled his voice. "You may wait until I am."

"I think I might need to cut and run, Mr. Quilty."

"You may leave as soon as you like, sir, but if you wish to leave aboard a navy ship you'll wait until I have signed your bill of health."

"But it's important, Mr. Quilty."

"Is it."

He thrust the tent flap aside and looked out at me. He had took off his wig, and pebbles of sweat glistened on his close-cropped head. His eyes sagged in his face, and blood crusted his leather apron.

"Is it," he said again. It was a denial or maybe a challenge, but it weren't a question.

I looked around at the sick men writhing under the awnings and suppressed a surge of anger.

"Not to anyone but myself, I guess, Mr. Quilty."

"Very well, then."

The tent flap fell back into place. A moment later I heard a stream of liquid tinkling in a metal bowl and smelled the iron tang of blood.

The tall lieutenant carried a hoop-handled wicker basket in his right hand. The basket, which he held away from his side as he hooked along, made him look like he was off to take yellow cakes and pink lemonade with a lady on a lawn.

It could've been coincidence that was bringing him to that particular spot on that particular island at that particular hour, as if to occupy the same place at the same time as me, but I doubted it. And it could've been that I was the furthest thing from his mind, but I doubted that, too. I had a notion that if I wasn't the center of his universe, I was one of its more important satellites. A guilty conscience will do that to you.

The clearing in the mangroves where he'd put a pistol ball through Billy's lungs lay just beyond the paw-paw grove, behind a derelict sugar shed with blue paint fading from its weathered boards. I could see it if I turned my head to look. The first fingers of a headache gripped the back of my skull.

He trudged up to where I stood, the basket dangling in his right hand and his hanger cradled under his left arm, hilt astern, and came to a halt. He gave the Frenchman behind me a look I couldn't read, though there seemed a hint of sympathy in it; and then he stared down at me from around a long, down-curved beak that dipped toward the tip of his equally long and up-curved chin. He was near a foot taller than me and about ten years older—no more than thirty, anyway. A lurid pucker on his right cheek showed where a French musket ball had knocked out some of his side teeth back in January. Without a word he held out the basket.

"Hello, Peter," I said. I looked at the basket but didn't touch it. "It's too big for pistols, and you ain't the sort for a picnic."

"Nor I am. Since you will not stir yourself to reach for it—"

He set the basket on the sand and flipped the lid. A long-haired gray cat lay curled up inside on a neatly folded piece of calico. It lay on its back with its paws in the air. Its mouth had closed with half the tongue sticking out.

I looked away. "Is it dead?"

"He is not."

He took off his hat and pressed his kerchief against his face: first his brow, then his upper lip, then beneath either eye. The Africa-shaped port wine stain on his brow stood out dark against the skin, as if it'd drawn all the blood of his face into it. That was usually a bad sign, but he seemed calm enough elsewise.

I looked in the basket again. "Near about the quietest cat I ever see."

"The consequence of a dish of rum and cream." The hat went back on his head, and the kerchief went back up his sleeve. "And Greybar is a *he,* not an *it.* He's a living beast. He needs someone to look after him."

Greybar yawned, showing a mouthful of fangs.

"Yes. Well," I said. "I guess you better keep looking, then."

"He's fond of you."

"He was fond of the fish I used to give him."

"You have an obdurate heart, Mr. Graves."

"It's a lie. Ain't nothing wrong with my heart," I said. Not that I knew what *obdurate* meant; I just didn't like the sound of it.

"Then take your cat."

"I ain't *got* a cat."

"No, but your cousin did. And now he is dead, and the *Rattle-Snake* is sank, and there is no one to look after the beast." He said it like he was explaining items on a bill.

"You shot Billy," I said. "You take his cat."

Its tail twitched.

"You *like* cats," I said. "You take it."

Peter looked at the Frenchman again. He was leaning against the paw-paw tree with his hands in his pockets.

"Greybar is not my responsibility." Peter closed the lid again and slipped the wickerwork latch in place.

I'd clasped my hands behind my back the way he'd taught me. The skeeter bites on my wrists itched like Old Harry.

"I don't guess you come all this way just to give me a cat."

"Nor did I. I came to say good-bye." He shook out his sleeves. "The commodore has ordered the *Breeze* home to Norfolk, there to be condemned and sold."

I squeezed my wrist, waiting for the burning to fade away, waiting for the ache to ebb from my heart.

"You're coming down in the world, Peter. The *Breeze* ain't nothing but an 8-gun sloop, and four-pounders at that."

He'd had her for a few weeks once before, with me as mate, and Billy had mocked us for it; it was one of many steps he'd taken on the way to his duel with Peter. I could see her out on the bay, now that I knew to look for her. She was hove up near to the *Columbia,* looking like a jolly boat beside the big 44-gun frigate. Peter deserved better than that.

I looked at Peter hiding his shame, joy, whatever it was he felt.

"Peter, she's barely big enough for a master's mate's command."

"Nonetheless," he said, "I require a command, and she serves my purpose."

He *required* a command. Yes, and I required a commodore's star and a thousand dollars a year, but I didn't see them lying around anywhere.

"Where will you go after you get to Norfolk?"

"You assume that I shall leave the service." He looked past my shoulder again, eyeing the Frenchman. A hint of a smile crept across his face and was gone again like it'd never been. "There's always the Africa trade."

"If I thought you'd stoop so low, I'd kill you myself."

"Gold? Ivory? Trading in these is low?"

"You know what I mean, Peter Wickett. I remember you sailed in the Bight of Benin, and was in Whydah. You said it way back when we first took the *Breeze.*"

"Did I? Well, then I shall go where the birds dwell," he said, by which I supposed he would take a ramble in the country till he found where he was going. He tucked his sword up under his arm again, where it would be out of his way while he walked. "You might wish to be more careful in your passions, Mr. Graves. People might make a connection between them and your complexion." He leaned forward. "And another word of advice, if you will allow me: When you fill your cup, as I have no doubt you will, drink deeply of it. Then tell me if it is as sweet as you thought it would be."

I sat on a palm stump and watched him trudge back down to Le Cap. He seemed to sink into the earth a little with each step, until he was no taller than an ordinary man.

The basket shifted at my feet. I lifted the lid and looked in. Greybar's head bobbled as he looked up at me, and I hauled him out by the scruff and set him by the side of the road. He backed and filled his way over to the paw-paw tree and puked against it.

The French lieutenant came up behind me and looked up at the paw-paws. *"Ah,"* he said, *"alors c'est ça une papaye."* Not the high-toned *"Voici donc a quoi ressemble une papaye"*—"Here it is, then, what a paw-paw looks like"—that I would've expected from the way he carried himself, but the common "Ah, so that's a paw-paw." It struck a jarring note, like he was pretending to be something less than he was.

Greybar stood with his head down. I scratched him behind the ears, and he took a swipe at me. I snatched my hand away from his claws and looked over my shoulder at the Frenchman.

"Why'n't you quit talking French? And don't stand behind me. You're supposed to be a prisoner."

"Pardon, s'il vous plaît, m'sieur!"

I looked at him close. I could've sworn he'd called me *môsseur,* a sneering way of saying *monsieur,* but he switched to English on me.

"But they are getting ripe, yes?" he said. "Soon they will be too ripe."

"What do you care? They ain't yours."

He shrugged as only a Frenchman can, with his whole body and a shake of the head, and his lips all twisted to one side.

I turned my head so he couldn't see my face.

"Listen, pal, go away. You make my head hurt."

"I think he is not I who makes your head hurt," he said, but low enough that he and I could both pretend I hadn't heard, and he wandered off to the other side of the camp.

I knelt down in front of the cat and held out my finger. He grabbed it. The pads of his paws were warm and rough against my skin as he pulled my finger closer and rubbed his cheek against it. He purred so low I could only feel the vibrations in my finger. I figured purring was a good sign. But he was also thrashing his tail, and that I knew was a bad sign.

Then suddenly he bit me and I smacked him on the forehead. He gave me a puzzled look as he fell over, like I'd done something unfathomably strange, and I remembered he was drunk. Careful of his claws, I put him in a shady spot next to Quilty's tent, with the basket nearby on its side where he could crawl back into it if he wanted.

"No, I do not wish for a cat," said Quilty. He'd come out from his tent to join me in the dubious shade of the paw-paw tree. He used my chin as a lever to move my head up and down and from side to side. He held up some fingers.

I'd gotten my cocoanut cracked a time or three in the past several months. It's what had landed me in that fever pit. First in the Bight of Léogâne off the western coast of the island, when we got swooped on by several hundred French picaroons and a gun blew up in my ear, and then when I fell off my horse during the assault on Jacmel, and then when I ran into a desk while Juge and I were fighting our way out of prison. There might've been some other times but I couldn't recall them offhand. I'd been subject to fits and spells, but I hardly ever fell down anymore.

"Three," I said, looking at the fingers. "And I didn't ask if you'd take him."

"I wish it to be clear from the outset," he said. "Two."

"You're sticking your thumb out." I made the European gesture for three—two fingers and a thumb. "That makes three."

He smiled patiently. He was about the patientest cuss I knew.

"It is the custom in such cases," he said, "for the surgeon to manipulate the patient's head, and for the patient to count the number of fingers that the surgeon holds up. It has been our routine these several weeks. There is comfort in routine, Mr. Graves."

His big square fingers were black around the nails and stank of blood. I pulled my face away.

"I myself cannot mend your head," he said, "any more than I can turn you back into the amiable young man you once were, but I can make you be still until you mend yourself." He held up a finger to shush me. "I am not proposing a return to strapping you into your hammock. Don't worry. I shall release you this very day to the commodore."

"Well, I am just joy itself," I said. "Now I can get back to shooting at people and sticking my sword in 'em. Where do I sign?"

I'd meant it to be funny, but he didn't laugh. He did give me a funny look, though, and said, "*You* needn't sign anything. *I* have to sign a certificate."

I followed him into his tent, where about the yellowest man I ever seen lay in a daze on a cloth-draped table. A pewter bleeding-bowl lay nearby with an iron-smelling, fly-crawling pint in it.

Quilty waved the flies away with an absent air as he fetched a printed form and filled in the spaces where my name and the date and what illness I'd had were supposed to go.

I craned my head around to see what he wrote. "How come you surgeons never write so's anybody else can read it?"

"We live in fear—" He blew on the paper to dry the ink. He looked at the paper again and handed it to me. "We live in fear that ordinary mortals will discover how little we know. Off you go to the *Columbia,* now."

"Good," I said, as we stepped once more into the tropical sunlight and the flower-smelling air. The Frenchman was still mooning around with his hands in his pockets. "Now I can be shed of Johnny Crappo over there."

"Who, Mr. Corbeau?" he said, summoning the French lieutenant with a wag of his finger. "I'm afraid you labor under a misapprehension, Mr. Graves. A prisoner is a military matter, not a medical one. The commodore has bade me send him along with you." He chuckled as he went back into his tent.

"Monsieur Corbeau," I said, patting the paw-paw tree. "*Faites-moi la courte échelle, s'il vous plaît.* Make me the short ladder, if you please."

He held out his hands, palms up and the fingers interlaced; I stepped onto the rung, as it were, and used the ol' death's-head sword to cut down a load of ripe paw-paws. It don't do to go empty-handed when calling on a commodore.

Commodore Cyrus Gaswell was transferring himself from his barge to the *Columbia* when Corbeau and I pulled up in a shore boat. I hardly recognized the old coot in his gold lace and epaulets, he sparkled so. There was even the golden eagle and sky-blue ribbon of the Cincinnati in his lapel. He'd fought in the Revolution from the beginning, which made him a Methuselah—fifty if he was a day—but although the seat of his white britches was stretched tauter than it might've been once upon a day, the muscles bunched and rolled in his thighs and calves as he hauled himself up the frigate's side, and power and woe lurked in the glances he cast here and there around his potato-like nose. He lingered on the spar deck while the extra attendants slipped away at the sight of my lieutenant's uniform, until there were only two side boys and a bosun's mate left to see me aboard. I did off my hat to the quarterdeck and the Stars and Stripes, and was about to do the same to Gaswell when he stuck out a paw for me to shake. He cast an eye on Corbeau coming up behind me and noted the basket of paw-paws that the sailors were handing up abaft of all, with Greybar perched in it with his ears laid flat aback.

Gaswell's splendiferous uniform weren't in my honor; nor in Corbeau's, neither.

"Mr. Corbeau," I said over my shoulder, "I'll need your parole."

"Oh, yes, of course," he said, gazing across at the *Breeze*. "I shall go nowhere."

"I'm leaving Greybar and the paw-paws with you."

"Yes, yes, they are safe with me."

I turned back to the commodore. "The paw-paws are for your table, sir, if you'll allow me."

"I'll have 'em for breakfast." He waved off the flock of lieutenants and clerks that had descended on him with their messages and papers, clapped me on the arm, and said, "Let's us have a dram."

"Things've gotten quiet as worms around here," said Gaswell. He led me past the Marine sentry into his day-cabin and shut the door behind us. "Drop an anchor."

He shucked his gorgeous coat and tossed it across his settee. The great cabin of the *Columbia* was near about big enough to stick Peter's whole *Breeze* sloop in it and not stretch the truth entirely out of recognition. The commodore's cocked hat followed the coat.

"Go on, sit," he said, and with a thrust of one thick forefinger he let me know I was to sit in the straight-backed chair on the forward side of the big Cuban mahogany table he used for a desk.

"Now that Toussaint's drove Rigaud into exile in France," he said, "he got time to spare to start thinking of me as a dog to sic on the Dons, as if I had no more manners than a Kentucky puke." He rolled up his shirtsleeves. "I just seen him over to town. I do believe he intends to invade Santo Domingo and free the Spanish slaves. Been sending battalions over all week."

He poured himself a glass of whiskey and put it down where he stood. Then he poured a couple more and set them on the table. He dropped himself into his chair and held out a plug of tobacco and an ivory-handled clasp knife.

"Chaw?"

"No thank'ee, sir."

"Don't tell me you don't chaw."

"I like a cigar now and again, sir."

"Smoking!" He reached out with his foot and drew a well-watered spitkid closer to his chair. "That's a damn disgusting habit." He carved off a hunk of leaf and stuck it in his cheek. "How ye been enjoying your stay in the island?"

"Depends, sir." I reached for my glass. "You want the right answer or the honest answer?"

He unbuttoned the knees of his britches and pulled his shoes and stockings off, saying, "I reckon ye know me well enough by now to guess the answer to that one." His feet didn't have an entirely unpleasant reek, but there was a power of it.

"Well, sir," I said, "then I will tell you I'm about as sick of this place as I can be and still stand to live." I watched him take a sip of whiskey. "Hell ain't in it—I never seen such a place for murder and mayhem as San Domingo. I figure anyplace else in the world 'ud be nuts in May compared to it." I stuck my nose in my glass. The whiskey smelled like buttered fire.

He looked at me over the rim of his glass with eyes like big blue eggs. "Scuttlebutt is you and Peter Wickett ain't gettin' along so well."

I lowered my glass, feeling the whiskey burning my lips and tongue. "Scuttlebutt ain't always accurate, sir."

"Well, is it this time?"

"I got nothing again' him."

He launched an amber stream in the direction of the spitkid and wiped his mouth with the back of his hand. "Ain't what I asked."

"I can't answer for him, sir. I can tell you this, though: he weren't too happy I sank the *Rattle-Snake*."

He chawed and spat, and spat and chawed, and took another mouthful of whiskey. It takes skill to chaw and drink at the same time, but spitting on top of it was just showing off.

"He ain't happy he was below decks when ye boarded the *Faucon*," he said.

"Weren't his fault, sir. The topmast cap fell on him."

"I *know* the topmast cap fell on him. But no one'll remember it that way. They'll just remember that you went across and he went below."

I threw back my whiskey and felt it boil in my guts. "I don't expect he much likes the sight of me, sir."

"Don't take yourself so serious—no one else does. I expect he's too tied up in his own misery to think about you one way or t'other. If he mislikes anybody, it's me, and I ain't required to care what he likes. I ain't *allowed* to care what he likes. Besides which, I told him I'd give him the best command I could as soon as I could."

"When was that, sir?"

"About a month ago. Been gettin' a mite sniffy. Thinks I don't notice." He shot me a wink, like he didn't mean it serious, and said, "What about you, are ye fit?" He waved off Quilty's certificate when I tried to poke it at him. "He wouldn't send ye aboard of me without he thought ye were fit. I'm asking *you*. Are ye fit?"

"Tolerable, sir. Just tolerable." It like to killed me to admit it, but it don't do to lie to commodores. They got ways of finding things out about you, things you might not even have knowed yourself.

He hooked a pair of spectacles to his ears and settled the lenses on his nose. "You need to find your strength, son," he said. He took a piece of paper off one of the neat piles on his desk and dipped his quill into the inkwell. "I'm sending you home. Somebody in the Navy Office wants to talk with you about the duel, anyway. I been putting 'em off for a while now." He looked at me over his glasses. "I don't guess it's anything to worry about. They ain't asked for Peter Wickett."

The way he said it, I felt like I'd stepped out on the front step of a winter's morning and found the door locked behind me.

TWO

Gaswell sent Corbeau and me over to the *Breeze* in his own barge. He probably only done it because it was convenient for the Columbias—the boat being already in the water—but it was handsome of him all the same. We rode in style in the stern sheets, with Greybar yowling in the basket between us, while I educated Corbeau on the advantages of the *Columbia* as we receded from her, and the fine points of the *Breeze* as we approached. They were a study in contrasts, them two.

The *Columbia* was a sister to the *United States* and the *Constitution,* rated as a 44 but built like a two-decker. "You can tell 'em apart mostly by the roundhouse," I said, pointing at the low structure that gave the frigate a sort of poop deck. "I mean, you could if the *Constitution* was here. *Constitution* ain't got a roundhouse, but the *United States* and the *Columbia* do. Don't ask me why," I said as he opened his mouth, "because I don't know." Our route took us around the bows and I pointed up at the figurehead, a fat lady with a gilt sword. "You'll note the Amazon with our coat of arms on her shield."

Corbeau's eyes were of such a dark blue that the colored part of them seemed to consist solely of pupil, and they appeared to look through things as much as at them.

"An escutcheon paleways of thirteen pieces, argent and gules; a chief, azure," he said.

"Come again?"

He smiled as if remembering a sad secret. "Heraldry is a foolish and unrevolutionary art. As you may see for yourself, it merely means thirteen red and white stripes with a blue band across the top. The arcane becomes simple when it is examined, no?" His eyes followed the line of the *Columbia*'s bulwarks as we pulled away from her. "How many guns has she?"

It weren't a secret how many guns she had, or what she displaced, or how high her masts were, but I would've guessed him to figure all that out for himself.

"Thirty long 24s and twenty-two 12-pounder carronades," I said. "Didn't you look around while I left you on deck?"

"No, *monsieur,* of course not. She is a 52, then?"

"I'll say she ain't." The British were all the time grousing about how the *United States* and her sisters were really ships-of-the-line, as they were bigger, faster, and more heavily gunned than the Royal Navy's frigates. But Corbeau had said it mild, as if he really was ignorant of the difference between a ship's rate and the number of artillery pieces she actually carried. I lightened my tone, the way you do with the softheaded.

"She's rated as a 44," I said, "but she's only got thirty carriage guns. They're down on her gun deck, of course. Twenty-four-pounders, like I said. The short twelves on her fo'c's'le and quarterdeck are carronades, y'see. But you're a navy man. You know all this."

He tossed his head. "I am from the artillery. I know not these carronades. We do not have them, *monsieur.*"

"They got a short barrel, mounted on a traversing slide instead of a carriage. They fire a larger ball with a smaller charge than a long gun. Lousy range, though."

"Then I do not care for them." He looked forward toward the *Breeze.* "This one is a lively little thing, *hein?*"

"Yes, we took her from some picaroons a few months ago over in the Bight of Léogâne."

"Picaroon?"

That boy didn't know his head from a turnip. "French-speaking pirates," I said. "Leastwise we guessed they was French. We had to—it was kind of hard to tell . . ." I swallowed a sudden squirt of saliva. "Well, anyway, she was *La Brise* at the time. We caught her unawares, otherwise she'd've had the heels of us."

"Fast, is she?"

"Like lightning. I warn you, though, she's tarnal cramped."

"Oh, you have sailed in her?"

"Sure, I was her first officer before I made acting lieutenant. But she don't rate two commission officers, and Peter and I both went into the *Rattle-Snake* when—when command of her came open."

"Peter?"

"Peter Wickett—the lieutenant who brought me that fool cat."

"You say she is cramped?"

"Crowded ain't in it. She only got but the one cabin, which is for the captain's use. We'll be slinging our hammocks in the bread room and counting ourselves lucky, I guess."

A seaman looked over the rail at us as we approached the *Breeze* and said something to someone I couldn't see. A moment later a petty officer showed himself.

"Ahoy the boat!" he called.

"Aye aye," replied the midshipman who was steering us, as a warning that he had an officer aboard, and held up two fingers to indicate my rank. We hove alongside and hooked on.

Corbeau tipped his hat and said, *"Après vous, monsieur,"* but I had little faith in his naval etiquette and was already climbing up the sloop's side. She only had about five feet of freeboard anyway, and I swung aboard before Corbeau even had time to put his hat back on.

A pair of ratty-looking side boys greeted me while the petty officer tweedled on a silver pipe. By the pipe I took him to be the bosun, and I took in his unshaven face and dirty shirt with surprise before doffing my hat to the colors and to the quarterdeck. Peter stood there, in the space cleared between the mast and the tiller, as remote and severe as when I'd first met him in the *Rattle-Snake* last winter. He turned away before I could salute him.

The handsome blond officer next to him, however, called me by name and stepped forward with his hand out.

"Shipmates again, by God," he said. "We'll be six to a bed, just like old times, hey?"

"Dick Towson! I thought you was third in the *Croatoan.*"

"And so I was, but it seems someone in the Navy Department wants a word with me."

I dropped my voice. "Yes, me too." Then louder I said, "Dick, allow me to make you acquainted with Lieutenant Corbeau of the French navy. *Monsieur Corbeau, j'ai l'honneur de vous presenter le lieutenant Richard Towson de la frégate* Croatoan."

"Enchanté de faire votre connaissance, cher monsieur," said Dick. He didn't have a lick of French, but he knew enough polite phrases to fill a boot.

Corbeau murmured something back at him and tipped his hat in return. It was an un-French gesture, but it exactly mirrored the extent of Dick's politeness, as if to return less than the same would be shameful and to give more would be like handing over the keys to the store.

But Dick was an old hand at that sort of thing. "Perhaps you'd like to go below, sir," he said. "We'll be getting underway shortly."

"A fair wind," said Corbeau, nodding his head. Much *he* knew. The long commission pendant writhed like a snake overhead as the breeze kicked up, and the telltales in the shrouds showed the breeze to be steady in the northeast—about as inconvenient a wind for getting out of the harbor at Le Cap as you could wish for. "I should like to observe the working of the boat," he added.

"She's no boat. She's a sloop," said Dick. "But not a ship-sloop or a brig-sloop or any of that nonsense. Just a regular old sloop." He waved his hat toward the forward hatch. "Now, sir—"

"A sloop!" said Corbeau. "How it fascinates. If you would indulge me—"

"Here's the pilot," I said, as a tidy black man in a French colonial uniform came over the rail. "The captain'll want everybody off the deck that ain't necessary to work her."

"Which, Mr. Graves, includes you and Mr. Towson," said Peter, stepping past me. "I trust you will not give me cause for complaint."

I'd only been funning Corbeau about having to sling our hammocks in the bread room, but I weren't too far wrong. There was exactly three feet ten inches of headroom in the *Breeze*'s 'tween-decks, and even so we slept in two tiers by night or day, swaying from side to side in the stenchy gloom. We could have had a canvas screen rigged to shield our delicate sensibilities from the eyes of the foremast jacks, but the air was solid enough down there without impeding its flow, and we passed on it.

By day we tried our best to keep out of the way on deck, which weren't easy, what with the sloop's thirty-five men swarming over her like lice in a bird's nest. Peter wouldn't let me and Dick so much as touch a rope, neither, much less stand a watch, insisting that we were passengers and not to be employed on any account. That might've been well and good for a fellow that likes to be idle, but I weren't one of them. Neither was Dick, though there'd been times in the past when I thought he was about as good at doing nothing as ever a mortal man could be and still draw breath.

We'd barely cleared the Straits of Florida before boredom of the crushingest sort come down on our heads, and us with still a thousand miles and more to sail. Peter compounded it by refusing to engage me and Dick in conversation while he was on deck, and refusing our visits when he wasn't, and spending a good deal of time with Corbeau to spite us. Even the smallest events became of great interest to us, because we had nothing else to do but watch and pass judgment.

One brisk afternoon about thirty leagues southeast of Cape Canaveral, Peter called up to the lookout to keep a keen eye out for Memory Rock. The lookout called down that he could see it about two miles off our larboard bow. The air seemed kind of empty afterward because the lookout hadn't said "sir," which was pretty familiar even in an American man-o'-war.

Dick and Corbeau and I were gathered around a pile of greasy cards in our cubbyhole right aft on the starboard side of the lower deck. Plenty of air came in through the open hatchway, along with just enough spray to keep us comfortable. We were playing a three-handed version of *Juker*, an Alsatian game that Corbeau had taught us. He and Dick found it appealing. Me, I disliked gambling in general and cards in particular, but I was tired of being tromped on every time I so much as showed a leg on deck.

After what seemed an eternity without Peter rebuking the lookout, I said low so only my companions could hear, "What the hell has gotten into that man?"

"He's been worse than usual ever since we fetched Great Inagua," said Dick. He dealt out four hands of five cards each and set the remaining four cards on the deck between us. He turned the top one over, revealing the jack of spades. "I suppose he's remembering how you sunk the *Rattle-Snake*. Your bid."

"*I* sank her? How you talk. Pass." I had nines and tens, which were miserably low, and nary a spade to match the one that Dick had turned over. I did have the other black jack, though, the "larboard anchor," which I remembered too late would count as a trump if spades were called. I glanced at Corbeau over my cards. "The *Rattle-Snake* took on a corvette and a frigate armed *en flute* a couple months back. The corvette had sixteen 9-pounders and the frigate still had ten 8-pounders in her, not to mention about two hundred infantrymen all popping away at us with their muskets."

"Pick him up, if you please, Monsieur Towson," said Corbeau, motioning at the jack on top of the pack of cards. "But what is this *Rattle-Snake* of which you speak?"

Dick took a card from his hand and slipped it facedown under the pack. "Schooner, fourteen sixes," he said. "Our former home." He picked up the jack, making spades trumps.

"Against the nine-pounders corvette? *Zut alors,*" said Corbeau. He picked up the dummy hand and sorted through it.

"*'Zut alors'?*" says I. "No one says *zut alors*."

"I do," said Corbeau. He smiled, showing his dimples. "It is the one thing I take with me from my childhood. It is your lead, is it not?"

I threw down my lone trump, the jack of clubs. Corbeau followed with a dirty look and the queen of spades, and Dick took the trick with the jack of spades and led the ace. I threw off a red nine, and Corbeau coughed up the king. We were well on the way to taking every trick—or Dick was, anyway—when the youngest ship's boy, little Freddy Billings, who was flat-nosed and wide-mouthed and curly-headed, like a lampoon of a miniature Irishman, came down the hatch with a note in his hand.

Dick glanced at it. "Goodness," he said. "We've hardly got time to dress."

Peter's cook started us off with steamed flyingfish on top of cornmeal mush and okra. The sailor who brought it to the table had tar on his hands and needed a shave, and from the smell of him he hadn't changed his linen for several weeks. Dick's slave, Jubal, a mountain of a man who considered his master his personal domain, near about snatched the platter from the sailor's hands and give him a look that like to have killed a normal fellow. I might not have noticed, except it was Peter's table. It wasn't like him to overlook slovenliness. But overlook it he did, in the person of Ben Crouch, the bosun that I'd remarked the day I come aboard. Crouch was dirtier than the man that Jubal had shooed away, and he was at our table, and he was drunk. He was hunched over his plate, and bits of fish and okra fell from his mouth as he ate.

"You seem nonplussed about something, Mr. Graves," said Peter. His tattered old calico cat, Gypsy, crouched in his lap, her eyes half-closed as he scratched her.

"Not I, sir." I watched Jubal, scrunched up against the bulkhead to make room for himself, offering Dick a choice of wine. Madeira, port, hock, and claret were all the wines I knew or cared about, but

Jubal seemed to think it went further than that. I looked back at Peter. "What's nonplussed?"

"Confused."

He toyed with his wine glass, and although he hadn't drunk much his eyes wandered as if he weren't entirely inside his own head. There was headroom in the cabin, so long as we stayed seated, but the room was so close that I had to keep my right knee tucked in to avoid touching his.

"Puzzled," he added. "Perplexed. Are you perplexed, Mr. Graves? At a loss for words?"

"I don't guess I am, sir." I poked at the fish with my knife. I could smell Crouch blowing on his food at the foot of the table.

"What an odd look you have on your face," said Peter. "Do you find the food objectionable?"

"No, it eats as good as anything. I guess I just never knowed Doc could actual cook." I looked at Corbeau. "A navy cook is always called Doc—don't ask me why. It just is so. Our Doc only got one eye and one leg, which is kind of usual, too, now that I think of it, but he's a terror against boarders. He was with us in the *Rattle-Snake* when we took on that corvette I told you about. Some Frenchmen got into his galley, and he pasted 'em with a skillet and his peg-leg both."

Corbeau smiled obscurely. "Certainly one must be wary of strange Frenchmen in one's galley."

"I doubt Mr. Corbeau understands what you mean by 'pasted,' or even what a skillet is," said Peter. Gypsy had been purring on his knee, but she broke off to look at me. "Yet you make an interesting point, Mr. Graves, which is that many people can do things about which one might not previously be aware. Some men, for instance, are even capable of performing their assigned tasks without sinking the ship out from under their feet."

"I guess sinking your own ship would be a pretty lonely feeling, Captain," says I, looking him straight on. "I can only guess at it, as I ain't never done it."

Captain because he was the skipper of the little sloop, and *sir* because he was senior to me, but that was just front-parlor stuff. He was still a lieutenant and didn't outrank me; and he'd said himself that losing the *Rattle-Snake* weren't my fault. I looked back at Corbeau.

"I misspoke earlier. It weren't the corvette we took, but the *Faucon,* the frigate that was with her. The *Croatoan* got credit for taking *L'Heureuse Rencontre.* That was the name of the corvette. Ain't that right, sir," I said to Peter. "Didn't Block come up in the *Croatoan* an hour after the shooting stopped and took possession of the corvette?"

Dick got a pained look. "We'd lost our fore and main-topmasts," he said. "There's shoals all around there. It was the Bahama Bank in the middle of the night, for goodness sake. We came up to you as quick as we could."

Corbeau glanced at Peter on his left and Dick on his right. "I see."

"Ye don't see nothin'," said Crouch.

"That was a shocking dinner, Mr. Corbeau. I hope you will forgive it," said Dick. The three of us had found a perch in the starboard chains where we could savor the breeze without its being flavored by the stink of the hold, nor Ben Crouch, neither, and where we were relatively safe from being trampled. "Americans pride ourselves on honesty, but sometimes I think we're just tactless."

"It is as nothing," said Corbeau, with a hint of contemptuous amusement in his eye. "Even *la belle Paris* suffered from perhaps an excess of enthusiasm when the odious constraints of authority were lifted. Sometimes even today, even in the high seats of government, the rod and fist are wanted when civility fails." He clutched the shrouds even though there weren't much of a sea. "Are we the macaronis, that we would scruple over the well-deserved thrashing of an upstart?"

"I'm no macaroni," said Dick. "My father was one, though. He met Lafayette once."

"Corbeau's having you on," I said.

It was a gorgeous afternoon, all racing clouds and spindrift, and the breeze already noticeably cooler as we left the tropics astern. My head hardly hurt at all, and I didn't care a hoot about Peter Wickett and his bosun. If Corbeau wanted to thrash either one of them, I'd hold his coat for him, but that was about as interested as I was in the matter.

"I don't care if he is having me on," said Dick. "I want to know what to do about Crouch."

"What makes you think we got to do something about Crouch? This ain't our sloop."

"This man is a churl," said Corbeau.

"That's the word for him," said Dick.

"A bit unrevolutionary, ain't it?" says I. "Calling him a name like that."

"Very well, then," said Corbeau, "let us say he is a boor. But you raise the good point. Aside from his being a boor, what is wrong with having the bosun in to dine? Is he not an officer?"

"Well, sure, he's a *warrant* officer," I said. "And he's theoretically equal in rank to any other senior warrant officer. But—"

"But in point of fact," said Dick, "your bosuns and carpenters and such are *gunroom* officers. Bringing them to the captain's table and expecting them to behave themselves is like squaring the circle—it can't be done. They're skilled mechanics, not gentlemen. They're *workingmen.*"

"Ah yes," said Corbeau, knowingly. "Workingmen. America and France alike fought to rid ourselves of the aristocracy, and yet we are still filled with contempt for the man who does the actual work."

"Now hold on there," Dick shot back. "X-Y-Z, my friend. X-Y-Z."

Corbeau looked at me and shrugged. "I know not this X-Y-Z. Is it some form of bourgeoisie?"

Liar, thinks I. The X-Y-Z Affair was how this whole undeclared war with France got started in the first place. If he wanted a lesson in affairs of state, then by gad I'd give him one.

"President Adams sent three agents to Paris," I said, "to talk to their counterparts on your side. They went by the code names of X, Y, and Z. They went to ask you nice to stop taking our ships."

"Three hundred of them," said Dick.

"But then Talleyrand demanded fifty thousand pounds sterling just to be sat down with. That's a quarter of a million dollars."

Corbeau shrugged.

"Talleyrand's your foreign minister," said Dick.

"Oh, la, I know this. But Monsieur Talleyrand, he wanted the money for to fight the British, no?"

"'No' is right," I said. "It was his personal walking-around money. He wanted another twelve million on top of that, and *that* was to go to the war effort."

I leaned out to watch a pair of sea pigs riding the bow wave. They glided along effortlessly, with their forever grins on their faces, and then they flicked their tails and were gone.

"Which you got to admit," I continued, "the British wouldn't look too kindly on it. It would've meant war with 'em, which between you and me I would've been just as happy to see. The Jeffersonians calculated there was a plot afoot to make France look bad, but Adams spilled the papers and there it was in black and white."

"But this makes me feel bad," said Corbeau. "I fight for the liberty, the equality, and the brotherhood."

"Well, we have all that already," said Dick. "So why don't you just pack your bags and go on home?"

Corbeau laughed. "There is nothing I would like better, but I am your prisoner."

"He got you there, Dick, ha ha!"

"I'll say he don't," said Dick. "He's Peter Wickett's prisoner, and welcome to him. But anyway, by 'you' I meant 'you French,' not Mr. Corbeau here. Say, either of you chaps care to continue our game?"

"I'd rather pound cockroaches with your hairbrush," I said.

"You mean *your* hairbrush," said Dick.

"What, and make mine all gloptious?"

"It's a moot point," said Dick, "as Ben Crouch complained to Peter Wickett about it. Said the noise was keeping the watch below awake at night."

• • •

About five leagues south-southwest of Cape Hatteras I was up in the crosstrees with a glass, admiring the lighthouse that had been built on the cape the year before. It was about ninety foot tall and its white paint gleamed in the afternoon light; even at that distance it seemed to tower over the low sandy ground on which it stood. It makes a fellow proud to see a sight like that, and I drank it in. *At long last and about time, too,* I was thinking—the cape was a notorious catch-hell for ships riding the Gulf Stream north or the inshore current south—when the lookout beside me sang out, "Sail ho!"

"Where away," called Peter from the quarterdeck, "and what is she?"

"Two points abaft the starboard beam. Ship-rigged, sir."

I thought he hesitated before the *sir* and that he glanced guiltily at me before he said it, but it could've been nervousness at my presence. I put my glass on the strange sail. She was square-rigged on fore, main, and mizzen—what *ship* means to a sailor—with a jaunty rake to her masts. She wore no colors that I could see.

"She turns toward us, sir," called the lookout.

She was still hull-down, but I'd seen enough. "Deck there," I called. "She looks to be French. Maybe a privateersman."

"What, this far north?" said the lookout.

"We're indebted to you, I'm sure, Mr. Graves."

Peter's voice had an odd note to it, aside from the usual sarcasm, and I glanced down. Every idle hand had turned to look at him, as well they might with a strange sail standing toward us and we armed only with eight small guns. But then I clearly heard Crouch say, "Nay," and the men seemed to lose interest.

"Bring us as near to the wind as she'll lie on this tack," said Peter, and the tillerman brought us on a course that took us farther west into the shoals, where the ship couldn't follow us.

THREE

We shucked the *Breeze* at Hampton Roads in favor of the Baltimore packet, and transferred at the mouth of the Potomac into a grubby old log canoe. Her sails were more patches than canvas, and Dick and I could've ruined any number of hairbrushes on her hordes of roaches, but I for one was glad to see the last of Peter Wickett and Ben Crouch. Corbeau elected to stay with Peter, which I thought was a pity; but as we approached the capital city on the last of the tide the next day, I realized I not only had no interest in prisoners or even the navy, but that I didn't even know what day it was. And I didn't care, neither.

High white clouds dotted the milky June sky, and the afternoon breeze smelled of dank woods and humid cornfields as we doddered along. Woodpeckers thumped in the forest on the starboard shore, and I thought there was a tarnal lot of them till I realized I was hearing the pounding of workmen's hammers.

A few men and boys swam naked in the stream. I shuddered to see it, for the sultriness of the West Indies lingered in my bones, and the northern air seemed thin and unable to hold its warmth. They stared at our uniforms as we lounged on the gunwale.

"Prolly don't even know dar's a war on," said Jubal.

"Hush, you," said Dick absently. He gripped the rail and stared off at the shore.

I didn't see anything remarkable. There was just a lot of trees and corn, and clay pits, and granite boulders among the stands of sweetgum and the sassafras thickets that choked the runs.

"Ignorantest fools I ever see," said Jubal, but he said it quiet and Dick ignored it.

I looked up past the swimmers, up and along a broad avenue that had been hewn out of the forest. It reached straight and true into the hazy distance for a mile or more, but the stumps hadn't been yanked out yet, and you couldn't have driven so much as a dogcart down it. At its junction with another wide avenue stood a cow, chawing her cud and waggling her ears.

"Say, Mr. Plank," I said to the master of the canoe, "where's the President's House? Where's the War Department? Where's the city?"

"They be there," he said, shifting his wad of tobacco to his other cheek. "They be new buildings all along in there, though you cain't see 'em for the trees." The canoe weren't more than about five foot wide, but he ejected a brown stream into the puddle that sloshed around his bare feet rather than rupture himself trying to spit clear over the gunwale. "Miz Adams ain't moved in yet. Reckon when the *quality* move in, that make it official."

"No," said Dick. "No. No. Surely this is not the capital of the United States." He glared at Jubal as if he had something to do with it, but Jubal wouldn't rise to the bait and Dick turned his glare on Plank.

"You bet it is," I said, waving at the woods and tidal marsh and a herd of hogs belly-deep in the mud. I could suddenly see it all, just as clear. "This here's the Federal City, a-building for the purpose."

"No, I guess not. We aren't *there* yet," said Dick. He said it fierce, like he'd set the words on his shoulder and wanted me to try and knock them off. He pointed upstream where some roofs and chimneys poked up out of the trees. "That's it up there, I suppose, isn't it, Mr. Plank? Those houses beyond that island?"

Plank shifted his chaw and spat again. "Naw, that there be George Town." Turning into a broad inlet, he nodded toward a tall square building on a hill that rose out of the woods to the east. Arched windows and white stone were visible beneath the scaffolding. "*That* be Washington," he said. "That there be the Capitol, where, come the fall, the congressmen and senators will pronounce they edicts like bolts of blue from the fundament."

"I guess you mean to say 'firmament,'" said Dick.

"I know what I said," said Plank. He pointed across the inlet to another pile of stones. "That be the President's House. Now, gents, the wind and tide be falling and we done made our offing." He spat out his chaw and yelled at his sole crewman, "Zeus, you lazy rascal, get ready to drop the hook!"

Zeus hefted the canoe's anchor over his bony shoulder and slouched up into the bows. I never seen a man slouch while climbing before, but Zeus did it. He had talent. Plank flew his sheets, letting the canoe's sails flap in the dying breeze, and fetched his moorings by throwing the tiller hard over and running the canoe up onto the muddy bank. Zeus dropped the anchor overboard with a splat.

"Gents," said Plank, looking down at us where we had tumbled in the sloshing bilge, "we be arrived."

"Plank weren't wrong about not being able to see the buildings for the trees," I said as we tromped down the brow and into the mud. The vale and hills for as far as I could see was all parkland and brushy woods, and not at all the pesty swamp that opponents of the relocation had made it out to be. It was marshy on the fringes, sure, and buggy where we happened to be standing right at the moment, but it's always that way along a river. Stumps and cornfields sprawled across the boulevards, and pigs and cows wandered the thoroughfares, but it's that way in Baltimore and Philadelphia, too, as anybody knows. I expect that's the way of it in London and Rome and the whole world over, and maybe even in the palace of the Grand Vizier of Arabistan, too, except for maybe not the pigs. Stones stood stacked up all round about, but gangs of black men were turning them into the temples of government. You could see where the city was a-going to be by the brick kilns and clay pits and piles of lumber that was scattered across the landscape. It was like a giant hand had flang down stacks of building stuff and was coming back any minute to do something about it.

"Will you look at that?" I waved my arms. "Will you just *look* at that?"

"I'm *looking*," said Dick. "But there isn't much to *see*."

"There will be." I throwed a glance at Jubal toting his and Dick's sea chests under his massive arms like they was little music boxes or something. I'd lost mine when the *Rattle-Snake* went down, but a sailmaker's mate in the *Croatoan* had made me a canvas carryall for what few duds I had left, and Jubal had slung that from his wrist like a lady with a reticule. "Ain't that so, Jubal?"

"Yassuh, Mars Matty," he said, but you can't trust a man's opinion when he's obliged to be agreeable.

I turned back to Dick. "Imagine it, a whole city built for the purpose. They ain't never been nothing like it!"

"Oh, the Roman army did it all the time. The scouts would show up and get the lay of the land, then the soldiers would lay out streets and set up the tents, and the sergeants would make sure they all lined up shipshape, and by suppertime they'd have paved streets and marble fountains, practically."

"Well, there you go," I said, laughing. "A modern Rome. There's even a River Tiber."

"Yes, which I read was called Goose Creek until recently." He turned around to see how Jubal was doing with the baggage. "Giving something a grand name doesn't make it grand. Here! You, Jubal—keep your station."

On the north side of a road that ran below the bluff where the Capitol was building, across the swampy place where Plank had landed us, and on up past the shell of the President's House, which asking around had told us the road was called Pennsylvania Avenue, we come to a group of six government buildings leaning against each other. The Navy Board made its temporary headquarters there in rooms owned by the War Department.

"Think we ought to go in?" said Dick.

I looked up at the halls of doom and glory. "I calculate maybe we ought to wash the taters out of our ears first."

"It might be good if we find a place to shift our clothes at least," said Dick. "Excuse me, sir," he said, planting himself in front of a gentleman in a torn coat and greasy britches. "Can you tell us where we might find lodgings?"

"Try New York," said the gentleman, giving us a long look. He was mud-spattered from the knees down and tobacco-dribbled across his chin and neck-cloth.

"You look like a congressman," I said.

"Well, I bein't one, begod," he said, baptising the oath with tobacco juice. "Them idjits broke for the summer a month ago, and they was still up in Philadelphia for the first session, regardless. They don't commence to conspire again till November. I don't expect the Adamses will heave in till then, neither. But I tell you what"—he jerked his thumb at a muddy walkway of badly laid stones that wandered off westward—"you'll find that most of Washington City lives cheek-by-jowl in rooming houses, back parlors, lean-tos, and cow sheds over to George Town." He walked away, chuckling to himself and saying, "Me, living on a congressman's six dollars a day! Haw haw haw, that's rich! Ain't it *just.*"

My excitement had faded away like dew on a summer's morning. I regretted it. After even burned-out Le Cap, Washington's namesake was sort of an afterthought of a city.

A Marine sentry in the War Department building directed me and Dick to "the sar'n on dooty" in the guardroom. The sergeant on duty glanced at our summonses and then marched ahead of us down a short hallway into what I took to be the navy's suite of offices. There he knocked on a door and entered. Dick and I pretended to examine the new portraits of the *United States,* the *Constellation,* the *President,* and the other three first frigates and their captains that lined the hallway, humming to ourselves and jiggling things in our pockets, until the sergeant came back out. He looked into the middle distance and bawled, "Mr. Graves! Mr. Towson! The gentlemen will follow me!" With our hats under one arm and our personal logbooks under the other, we entered the room.

I would've expected Captain Thomas Tingey, late of the *Ganges* and now superintendent-to-be of the still largely fictional Washington Navy Yard, to have a more impressive office. From the look on his face, he'd expected it, too. The room was well lighted by three tall windows, but that's about the best that could be said for it. Like near about everything else in Washington, it was unfinished and didn't look to be finished anytime soon. There were no curtains or shutters, no rugs, no plaster on the walls or ceiling. It was higher than it was long or wide, which didn't strike me as a very useful arrangement, and the desks and bookshelves and Tingey and his two assistants were crammed in there like twenty pounds of turnips in a ten-pound sack. Tingey, bald and bloated, didn't look any too happy to see us, but that was fair enough. We weren't happy to see him, neither.

At a desk to his right sat a gray-faced lieutenant, with silver in his side-whiskers and his throat puffed out like a bullfrog.

"This is Mr. Crawley," said Tingey. "He will keep track of events during this inquiry."

At the word *inquiry* I snuck a peek at Dick out of the corner of my eye. He'd assumed an expression of polite expectation, which seemed a good way to look. I adopted it for myself.

Tingey pointed at the other man in the room, a dumpling in a plain blue frock coat. "Whitlow, my clerk, will write down everything." He pronounced it "clark," though I doubted he'd been in his native London since before he'd joined the Continental Navy. He was half a century old if he was a day, and looked every second of it.

Whitlow was perched with his back to us on a high stool in front of a standing desk; he didn't acknowledge us, but moved his pen across a sheet of paper—writing down what Tingey had just said about him, I guess.

"First order of business," said Tingey. "You gentlemen are out of uniform."

Dick and I looked at each other. We'd changed our tropical whites for buff britches and vests, same as what the three of them had on, and we both of us had worn our best blue long-tailed coats with the three yellow metal buttons at cuffs and pocket flaps.

"I don't understand, sir," I said. "Did the uniform change since we been at sea?"

"Tell them," said Tingey.

"It's the epaulets, boys," said Crawley.

The bullion of Dick's epaulet shone on his shoulder in the sunlight streaming through the windows, and I didn't see how Tingey could fault it. My own swab was sprung and brassy, as I said before, but it was regulation for all that. I hoped the new navy hadn't followed the British example so far as to deny epaulets to lieutenants.

Dick was quicker off the mark than I was. "I beg pardon, sir," he said, "but we've both been appointed acting lieutenants by Commodore Gaswell."

"Yes, and I hereby *unappoint* you," said Tingey, "at least whilst this dueling business is being straightened out. Until such time you are merely unemployed midshipmen as far as I'm concerned, and you'll find my concerns carry great weight around here."

Tingey had commanded the Santo Domingo squadron before Gaswell did. I would've guessed he'd harbor a grudge against Gaswell, and maybe even some hard feelings, but I hadn't expected him to extend them feelings to us. Stunned, I reached for my epaulet to unship it.

Tingey threw up a damp-looking hand in horror. "Oh, don't compound your error by disrobing," he said. "Good God, man." He waved his hand around, like he was drying it, maybe. "Whitlow, read the opening statement. You know, the thing that says what we propose to accomplish by being here in the first place."

The clerk picked up a neat letter-book and turned to a closely written page. "'The late Lieutenant William Trimble,'" he read, leaning close and lifting his specs so he could peer out from under them, "'having been deprived of his command, the armed schooner *Rattle-Snake,* by certain of his officers and men on or about the afternoon of January *blank'*—that's to say I put a blank there, sir," he broke off, "pending our acquisition of the proper date—'of the present year, thereby preventing his defeat of a force of French picaroons intent on capturing the convoy which the said schooner was then engaged to protect, developed a mutual resentment of such intensity with his inferior, Lieutenant Peter Wickett, that the two subsequently met near the town of Cap Français in the French colony of San Domingo and engaged in a duel with pistols, which subsequently proved fatal to Lieutenant Trimble.'"

"Sir," I said, "that ain't true."

Tingey's face quivered like a slice of pork-fat pie. "D'ye mean to say that Mr. Trimble didn't die?"

"No, sir. I mean we didn't deprive him of his command—"

"D'ye mean he wasn't locked in his cabin for most of the fight with the picaroons?"

"No, sir, he was, but it weren't Peter Wickett that locked him in." That was shoal water for me, as I'd been the one who'd locked Cousin Billy's door. I'd done it because he was sloppy drunk and I didn't want him found in a puddle of his own piss, but I didn't guess Tingey needed to hear it. His clerk would just write it down. "Captain Trimble—he left the deck by his own choice, sir. He put it to a vote whether we should surrender. And we all demanded the right to defend ourselves. It was our right and duty, sir."

Whitlow scratched with pen on paper.

"You have the right and duty," said Tingey, "to obey the lawful orders of your superiors."

"That we do, sir," said Dick. "Lawful orders."

"Are you a lawyer, that you know what is lawful and what is not?"

"It's our right as free men to defend our flag against dishonor, sir, and our duty as officers not to cry for quarters."

"I see. What about the report by Mr. P. Hoyden Blair, the assistant U.S. consul to San Domingo? He was aboard, and he has not a good thing to say about any of you."

Dick's face twisted in a sneer. "Maybe that's because he was hiding below decks during the fight, too, sir."

Crawley jerked his head back. "Do you mean to disparage Mr. Blair?"

"I do," said Dick. "He even took a shot at Mr. Graves here when he went to check on the captain."

"Twice," says I. "With the very same pistols—"

Tingey held up a hand. "Continue, Whitlow."

"Aye aye, sir. 'Death was by a single gunshot wound to the right breast. It was attended by the *Rattle-Snake*'s surgeon, Humbert Quilty, and witnessed by the principals' seconds, Mr. Graves and Mr. Towson.'"

A fug crept into the closed room as Whitlow read. When the clerk paused for breath, Crawley said something about someone having had a bad oyster for dinner, which I guessed he was joking because it was getting on spawning season for oysters and no time to be eating them, but he clammed up when Tingey turned his eye on him.

Tingey and Crawley leafed through the logs that Dick and I had kept at sea, commenting to each other on the contents while Whitlow scratched notes. Every time they asked one of us a question, the clerk set down what we said, and it soon got to the point that we couldn't so much as twitch without sending his pen whispering across the page.

Crawley read excerpts from Billy's log as well. It was inaccurate when it wasn't incoherent, and dwelt on his attempts to stay in the good graces of the crew.

"That last," said Tingey. "How did he go about it?"

"Extra grog, sir," I said.

Tingey looked puzzled. "What about disciplinary measures? Any floggings?"

"One, sir. It made him sick."

"Strike that, Whitlow, and continue with the recitation."

There was a lot about how Peter had questioned everything Billy did, from when to get the topmasts in during a blow to whether it was permissible to allow one of His Majesty's frigates to send British marines aboard to search for deserters—which it wasn't, and which hadn't stopped Billy from allowing it anyway.

"You were boarded," said Tingey. "Does he give any particulars, Whitlow?"

"Says here, 'H.M.'s frigate *Clytemnestra*, Captain Sir Horace Tinsdale,' sir."

"Yes, but how many men did they press?"

Whitlow looked at it near and far, and up and down and sidewise. "Doesn't say, sir."

"They pressed no one, sir," said Dick.

Tingey turned a frown on him. "And how was that?"

Whitlow spoke without looking up. "A Frenchman hove into view and the *Clytemnestra* crowded on sail in chase of her, says here."

"Yes," said Dick, "but before that, Mr. Wickett hauled down our colors."

Tingey raised an eyebrow. "Did he, then? Why so?"

"So Tinsdale would have to accept our surrender."

Tingey almost smiled. "And force him to commit an overt act of war in the doing of it," he said. "A clever fellow is your Mr. Wickett, and I dare say Mr. Trimble resented it. But let us dispense with that. The unfortunate Mr. Trimble's squabbles with his lieutenant are not germane to these proceedings."

If they weren't germane to the proceedings then I didn't know what was; but if he wanted to let them dogs lie, I wasn't about to rouse them up again. He shifted uncomfortably in his chair, leaning over on one ham with a preoccupied air for so long that I wondered if it was he that had consumed Crawley's bad oyster.

"Very well, gentlemen," said Tingey at last. "Synopsize for me the more salient points of your late cruise, after which you may go as far as George Town, but leave word where you may be reached. Today is . . ."

"Friday, sir," said Crawley.

"Today is Friday. We have too much work for us to resume this tomorrow. Return here at noon on the Monday, unless you hear otherwise from me. But before you go, gentlemen," he said, holding out a hand as we made ready to haul our wind, "Whitlow will supply you with pen and paper. I require a full report, as best you are able to remember, of the events that led up to the unfortunate death of your late commander."

Whitlow put us each into a separate room. I sat at the desk I was shown to, ignoring the civilian clerks shuffling their papers to let me know I didn't belong there, and cut a new quill with my clasp knife while putting my thoughts in order. I had no idea where to start. So I started at the beginning, continued till I'd finished, and then stopped. I spared Billy, Wickett, and myself nothing. I didn't condemn or hedge or embellish. I merely put down what had happened and when: Billy's drunkenness at all hours, his attempting to surrender when the picaroons attacked us and then hiding below with a bottle, his publicly accusing Peter of lying about the fight and then refusing to explain or apologize, his refusing to let me be his second—and, God help me, my siding with Peter. Dick had stood up for Billy—long enough to see him shot, anyway.

I sat looking out the window. The whiteness of the clouds was so pure that I could've wept. The room was dark when I returned my eyes to my paper.

I dipped my pen again and wrote: *Believing it necessary for his protection, I locked Capt. Trimble in his cabin during the fight with the picaroons.*

The room Dick had gotten for us was in an old stone house, hard by the waterfront on Bridge Street in George Town. It had an iron bed in it with a cob-filled mattress for me and Dick and a pallet on the floor for Jubal.

"I'm cutting out," I said. "You hear *me,* Dick Towson. I'm through with the sea."

It was a black night, no moon. It was warm, too, the first evening of summer, and the air hung damp and heavy over the Potomac. If quiet was a prime need for speechifying, George Town had it in spades. Besides my own steps, all I could hear was the water swirling around the granite boulders upstream at the falls of the Potomac, and every fifteen minutes the chimes of the town clock a few blocks east over by the market. My pacing was more careful than I would've liked, what with Greybar trying to rub his head on my ankles. Cats make terrible noises when you step on them.

"There's a reason Tingey's still a captain," I said. "He got spine."

I'd been thinking about it all evening, kind of pulling at it, the way you do a rotten tooth. February before last, back when he was in the *Ganges* and still commodore of the Santo Domingo squadron, Tingey got boarded off Cap Saint-Nicólas by His Majesty's frigate *Surprise,* Captain Edward Hamilton commanding. "I say," says Hamilton, "do you hand over any Englishmen you happen to have lying about." I'm only guessing about the exact words, mind, but you bet he mustered the crew and started picking out the likeliest-looking topmast Jacks. So Tingey gets his back up and says, "A public ship carries no protection but her flag"—which was pretty good stuff, considering he shouldn't have let them aboard in the first place—and tells Hamilton to vacate the premises forthwith.

The clock down the street jangled out another quarter hour, then bonged twice, out of tune and dismal.

"Dick."

"Mmph."

The ships were a fair match on paper—*Surprise* was rated as a 28 and *Ganges* as a 26—but *Ganges* carried long nine-pounders while *Surprise* carried thirty-two-pounder carronades. That gave Hamilton a considerable advantage at close range—which is exactly where Tingey had let him get. I had to hand it to Tingey, though, he brassed it out pretty good once he seen what a bind he'd gotten himself into. He said he didn't guess he'd prevail in a fight, but he'd die before he let the British take off any of his crew.

"Dick, wake up."

"No." The husks rustled in the mattress as he rolled over.

I took a couple-three more turns up and down the room in the dark. There was a clear space between the door and the window along the wall, except for Greybar trying to attack my feet. He wrapped his paws around my ankle, and I stopped to look out into the blackness. The breeze shifting the curtains around smelled of river mud and the outwash from the paper factory.

Edward Hamilton was no lace hanky. He was the same Hamilton that cut out the mutinied *Hermione* right from under the Dons' noses at Puerto Cabello in New Granada last October, killing over a hundred of her crew, but that day in the *Ganges* he'd discovered he had somewhere else to be and buggered off empty-handed. I'd thought it was fine stuff when I read it in the papers, for a man to be willing to take such a decision as Tingey did against such odds.

But now something wasn't sitting right. If you'd asked me yesterday did I think Tingey would like how Peter had forced Sir Horace Tinsdale's hand under similar circumstances, I would've said yes. The parallels were obvious: Tingey had forced Hamilton to decide whether pressing a few men was worth committing an act of war, and Peter had done the same when he hauled down our colors and dared Sir Horace to accept our surrender. When I first seen Tingey earlier that day I thought some of the benefit might could rub off on me, but he had shied from the similarity like it was corn liquor at a camp meeting. I kicked the bed.

"Dick—wake up, dern ya."

"Please shut up."

I grabbed his foot and walked away with it.

"Hi!" he said, and added some interesting embellishments when he hit the floor.

Jubal sprang up in the dark. "Is you well, Mars Dickie?"

"Yes, Jubal. Go to sleep now." Dick said it like shushing a child.

When Jubal had stopped thrashing around on his pallet and fussing with his blanket, I said, "Dick, listen, I'm going to cut and run."

I couldn't see him at all in the dark, but there was a sort of billowing sound like he was tucking his shirttails under himself where he sat on the floor.

"Well," he said, "of all the darn fool—"

"Shhh! Hear that?"

"I expect to hear myself snoring in about a minute. I'd get back in bed but I can't—"

"*Listen.* Hear that?" I held still, and the distant sound of the falls at once became clear. "General Washington was building him a series of locks up there before he died, and Lighthorse Harry Lee is keeping on with digging the canal. I guess if I wait long enough I could float all the way to the Ohio, never once set foot on solid ground if I didn't have a mind to. Or I could just walk up to Hagerstown and catch the stage. Inside a couple weeks I could be rolling into McKeesport. See my old man. I'm going to make whiskey. It won't be so bad."

"Walk, it'll be faster." He yawned. "What are you on about, anyway? It must be four bells in the middle watch." He yawned again.

"Two A.M.," I said.

"Oh, good guess," said he. "Huzzah for me." Greybar purred in the blackness, and I guessed that Dick had picked him up and put him in his lap. "Besides, I thought you hated him."

"My pap? I never said I hated him."

"That's right." The mattress rattled as he climbed back into bed. "He hates *you*. You really ought to make that up with him, if you don't mind my thrusting in my oar. Fathers with money come in handy, especially when you're supposed to be courting a rich man's daughter. Like my sister, f'rinstance." He yawned hugely.

I touched the front of my shirt, feeling for the pewter locket with its miniature portrait of my dead mother. She was white, and my father was white, but somehow, somewhere, I had gotten *amalgamated*, a mix of the white race with another, the exact identity of which had been denied me. I was light enough that I hadn't even knowed until Commodore Gaswell told me, and dark enough that I believed it the moment he said it. I still wasn't sure as sure of it. I had some questions that needed answering. But no, I didn't guess the old man would be any too happy to see me.

"There's money to be made out west," I said. "With a raft of whiskey and a Spanish trading license, I'd have to be dumber as a rock not to turn a profit."

"Well, I guess you are that, then," said Dick. "Where do you figure on getting a Spanish trading license?"

"In Saint-Louis on the Mississippi. My mother was born there. Maybe someone remembers her."

"Stay out of Louisiana. The Spaniards are crazy."

"Hang the Spaniards and New Orleans too." I could walk all the way to New Albion on the far side of the continent. All I would need was a bag of corn and a shotgun. "Why don't you come with me? We could be the first white men to set eyes on the Lost Tribe of Israel."

The mattress crackled as he sat up. "That's an idea."

"Thomas Jefferson says—"

"That's a dang crazy idea," he said. "I got a better one. You come with me to White Oak for the summer. Let's think on it for a month or two. Tingey will give us permission to ship out as soon as we find a berth, you'll see."

FOUR

Dick and I hired a boat to take us across the upper Chesapeake to White Oak Plantation, the Towson family holdings on a spit of land between the bay and the Chester River. As we sailed north along the eastern shore of a large island dedicated to wheat and tobacco, with the red-winged blackbirds creaking like rusty hinges in the cattails along the shore, Dick pointed past the salt marsh to the fields blowing green and silver in the breeze off the river, and beyond them to the gables of a mansion on a hill amid a grove of sycamores.

"That's where Lambert Wickes and his family have lived for the last couple of centuries," he said.

"Why, how you talk. How could he live for a couple of centuries?"

"*He* didn't. His *family* has, you ignoramus. Besides which, he's dead anyway. Foundered off the Grand Banks of Newfoundland back in 'seventy-seven on his way home from taking Benjamin Franklin to France."

"Then why'd you—"

He laughed. "Did you know that the cook was the only survivor?"

I thought of Doc and how he'd fought in the old *Rattle-Snake*. "That don't surprise me. Cooks is tough."

"Say, look," he said, taking in the dozens of small craft on the broad river with a wave of his hand. The men in them were bending and heaving over nets stretched across the shallows. "The shad must be running. Do you like shad?"

"No idea—"

"They take some getting used to. They're awfully bony, but oh! So fat and delicate! And their roe is something."

"What's roe?"

He looked at me like he wasn't sure if he wanted to be astonished or amused.

"Why, it's fish eggs, of course. We'll have some for breakfast. You just wait—they're superb."

I guessed I could wait a while; a good long while would do. What was superb to me was the sight of Arabella Towson, blond and pink and dressed in white, waving from the dock as we pulled into the cove at White Oak.

I noticed straight away that Dick's sister had changed considerable since I'd seen her last. For one thing, her bosom had growed, which she'd emphasized with a low neckline and then obscured with a kerchief. Her dress was of some white gauzy stuff, and the afternoon sun behind her skirts caused my glance to linger below her waist. I thought I was being clever, taking it all in as I bent to make my leg, but as I rose my eyes met her sky-blue ones and I knew she'd seen me looking.

She threw a deep curtsy that had more sass than courtesy in it, cocked an eyebrow at me, and said, "What a pleasure to see you again, Mr. Graves."

I bowed again, annoyed at the confusion that roared in my head. I would've recovered from it with grace if she hadn't throwed her arms around me and kissed me. Her dress was as soft as clouds and she smelled like an orange tree in bloom, and it got me all tongue-tied and gangly. And then, as if she'd just then realized that her brother and a boatman and two Negroes were watching—or most determinedly *not* watching—she straightened her kerchief and said, "Well! Come, Matty. Come, Dickie. Papa and his lady are waiting. We saw you rounding the point. There are cool drinks and petit-fours in the garden."

She led me by the hand up the oyster-shell path while Dick strolled along behind with his hands in his pockets, whistling. Behind us, Jubal hauled the bags and chests out of the boat and piled them on the dock. Ahead of us, the red bricks and white columns of the manor house rose above the white oaks that give the place its name.

I give her hand a squeeze. "Missed you, Arie."

She dropped my hand. "I am glad to see you still have the use of all your limbs, Mr. Graves." She pinched my arm hard.

I resisted the impulse to rub it. "Well, why wouldn't I?"

"When a gentleman goes off to cruise against the enemy and doesn't write his lady for a year, naturally she frets."

"It weren't neither a year. It was six months."

"Six months!" She said it like she'd caught me in some monstrous deed. "Six months without word! A gentleman needs to be more considerate of his lady."

"That was wrong in me." *His lady.* I was pretty sure I liked the sound of that. I looked over my shoulder at Dick. He pretended to see something interesting in a nearby gum tree.

"But hang it, Arie," I said, "I was a mite busy, you know. I got captured and hit on the head some fierce. Want to see the place?"

"No." She gave me a hidden sort of smile and turned her face away. "Yes."

We walked along a bit, our hands brushing against each other until I held mine open. She smacked her palm against mine a couple of times and then laced our fingers.

We met Jubal's father strutting along with his cane, bringing the pony cart down for the luggage. He looked fine in his blue and silver livery, and his white wig gave him a distinguished air. He took off his hat and bowed.

"Welcome home, Mars Dickie," he said, smiling beautifully. "Hello, Mistah Graves. Pleasure to see you ag'in."

"Hello, Uncle Jupe," I said. "Glad to be back. How's the missus?"

"She fine, she fine. She over to da Woolsey place now." Just the slightest of hesitations, and then he smiled beautifully again and said, "I see her 'most ebber week, I thank you, sah."

"And how's the leg?"

"Oh, fine, fine, I thank you, sah. Bit o' da rheumatism, is all. It get in my bones, sah, I thank you for askin'."

"He's a little old to be working, ain't he?" I asked when we had passed out of earshot.

Arabella frowned in puzzlement. "Who, Uncle Jupe? Don't be silly. I don't think he'd know what to do with himself if he didn't have us to care for. Besides, he must work to earn his bread. The Bible says so."

"But even mules get put out to pasture when they're used up."

She swung her hand, swinging mine with it. "Silly, Uncle Jupe's no mule!"

"What happened to his wife?"

"She never could make a pie. I said to her, 'Easy as pie,' but it didn't take. We had to buy a new cook."

That brought up a memory I didn't care to mention—my friend Juge in our prison cell in Jacmel, telling me how he'd put his former owner into the oven for burning the pastry.

I shook my head. "That's a shame."

"Yes, there's nothing I like so much as pie."

Dick laughed. "I think he meant it's a shame for the niggers, Arie. He fought alongside 'em in San Domingo and they put bugs in his ears."

"Pish, pash, and posh," said Arabella. "Don't pay any never-no-mind to Dickie, Mr. Graves—nor to Uncle Jupe. The Woolsey place is only five miles away, and he can walk over and see her any night he wants."

Side by side in tall-backed cane chairs, Mr. and Mrs. Towson drank lemonade under an ancient, laurel-smelling sweet bay magnolia, festooned with leafy white blossoms, that was the centerpiece of a trim garden at the end of the path. Although Elver Towson had served with a macaroni regiment during the Revolution, he hadn't awarded himself an honorary colonelcy, being afflicted with an inconvenient honesty. He was yellow-haired and blue-eyed like Dick and Arabella, but silver had shot through the yellow, red had rimmed the blue, his jaws had become jowls, and whiskey roses had gone to seed on his nose and cheeks. Lily Towson—the second Mrs. Towson and about twenty years younger than her husband—was slender and redheaded, with small creases at the corners of her mouth that disappeared into dimples when she smiled. She was dressed in white muslin, with an upside-down flowerpot of a straw hat secured by a sea-gray ribbon that matched the color of her eyes. On a marble bench to her left hunched a lank-haired lout with no eyelashes or brows that I could see, and no color at all in his face except a rash of raspberry pimples across his chin, cheeks, and forehead. He smirked at me.

"Mama! Papa!" said Arabella, tugging me along. "See what I have brought."

I don't expect my own homecoming could've been any solemner. Mr. Towson rose to shake his son's hand, but that was about as excited as they got. It was just their way.

Mr. Towson took in our midshipmen's uniforms and waved his hand at a pitcher on a silver tray. "D'ye care to take anything in your lemonade, Mr. Graves? We have the ladies' indulgence."

"Thank'ee, Mr. Towson, but I guess I'll pass."

"It's your father's own stuff."

"Sometimes I'm of two minds about whiskey, Mr. Towson."

He looked up sharply. "Not gone temperance, have you?"

"Oh, I'll say not, sir. It's just that I floated Billy in a barrel of it after his duel with Peter Wickett. I had to get him home somehow, and—"

"Sir, I don't believe the ladies needed to hear that."

"Well, I don't guess I will have any right yet, sir, thank'ee."

"Suit y'self." He topped off his glass from the decanter. "Dick?"

"If it doesn't misplease the lady." He bowed to his stepmother. "Good afternoon, madam."

"Good afternoon, Dickie dear. Refresh yourself as you will." She smiled at him, and then she turned to me and showed me her dimples.

I got my hat off without dropping it. "I hope I find you well, ma'am."

"I am, thank you, dear." She held out her hand to be kissed. "How handsome you have become!" Her smile faded faintly as she indicated the lout. "This is Mr. Roby Douglass of Delaware. New Ark, isn't it? He has come to stay the summer, I think."

Douglass had gotten to his feet, though I didn't bet it was on my account.

"Pleasure to make your acquaintance, Mr. Douglass," I said, but I said it to the back of his head. He'd taken Arabella's hand in both of his and leaned over it as if he had every intention of kissing it.

"Oh ho," he said, like a stage Frenchman. "We are meet again, *mam'selle.*"

She giggled and pulled her hand away.

"Well!" said Mrs. Towson, fixing a smile on her face. "Isn't this grand. Do be seated, my dears. Mr. Graves, why don't you join Arabella on the marble settee. I'm certain you were comfortable where you were, Mr. Douglass. I'm sure you're hungry as ever, Dickie. Shall I pour you some lemonade, Mr. Graves? Why, Arabella, don't crush the poor boy. You'll be in his lap in a moment."

"Yes, ma'am." Arabella lowered her eyes and moved an inch or two away from me on the stone bench. Hanging her head had the advantage of bringing the wide brim of her straw hat between her face and her stepmother's eyes, and she looked sidelong at me and grinned before turning herself once more into a young gentlewoman. "Will you have a cake, Mr. Graves?"

"Yes, thank'ee."

Mr. Douglass leaned forward and snatched a petit-four before Arabella could bring the tray within my reach. "Oh ho," he said and stuffed it in his mouth.

"Well, really," she said, giggling.

"Mr. Douglass is here on . . . business of some sort, wasn't it?" said Mrs. Towson.

"Y'm," said Mr. Douglass. He swallowed and said, "Beg pardon, ma'am." He showed his teeth charmingly.

"Mr. Douglass is the son of . . . well, of Mr. and Mrs. Douglass, of course—silly me!" said Mrs. Towson. "His family have been in Delaware for some time, I understand. Since the Swedes, wasn't it?"

"That's right."

I said, "Is Douglass a Swedish name, sir?"

"No, 'tisn't. Say, what're you questioning me for?"

"I ain't."

He showed his cake-covered teeth again before setting them into another petit-four.

"You seem remarkably well, Mr. Graves," said Mrs. Towson. "I understand you were in your sickbed for some weeks."

"I'm tolerable, ma'am, thank'ee. My wounds were mostly to my head. Our surgeon, Mr. Quilty, thought that in itself disqualified me from the sick list."

"Don't listen to him," said Dick. "He took the *Faucon* frigate nearly single-handedly, and dressed only in his shirt."

"And a belt," I said.

"There wasn't much left of the shirt afterwards, though," said Arabella.

Her father dang near spilled his lemonade. "Arie!"

I was surprised to hear her say it, myself. I looked at her, wondering how she knew it, and she held herself very straight like she was trying to hold her breath and laugh at the same time.

"Dickie tells such funny stories in his letters," she said, turning the look toward me. "Are they true?"

"He must've been flattering me, ma'am," says I. "There was a good fifty Rattle-Snakes left when we boarded. They deserve the credit as much as anyone."

"That isn't what I—"

"Yes," said Douglass. "The way I heard it, you were running around San Domingo in the stark-staring altogether with a bunch of niggers you'd taken up with, and—"

"I weren't *either* naked—"

"More lemonade, Mr. Douglass?" said Mrs. Towson. "Do have a cake." She nudged him with the tray until he took one. "Dickie, dear, surely you had some adventures?"

"No, ma'am, except I got to take a pair of twelve-pounders ashore at Jacmel and pound the fort with 'em."

"Yes!" said Mr. Towson. "I read that to you from the *Gazette,* Lily. Routed the nigger army."

"I guess you'll forgive me, sir," I said, "but it was the *colored* army he routed."

"That's what he *said,*" said Douglass. He looked at me like I needed a drool cup.

I opened my mouth, but Dick beat me to it. "They have different degrees of niggers down there. Most of them are black as sin, but there are some mulattoes," he said. "The coloreds—seriously, that's what they call 'em in French, *free coloreds.* Isn't that right, Matty?"

"*Gens du couleur libre*—'free people of color,' sure."

"The coloreds were under a chap named Pétion, who was under Rigaud, who's the leader of the mulattoes."

"Till he ran off to France, anyway," said I.

"Yes, before then," said Dick. "The niggers, they were under Toussaint L'Ouverture, whom you'll have heard of."

"Not I." Douglass reached for the petit-fours. "Not that it matters anymore, does it? Isn't it over now? You lost, the niggers won, and here you are and not even a lieutenant for your troubles. That's a midshipman's uniform, isn't it?"

"That'll come with time, sir," said Mr. Towson. "The military's like the weather—no accounting for it, but you can turn it to your advantage if you're smart. Now tell on, and no more interruptions."

We took turns relating our tales, leaving out the more bloodthirsty bits so as not to distress the ladies, and so Mr. Towson could savor them himself after dinner.

Arabella clung to my arm and shuddered when I described my captivity in Jacmel. "It must have been *horrid,*" she said, "surrounded by all those nasty niggers!"

Her clutching me like that had the pleasant effect of pressing her breast against my arm, but I found the touch of her fingers unaccountably unpleasant. "I wouldn't say that, not at all," I said. "Toussaint is about as magnificent a fellow as you'll see anywhere. And I had a friend on his staff, a major name of Juge. We got captured in the same assault.

He was a great pal to me, and you couldn't beat him for bravery and honor." Which was what got him killed in the end, but I didn't say it. "He was all the time laughing, no matter how bad things got."

"Yes," said Mr. Towson, "the nigger is funny that way. It has to do with the simple nature of his soul."

"Oh, pooh, papa," said Arabella. "A nigger hasn't a soul. Reverend Thomas says so. Everybody says so. Matty, you didn't bring this ol' Juge with you, did you?"

"No, he was killed aboard of the *Faucon.*"

"How you prattle, child," said Mrs. Towson, and for an instant I wasn't sure if she meant me or Arabella. "More lemonade, Matty dear?"

"Yes, please."

"Do continue—you were interrupted."

"Yes," said Douglass. "Tell us about the duel."

"We've heard enough of that to last us a lifetime, I guess," said Mr. Towson. "Some folks have no notion of what the Code Duello means. You boys behaved honorably, we've sent our condolences to the family, and that ought to be the end of it."

"The end of Billy Trimble, you mean," sniggered Douglass.

I stood up. "He was my cousin, you—"

But Elver Towson leaned over and shook a finger in his face. "You embarrass yourself, sir!"

"No need for shouting, Elver," said his wife.

"Damnation, I'm not shouting!"

Ha ha for you, Mr. Douglass, thinks I, sitting down again, but he was cunninger than I thought.

He smiled at Arabella. "I believe the lady promised me a walk."

"Oh . . . but I meant later!"

He pouted. "But you promised."

"Yes, do be a dear girl," said Mrs. Towson. "Mr. Graves and your brother have weeks and weeks to tell you all that has transpired, but Mr. Douglass is our guest and he must be humored. I mean, indulged. Goodness," she said, fanning herself, "it's rather warm for June, isn't it?"

I regarded Arabella's eyes, the color of the sky behind their long lashes, and was moved; I regarded her figure as she rose from the marble settee and was moved again. Beneath her broad hat her yellow hair was cut short in the new French fashion, and I'd disliked it at first, thinking it made her too boyish, but it really did something fine for the slenderness of her neck. Which I wanted to squeeze when Douglass held out his arm and she took it.

The candle Dick carried was an island in the darkness. Down the hall to the left, dim lights showed under Arabella's and Mr. Towson's doors; to the right, Mrs. Towson's and Douglass's were dark. Time ticked away in the clock beside us at the top of the stairs. We turned right. At the far end of the hall, Greybar's eyes flashed yellow in the candlelight as he turned away from Douglass's door and stared at us.

"Who is that wart, anyway?" I whispered.

"That's your cat."

"No, that *wart.*"

"*What* wart?" We'd been through a couple-three bottles of Mr. Towson's port wine after the others had gone upstairs, and Dick spoke overloud.

I draped an arm around his shoulders. "Sh!"

"Sh!" he said back. Then, "What wart? Roby Douglass?"

"No, your granny! Of course I mean Douglass."

"Oh, ho! Jealous, brother?"

"Sh-sh-sh! Not I, mate. Curious, is all."

"Yes, sure. Well, he's one of the Delaware Douglasses, of course. Armaments, I believe." He put his finger to his chin, and then held it up. "I remember now. His father owns a gunpowder factory. But—trade and manufacturing, Matty, not at *all* our sort."

"Pipe down."

"*You* pipe down."

We stopped to put our fingers to our lips and shush each other.

"Anyway," he whispered, "I shouldn't worry about it."

"But I'm trade and manufacturing myself, come to that."

"As long as you're an officer, you're a gentleman."

"That's true, so true." However long it might be till we actually were officers again. We bumped into my bedroom door. I opened it. "I always thought your old man looked on me kind of favorable."

"Well, so he does." He followed me in and shut the door. He lit the candle on the nightstand. "But you're different, almost one of the family. I've always thought of you as a brother, brother."

"Maybe that's just it." I sat on the bed and kicked off my shoes. I couldn't tell anymore if I liked Dick because I liked him or if I liked him because he was rich. Uncle Jupe had turned down the bedclothes and laid out my nightshirt. "If I'm a brother, I can't very well be a brother-in-*law.* Your pap was awful reserved today, don't you think?"

"Not a bit of it." He stretched out his arms and yawned, the candle in his hand throwing shadows on the wall. "Say, now that you mention it, he *was* unusually polite. I remember marking it: Mr. Graves this and Mr. Graves that, and never a 'Matty' or 'dear fellow' in it. I put it up to our having been blooded. Did you see the way he got his color up when you told him how the old *Rattle-Snake* got sank? It's a good job you saved that part for after dinner. Though I expect Arabella would have enjoyed it. She's a bloody-minded ninny, you know."

"No, I didn't know." I got up and hung my coat on the back of the chair.

"Why, sure! She sets her suitors on each other like fighting cocks."

"What suitors?"

"*What* suitors? Half the Eastern Shore, of course—the male half. As her brother I hate to admit it, but she's kind of a peach, don't you think?"

"Yep." When he said *peach* I had such a vision of soft juiciness that it give me a third leg, and I had to sit down again to hide it. I'd gotten it into my head that I was undressing for bed, but I sure couldn't take my britches off right at that particular moment, so I unbuttoned the knees and yanked my stockings off.

He yawned again. "I don't know what she sees in that Roby Douglass fellow."

I balled my stockings up and heaved them against the wall.

"Goodness, Matty, you have it bad, don't you!"

"Well, I guess I know it, don't I? It's just that . . . that toad has throwed me. Only temporarily, mind you, and don't you dare allow I said it."

"Him! Arabella's snubbed him since he first began coming around."

I rubbed my bare feet on the floorboards. I looked at Dick, trying to gauge what the truth was. "What d'you mean, since he first began coming around? How long's that been going on?"

"He was here last Christmas, which you would've known if you had come like you said you would."

"I had some family business to take care of with my brother Phillip, which I guess you know." Phillip had managed to get the shipping business he owned with my father into shoal water and had cut off my allowance. I'd also been a-whoring that day, it being my birthday as well as the Lord's, but I didn't guess Dick needed to know how I spent my time. "How come I never heard of Roby Douglass before?"

"Good fortune, I suspect."

"But why nary a mention of him?"

"Because Mrs. Towson despises him. Look, I shouldn't worry about him. So what if he's awful rich—just *look* at him." He shuddered. "Not even Arabella is that stupid."

After Dick left I lay awake in bed, staring at the dark and turning visions of Arabella and Roby Douglass over and over in my head. The more I tried to put it from my mind, the more I thought about it. I thought about how she'd looked at him as he led her away from the garden that afternoon, and I thought of how they probably looked praying together at church of a Sunday morning, as if nary a wicked thought ever passed through their heads. I thought about—

"Good Lord!" I sat up in bed. I'd dozed off and had an awful dream.

The door was rattling. I opened it to let Greybar in, but when I reached down to pet him, the little bastard scooted across the hall to Douglass's door and meowed.

FIVE

Elver Towson wouldn't never have admitted it. He would've been tarnal put out if I could properly take affront at anything he said or did; yet he managed to make it clear I was about as welcome as a wild hog at a church social.

"Dick has gone up to Chestertown to fetch the papers," he said in his study one morning. The room smelled of old leather, old whiskey, and old cigar butts. Sipping from his glass, which was one of them little thimble-sized things old ladies use for sherry, he looked at me standing by the window. "He tells me you've some notion to go west."

"Yes, sir. I got an idea to open up some markets out in Kentucky or down in that area. Tennessee, maybe, or maybe all the way down to New Orleans."

He finished his glass and waggled it. "Sure you won't have a sniff?"

"No, thank'ee, sir. If one bit of advice stuck from my pap, it was never drink and do business."

"Oh, you don't say?"

At the sideboard, he poured himself a bumper and lifted it to his lips, slowly so as not to spill it, and stood there holding it to his mouth as if he was soaking it up through his tongue. When the glass was half empty he sat down again in his wing chair, one knee over the other, and looked past me out the diamond-paned window onto a bed of roses and the broad side lawn. Some Negroes were out there cutting the grass with scythes. It was warm out there, and the sweat shone on their skin.

If Elver Towson knew what I was, I'd be out there with them.

Certain sure I wouldn't be in his study breathing the sweet fumes of his whiskey. By God, I was thirsty.

"How much do you need?" he said.

About a barrel would do it, I thought. I looked at the nude Aphrodite on the wall behind him. She was smiling past one hand, the other hand being more strategically occupied. Strands of red hair streamed across her face and breasts.

"Are you well, Mr. Graves? I know a head wound can be a dangerous business."

"I'm fine, sir. I just got kind of a permanent headache is all."

"Son, I'll give you a little tip about business. When a man mentions a venture of yours and asks you how much money you need, you're supposed to tell him how much money you need."

The whiskey glowed in his glass. I wondered was he ever going to finish it.

"Yes, sir."

"So, what's your proposal? How many men will you hire? How much is a flatboat man getting these days? How much is a barrel of whiskey wholesale, and of what quality?" He waved his glass around as he talked, and I watched it lest he spill it. "I'm sure you'll not have much trouble with those latter two things," he said, "considering your daddy produces a good deal of good drink. Top-quality stuff. You have written to him to set up the scheme, I hope."

"Well, I need to get me a trading license from the Spaniards."

"Not a bit of it! Pinckney's treaty solved that four years ago. Free trade along our side of the river all the way down to West Florida. Write to your father. If you can't take advantage of your family, who can you take advantage of, I always say."

"I confess I ain't wrote him these six months and more, sir."

"Then I suggest you do so," he said. "Better yet, go see him in person. That's far and away the best thing to do. Perhaps we'll talk about it again some other time."

He drank his whiskey at last, throwing it back like it was air. Then he put his glass down.

"There," he said, "I'm done drinking for the day." He winked. "And I'll commence again at sundown. But say, I hear my daughter and her gentleman friend are going riding this morning." His laugh rattled low in his chest, like he had water in his lungs. "Do you like horses, Mr. Graves?"

I hated horses. I'd charge across a burning deck with grapeshot howling past my ears. I'd go aloft in a roaring gale, blindfolded and with one hand tied behind my back. I'd swim naked through shark-infested seas, even, to save Arabella from the evil clutches of Roby Douglass, but hell if I'd do it a-horseback. On a plow nag, maybe, but not one of the Towsons' riding horses. No, sir; last time I got astride a galloping horse the tarnal thing took me into the middle of an infantry assault on a fortified town. I'd be dogged and double damned afore I got on a horse again.

I got to the stable yard just in time to see Douglass helping Arie get settled sidesaddle on a piebald mare. Arie wore a black, flat-topped round hat and a high-waisted, tight-sleeved red riding habit with long skirts flowing down the horse's larboard side. Mr. Douglass wore a smug little grin that I didn't like at all. He threw his leg over a bay gelding and glanced back at me.

"C'mon, Arie!" he whooped, and touched heels to his horse.

She tapped the long whip in her right hand against the mare's odd side, and away they trotted down the road. Her perch looked mighty precarious to me, but then they broke into a canter and disappeared behind a stand of sweetgum trees down at the end of the lane.

"Hey! Ahoy!" I ran into the stable. "He's riding her too fast!"

"Oh, *no,* suh," said the groom, leading a saddled chestnut past me into the yard. "Dat Mars Roby be ridin' a gelding. Dat ain't a her. Dat's a fella what used to be."

"He'll 'used to be' a fellow when I get done with him, I guess. He's like to break her neck."

"No, suh, I'm sorry to say again, but Miz Arie got da mare. An' it take a lot to break a hoss's neck, I can tell you from experience. Yes, suh." He held out the chestnut's reins. "I expected you'd be along, so I done saddled—"

I grabbed the reins. "Hold his head while I get aboard."

"Yes, suh," he said with the patience of an old bosun obeying the orders of a boy midshipman. He wrapped a big fist through the bridle.

The chestnut seemed to be biding his time; he stood still enough with his head in the groom's arms, but his rump was a-quiver.

"You want I should fetch you a bar'l to stand on, suh?"

"No." I reached up and grabbed the pommel, but still I hung fire.

The groom pointed at the stirrup. "You puts your foot in dere, suh."

"Well, I guess I know that much, don't I?" I put my foot in the stirrup, but the groom grabbed my ankle.

"Beg your pardon, suh, but you wants to put it in da other side. Like dis here." He turned the stirrup around and slipped it over the toe of my boot. "Try it dat way, suh."

I boarded at last—clutching handfuls of reins, mane, and pommel—and set out at a brisk trot, the chestnut snorting and shaking his head and me bouncing all over Sunday and back. I never could get a hang of riding proper—all that rising up and down while standing in the stirrups just confuses me and makes it double hard to hang on. I'll tell it true, though—a trot may be an easy gait for a horse, but it's a power uncomfortable on Charlie and the boys.

The chestnut turned right at the stand of gum trees. Dust hung in the air in that direction. I didn't bother looking down, though, calculating I could trust the horse to watch the road; I watched his ears and head. When we jolted past a patch of pine waste he twitched his ears and raised his head, and I let him pull in where he wanted to go. He nickered, and from beyond a thicket of bushes Arabella's piebald raised her head and neighed in reply.

I found Arabella and Roby Douglass in a cozy little grassy place. Douglass's shirttails were out, and Arabella had leaves in her hair. She'd lost her little hat, and her skirts were muddy in the back.

"Oh, Matty!" she said. "You won't tell, will you?"

"There's nothing *to* tell," Douglass snapped.

"Oh, I think there is, mate."

"Yes, that you're a peeping Tom!"

"Mind yourself, pal, or I'll knock you down!"

"Roby! Matty!" Arabella clapped her hands like a Sunday school teacher. "You stop it this instant. Why, you'd think you were a couple of dogs, the way you sniff and growl around each other."

"Well, thank you very much," I said. "I guess you *wouldn't* want me to come along and help you if you'd fell off and broke your neck."

"Oh! Never you worry about *me,* Mr. Graves, I'm sure," she said, sweeping by me. She marched up to the piebald and grabbed the reins. "You go ahead and tattle if you want. Papa will know Dasher never meant to throw me. It's that stupid sidesaddle."

I scrambled down to help her and Douglass elbowed me out of the way, but Arabella stuck her nose in the air.

"I don't need help from either of you," she said. And she didn't, neither. She put her left foot into the single stirrup, hoisted herself up as easy as climbing into bed, and hooked her top leg between the two prongs sticking out of the side of her saddle. I guess that's what she did, anyway; with all them skirts, it's kind of hard to tell what a woman's doing with her legs. She held out a hand, still with her nose in the air. "My whip, if you please."

I found it before Douglass did, and I held it out to her.

"Thank you," she said, cold enough to freeze a fire in August, and kicked her heel against the horse's larboard side and tapped with her whip on the starboard.

I was so mesmerized by the way the damp skirts clung to her thighs that I forgot to keep an eye on the enemy. He rode up behind me, and as I turned to get out of the way he gave me a boot in the head.

"Come along, darling," I heard him say as I tumbled into the bushes. "I fear the lout means to do you harm. I shall protect you. Also I have found your hat."

I lay peacefully in the bushes while the thudding of their hooves faded, and soon the only thudding was in my head. I wondered if he was a good shot. Certainly he had the reach on me with swords, but if I could rush inside his guard I could gut him.

The summer sun was piercingly bright even in the shade of the woods, and the air was breathless and sodden. After a time I found myself down by the shore, and I stripped off my clothes and swam in the bay until I could think of things other than murder.

We spent that evening on the veranda, listening to the crickets and fanning ourselves while the ladies drank lemonade and the gentlemen drank julep, which Lily Towson allowed of an evening and which Uncle Jupe made so well. Manners dictated that we call the julep something else, though.

"How do you find your lemonade, Mr. Graves?" said Arabella.

"Delicious, ma'am." I allowed myself a deep pull at it. Jupe had gotten the mint, sugar, and whiskey mixed so well together that I couldn't tell where one ended and the next began. I held the dewy glass against my temple.

Arabella perched in the middle of the cane settee with me on one side and Douglass on the other. Elver and Lily Towson sat in high-backed cane chairs across from us, while Dick lounged off to the side, reading one of his newspapers in the light of a lamp in the window. Greybar crouched at Douglass's feet, staring up at him.

"Say, Graves," said Douglass, holding out a finger for the cat to bat at. "Who're your people voting for?"

"How would I know?"

"Why, don't you care who's president?"

"I don't get a vote."

He leaned past Arabella and gave me a sly grin, all teeth and chin. "That's right. No property."

"I ain't old enough and neither are you. And my father owns plenty of property."

He snorted. "Pittsburgh, isn't it?" He patted his lap, and Greybar jumped into it. "Away off in the mountains with nothing on it but rocks. Who would want such land as that?"

"General Washington, for one," I retorted. "He owned a passel of it. That's why he was so eager to put down the Whiskey Rebellion." That stupid cat was purring. "What do you care who we vote for? I don't see how it's none of your business."

"Jefferson's bound to cause another rebellion if he gets elected," he said. "You ought to read the papers."

"I guess if it's important someone'll tell me about it."

"I don't suppose we need discuss politics," said Mrs. Towson, "any more than we need discuss which church to go to on Sunday. Tell me, Mr. Graves, have you read the new edition of the *Letters from an American Farmer?*"

Hector Saint John's collections of essays had been a mainstay of discussion for years. "No, ma'am, I didn't know he'd published a new one."

"It isn't doing nearly as well as his others." Douglass smiled condescendingly at Arabella. "It's in French."

"What," I said, "ain't you got any French?"

"I've never heard a Frenchman say anything worth listening to." Again he smiled at Arabella. "We're at war with them, you know."

"Says here," said Dick, holding his paper closer to the lamplight, "that Bonaparte has crossed the Alps on a mule."

"A mule," I said. "Why'd he do that?"

He looked at me over the folded sheet. "To attack the Austrians, says here."

Arabella fidgeted beside me. "Why didn't he attack the Italians?"

Dick and Douglass and I all looked at her. "What?"

"The Alps are in Italy, aren't they?"

"Yes, Dick," I said, slipping him a wink. "Why *didn't* he attack the Italians?"

Douglass gave me a pitying look. "There's no such thing as an Italian. You got your Genoese and your Ligurians and your papists, but never a plain old Italian. You ought to look at a map sometime."

Dick raised an eyebrow at me. "And here I thought Genoa was in Liguria."

"I guess gunpowder's a pretty good business to be in, what with the war and all," I said. "Ain't it, Mr. Douglass."

"About as good as selling cheap whiskey, Mr. Graves."

"Gentlemen," said Mrs. Towson, holding up a slender hand, "I must disallow this topic as well." She plied herself with her sisal fan. "I suppose discussing Hector Saint John will necessarily lead us back to religion. Oh dear."

We sat a while in silence, except for a rustle or two from Dick's papers and now and then someone slapping themself on the cheek. I was thinking about asking Mrs. Towson could we smoke on account of the skeeters—she'd already indulged us with whiskey in mixed company, after all—when Arabella ran her fingers lightly across my own. I thought maybe it was a centipede or something at first, she did it so light, but then she took my hand in the dark and give it a squeeze.

"Here's an interesting item," said Dick. "Says here, 'Norfolk. John Kendle, master of the *Liza* of this place, having lately returned from Europe, reports that on the twelfth instant—'"

"What's the twelfth instant?" said Arabella. "And why are there twelve of them?"

I heard a wheeze as Douglass opened his mouth, so I said, "It means on the twelfth of this month."

"Which is June," said Dick, "in case you have forgot. Where was I? 'On the twelfth instant, Cape Henry bearing northwest a half west, distant nineteen leagues, after a chase of four hours, he was captured by a French privateer sloop, Citizen Captain Mesh, from Guadeloupe, mounting eight carriage guns. The French captain, exceedingly tall and beautifully mannered, took from the brig some pots of paint and other ship's stores, along with the better part of a hogshead of rum, and several Negro sailors belonging to the ship's owners. Upon being told the *Liza* was short on provisions, Captain Mesh supplied her with a barrel of beef and a bag of bread, expressing much regret that any difference should have taken place between the two republics, and released her with a profound *merci*.'"

"That was droll of him," said Mrs. Towson.

"Surprised that Master Kendle didn't notice a few hundred dollars was missing from his strongbox while he was at it," said Mr. Towson. "Yankees have a sad lack of imagination."

"Why, Elver!" said Mrs. Towson.

"I'm joking, my dear."

"Well, if the Frenchie released him out of profound mercy, why'd he steal the strongbox, then?" said Douglass. "That doesn't sound so merciful to me."

"What?" said Mr. Towson. "Who said he stole the strongbox?"

He gazed blearily at Douglass, who was explaining about Yankees to Arabella.

"That was pretty dang funny, Dick," I said. "Why don't you read—what's the matter?"

"You won't like this one as much," he said.

"Read it anyway."

"Very well. 'Washington City. A duel took place on the ninth instant at Bladensburg between Lieutenant Peter Wickett of the United States sloop *Breeze* and Lieutenant Danville Crawley of Captain Tingey's staff. Mr. Crawley was so badly wounded that it was supposed he should succumb to his death. Two shots were also exchanged by the seconds, neither of whom was wounded. Mr. Wickett is desired to return to the federal city to answer to a charge of attempted murder.' Hmmm, what do you know."

He looked more cheerful than alarmed, but was doing a good enough job of hiding it that I didn't guess I could mention it.

"That's kind of strange, ain't it?" I said. "Peter must've been tarnal provoked."

"Yes," said Dick dryly, "considering how dead set he is against the gentlemanly art of the Code Duello."

"That isn't the half of it," said his father. "Since when is dueling illegal?"

Dick shook his head. "Doesn't say. It's just the one paragraph."

"Oh, for—it *isn't* illegal," said Mr. Towson. "Not in this state, begod! Good gracious, what's this world coming to where a man can't defend his honor without having to answer to trumpery? It's a disgrace."

"I don't believe it," I said. "Crawley must've provoked him some awful."

Dick snorted. "Him! He probably figured that Wickett only fought Billy because he couldn't get out of it. If he provoked him because he didn't guess he had the stomach for it, it serves him right."

"That's downright uncivil," said Mr. Towson.

"For shame, Dick," said Mrs. Towson. "You ought to send him your best desires for a speedy recovery."

"You're right," said Dick. "I'll send him a basket of oysters."

Arabella giggled. "June hasn't an *R* in it. It's no month to be eating oysters."

"All the more reason to send 'em," said Dick. He went back to reading his paper.

One good thing about it all, I thought: They wouldn't be desiring Peter to return if they already had him in custody. I let the others talk. I watched Arabella watching Douglass, and I listened to him mewling when the conversation outdistanced him, and braying when he managed to catch a hold of it. She smiled at him with her lips half open, full and moist and shining in the light from the window, as if she was so enraptured by him that she couldn't remember to close her mouth, and giggled at his jokes, and carried on so transparently that I wondered he didn't tumble to it. But even Mrs. Towson listened politely while he nattered on about himself, and Greybar was a gray puddle of fur in his lap. Arabella had let go of my hand long since. I couldn't wait to head out for Kentucky. I guessed maybe I'd better talk to Elver Towson again about money; maybe he'd have some ideas. At any rate I guessed I'd go in the morning, and Arabella could go hang.

And then I ran into her in the upstairs hallway on my way to bed. She slowed as I passed, and her hair smelled like cedar.

"If someone were to walk in the garden at midnight," she whispered, "he might find something that would please him."

When the clock at the top of the stairs had whirred and clonged twelve times, I rinsed my face and teeth at the washstand, picked up my shoes, and crept into the corridor. I held my breath as I passed by Mrs. Towson's room. A faint light came from beneath the door, and through the panel I heard Mr. Towson's voice mingled with his wife's. I grinned in the dark. "Go it, you old goat," I whispered as I drifted down the stairs, thinking of Mrs. Towson instead of Arabella, till I remembered the mission I was on.

Half a crescent moon peeped over the trees to the west. Crickets in the bushes stopped in midsong. I crept across the veranda and down the steps to the garden. I walked on the herbs that lined the path so as not to crunch on the oyster shells.

An owl screeched from the other side of the house. It screeched again as it passed overhead and swooped toward the bay, a ghost in the rising mist. The crickets began chirring again as I stood there. Down in the cattails a late shorebird gibbered.

The marble benches by the magnolia were soaked with dew. I put my foot on one, with my elbow on my knee and my chin in my hand, looking toward the bay but seeing nothing out there but a pale halo where the moon had dipped below the horizon. It faded. I turned to go.

A shadow came toward me—Arabella in a dark cloak. She looked back toward the house, then at me, and then fumbled at her throat. Her cloak fell away and she put her arms around my neck and my hands were around her waist, her skin exquisitely warm beneath the thin muslin of her nightdress. Her breath was in my ear. She bit my ear and I kissed her throat and the sound of her kissing my ear snapped in my head. I put my left hand on her hip with my thumb in the depression by her belly, and I could feel soft curls there through her nightdress. My right hand pressed into the small of her back and then ran over the smooth muscles and the base of her spine and out over the excruciating curve of her buttocks. Before I knew what I was doing, my fingers slid into the warm furrow between them. Her breasts pressed against my chest and through my shirt I could feel her nipples hardening. I put my left arm around her lower back and with my right hand I lifted her thigh. She twined her legs around me, and her arms were still around my neck and her lips sucked on my lips and my tongue, and her hair smelled like the cedar box someone had brought me once, one of Phillip's captains had brought it to me all the way from Tangiers, but she smelled like something else entirely, not entirely sweet but delightfully brown and rich and smelling like the sea and it was the most wonderful thing I had ever smelled.

Shocked weren't in it—I was scared. But I didn't want to be anywhere else, I tell *you*. I turned and set her on one of the marble benches, her bare feet slipping at first, and she knelt on the bench and her mouth was still melting into mine but now she could run her hands over my body and she thrust my shirt open and ran her nails excruciatingly down my chest and I wondered who she'd done this with before.

"We oughtn't," I said. Her nightdress was up around her thighs, and my hand was sliding around like butter in a skillet.

"That's so," she breathed. "We really mustn't." She took my hand and pressed it deeper into herself. It was like getting a handful of hot custard. Then she squirmed away from my fingers and stepped off the bench. She came around it toward me, and as I wrapped her in my arms she turned her back to me.

I reached around her and cupped her breasts. The nipples were like thimbles under my palms.

She grabbed my hands and held her elbows tight against her sides and folded her arms, trapping my hands.

"Sorry," I said. I tried to take my hands away but she held onto them.

"Nothing to be sorry about." She said it resigned, like she suffered from hurts I couldn't begin to fathom.

"I guess you're in love with Roby Douglass."

"I hate him."

"Then make him leave."

"Silly! I shall marry him."

I pulled free and tucked my torn shirt back into my waistband.

She tilted her head back and leaned against my chest. She looked up at me. "I thought you knew."

"I had an idea *we* was going to be married."

"Oh, what a lunkhead you are."

"Me!"

"Shhh!"

A light flickered upstairs behind Mrs. Towson's curtain. A figure moved against the light, and then withdrew as Mrs. Towson's voice rose angrily. The words weren't clear, but I could hear the tone of it just fine. She was delivering an ultimatum of some sort.

"So that's what you've been playing at," I whispered. "That's why your father's been treating me so. I couldn't understand his reserve before, but now I see. He played a joke on me today. He had me in his study to discuss a little business proposition. He told me you and Douglass was going off riding. He meant for me to catch you. I wondered why he laughed when he said it. Well, I see the humor in it now."

She had gathered up her cloak again and pulled it around herself. "Don't be beastly. Do you have any idea how hard it is to fall off a sidesaddle? On purpose, I mean, without breaking your limbs?" She wiped at her eyes.

"What in the tarnel hell has got into you, Arabella Towson?"

She shivered. "You— I thought— You're nearly broke, and—"

"I have some prize money."

"You don't have a position. The navy doesn't want you after the scandal you caused with the duel—"

"The scandal *I* caused!"

"And your family's business is nearly bankrupt. Everybody knows—"

I squawked.

She held a frantic finger to her lips.

"Hush." She looked up at the house, but all was dark and quiet. "Well, I don't know who caused the scandal, *dear* sweet Matty, and I don't care. But you can *hardly* expect me to *marry* you with that *cloud* over your head."

"Then why did you ask me to meet you here?"

She leaned harder against me. "Because . . . I love you." She used a little-girl voice.

I stepped away from her, and she fell on her rump.

"Oh!" She sniveled for a while. Then she wiped her eyes, straightened her back, and said, "Then I must get Papa to shoot you, or Dickie." She waved her hands around. "I mean, get Dickie to shoot you, not get Papa to shoot Dickie. Here, help me up."

I pulled her to her feet. "You do love me."

"I do not." She passed the back of her hand across her nose.

It would be a grand gesture to kiss her tears away. Snot shone on her upper lip.

I spent the night on the dock, looking at the fog and listening to the bullfrogs groaning in the marsh.

Saying good-bye was harder than I thought it'd be, not just because I hated to leave when things was getting interesting but because it had begun to dawn on me that striking out on my own down the Mississippi, with no prospects before me but a vague idea of finding a place for myself in the western wilderness, was ridiculous. Even Dick had said it was a crazy idea, and he was usual up for all kinds of foolishness. Elver hadn't mentioned money again, and I didn't guess he would unless I brought it up first.

I found Roby Douglass around the side of the house. He was alone for once, and happier than a dog with two tails when I told him the news. "Good!" he said, "that'll save me the trouble of calling you out. I feared I would have to before long. I'm a crack shot, you know. I only restrained myself on Arabella's account." He clapped his hands like it was his birthday. "Oh, the insults I endured! But that's all in the past, old man. I can be big about it. Yes, sir. Put 'er there."

I submitted to his clammy handclasp and smiled while I did it. Him with his rash of pimples and his furry teeth—I didn't know who I was sorrier for, him or Arabella. I looked down at Greybar, who was bonking his head against Douglass's ankles.

"You'll want Greybar," I said. "That's all well with me. You can have him."

He looked at me like I puzzled and amused him at the same time. "I don't want your fool cat," he said, and gave him a kick.

Greybar dodged it easy enough, but it was the principle of the thing. I looked larboard and starboard, and aloft and alow, and weren't nobody around to tell me different. So I knocked Roby Douglass into a rosebush. He couldn't have looked more surprised if I'd grown hooves and a pointy tail.

"You want to call me out," I said, leaning over him, "I'm choosing swords. I got a good one I already used on a couple fellows. The scratches you got from them thorns ain't nothing like."

But I knew he wouldn't say boo to a goose. Greybar followed me into the house.

I found Elver in his study with his whiskey. He was gazing out his window at the rose bushes.

"I detest the fellow," he said, "but Arabella has expensive tastes. And between you and me, son, I think she would have used you badly. She'll make a cuckold of her husband—hear you *me*. I'd rather it was Douglass than you."

I put my hands behind my back and stood up straight. "Mr. Towson, I've reconsidered your kind offer to invest in my venture out west—"

"Now there's a coincidence," he said. "I've reconsidered it, too. I've decided to invest elsewhere. Good day to you, Mr. Graves."

I spent the rest of that last morning with Mrs. Towson in the drawing room, standing uncomfortably in my dress uniform with one arm cradling Mr. Towson's old cavalry saber, which she had insisted I pose with despite my protests that it was entirely the wrong sort of sword and I had a perfectly good one already. I had even brought it downstairs to show her.

"That horrid thing, with the *memento mori* on the handle?" she said, looking at it lying on the settee. "I'll not paint you holding that."

"It's become sort of my visiting card," I said. "I don't rightly know that anyone'll know it's me without it." She gave me half a frown, and I realized what I'd just said. "I mean, of course they'll know it's me from the *painting*. Of course they will—it'll look like me," and after she let me sweat a bit she laughed outright, and I let her make me hold the sword the way she wanted it.

"Besides," I said, "I could always cover the pommel with a sword knot." Elver Towson's saber had a beauty, of soft, heavy blue rope worked with thread of gold.

She gave me a secretive smile.

"That ain't a hint," I said, all in a hurry. "And anyway, I'm not sure as I like this business of sitting for a picture in a midshipman's uniform. I aim to be a lieutenant again pretty soon."

"Oh, that's well enough," she said airily. "I intend to add an epaulet or two anyway."

She took my free hand and placed it palm upwards on a waist-high marble-topped table. She'd scattered the tabletop with old maps and charts, and we managed to knock a sheaf or two of them off before she got me the way she wanted. Finally she stuck a brass telescope in my hand and commenced to sketching my likeness with charcoal into a fresh canvas.

"It's just as well, really," she said, gazing at her sketch with her head tilted. Then, "No. No, it's not just as well. It's sad, is what it is. So unnecessary. It was Elver's decision, dear heart, not mine. I hope you understand that. You will always be welcome here, but now—oh, now it will always be uncomfortable, won't it? You've moved, dear. Tilt your chin a little to the left. That's right. Ah me, I've made such a mess of it."

"You! You didn't do anything wrong. It was me."

"No, sweetness, I mean I have made a mess of the sketch. No matter; we'll just start anew, that's all." She rubbed at the canvas with a rag. "Wouldn't it be nice if we could start over as easily as this? Just wipe away the missteps and sketch again until we have a good foundation, and then begin painting. But we get so caught up in the missteps that sometimes we never even get to the painting. I have been painted, you know."

"Yes, I've admired it many times."

"Have you?" She looked at me absently, and then smiled up at her portrait above the fireplace. "No, not that one, though I admit I'm fond of it. A bit prissy, I think, but it flatters me. No, I was thinking of a series I posed for when I first met Mr. Towson. Actually, that was how I met him. I lived in Paris when I met him. Did you know that?"

"No, ma'am."

"If you must scratch, please do so instead of fidgeting. There. Your right hand is out of place. No, let me show you." She came out from behind her easel to readjust me. Her hand lingered a moment on mine. She smiled. "There. Stay just so, please. Yes, I was a painter of some promise," she said as she resumed her seat. "To dabble in painting is proper for a young lady, but oddly enough to be good at it is not. I was quite good. I am not being immodest, I think—I've heard you admire the still lifes in the hall. I hope you didn't know they were mine."

"No, ma'am, I didn't. I especially admire the plums with the earthenware jar. You sure captured the blue dust on 'em."

"Thank you, dear. I do believe your admiration is honest and not just flattery. In that case, I would be honored if you would take it for your own. You'll have a house one day. Send for it then, and it will be yours."

"I'd treasure it."

"As I treasure you. You know, Matty, I am aware of your regard for Arabella. You have made that plain enough. But she is a ninny." She frowned past her canvas at me. "You needn't defend her to me. I was very much like her once. Or she is very much like I was, take your pick. I know I seem flighty at times, but I see what goes on around me. I had her same dilemma when I was just her age, and I solved it the way she tried to. I was in love with a beautiful man, but he was not the sort of gentleman my parents wished me to marry. For one thing, he was already married. For another, he was more than twice my age.

"The man my parents had picked out for me was an absolute *toad.*" Her mouth broadened and grew ugly around the word. "Even more repulsive than Mr. Douglass, if you can believe it." She smiled faintly, and her lips grew plump again. "The man I chose for myself was entirely a nobody, a dashing fool on the loose in Paris. Full of all sorts of dangerous revolutionary ideas. And an American, to boot. Well, I was gently raised, of course, in Virginia, and my parents hadn't taken me to France to marry a Yankee Doodle. We were Tories, Loyalists, and we had lost our lands in America and a good deal of our fortune.

"His wife had given him a daughter the previous autumn. It was a dangerous birth, her second, and she could no longer accommodate him. She never rose from her bed again.

"Your left arm is drifting, dear. Raise the sword up. There." She rubbed at the canvas with her cloth and then commenced again with her charcoal. "I suppose you've also admired the Aphrodite in Mr. Towson's study. Now you're blushing, dear, so I'm certain you have admired it. Or examined it, at least."

"Admired, examined. I—yes."

She smiled. "It was painted from life, and yes, I was the model. One mustn't be shocked—to find models, a painter must often pose as well. There can be no modesty in pursuit of art. It's quite usual in Europe, I assure you. And it can be useful, too. It was how I assured my marriage to that beautiful man instead of that insufferable scrub I spoke of. My husband painted it, though I think maybe he has forgotten the circumstances behind it . . . or what transpired during the painting of it, I dare say."

She looked up from her work. "Do I disappoint you? Shock you?"

I shook my head. After last night with Arabella, I calculated it'd take a lot for someone in that family to shock me.

"I mention it for a reason," she said. "My husband has forgotten many things over the years, but I never thought he would forget that. I know perfectly well what happened between you and Arabella in the garden." She rubbed her brow, leaving a comma of black soot. "Elver was determined to go downstairs and 'catch' you, as he said. I reminded him of how he seduced me. Even if he didn't still believe he seduced me, naturally he would never admit that I might've had some volition in the matter. Men think only they have desires." She smiled, and then the smile faded. "I told him that if he went down and disturbed you I would leave him. I was quite adamant, and he believed me, if only for a short while. But Matty—" She shot me a look so filled with woe that my heart just about jumped out of my shirt. "Oh dear love, whatever dissuaded you?"

I didn't ask her how she knew; it was enough that she did. I didn't know whether to be proud I'd kept my britches on or feel stupid that I hadn't taken them off.

"I couldn't go through with it, that's all." I shrugged. "I thought it was wicked."

"Of course it is! Women are entirely wicked. Have you never been to church? Often the sermon is about nothing else. But men are much wickeder, otherwise what's the point? What's the point of being a man if you do not take advantage of your capacity for deviltry?"

The dimples were deep in her cheeks and her lips were flushed a rich pink, and she smiled with such impishness that I had to smile back.

"There, that's better," she said. "Well, I knew Elver was a fool when I married him, so it should not surprise me now that he still is a fool and that he has a fool for a daughter, too."

"She's not so foolish, Mrs. Towson. She knows she's marrying for money, but she offered to . . . you know."

She examined her charcoal, and then smiled brightly. "Do I?"

"She—she intimated a continued liaison."

"Did she! Then she is even more foolish than I thought. An *affaire de coeur* must be sudden, glorious, and soon ended. Otherwise one is found out, and that is unpleasant for everybody."

She set her charcoal down. "There now, I think I have got enough of you into this sketch that I can finish it without you, Mr. Graves. Thank you so much for sitting for me. I think Dickie has got the boat—" She looked out the window. "Yes, I can see Jubal has fetched the pony cart and has put your baggage in it. And oh, look, see! Your silly kitty has perched atop the pile."

She took my hand. Her fingers were cool and dry.

"Do visit us again some day, won't you?" She smiled sadly, as if I'd hurt her or was going to.

As I walked ahead of Jubal down the oyster-shell path, I saw Dick waiting on the dock to run me across to Baltimore in his boat. I felt low and mean, with the sword knot hidden in my pocket. Mrs. Towson had slipped it off her husband's saber and insisted I take it. It wasn't the only thing I wanted, neither, and I hoped to sweet God almighty that Dick wouldn't wonder why I was walking with one hand in my britches pocket.

SIX

A military band was playing "Roslin Castle" on the waterfront as we tied up at Bowley's Wharf in Baltimore. It's a jaunty air despite being solemn as Sunday, but the bandsmen in their gaudy red musician's uniforms were playing it fit to bust out crying. The sergeant that led them was sweating a river as he marched backwards in front of them along Pratt Street. He was getting dished out the devil's own portion in keeping the hornsmen tootling their cornets and serpents in time with the funeral pace that the drummers were marching them to, and the company just about fell apart when he executed a starboard tack to head up toward Baltimore Street, which is where your mobs of any consequence assemble. Half the band was in tears. The tune had been one of General Washington's favorites, and he'd only been moldering in his crypt these seven months. But the old man was entitled, whether I liked it or no, and because of the mood I was in I sang the last verse low to myself:

O hither haste, and with thee bring
That beauty blooming like the spring,
Those graces that divinely shine,
And charm this ravish'd breast of mine.

My breast felt ravish'd, all right, and I had aimed to do something about it, but sure as certain I'd be thwarted in my intentions that day. I'd known it was a Friday and that it was the fourth day of July, but I'd forgotten it was also Independence Day. Bawdy houses might contrive to stay open on Jesus' birthday, but there'd be tar and feathers if they dared to engage in commerce on the Nation's.

The bandsmen passed out of sight between the rows of narrow brick houses, followed by a fleet of children and a handful of old soaks in Continental uniforms they'd filched from somewhere, but you could still hear them honking and thumping as they traipsed along. Then twenty-one guns roared out down the Patapsco at Fort McHenry, one after another. Such a thing commands your attention, and we sat and gloried in it till the guns fell silent and a gloom of smoke cloaked the point.

At last Jubal heaved out the old sea chest that Dick had given me and plunked it down on the tarred planks of the pier. He hopped back into the boat and handed up my carryall. Last of all came the wicker basket with Greybar in it; the lid was open, and he sat upright, staring haughtily over the edge like a squire riding in his very own sedan chair.

"Come with me, Dick," I said. "Let's have us a dram for old times' sake. There'll be toasts a-plenty. Free drink, too, I bet."

He glanced at the sun. "It's a good four hours even if this breeze holds. I'd like to be home by suppertime."

"Aw, Dick, it ain't like you to be so responsible."

He kind of nodded and shrugged at the same time.

I thought guiltily of Arabella and Mrs. Towson. "C'mon, now, a little caterwauling'll do you some good. Shake some of them frogs outta your hair."

He shook his head. "No, I don't suppose I will. You hoist a couple for me and say hello to your brother."

"My brother is Geordie, and he's been dead these eight years. Phillip's my half-brother, I'll thank you to remember. At least let Jubal haul my baggage up the house. It ain't half hot out today."

"Now, there, see?" said Dick. "That's exactly why I'm not going to do it."

And with those last words to me he told Jubal to cast off, and they glided away across the Basin. He looked back and give me a wave, but

I didn't bother returning it. Then they rounded Fell's Point, and he was gone.

A great huzzah rose up from the direction of Baltimore Street, which was a few blocks north and was the main east–west thoroughfare. I guessed I might as well go that way to get to Phillip's house in Fayette Street, after a stop at the Graves & Son offices in Commerce Street. I didn't expect them to be open, but I'd hate to have to go all the way out to the house and find Phillip had only been a couple blocks away.

A raggedy kid was eyeing me from his seat on a barrow in the shade.

"Here," I said. "Are you your own man?"

He looked me up and down, and kind of smiled to himself. "Might be I ain't. Might be I is. What you axin' for?"

"I need someone to haul this here chest and carryall."

"How far you goin'?"

"Might be just around the corner on Commerce. Might be over to Fayette and Sharpe."

He held out his hand. "I'll do it for half a dollar."

"Half a dollar! That's kind of steep, ain't it?"

"It cheaper'n replacin' all your duds, brother."

Which is what I'd have to do if I left them around there.

I gave him a Spanish *real.* "That's twelve and a half cents American."

"I knows it. I wants half a dollar."

I gave him my best grin. "And you'll get it when we get where we're going—*brother.*"

The warehouses west of South Street had been rebuilt since the big fire a year ago last May, and the brickwork shown a deep red where it hadn't been painted over. The iron-wheeled drays that usually rumbled along under loads of shad, herring, and oysters coming in from the bay and barrels of flour going out, stood idle for the holiday, and the great doors of the warehouses were closed and the windows shuttered. The fire hadn't touched the stock exchange and counting houses on Commerce Street, but a spider had built its web across the doorway of

Graves & Son. The front window was grimy, and when I wiped a clear space and pressed my hands and face against it, all I saw inside was bare walls and dusty floorboards.

"You done come to the wrong place, brother," said the kid, peering in beside me. "This place is full of nothin'. Maybe I better charge you a dollar."

"A dollar! That's more'n a day's wages for a *white* man."

"Yes, an' if you can find one to be about yo' business all day for a dollar, you show him to me."

He grumbled about it all the way down Water Street, which we had to take to get around the wharves and warehouses at the foot of Calvert; but he was quick and sturdy with his wheelbarrow, and I guessed a man who commanded such wages as he did could talk all he wanted. We sallied down Pratt Street again till we'd made our westing at Sharpe, where we turned north, and by and by we fetched Baltimore Street on a surging tide of mechanics, fishmongers, clerks, sailors, women, children, and a fair sprinkling of French émigrés who'd fled the slave rebellion in San Domingo. Everybody seemed to have put on their Sunday clothes, but for sheer finery the Negroes and sailors outdone them all. I felt downright dull, although I'd bathed that week and Old Jupe hadn't let me leave White Oak without he'd brushed my coat and greased my shoes first.

Baltimore Street was a mighty tangle of militia in their trim new uniforms and veterans in their quaint Continental ones, all long-skirted vests and oversized coats that looked mighty sweltering in the sun; and dogs and pigs darting in and out of folks' legs, setting the girls to shrieking and the men to roaring; and boys in paper hats, waving wooden swords and following the soldiers around.

My faithful companion eyed the crowd and then give me a look like he was about to reopen negotiations.

"C'mon," I said, stepping out before he could up his price again. We drifted along with the crowd, me touching my hat to the officers and the kid doing who knows what behind me. He must've been doing something because the people watching from the side of the road kept a-laughing, but the couple times I turned around quick to catch him, he was just trundling along with his barrow and not bothering anybody. Maybe we just looked funny, I don't know.

The current shoved us down the long block back to Charles Street, where we finally forded the stream. There we turned north again and then west by north up Fayette, till at last we stood in front of a tall yellow house with pale green shutters and white marble steps. The kid stared up at it and whistled.

"Man," he said, "this here's a regular castle. I ought to charge you two dollars."

"What for?" The house wasn't notably larger than any of the others on the street, and smaller than many. The marble steps were cracked and stained, and the bricks had begun to show through the paint.

He ducked his head and kept his voice low. "This a white man's house, brother. Is you sure you can pass?"

"Just you watch if you don't believe it—*brother.*" I put a silver dollar in his hand.

He hid a grin. "Naw, sah. For that kind of money, I believe you."

He rolled his wheelbarrow away, whistling. I waited till my heart had stopped pounding before I lifted the tarnished brass knocker.

"It will be hard on us, having another mouth to feed," said Phillip, setting down his fork. He crossed his knife on top of it and pushed his plate away. "But however it may be that God finds for us to be of service, we must turn our hands to it and give thanks."

"Amen," said Constance. She had a girlish look to her, though she kept her long, dark hair tucked up in her mobcap, and kept her high collar and her cuffs fastened, and though she must've been in her thirties by then. She made a brushing gesture at her chin.

"Whatsover thy hand findeth to do, let it do with all thy might," Phillip was saying. "Who said—"

"Husband, thee has a bit of mustard in thy beard."

He dabbed at his chin whiskers with his wipe. His beard was shot with gray. So was his hair, cut off blunt at the shoulders. Despite his clean-shaven cheeks and naked upper lip, he looked older than he was.

I stole a glance at myself in the mirror on the sideboard behind him, trying to see a resemblance between us. We'd had different mothers, but surely we had a father in common.

"So tell us, then, Matthew—" He got the nod from Constance and put down his wipe. "How long does thee intend to stay?"

I shrugged. His thin lips tightened at the gesture, and I changed it to a shake of my head.

"I don't know. I hadn't thought that far ahead. Unless I can get another berth or find some other way of situating myself, I don't know what I'm going to do. You got an open berth?"

"Thee is a lieutenant now."

"I could go as supercargo. I done it before. I know my bills of lading—"

"I have no doubt being a lieutenant counts for something."

I held my arms open, as if to show him the difference between the uniform I was wearing and the one I no longer had a right to. Not that he'd be able to tell them apart, I didn't guess.

"It was only an acting lieutenancy," I said. "My official rank is midshipman, and I've been put on the beach."

He nodded. "I see. But although this enforced idleness is vexing, it carries some remuneration, I believe."

"If you mean half pay, that's for lieutenants and captains. And by lieutenants, I mean lieutenants with actual commissions."

He looked at Constance, who gave him a sharp look. "I see," he said. "Thee will attend Meeting, of course."

"Or whatever service thee wishes," said Constance. "Or none at all, if thy conscience directs thee so."

"He must attend to *some* spiritual guidance."

"He must find God as he will."

"My gun and head money ought to be ready by now," I said. "We took a couple of prizes in the old *Rattle-Snake* before I—before she sank. Our agents are here in town. I'll get a draft on Monday."

"Gun and head money?" said Phillip. "That is thy word for blood money?"

I pushed a piece of ham rind across my plate. It hadn't been much of a holiday meal—just the shank end of some mummified pork and a few boiled potatoes.

"It means the prizes we took weren't national ships. You know, proper men-o'-war. When you take a man-o'-war and she's condemned, she and everything in her gets sold and the proceeds are divvied up between the captors and the government. That's called prize money. With a private armed vessel you only get paid for the number of men and guns she carries, and the government takes everything else. Then there's more rules about salvage and pirates, which as a shipowner I guess you know all about already."

There was a little lump of potato left on his plate. He sliced it into quarters and put one of the pieces into his mouth. From around it he said, "Is it a sufficient sum?"

"For a while. I'll give more than I take."

"That will be well." He scratched at the hairs beneath his chin. When he realized what he was doing, he pulled the ends of his neckcloth a little tighter.

Constance began gathering the dishes. "It's a disgrace, asking kin for money."

"Does thee like doing the washing up for thyself?" he called as she marched off to the kitchen. "Does thee like to eat? Does thee like a roof over thy head?"

"Does thee prefer thy bed to a chair in the parlor?" she retorted, and he ducked his head so low it near about disappeared into his collar.

Constance Graves was happy to have me underfoot, but it was hard to tell with Phillip. I'd been hoping to indulge my natural laziness for a few months, except that Phillip despised inactivity in others. He spent most of his time at coffee houses, trying to drum up business to reopen Graves & Son, the concern he ran with my father—who, of course, was two hundred and fifty miles away in Pittsburgh—and I rarely saw my half-brother except at dinner and at Sunday worship.

Attending the Pacific Brotherhood meeting with Phillip and Constance had seemed convenient and obvious. The Brethren were good folk, but there was a brusqueness in their speech that made me entirely too aware of my errors, and among the Elders there was an unshakeable self-certainty that made me want to catch them in something just so's I wouldn't feel so wanting. Besides, I had no clothes but my uniforms, and the Brothers and Sisters were Quakerish in their belief that no problem ever merits a violent solution. Even my plain blue workaday frock coat, with no insignia on it at all, made me conspicuous among the congregation's gray and brown and black; and if looks could kill, I calculated some of them good folk would have problems in the hereafter that they hadn't expected.

The meetinghouse stood away across town in Fell's Point, on Pitt Street where Harris's Creek runs across the road above the York Street bridge. Few houses had been built that far north yet—a couple dozen shacks lined the next street south on the other side of the creek, but most of the building in the Fifth and Sixth wards was down by the Basin and on Fell's Point. Although Pitt Street had been laid out properly straight, it had more the feel of a country lane than a city street, and the Brotherhood Meetinghouse looked more like a barn than a church.

The Brotherhood had no preacher, no deacons—no officials of any sort. There were officers elected every solstice, but they were more in the line of servants than leaders. They lit the fires in winter—more a concession to the needs of the building than to the comfort of the parishioners, I guessed—and washed the windows in spring, and swept up after meetings, and made minor repairs, and collected tithes; they could wield shame like a bludgeon or a dagger, but in theory they had no power.

The pews didn't face an altar; there wasn't one. Instead, they were arranged in three concentric squares around the center of the room, which was empty to my eyes, but to the Brethren it contained the Holy Spirit. Or perhaps the Spirit was in all of us, except in those it wasn't; I was never quite sure what they were on about. What I was sure of was that the arrangement gave the younger men and women plenty of time to eye each other when the elders weren't looking.

A girl of about my age had been giving me the eye all morning. She had a blush of freckles across her nose and cheeks, and eyes as blue as the Caribbean on a clear day. A few orange curls had fallen loose from her mobcap, and she smiled at me with the directness that is the Brotherhood's way. I noticed that she also kept an eye on her parents, who sat on either side of her like a pair of stone lions. For all the attention she gave me when they were looking, I might've been Satan's half-brother that the Beelzebub family didn't like to talk about; but when they were distracted, as right at that moment, she looked like she might like to give Old Scratch himself a go. I raised an eyebrow, she smiled and ducked her head, and I decided I'd give her the chance to talk to me after the meeting was over.

Which seemed like it might never come. The Brotherhood's method of communion was to sit around silently waiting for the Holy Spirit to enter somebody, or at least till someone couldn't stand the suspense and started jawing about whatever was itching him. Failing that, there was the Topic of Examination, which was written on cards that was placed on the pews. The Topic of Examination that morning was the abolition of slavery—they were all for it, which I would've guessed would kind of put a damper on the debate, but they managed to bring up some things I hadn't thought about, such as the cost to the owners. There was some talk about the road to Mammon, wherever that was, and not serving two masters, though I would've thought just one master was plenty enough for any slave. At any rate the wind went out of it after a while and they turned their soul-searching lamps on the question of manumission and returning free blacks to Africa. They were for that, too, till someone readmitted the question of money. The silence got longer and longer.

So I said, "Suppose they don't want to go?" and that livened things up again.

I felt some pleased with myself as I followed Constance and Phillip out of the meetinghouse. There was enough of the afternoon left for a ramble, and maybe once the sun went down I could find a tavern that dared stay open on the Sabbath. And who knew . . . I slowed down to let the orange-headed girl walk by with her parents.

Mama and Papa nodded at me, despite my uniform, and Papa said something about business to Phillip. The girl give me a flicker of a smile, and then both barrels when she seen I noticed her. With an amused light in her eye, Mama took Papa by the arm and maneuvered him alongside of Phillip.

It was easy enough for the girl to match my step, and easy enough for me to fall off a little more. Already deep in conversation, the oldsters headreached on us and began to draw ahead.

"I'm Matty Graves."

"I know it."

"Might I know your name?"

"Thee might."

She smelled like peaches, or maybe she just looked like one. Her skin was a delicate pink beneath the freckles, and softened by a pale down. It had rained that morning, and the clogs she'd worn against the puddles gave her a long-legged stride and put her at just my height. They also made her a little wobbly.

I reached out to steady her, and she put both her hands on my arm.

I nodded toward Phillip and Papa. "Them two know each other. It'd be easy enough to find out your name."

"Yes, but then thee would have to explain why thee wished to know."

I give her the ol' twinkly eye. "Oh, I doubt they'd wonder why."

Her eyes turned into little upside-down crescent moons when she smiled.

I pulled my elbow in to squeeze her hands against me. "Perhaps a fellow could come a-calling of an evening?"

"We do not admit visitors after dark." She glanced at her parents, who were still exchanging opinions with Phillip and Constance. Then she gave me an address in Albemarle Street. "The left-hand window on the second floor. I will go to bed early with a headache."

Oh, what a joyous world, thinks I, hauling out my watch to see how long I'd have to wait. Dick Towson had give it to me last Christmas. It was something to see, a fine silver piece with raised figures of dolphins and mermaids around the rim, an engraving of the *Constellation* taking the *Insurgent* on the lid, and a sailor and a half-naked Liberty tromping on the British crown on the back. I popped the lid and held it open in my hand like an oyster, the better to make it sparkle.

"Shortly after supper, then," I murmured. "Make it nine o'clock . . . Say, are you well? You seem took sick of a sudden."

"Brother," she said, staring at the watch, "it is the intolerable hardships of the Indian slaves in the Mexican mines that make such frivolities as silver watches possible. I'd expect a man of color to know that."

"Man of color!" She had a prim look on her, like I had disappointed her after she'd overlooked some defect in me. I swiveled my head around in a panic lest someone had heard her. "Man of color? I am a sailor, Sister, which you'd expect me to be burned by the sun."

"Brother, thee is certainly burned as brown as a Negro."

"It's from the sun."

"The right-living man is grateful to be what God has made him."

"And who are you to decide what I am?"

"It is not I, Brother, but God." She stepped along, pulling out ahead. She took her mother's arm, and they made their good-byes.

I resolved to spend my future Sundays loafing along the waterfront and letting Phillip believe I had joined the Episcopalians.

"Thee mustn't accost the Brethren," said Phillip over dinner. "At least not their daughters."

"Remember my place, you mean?"

"I did not say that."

Supper was a stringy hen that had stopped laying. Phillip's embargo against violence didn't extend to animals, I'd noticed.

I picked a pinfeather off the tip of my tongue. "I wish you'd let

Constance buy her chickens in the market. You ever seen her try and wring a chicken's neck?"

"No, nor have I seen thee do it."

I poked at the body in my plate. "I'm kind of delicate that way."

He looked at her, eating silently with her head down. "Dressed chickens are too dear," he said. "We will do for ourselves."

"I will do for us, you mean," said Constance.

And then they did something I didn't understand at all. He reached across the table, and she took his hand.

The sulphurous reeks of gun smoke and asafetida filled the streets as July crept into August. The ordinary summer influxes of influenza and scarlet fever stalked the narrow streets, and more than one open window exhaled the stench of a corpse in the front parlor. Anybody who could afford them smoked cigars to purify the air—a lesser defense against fever than firing muskets into the air and wearing asafetida bags, but easier on the nerves. The high-tone people had cleared out of the city entire, not to return till the fevers vanished with the October frosts. Usually Phillip and Constance summered in the woods around upper Gunpowder Falls, but they didn't go that year. Phillip had sold the cottage. I thought about going to sea again—which was about as far as I got with the notion at first. I felt like my brain was stewing inside my skull.

To say the heat in Baltimore was fierce is to do it an injustice; Beelzebub's left armpit weren't in it. Stinking water collected in the gutters, and the skeeters bred in such numbers that sleep was a misery of tossing and turning and slapping. A dead horse lay in a pool of stinking ooze beside Jones's Falls for six days before someone finally hauled it away; its stink permeated the brick walls of the houses even yet, and the muddy pool still swarmed with maggots. The sluggish water of the Basin stank. The piles of parings and bones and fish guts in the market writhed like living things; they stank. The people in the street stank. I stank.

I was forever remembering a night in Port Républicain, coming down a stinking alley into the market. The paving stones were carpeted with chewed-up cane, and the air had smelled of sugar. And at the end of another alley had waited a man with a sword that was a twin to my own.

I took to spending my afternoons in the coffee houses of Baltimore Street, spinning yarns and smoking myself into the jitters. In the evenings I tramped over to Reynolds's Quid Nunc Club in Lovely Lane, a greasy back alley despite the name, where I tempered the effects of the cigars with frosty tankards of whiskey julep. The Quid Nunc was nothing more than a tavern in a damp and close series of low-ceilinged half-basements, not what your better sort of gentleman would call a club at all, but you could count on it to be open no matter the day or the weather—and you could count on Reynolds to find ice in August, which was handier than in January, when most folks have it. Those were its primary assets; it had few others.

I sauntered in one evening to take up my usual station at a corner table in the best back room—"best" being a comparative and not an absolute, but it suited me. The night air had a tang to it from a load of salt cod down at the docks that had gotten prematurely reconstituted en route and hadn't found any takers. It lay there yet, dripping and ghastly. I'd just about swear it emitted its own light. Runny cabbage and furry beans were weak sisters compared with that cod—puny invalids, hardly to be trusted outdoors on their own—but as I didn't have the proper instruments to hand, I couldn't do more than guess as to its strength. For sheer penetrating power, though, I gauged it to be the pure stuff.

I was feeling a good deal content with myself as I come in. I had paid a call on a freckled dolly at a house I knew down in Fell's Point. There's something about a pumpkin-colored angel's nest that makes a fellow want to holler heigh-de-ho—which I did, twice, and worth every cent. If it's possible to feel any better than I did it's probably illegal.

As I ducked under the low stone archway and pushed open the familiar door, the memories flooded past me like a receding tide washing the sand out from under my feet. The Quid Nunc was where I had first seen Peter Wickett in action, the day after Christmas last year. We had been drinking there at Billy's expense. Peter had had a few caustic things to mutter about the Royal Navy officers who had taken up the front room—they were from H.M.'s frigate *Clytemnestra,* which meant nothing to me at the time—and about P. Hoyden Blair, who was on his way with us to Port Républicain, there to take up his duties as assistant U.S. consul. Phillip had found me there at the Quid Nunc, and delivered to me a pair of dueling pistols—a gift from my father that later went down with the *Rattle-Snake* in the fight with the *Faucon* and *L'Heureuse Rencontre.* All the memories were jumbled together, like they'd been throwed into a box. I remembered a sunlit Peter in the Bight of Léogâne, pulling a broken tooth out of his jaw and telling me to go below and see to Billy. I remembered him later with one of my pistols smoking in his hand, and Billy's breath coming out in a fine pink mist.

It was a quiet night at the Quid Nunc. I was the only customer, and Fugwhit, who had recently been promoted from bar boy to bar man, gave me a grin that showed the stumps of his front teeth to advantage. "The usual?" he said, breathing through his mouth and talking through his nose.

I nodded; he served me up a cold whiskey julep and went about his business. I took the tankard to my table in the back room, where I sat with my head tilted away from the smoke of the cheroot between my teeth and sorted through some recent numbers of the New York and Philadelphia papers.

The War of Knives was sure as certain over down in San Domingo, in spite of a few misdemeanor murders and some inconsequential atrocities here and there, and editors were finding other things to blow about. By wading through the back pages, though, I was able to get some idea of what was transpiring in the nominally French colony. Toussaint would be taking over the Spanish side of the island soon, which was well with us as long as we were still fighting the French. It'd keep them occupied.

I scanned the other columns. The madman John Chapman, who affected rags and preached Swedenborg's Church of the New Jerusalem, had left western Pennsylvania and moved along to the Ohio country, planting huge numbers of apple trees and giving away seeds by the bushel. Over on the next page, Lieutenant Shaw of the 12-gun *Enterprize* schooner had captured the 10-gun *L'Aigle* on Independence Day. And below that was a paragraph about that impeccably polite French rascal, Captain Mesh—or Mèche, as the paper now had it—that Dick had mentioned. He had struck again, this time stealing four barrels of potatoes and a Negro sailor out of the *Eliphelet G. York* off Cape Fear.

But here was something more immediately interesting to me: Master Commandant Asa Malloy, former captain of the *Aztec*, had returned from a cruise in the *Insurgent* frigate. She was the very same Frenchman that had forced us to run in '98, and that Truxtun in the *Constellation* had captured off Nevis the following February—which was immortalized on the sinful silver watch that, in my vest pocket, even as I sat there, was ticking away the misspent moments of my life. I had to read the item again to be sure of what I was seeing, but there it was, sure as eggs is eggs: Now that Truxtun had been promoted into the *President*, a forty-four that was a-building in New York, Malloy had managed to talk his way into command of the *Constellation*. He'd be recruiting pretty soon.

Which I needn't even think about. Malloy had written me after Peter and Billy's duel, and I calculated I could remember every word of his letter. He'd wrote it to express his "surprise and dismay" that his "former protégé had disregarded the laws of our country in pursuit of a false notion of honor." He had "no doubt that, had a proper investigation been made into his appointment, the son of an obscure tavern-keeper would not have received a warrant." Not that Malloy had taken any pleasure in writing the letter, of course, except in that it gave him "the opportunity to offer some healthful and necessary advices."

But I'd been called worser things than the son of an obscure tavern-keeper—worser things than that name, I mean; I guess obscure tavern-keepers get called all sorts of things—and there were worser things to *be* than that, anyway, which I wasn't in the first place. It was an idiotic insult. I was stupid to be angry about it. God *damn* it.

"Hey, in the front room, there," I called. "More julep."

Fugwhit poked his head in, his mouth hanging open like he'd forgotten to shut it. He was smearing a glass with a dirty towel.

"You sure?"

"Yes, you slack-jawed drool-bucket. Look lively now."

It didn't rectify the insult any that it fit him so well. Made it worse, really. I felt lower than before I had said it. The world's coming to a pretty fix when you can't even make yourself feel better by cussing somebody out.

I remembered some American sea officers cussing up a storm one night in the Amiral de Grasse in Cap Français. A gang of British lieutenants had stood a midshipman on a table and were making him sing "To Anacreon in Heav'n," which the Americans were throwing coppers at him to try to get him to shut up. His voice hadn't cracked yet, and he'd been murder in the high ranges. Peter had stood drinks for us—"wetting the swab" as I'd just gotten my lieutenant's epaulet. We'd had stewed goat washed down with *sanguinaire,* a punch made with rum, wine, and chunks of tropical fruit. Peter had been as cheerful that night as I'd ever seen him. And then Billy had come in.

I reached for the Philadelphia *Aurora.* Matthew Carey, printer and bookseller, was offering a new volume of Parson Weems's *The Life and Memorable Actions of George Washington.* I threw the paper aside. The General was barely half a year in the ground, and the cult that had surrounded him in life was now raising him to quasi-deity in death. Reynolds had taken his old engraving of Washington from over the fireplace—where it had been obscuring a particularly interesting Leda and the Swan since the General's proxy funeral last winter—draped it in the Stars and Stripes and promoted it to the main room. He filled the urn below it daily with fresh laurel boughs. What most give me the snorts, though, was that he'd tossed out the Leda and replaced it with a new nude: the American Cincinnatus, bare-chested and barelegged, with three winged fat ladies clutching banners embroidered with Latin mottoes in their teeth. The artist had depicted the old man with one hand clutching a cloth across his middle and the other raised heavenward, perhaps in beatitude, perhaps in mortification—it was hard to tell.

I had wandered out into the front room in my distraction and came to rest in front of the table where Reynolds kept a pile of the smaller and local papers. I sorted through them while I tried to decide whether to go up to Fayette Street and bed, or drink till I keeled over somewhere.

Here was a promising item in the Norfolk *Herald.* Patrick Fletcher had replaced Malloy in the *Insurgent,* and was even then lying in Hampton Roads assembling a new crew. The article didn't spell it out, but I was stupid not to have thought of it before: the *Insurgent* had been forced to leave Baltimore last month after her midshipmen had started a brawl in Fell's Point. They'd been carrying one of the lieutenants around from tavern to tavern in a chair and knocking peoples' hats off—well, it was a funny story, but the point was that one of the young gentlemen, a Mr. Brown, had lost the use of his left hand in the brawl that followed and had been put on the beach. If the transfer from Malloy to Fletcher had been an amicable one, and assuming Malloy hadn't poisoned Fletcher against me . . .

But no. Fletcher didn't know me. He wouldn't be interested in taking on his predecessor's former shipmates, even to pull the nose of a snob like Malloy. My eye wandered down the page.

And here was a paragraph that stopped me dead.

"What is it, Mr. Graves?" said Fugwhit. He held a dewy tankard of julep out to me.

I searched his face. "What?"

"I were comin' up the cellar stairs just now, sir, having gone down to see was there some ice left, which there was, which is how your punch come to be cold—"

"And what of it?" I took a good long pull at the delicious whiskey.

"And you shouted, sir."

"Shouted." The tankard was empty, just chips of ice and green wads of smashed mint. I gave it back to him and wiped my mouth on my sleeve.

"Yes, sir. Like this." He throwed back his head and let out a caterwaul that sounded like a goat with the bellyache.

"So what if I did?" I rubbed my head. The constant headache had grown insufferably worse.

"Now, look here, sir," he said, snatching up the *Herald*. "You've gone and crumpled the sheet all up. Someone else might wish to read that, you know."

"You're right." I took the paper back and smoothed it out on the tabletop. It didn't get all too flat, but it was enough to mollify him. When he'd gone away I reread a passing mention in the closing paragraph of a reprint of one of Commodore Gaswell's letters to the Navy Board:

"Lost. Sloop '*Breeze*,' of 8 guns, Lt. Wickett. At Sea the 14th ultimo, her People presumed drowned."

SEVEN

My letters to the Navy Board went unanswered. Catching the packet to Washington got me out from under Phillip's eye, but waiting two hours for an interview with the Secretary, only to see his back as he stepped out, didn't do much for my sense of well-being.

I buttonholed a passing clerk. "Did Mr. Stoddert get my note, sir?"

He reared his head back and give me a look like he was of a mind to crush me with his brains. "He's a very busy man, sir," he said. "Much too busy, I expect, to bother with an unemployed midshipman."

I did not kick him. I smiled at him. Sunshine and bluebirds weren't in it. I *had* seen the Secretary, and I guessed I'd probably better accustom myself to a sternmost view of him if I wanted to get my career underway again. In the meantime I needed to find me some productive employment that wouldn't take me too far afield of the navy's fold.

There wasn't any lack of privateers coming and going on Chesapeake Bay. Two even lay right there across the Potomac at Alexandria, but they both of them was shabby tubs with dirty officers and roisterous crews, and I steered clear of them. I found four more at Hampton Roads. They were fast-looking Virginia pilot-boat schooners, sharp at the bow and with deeply raked masts; but two were outward bound when I got there, and a third was getting underway. So I went aboard of the fourth one and said I'd like to see the master.

Josiah Pratt, master and one-eighth owner of the six-gun *Luther,* was happy to see me when I mentioned that I might be induced to invest in the proper venture. Then I asked him did he need a mate as well.

He brought his eyebrows together like bull caterpillars at rutting time. "Hell no."

"Say, listen," I said, "I got to eat and I ain't shipping before the mast. I been an acting first lieutenant, and I can handle all the things you don't care to handle." His eyebrows was raring up for another go, so I said, "What about supercargo? I can keep books and find the buyers for whatever we pick up while we're cruising. I've done all that for my brother, Phillip Graves in Baltimore."

"So you're one o' *them* Graves, are you? And if you're so itchy to get to sea again, why don't he make you master in one of his bottoms?"

"I like a scrap, but he ain't much in the fighting line."

He stroked his chin. "That might be one way of putting it, I reckon. You like to fight, do you?"

"Yes, sir, I purely do."

He shook his head. "I tell you, son, I ain't needing a mate. But maybe as supercargo, as you say, with a proper share of course. And how much was you figuring on investing?"

"We picked up a fair amount of gun and head money when I was in the old *Rattle-Snake*," I said. "I got me eighty-seven dollars and fifty-three cents left. Cash money."

"Oh, cash money, hey?" says he. His eyebrows commenced to gouging and biting each other like a couple of backwoods hoo-roarers. "All eighty-seven dollars and fifty-three cents of it in bullion, hey? Well, well. Son, I tell you what," says he, "your reputation precedes you. I read about you in the papers, and I jawed about you, too. So did a lot of the fellows round here. And it's out of respect to your handsome behavior in that fight with the picaroons in the Bight of Léogâne that I ain't laughed in your face and throwed you in the drink yet. But I got to be straight with you. Normal buy-in is more in the order of several hundred dollars a share. And I tell you what. When they talk about you, they call you 'Little Matty' Graves, and just between you and me, son? You're a mite puny. Now, I'm sure you're a holy terror—your reputation precedes you, don't be taking it the wrong way, now—but privateersmen is a rough-and-tumble lot and I don't expect you've much experience keeping discipline with your fists. No, son, I think you'd best stick to the navy."

And with that he showed me where the side was.

"There ain't nothing for it, then, I guess," I whispered to myself. The *Insurgent* frigate lay nearby, splendid in her new yellow paint and sparkling brass. I sent a note to Patrick Fletcher, her new commander, who surprised me by sending a midshipman and a boat to fetch me aboard.

Fletcher sat in his cabin, unshaven and shirtsleeved and looking lost behind a desk adrift with documents. "As it happens," he said, "the *Insurgent* is short a midshipman. But a friend of a friend up the bay has a son that's in need of a berth. He better get here soon, though. I got a fair wind and plenty of shot and powder."

"Well, sir, I don't guess you would've been so kind as to send a reefer for me if you wasn't considering me for master's mate."

"That's so," he said, smiling for the first time. "I allow I wanted to set my eyes on you. Natural curiosity." And then he sat there looking at me with his face all closed up, as if to say he'd seen me and reckoned one look was enough to satisfy *him.*

"May I wait on you tomorrow, sir, in case your boy don't show?"

"Certainly you can wait on me tomorrow." He picked up a handful of documents and shook them at me, as if to show me what a true burden was. "And the next day and the next after that, too, if you want, and you may take a long walk off a short pier as well, if you care to." The lines in his face softened a little. He set the papers back on his desk and straightened the edges between his palms. "But should you call again in a week, you'll have your answer. No, you needn't show me your credentials. Our mutual friend Peter Wickett, rest his troubled soul, often spoke well of you in his letters. 'Steady in action,' he used to say, 'a reliable navigator, an amiable companion that knows his letters from Agamemnon to Zeus.' Now tell that boy that brought you that he's to take you ashore."

What a wonderful world this is, and all things in it! I chuckled as Fletcher's mid fetched me back to Norfolk, and I laughed all the way up to the Connaught House, where I was staying. With a friend in common with the captain, especially a dead friend, surely the berth was mine; indulging myself in a long dinner and half a bottle of wine, which became a whole bottle and then another, I tried but didn't entirely succeed in disguising my joy. And why should I disguise it? I was aware of meeting some amiable fellows, and calling for whiskey, and then I disremember what happened for a while. Then there was a midshipman who looked like Dick. He talked just like him, too, speaking so mild and sensible and all-fired reasonable while tugging on my coat sleeve that I hauled off and popped him one. He swam out of my sight, and I forgot all about him. The amiable fellows laughed, and I laughed, and we got to singing songs and carrying on.

If I was under the hatches from drink the next morning, my joy held it at bay. I had completely almost forgotten my headache and the muddy boots of the two men who'd also rented shares in the bed, when the landlord interrupted my breakfast. He held out a letter that looked like it had been tromped on a time or three.

"What's this?" says I.

"What that fellow from the *Insurgent* brung."

"What fellow from the *Insurgent?*"

"The one that wanted you to step along, but you wouldn't go with him without he had a dram with you, and then another, and then you wouldn't go at all. When he pressed the matter, you blacked his eye for him."

"No! I didn't." I looked at the back of my hands. The middle knuckle on my right hand was split, but a sailor's hands are always banged up. "Did I?"

"You did, sir. And you forgot the letter and left it on the floor. I guessed you'd want it come morning, though, and here 'tis."

I took a walk along the waterfront before I read that letter. A western breeze blew just strong enough to wrinkle the surface of the roadstead and hound the few fleecy clouds out into the Atlantic.

The *Insurgent* had left her moorings. Obviously Fletcher had completed his stores and had taken his ship farther out into the roadstead in case some new recruit figured on absconding with his enlistment bounty. Any prudent captain would do that.

I strode along the Elizabeth River past the fort till I come to Tanner's Point at the north end of town, where I could see farther out into the roadstead and up the James River. No *Insurgent.* I begun to grow alarmed. I couldn't see east, though, out into the Chesapeake, where there might be a hundred ships and vessels at any one time. A broad slough stood between me and the north end of the peninsula, and I had to pick up my heels and run off a good deal of southing before I could cut back across the neck of land and fetch the Chesapeake side. I sloshed and staggered across the low ground till I come up against the bay, but I already seen all I needed to. Away on the horizon, a good five miles out and halfway to the Capes, the *Insurgent* was shaking out her topgallants and royals as she stood out to sea.

I went back to the inn and read Fletcher's letter in the soothing dimness of the taproom:

Fri., Aug. 8, 1800
U.S. Frigate Insurgent
Hampton Roads

Dear Mr. Graves,
My regrets at the haste of this Message, but Tide and Wind are fair and I am to proceed to the West India Is at once. My wayward Midshipman having come aboard, but another having gone ashore, I find I can accommodate you should you come at once.

Yr. obd't servant, &c
Patk. Fletcher, capt.

P.S. *To speed you on your way and that you might sooner wish him joy, I send this by way of yr. new and former Ship mate Mr. Towson.*

EIGHT

When I got back to Baltimore I was fit to be hanged. Slogging through the August afternoon out to Phillip's house in Fayette Street was like trudging around inside a dead turtle. The sky was the color of a boiled lung, and the pewter locket slipping around on its chain beneath my shirt weighed on me like an overripe conscience.

The heat was worse indoors. I could feel my innards baking as I wandered through the rooms upstairs and down in search of someplace cool. At last I found Constance and Greybar out in the kitchen yard with the pig. Greybar had stretched himself out along a narrow strip of shade along the fence; the pig lay with his head in a draggle of kitchen scraps in a patch of mud in the corner by the alley, watching Constance through little red-rimmed eyes as she shoved clothes around a steaming cauldron with a long stick.

"Hello, Greybar," I said. He flicked his tail sleepily. "Hello, Constance. What for's that pig watching you so?"

"I imagine 'tis the lard in the soap." She swiped her forearm across her brow. Dark strands of damp hair hung down from her mobcap. "Smelling it makes him hungry."

"Pigs're always hungry."

"So are boys, I find. Is thee hungry?"

"Not particularly, thank'ee."

"That's as well, as thy brother has not returned from the market—"

"Half-brother."

"Half-brother or no, he is still thy brother."

Greybar sauntered over and rubbed against my leg till I scratched his head. Constance stirred her pot for a while.

"Not that I am ungrateful for what the Lord provides," she said, "but sometimes I think our pig eats better than we do."

"We'll change that come hog-killin' time." I looked at the pig. He'd fallen asleep on his garbage. "I guess he'll eat pretty good then." I meant he would be good eating, you understand, but it was an undersized joke and she passed on it.

"It won't be cold enough for that till months yet," she said. "I am glad I never named him." She hoisted a shirt on the end of her stirring stick. "Is that clean?"

"How would I know? I never b'iled a shirt in my life."

"Well, what makes thee think *I* have?" She slopped the shirt back in the cauldron and thumped it a bit with her stick. "Will thee stand there all day?"

I looked around, but the back step was full up with baskets of wet clothes. "There ain't no place to sit."

"I meant will thee help me."

"Sure I will."

"I should have asked direct, rather than assume thee wo—"

"I said I'd do it."

"Will thee tie a line for to hang the shirts on?"

"Didn't I just say I would?"

"The one Phillip did for me came down when I tried to use it, and now I've had to wash his shirts twice."

"I guess I know how to tie a knot." I rigged her up a four-line clothes rack out of reach of the pig. I looked at her sweating over the cauldron and felt some disgusted with myself.

"Connie, I repent of my anger."

"I know it," she said; and before I knew what she was about, she had me twisting the water out of the clothes and draping them across the lines.

"Say, Connie, ain't you supposed to have a wringer?"

She put her hands in the small of her back and stretched. Suddenly she laughed. "I suppose there must be one in the cellar," she said. "I have never been down there, and when the girl left, she didn't tell me where things were. But never thee mind about that. I shan't burden thee with my troubles."

I laid a shirt out on the line. Little pink and green bubbles shone in it and the inside of the neck-band was dingy. I started to give it back to her, but then I thought if someone done it to me it'd make me sore. Besides, it was cleaner than it had been.

"It's no burden," I said. "Is things really as bad as that, Connie?"

Through the open kitchen door I heard the front door open and shut, and then men's voices in the hall.

"Here are the fellows who would know," she said. "Why does thee not ask them?"

There was a clomping of feet in the kitchen, and here was Phillip, smiling as he stepped wide with his long shanks to clear the baskets on the back step, paying them no mind except to avoid them as he called out, "See what I have brought!" In his hand he held a reticule filled with leafy summer stuff, and the smile died on his lips when he saw me.

Behind him in the doorway stood a well-dressed gentleman farmer, taller than I remembered, and older. Like Phillip, he was bearded, with the mustache shaved, ropey in the neck and lean as jerky-meat in the arms and legs. His gray hair hung straight to his collar. He held his broad-brimmed hat in his hand, but I think it was only happenstance, as it wasn't a usual posture for him. He looked at me the way he'd always looked at me, like I was a runt piglet and his sow was one tit short. I'd have knowed him if he was a hundred and twenty years old, and forty of them in the grave.

"Hello, Father," I said.

Constance brought us tea in the downstairs parlor, like we were guests. She served it in the old chipped delftware service. I thought maybe we didn't rate the silver set till I realized she'd probably sold it. She cut the piece of cake she'd brought into two pieces and put them on the blue and white plates.

"No, thank'ee," I said.

"Suit thyself."

The old man dunked his cake into his tea and filled his mouth. "Light as a brick, Connie," he said from around it. "You'll excuse us now."

She topped off his cup and went to the kitchen. I heard Phillip say something about extravagance and vanity, and then she shut the door and I missed her reply. He came out a moment later and went upstairs. The old man ignored it, like it was flies buzzing. He stuffed his maw with another wad of cake and worked it down.

"She's a good 'un, your sister-in-law," he said. "Phillip did well."

"I like her. This here's the last of the tea, I bet."

"There's plenty of tea in the world, and more will come this way eventually. You're a burden to your brother, Matthew."

I took a slow sip. It just about burned my lips off, but I would not give him the satisfaction of knowing it. "I haul my own freight," I said. "I don't guess we'd have eaten at all this week without I kicked in. That's probably tomorrow's breakfast you're eating."

"That ain't the kind of burden I mean." He took the other piece of cake and engulfed that, too. A light snowfall of yellow crumbs drifted across the front of his vest. "I got a few letters from my old friend Cyrus Gaswell these past six months, but none from you. You must've run out of ink, I expect."

"How is the commodore?"

"You tell me." He brushed the crumbs off onto the floor. "You seen him more recent than I have."

"He's throwed me over. He sent me and Dick Towson off to answer for Billy's duel. I'm Captain Tingey's man now, whether I like it or not. Which I don't much."

He sloshed tea into his saucer and blew on it. "I'm surprised to hear Cyrus has throwed you to the lions. Are you sure you read him right?"

"Tingey busted me back to midshipman and put me on the beach. Said I was free to ship out if I could find a captain to take me on."

"Ain't what I asked."

"There it is anyway."

"Have you found a captain to take you?"

"I have an idea of going out west."

He slurped from his saucer, holding it with his thumbs and first two fingers, with the other two sticking out on either side.

I shrugged. "You're right, I'm a burden to the family. I don't understand how, but I sure feel it. I could make something of myself out west. I'm through with the service."

He nodded, like the way he did that time I told him I was going to go live on the moon. He'd asked how was I going to get there, and I'd told him I'd just wait till it got close enough and use a ladder.

He reached into his coat, but then he pulled his hand out again. "Just to satisfy your old pap's curiosity, what do you propose to do out west? Sell whiskey to the Indians?"

"Why not? Ain't no worse than selling it to riverboat men and backwoods pukes."

"Indians killed your mother. Damn near done for you, too."

"Well, I guess I disremember it, as I was kinda young at the—"

He swept his paw across and knocked me out of my chair. I waited till the stars cleared. He was standing over me with his hand out, but I pushed it aside and he stepped back and I got to my feet. I squared up the chair with the table and sat down again.

"I ain't gonna let you do that again."

He sat down. "I won't."

He looked so small that I believed him. "You know I won't raise a hand to you. But I ain't gonna let you."

"You were cut out of her living flesh, Matthew. Don't you never forget that."

"You weren't there." He didn't say nothing to that, so I said, "I've heard all them stories. I was born with a full head of hair. I cussed her murderer with an Irish hex. All kinds of fool stories. But ain't a one of 'em got a mention of *you* in it. Every time I asked about you, they just told me to tend to my own affairs. Well, if this ain't my affair, I don't know what is."

"What did Cyrus tell you?"

I yanked my neck-cloth loose and unhooked the chain from around my neck. The dented pewter heart looked small and grimy in my hand. "He give me this."

He looked at me like I was hurting him. Or maybe I was just making him tired. "That's an odd thing for one man to give another."

"You saying you never seen it afore?"

He turned his head to one side, holding his yap shut tight like he was trying to avoid a dose.

My hands trembled so, I couldn't hardly spring the latch. But I got it at last. The lid popped open, and I held it so he could see the portrait inside. "There. My mother."

He took it from me. His hand was softer than I expected. So was the look on his face.

"That's her," I said. "That's her, ain't it? Ain't it?"

He half smiled, shaking his head, his eyes closed. "That's her. Course that's her. Can't you tell by looking?"

"I can tell by looking I don't take after you. Phillip looks like you. Geordie looked like you *and* her."

"Geordie's dead. Let him be."

"He had the same mother as me. I just always guessed we had the same father, too. I ain't no kin to you nor Phillip. Am I."

"I guess we done all right by you, Matthew. I might've done better, but another man might've done worse. And Phillip knows he don't owe you, yet here you are in his house."

"He knows?"

"Of course he knows." He snapped the locket shut. "Tell me now, what did Cyrus say about her?"

I dragged my mind back to last spring, when Gaswell had sent me into San Domingo. I remembered him sitting behind his big mahogany table, in his shirtsleeves and bare feet, telling me he'd seen a portrait of my mother in a locket that my father wore at Yorktown. And then later he gave me the same locket that the old man now had in his hand.

"He said she was a great beauty, and you talked your head off about her at Yorktown. You never talked about her around me."

"I talked about her all I needed to. Go on."

"He said I had the same features as her. Same cheekbones. He said, 'A woman like that, you keep next to your heart.' And he said . . . He said she was Creole and I'd gotten a lick of the tarbrush from her. But the woman in the locket is white."

"Portraits lie. She was dark enough." He said it like I had something to do with it.

"All I know is stories. You tell *me* what happened."

"What happened is, I'm all the father you got." He reached into his coat again and took out two letters and set them on the table. "Cyrus wrote me you might get a notion in your head. So I took the caution of calling in a few markers and otherwise annoying some old friends. I think it'd best be the last thing I do for you."

He put the locket in his pocket.

If anyone had asked, I would've said the locket was the most valuable thing I owned. If anyone had asked, I'd have said I wouldn't take house or fortune for it; it couldn't be replaced. But he needed the past more than I did, and I was willing to trade.

The letters were from the Secretary, on heavy paper and properly sealed with wax. One was addressed to a Lieutenant Graves, the other to a captain of the same name:

> *Washington City*
> *Navy Department 13th August 1800*
> *Lieu^{t}. Matthew Graves*
> *Baltimore—*
>
> *Sir I am honored to inclose an acting order as lieutenant— You are entitled to your pay and emoluments from 15 June 1800 & Mr. Archibald Campbell Esqre the Navy agent at Baltimore upon shewing him this will pay you from that date—I assume you still to have your uniforms, &c.—*
>
> *Your obed Servt*
> *B Stoddert*

Reading the first one got my heart a-thumping, but as I read the one addressed to "Captain" Graves it like to hopped right out of my chest, even with the pro forma second paragraph:

> *SIR It is the command of the President of the United States, that you repair at once to Norfolk, Virginia—there to assume command of the schooner Tomahawk, and then proceed to Cape Francois in St. Domingo & join the American Squadron on that Station, placing yourself under the command of the Commanding Officer of the Vessels of the United States—he is to acquaint you with your purpose—*
>
> *You are to use all your efforts to protect the American Commerce, to capture French armed Vessels, which are to be sent to the United States, and always with some of the persons found on board at the time of capture & to treat the vessels & people of all other Nations with civility & friendship—indeed French Vessels if not armed, are not to be molested—*
>
> *Wishing you great Success & Glory*
> *I have the honor to be Sir*
> *Your most obed Servt*
> *B STODDERT*

I was aware that the old man stood by the stairs for a time, looking at me as I read the sheets over and over; and then he went and got his bag and walked out the door. His footsteps faded away, and after a while Constance came and lit the lamp.

NINE

A pair of armed schooners swung to their anchors in Hampton Roads. One of them was tiny, probably no more than sixty feet long on deck and eighteen or twenty on the beam, and maybe of eighty tons burden. She had a stepped quarterdeck and wreaths around the arched quarter-galley windows on either side of her after-cabin, and was a quarter of a century old if she was a day. Even from the quay I could see remnants of blue paint and yellow trim through the black coat that had been slapped on her. I would've taken her for a trader, except the Stars and Stripes fluttered at her peak. "Supply ship," I muttered. She even had a lumpy pile of something amidships under a tarpaulin.

The schooner that rode alongside her, now—she was a beauty. The rake of her masts and the sharpness of her bow hinted at great speed, and she was pierced for sixteen guns. She was a senior lieutenant's command, or maybe even a master commandant's, but with orders from the president in my pocket—even at second hand, given by the Secretary rather than His Rotundancy himself, they were enough to swell my head and more—I say, with orders from the president in my pocket, I was willing to take on all comers.

"Here, you," I said as I stepped into the boat of one of the men that had been trying to catch my eye, "take me out to the *Tomahawk*."

"Aye aye, Cap."

He said it with a smirk, as a man well might who went home every evening to a soft bed and a warm wife, and never had to lay aloft on a stormy night. No doubt he was making more than the seventeen dollars a month I could offer him, too. I studied the big schooner's lines as we approached, with all the desire I ever felt for anything I could not have. We rounded her stern and passed abaft the little schooner I'd taken for a transport. She was handsome enough, despite her age, and on her transom, picked out in gold over the five arched stern windows, was the name I knew in my heart would be there.

"Tommyhawk," said the boatman, nodding up at her. "Bein't you a mite disappointed, there, Cap?"

"Nothing wrong with her and plenty right. Why should I be disappointed?"

He shifted his cud into his cheek and spat to leeward. "I were right disappointed when I saw what my missus looked like under her shift. But there be plenty of gals about, while you bein't so free to take another."

"I am content. Lay us alongside."

A white-faced midshipman looked through the open rail in time to see us hook on. "Oh, Lordy," he said, and ran to the hatchway. "Hey, there! Somebody's coming aboard of us!"

"I'll thank you to quit your dern laughing," I said to the boatman, who was not laughing, and swung myself aboard. The open rail only extended around the quarterdeck; from her mainmast forward she had just enough bulwark to trip over, though it rose a little as it ran around the fo'c's'le. She carried a trio of three-pounders on either side. Just abaft of the foremast was a windlass, rather than a capstan. While I waited for the midshipman to collect himself and whoever he was squeaking at below decks, I glanced aloft. She had her topmasts up, and despite her small size they were crossed for square topsails, fore and main, which would help her before the wind.

At last a gray-bearded petty officer in wide slop trousers and a faded blue jacket, a black bosun with a brand-new silver whistle on a lanyard around his neck, and a pair of foremast jacks turned out from below. The midshipman turned toward me with something like triumph on his face. He lifted his hat and held it over his head, the enlisted men doffed their hats and knuckled their foreheads, and the bosun, a big dark man who wore his hair in long, matted braids, lifted his hat with his left hand and fluttered the fingers of his right hand over his silver whistle as he piped me aboard.

I took out and read aloud my letter from the Secretary that gave me the authority to command the schooner. Afterwards, I gaped around like a looby. I don't know what I was expecting—shooting off thirteen guns for myself, maybe. Shit and perdition! Four men, a boy, and a two-masted jolly boat weren't much of a command, but begad it was mine.

"Welcome to the *Tomahawk,* sir," said the midshipman as the wailing died away. "My name is Peebles. These here are the standing officers—I mean, *the* standing officer, Mr. Horne, the bosun. And the old fellow is Gundy, the quartermaster—"

"Thank'ee, Mr. Peebles," I said. "Mr. Horne and I are old shipmates." I couldn't help grinning at the bosun. "What brings you to this tub, Mr. Horne?"

"An acting warrant as bosun, sir," he said, shaking the hand I offered.

"I guess you'll have a proper warrant before the year's out. We're to rendezvous with the San Domingo squadron as soon as we can. Are her stores in her yet?"

"Aye, sir. Bread, water, beer, salt junk, peas and beans, guns and small arms, powder, shot—we just finished stowing the last of it."

I looked at the two jacks. "The five of you did all that?"

Horne smiled. "I had a few favors owed me by the along-shore men, sir."

I nodded. A good warrant officer was a fiefdom unto himself, and it didn't do to pry. I held out my hand to the gray-bearded quartermaster. "Gundy, is it?"

"Iss, zur."

"That's quite an accent you got there. West Country?"

He gave me a gap-toothed grin. "Us call 'un the *wet* country, zur, as rains zo much."

"Where abouts? Bristol? Cornwall?"

"Blaamed if I know, zur. My vaather was a gadabout." He indicated the blue-eyed, yellow-haired seaman; chubby as a Dutchman, but tough-looking for all that. "Eriksson, a Svensker." He pointed at the little dark-haired one. "And the go-by-the-ground—O'Lynn, an Irishman. Both can 'an', reef, and steer, zur, and come rated able."

"I'm pleased to meet you men." They made agreeable noises, strongly flavored with their own accents, and I glanced around the deck. Right aft was the tiller; forward of that was the binnacle, where the compass and other navigation equipment would be kept, with a low door in the forward part of it that I expected was the top of the companionway to the after-cabin—*my* cabin, I thought with a surge of pleasure. At the fore part of the quarterdeck was a pair of three-pounders with their noses poking through the rail, a pair of pump shafts side by side near the midline, and the mainmast, which had a good deal of rake to it; forward of all was a small hatchway. Then came the open waist with another pair of three-pounders on either side, the main hatchway, the windlass, the foremast, a tiny fo'c's'le, a short chimney right forward, and the head. That was about it, except for whatever it was that lurked beneath the tarpaulin.

"Mr. Peebles, what's under here?"

He beamed like a parson at Easter dinner. "It's our stinger, sir! Here, Mr. Horne, help me unveil her."

They tugged off the canvas, revealing a squat iron gun. It was mounted on a slide instead of a carriage. A little wheel under the after part of the slide would allow it to traverse from side to side.

"Twelve-pounder carronade, sir," said Peebles. "This little beauty gives us twenty-one pounds of metal on both sides. We could take on an eighteen-pounder gunboat, sir!"

I could dismiss that last part out of hand. Our carronade's effective range was only about two hundred and thirty yards, while an eighteen-pounder long gun could throw a five-inch ball more than a mile. I hated to think of what would happen to the schooner in the time it would take her to make up the distance. Worse, the carronade wasn't much more than two foot long. The damned thing was like to fling flaming wads into our own rigging when firing to windward, and maybe right into the belly of the forecourse when firing to leeward. The tarred lines and sun-bleached sails would go up like a candle. Still, I mused, a carronade was fast to load; with the foresail brailed up and fire buckets ready to hand, we might could play merry hell alongside anything close to our size.

"Gundy, replace that tarpaulin. Mr. Peebles, show me my cabin."

The after-cabin was near about palatial, even when Horne and Peebles followed me in. There was a good six feet of headroom between the beams, which was eight inches more than I needed; and the deck was about eight feet long by twelve wide. No doubt it looked bigger than it was because there was nary a stick of furniture in it, except for the long, padded locker built under the stern windows. Beneath the deck was a storage place. I lifted the hatch and looked at several kegs of liquor and a barrel of apples, the kind of stuff that the people would get into if no one was looking, along with a barrel of potatoes and several jute sacks of turnips and parsnips. The turnips they could have and welcome to 'em, but the other goods would come in handy.

"The powder and shot are forward—" Peebles caught himself with a quick glance at Horne. "I mean, *forrard* with the . . ." He glanced at Horne again, who touched himself on the breast. "With the bosun's stores, sir."

"There'll be no smoking below decks, then," I said. "Any man who violates that order will get his pipe broken and a dozen at the hatch grating."

Horne give me a look when I said it, but I guessed he knew me well enough to know I'd just said it for effect. Gundy, O'Lynn, and Eriksson might be out of eyeshot, but they could hear; word traveled fast in a vessel as small as the *Tomahawk.* It would be law in the fo'c's'le soon enough without my having to do anything more about it.

Forward, under the ladder, was a cubby with a small table and a store of charts. To larboard was a small sleeping cabin for the mate, which was Peebles, and a larger one to starboard for the captain— "Which is *me,*" I thought with a jolt. My sleeping space had a privy;

there was a corresponding one on the larboard side for Peebles and the warrant and petty officers, in the after deck's forward-most cabin, where Horne and Gundy had slung their hammocks. Their cabin was barely six feet long and was divided down the middle by the pump shafts, but it was sited right about where the schooner reached her full width of beam, giving them a good eighteen feet athwartships. There were lieutenants in frigates who didn't have as much room. A table on the larboard side showed that the cabin was also the gunroom. If we had a carpenter aboard, he'd probably have built collapsible bulkheads already, and shelves and cupboards, too.

"Show me where the men sleep."

From the gunroom we climbed a ladder that ran up the forward side of the mainmast, through the small hatch at the fore part of the quarterdeck, and stepped down into the waist and over to the main hatch. Peering down into it revealed an open hold, filled in its lower parts with barrels and bags and sail lockers and the cable tier. Eriksson and O'Lynn had plenty of room for now, but it would get crowded soon enough with a couple dozen others in there. Full complement would be about thirty all told.

I thought of the chimney I'd seen up in the bows. "Is there a galley, Mr. Peebles?"

"Yes, sir. Right forward under the forecastle. I mean, right *forrard* under the *fo'c's'le.*" He repeated the words to himself in a whisper, like he wasn't entirely convinced yet that people actually talked like that.

The galley ran the width of the bows and had a sink as well as a brick and iron stove, but there was barely four feet of headroom in there, and the hawse boxes for the anchor cables ran through it from the deck to the hawseholes, and the foremast stood right spang in the middle of all. I could feel the heat rising through the hatch already. It would be a fair bit of hell in there once we reached the tropics.

I turned around and ran my eye along the length of the schooner, and on up her masts, and then down again toward our three enlisted men chatting away by the starboard three-pounders. "Very good, Mr. Peebles. Was there any letters for me?"

His face went paler and he ducked his head. "Yes, sir. In my cabin, sir."

"Well, God rot your fucking eyes, Mr. Peebles! Go fetch 'em this instant!"

"Aye aye, sir!" He scampered off, I winked at Horne, and Gundy and Eriksson and O'Lynn pretended there was something interesting to see off the starboard beam.

The Secretary was keeping a close watch on me. I couldn't decide yet if that was annoying or reassuring:

> *Sir The preparatory steps to be taken are—to call on all the officers formerly attached to the Schooner, not otherways appropriated to place themselves under your Command—and immidiately to recruit a sufficient number of Seamen, for the accomplishment of the present object—which may be entered either for the trip, or for 12 months—you may advance their pay up to two months, provided the proper security has been obtained, able Seamen at 17 dols. a month and ordinary at 14— As time is of the essence you are to proceed immidiately you have sufficient men to work the Schooner—any difficiency will be made up on your making station— Do not delay on any account—*
>
> *Wm. Pennock Esqre the Navy Agent in Norfolk, will furnish monies upon your requisition to enable you to carry these orders into effect . . .*

Monies would be good. I could sail the schooner with the men aboard her now, but shifting sails would be slow work, and an emergency could get dire plenty quick with only a couple of men on watch at a time. The first order of business would be to call on Mr. Pennock for some ready cash for recruiting. A dozen hands, half able and half ordinary, would be a hundred and eighty-six dollars—twice that if every one of them demanded the full advance. With wages in the merchant service coming a bit higher than that, sure as certain they'd demand everything they could get. Still, the navy had it all over the merchants when it came to victuals . . . which reminded me I needed a cook, which would fetch another eighteen a month. I amended the figure in my head to two hundred and four dollars, and hollered out, "Mr. Horne, get the jolly boat alongside."

I calculated it would take several days to get even a dozen hands, and I dasn't wait to get any of the senior ratings and ship's officers I needed, what with the Secretary breathing down my neck; but even if our mission was all-that-fired important, I still needed a few days to get some uniforms made. My reefer's jackets would do for daily wear, but I only had one lieutenant's uniform coat, which I had on, and no proper dress coat worth the name. And there were cabin stores to be bought, and furniture, and blankets, and oilskins; hell and damnation, I didn't even have a piece of paper to write it all down on.

I had given half my back pay to Constance, and now I regretted it. But if I could be said to be fond of anyone in the world, it would be her, and I put the resentment from my mind. I would go ashore, fetch my sea chest and that dratted cat, who'd begun to grow on me, acquire what clothes and furniture I could, and make do with that. I knew what my next meal would be, and that would be good enough. That's what I told myself, anyway.

When I set up my recruiting table at the Connaught House, the same as where I had stayed before, there was so much to do that I hardly knew where to begin. I got through it without going aground, though, having handbills printed, sending Peebles and my little band of Tomahawks out with hammer and nails to post them, and sitting in that tarnal taproom all day without allowing myself a drop, not so much as small beer, while a trickle of no-account sailors came and went. The ones with four limbs were missing an eye, or were ruptured, or were old; the ones with only two or three limbs all said they could cook, but they didn't look worth the trouble it'd be to get an acting-warrant for them, much less the pay.

I was *Tomahawk*'s commander, master, purser, surgeon, and clerk. I was also my own first lieutenant. Despite the Secretary's advice to call on the schooner's former officers who were "not otherways appropriated," I had soon discovered that not only were they otherways appropriated, they'd absconded with themselves and the dishes too. The shortfall was reflected in the gunroom, as well; except for Acting Bosun Horne, the standing crew—carpenter, sailmaker, and gunner, who were supposed to be attached to a vessel rather than a ship's company—had been pulled out and distributed elsewhere. It was entirely illegal, but there was nothing I could do about it without sounding like a bellyacher. I confirmed Gundy in his rating as quartermaster, which he accepted without comment beyond his usual "Iss, zur." Peebles, with his enthusiasm for that tarnation carronade, could be our gunner if it turned out he could be trusted not to blow us all to hell. Horne and I would be everything else between us.

At any rate, at length I assembled a respectable assortment of ordinaries and enough ables to keep them honest. I could allow I'd done good enough, and with a fair wind and a favorable tide I could no longer get around that clause in my orders about having sufficient men to work the schooner. I calculated I could sail her with four men per watch and another at the tiller. It might take a while to do anything, and nothing fancy, but we could do it.

"Very well," I gulped, taking a last look around the roadstead and noting the ships in motion and the direction of the wind. I was wearing Juge's beat-up old hat for luck. Juge wasn't scared of anything when he was alive. I pulled it down snug and felt some of his cheer coming over me. I grinned at Gundy and Horne. "Let's get underway."

"What 'ee gaakin' at?" said Gundy to Eriksson, O'Lynn, and the new Tomahawks. He pointed his thumb aloft. "Get abew and loose the tops'ls."

"D'ye hear the news there?" cried Horne, stalking the length of the deck and looking for shirkers. "All hands to make sail! All hands!"

One man elbowed his mate in the ribs. "Listen at that nigger making a noise like a bosun! It ain't natural, Bob Wilson."

"I should say not," said Bob. "I don't think we got to obey a nigger, do we?"

Before I could open my mouth, though, Horne solved the problem by clopping Bob Wilson across the back of the head. Bob went sprawling, and Horne leaned over him, roaring, "It's heavy duty for you, man! Get forrard to the windlass! Go! Go!" He reached out for Bob's mate, too, but he scampered off on Bob's tail, crying, "Anchor cable, aye aye, Mr. Horne!"

With half a crew we passed through the Capes and struck out east to give Cape Hattaras a wide berth. After five days we got out of the Gulf Stream and into the true green of the deep Atlantic. There we turned south and boomed along, which I accomplished by letting Horne and Gundy see to the work and showing myself on deck whenever we needed to shift sails or shoot the sun. Mostly I paced the quarterdeck, looking officer-like and impressing Mr. Peebles, who needed impressing, it seemed to me. My first command—*my first command!*—and it began to dawn on me that I wasn't entirely sure what to do about it.

Tomahawk turned out to be nimbler than she looked, an eager and agreeable boat, not brilliantly fast but easy to work to windward. I tried not to love her; I guessed the Secretary's haste was just his way of seeing I got down there without wasting any time, and that I'd be turning her over to some lieutenant with more experience and greater clout. But my chronic headache lifted in the sea breeze, so clean and cool after a summer in the city that I woke at first light every morning, even when I'd been on watch half the night, with energy and joy surging in my veins. And as I paced her spray-damp planks, I'd find myself patting her railings or gazing aloft just to see how prettily she carried her square topsails on her swept-back masts.

The only mar in my happiness was a recurring nightmare in which I saw Peter Wickett in the *Breeze*, her decks awash and dismasted as she broke up beneath his feet. In the dream I saw his mouth working as a maelstrom sucked him down to the bottom of the sea; I couldn't hear what he said. And then when the sea had calmed and closed, and I thought it was all over, he rose like a hideous fish to lie bloated and stinking among the wreckage. The port wine stain stood out like a bullet hole in his pale forehead. And then he opened his dead eyes and stared through me.

Ten days out we spoke the *Pickering*, one of the fourteen-gun jackass brigs that had been laid down a few years earlier for the Revenue Cutter Service and that had been turned over to the navy, Master Commandant Benjamin Hillar commanding, that was wallowing along in the company of a couple dozen merchantmen out of New Castle, Delaware. She was the new darling of the *Rattle-Snake*'s old sailing master, John Rogers, who looked as indestructible as ever with his granite jaw and oaken arms, and his tarry queue leaving brown dabs on the back of his white shirt in the heat. The day stands out with unnatural clarity in my mind, as if it shone through a camera obscura, but in truth it was an entirely ordinary day. As the breeze was gusting up about as windy as a mouse fart, I accepted Hillar's invitation to dinner, and over his second-best Madeira I caught up on news and gossip.

"Did you hear about the *Breeze?*" I said.

"Aye, I read it in *Claypoole's Advertiser,*" said Rogers. "*Her people presumed drownded.* That just means no one saw it happen, nor found any wreckage. But as you know Peter Wickett and I didn't get on in life, I don't guess I'll humbug myself by grieving for him." He thought about that, rubbing the bristles on his jaw. "I guess enemy is too harsh a word, but if ever there was a dangerous man to know, it was him."

"Why, how you talk! He never posed a danger to neither one of us. And he's past that now, anyway."

He shrugged. "A dead snake still bites."

"Listen at how solemn you are! Now, see here, John Rogers, I recollect perfectly well how you two got along." I caught Hillar's eye and laughed as I remembered. "You won't credit it, sir, but them two was like brothers—whatever one wanted, the other was again' it. One of 'em couldn't say it was Tuesday without the other one taking his affidavit it was Sunday."

"Can I help it he was ornery?" said Rogers, breaking into a smile. "And I allow his mean streak come in handy in a fight. I got no doubt them picaroons would've gotten the best of us if he hadn't insisted on fighting." He glanced uncomfortably at Hillar. However remote the chances might be, a charge of mutiny could still be levied against us if someone had a mind to.

"I know all about that," said Hillar, before I could speak. "Leastways enough to guess that what really happened isn't what really happened, if you follow. I won't ask you to tell me which stories are true and which aren't. Were it my business to know it, I guess you'd have told me already. But say there, Mr. Graves! You ain't told us about that fight betwixt the *Rattle-Snake* and those two privateers, and how she came to grief."

Hillar was a big pink man and had unshipped his seagoing face when we sat down to table. No doubt he'd put it back on as soon as we went up on deck again, but for now he was as mellow as brandy.

"Oh, as for that," I said, "I guess Mr. Rogers here has told you all about it."

"Why, yes, he did," said Hillar. "And from what I can gather, you did it blind-staring naked, with a cutlass in every hand and a bandage over both eyes. He thinks you're a lunatic."

I smiled at Rogers. "That right, John?"

"Maybe that's coming it a bit high." He laughed, but he kept an eye on me. "Let's just say *unpredictable.*"

"There," said Hillar. "Can't say fairer than that." He leaned sideways so he could see past me to the passage and shouted, "Hi, there! Fetch us in another bottle! Now, then, Mr. Graves, I hope you'll do us the kindness of spilling all."

"Well, sir . . ." I waited for the steward to open the wine, till I realized he was taking his time about it so he could hear the story too. "Well, sir," I said again, "I had been banished below when it all began, as Surgeon Quilty had taken the notion that I was out of my wits from having been kicked, stabbed, and shot out of a cannon five or six times."

"That's putting it mild," said Rogers.

"Not a word of truth to it," I said. "I just had been larruped in the head a couple more times than was good for me."

"You were addled-pated," said Rogers. "There was some as wanted you put over the side."

"No! Say it ain't so."

"It's so. It made Peter Wickett plenty sore, too."

"That's just like him not to mention it." I weren't sure if he meant Peter had been sore because someone wanted me gone or because I'd been a-booming along with all sails set and no one at the helm, so to speak. "Anyway," I said, "I disremember exactly how it come about, for I had been strapped down, but suddenly there I was on the quarterdeck in nothing but my shirt. It was the first I knowed of it. I can't hardly explain it, except it was like I was sleepwalking and then all on a sudden I woke up. 'Where's the captain?' says I, peering around in the smoke. 'Taken below just the minute, sir,' says the quartermaster, an Irishman name of Brodie, 'for the topmast cap has struck him a cruel blow.' Smacked him, sir, right here on the brow, I believe," I said to Hillar, tapping my forehead, "right where he has the port wine stain. Have you ever met him, sir?"

Hillar had taken out a jackknife and was whittling himself a chaw off a plug. He shook his head. "Can't say as I have."

"You can't miss it when you see it, sir. It's in the shape of Africa."

Rogers gave Hillar a look, but it wasn't till later that I realized I'd been speaking of Peter in the present tense.

I got through the story all right, judging by Hillar's contented chawing and spitting, and the way the steward and the mess boys lingered in the passage instead of getting on with the washing up. If I faltered a little when I got to the part where Alonzo Connor, the conspiring blackguard whose treachery near cost us all our lives, stuck himself through the throat on my sword and then heaved himself to the sharks, or the part where I found my friend Juge surrounded by the bodies of Connor's followers, croaking at me about honor and glory as the life leaked out of him—if I quavered, nobody told me about it. I could see the uneasy glances Hillar and Rogers gave each other when I finished the story, or rather when I got tired of it and just stopped talking. I drank off my wine and poured myself another.

Rogers cleared his throat. "How's your mate Dick Towson getting on? Last I heard, you two were waiting on Captain Tingey."

"Dick's no mate to me."

"Oh, is that so? How'd that come about?"

"He beat me out for a berth in the *Insurgent.*"

"Berth as what?"

"Fletcher wanted two mids and would've took me as senior. We spliced the mainbrace a time or two, me and Dick. Next thing I knew it was morning and he had shoved off without me."

Rogers and Hillar stared at each other, the way you do when you're not sure how to react to what someone's said. And then they both laughed, and before I knew it I was laughing right along with them.

"Well, if you aren't an ungrateful pup," said Hillar, slapping the table. He was laughing too hard to get any more words out for a while, but at last he managed, "Here you are a lieutenant—with a command—and you're—har har!—you're crying because your best pal is a reefer and you aren't. That's just too many," he said, wiping his eyes with the heels of his hands. "I am flummoxed."

I watched the watery track my tumbler made as it rolled along the tabletop. A wicked swell was coming up from the south.

"I guess maybe it's his sister I'm put out with," I said—to my instant regret, for it obliged me to sketch out my failed courtship of Arabella Towson. I even had to tell them about Roby Douglass.

"Aye, she's a looker, all right," said Rogers. "But flighty. She'd never do as a wife, except for her father's money. Ever an eye for the next chap. Word is she played merry hell with the young bucks of the Eastern Shore, you don't mind my saying."

"I do mind you saying. But I calculate you're right." I took a little more wine. "With a stepmother like that, how could she be such a bitchy sailer?"

"I've met Lily Towson," said Rogers. "There's an angel among women."

"You've met her? Where?"

Rogers put a finger alongside his nose and said, "I dasn't be telling tales." He winked. "But I will say she was gentleman's friend in her day. Delightful and handsome. Cake and lemonade with her offered a more satisfying memory than a week with the finest whore in Philadelphia."

"I'd place a higher value on her than that," said I. "She's a first-rate among a fleet of wormy tubs. So say I with all my heart, John Rogers, and I'll knock you down if you say other."

"You'll get no argument from me. And don't think anything ungenteel happened betwixt us, because it didn't." He put his hand on my arm, and I pulled away. "It appears to me someone's fonder of the hen than of the chick," he said. "Dick Towson wrote me you'd spent your mornings with her and could scarcely take your eyes off of her. He thinks of you as a brother and gave it no deeper thought. But d'you think of her as a mother, I wonder?"

As he spoke, my resentment of Dick came flooding back worse than ever. I guessed he could've stood up with me if he'd wanted. It didn't matter if it didn't make sense—I just couldn't shake it.

"You're stepping on dangerous ground, there, John Rogers. I'm warning you fair and square."

His honest brown eyes grew troubled. "Ease off, Mr. Graves, I meant no offense."

"Well, let's just say Dick Towson is no brother of mine."

"I'm sorry to hear it. You'd do worse for a brother than him. He's a good chap with only the kindest of motives, despite his money. Less wicked than some, says I." He rapped his knuckles on the table. "Though I hate to speak ill of the dead, lest I meet the same fate."

I'd been listening with half an ear to the creaking of the rigging and feeling the motion of the *Pickering* with my belly as much as anything. I glanced out the stern windows at the breeze playing across the sea, and saw the topsails of the brig astern of us begin to fill and shiver, and heard footsteps crossing the deck overhead toward the after hatchway. Before the man could call down that the wind was fetching out of the southeast, I stood up so sudden that I even surprised myself.

"Thank'ee for a most excellent dinner, Captain Hillar." My headache had roared back up, and I had to think about each word. "I'll see you both in Le Cap, I guess. I don't expect you aim to keep company with this lubberly set of merchantmen."

Hillar had shipped his seagoing face again. "I do, sir, and so will you. I'm busier than a three-legged dog with a new set of fleas, and you're going to help me shepherd this lot to Saint Kitts."

"No, sir, I'm sorry to say I ain't," I said right back at him. "'Do not delay on any account' is my orders, and 'time is of the essence.' There's saucy Johnny Crappo waiting for me in the Leeward Isles, and I mean to pull his nose for him."

Once I was on my own quarterdeck again I waved farewell to John Rogers. He lifted a granite hand in return, looking as indestructible as an oak as he stood by the *Pickering*'s wheel. I say indestructible, for that is how he appears to me in memory; but even oak and granite will break, and in fact the brig soon after vanished from the face of the sea, and her ninety men and boys were never seen again.

TEN

The view was fine from the quarterdeck of the *Columbia* frigate. Dick's old ship, the *General Greene,* cruised in our wake; the *Tomahawk* glided along off the starboard quarter; and the mountains above Le Cap Français on the north coast of San Domingo showed as a blue smear of clouds to the southeast. The ships and clouds I saw from around Commodore Cyrus Gaswell's bulk as he and I fetched the sternmost reach of our stroll. Just shy of the larboard eighteen-pounder stern chaser we both turned inward, so as not to interrupt the conversation, and continued forward till we come abreast of the forward thirty-two-pounder quarterdeck carronade, where we turned inward again and retraced our course.

Informing him of the results of Captain Tingey's examination of me and Dick had took all of five minutes. Our conversation during the other forty or fifty minutes we'd been walking up and down consisted mostly of Gaswell saying, "Hmmm!" and "Well . . . hmmm," which I couldn't think of nothing to add to. Sweat streamed from beneath his cocked hat and soaked his neck-cloth, and from the smell of damp wool it weren't doing his old frock coat much good, neither. I wouldn't have minded stopping for a second so I could bail out my shoes, but we just kept a-walking and a-turning, walking and turning till finally he fixed me with a stare from his pale blue eyes and said, "How many hands do you need?"

Two had always served me well enough, I thought, but I didn't guess he was in a mood for foolery. "I could use a cook, sir, a sailmaker, and another dozen foremast jacks. But as I don't know where I'm bound or what I'm to do when I get there, I can't say further than that."

"Where you're bound, yes," he said, like it was the great mystery of the age. "Ye've put your finger on the problem right there, *I* allow." He mopped his face with a bright blue wipe, and then ran it around his jaw and neck. He looked sourly at the sailing master and the *Columbia*'s dozen midshipmen as they climbed up from the waist, doffing their hats to the quarterdeck and fiddling with their sextants.

The sailing master took off his hat again at Gaswell's glance and said, "Just come to shoot the sun, sir. It's nigh on noon."

"And it'll be the middle of the first dogwatch," said Gaswell, "afore that lot of fatheads discovers our whereabouts."

The master nodded cheerfully. "That be true, sir."

Gaswell leaned toward me and muttered, "A man that stays sober after noon ain't no more use than tits on a schoolmarm. Let's you and me step below and have a snort."

He called to his steward for calibogus, which he brought us half a dozen bottles of spruce beer and another of rum. "Pull them corks," said the commodore. "Now then, Mr. Graves, strong or weak?"

"I guess that depends on how strong the spruce beer is, sir."

"Not too strong, not too weak," he said, handing me a frothing glass. It smelled like flowers and lemons with just enough rum to give it some heft, and when I poured it in me it tasted of hops and molasses, not piney at all like your inferior spruce beers. I licked the froth off my upper lip and said, "That's right good, sir."

"Yes, it is." He took a long pull and sighed. "Don't mean to be complacent about it, but the daughter-in-law makes it and I'm partial."

I realized suddenly that I had never thought of him as having a family. I'd never thought of him as anything but the large fellow who set me to strange tasks.

He drank off his glass and set it on the table. He had never set himself down, which weren't like him at all, and now he began to pace back and fro in front of the stern windows.

"I'm a-going to let you in on three joys," he said. "The first is that, yes indeed, you are that lucky commander that's to be entrusted with the *Tomahawk.* Bet ye had just a *leetle* shred of doubt about that, didn't ye?"

I allowed as how I did, and he held up a blunt hand.

"Don't thank me yet. Your second joy is that your acting order as lieutenant really did originate in the Navy Department and not with me. Not that I don't value your services and would've been glad to write ye out another, same as before, but the Secretary's good favor is more useful than my own."

The third joy was a little longer in coming, as I shall tell in a minute; but regardless of that, I knew full well he'd balance each joy with a corresponding burden. I sat in the hard chair, doodling my finger in the water rings that my glass left on the polished mahogany table and sipping calibogus while he backed and filled and tried to cough up whatever it was that was stuck in his craw.

"You're to suppress piracy, o' course," he said, "and 'otherwise advocate the free use of the sea lanes by all ships public and private not at war with the United States,' which I guess ye know is standing orders for every commander. But there's complications." He stopped to mix himself another drink. "Won't you take a drop, Mr. Graves?" he said in the country way, as if I hadn't had any yet.

"Why, yes sir, I believe I will."

He talked while he mixed the rum and spruce beer. "Our alliance with the British and Toussaint ain't anything more'n an informal agreement . . . the British give us copies of their signal books, and hardly ever shoot at us anymore . . . How's that taste?"

This time I remembered to use my handkerchief to wipe my mouth. "It's right good, sir." It was strong, too; I had to throw a round turn over a bollard, so to speak, to keep myself from drifting off in the current. I wasn't sure yet which way it was headed.

"The alliance, if I can call it that," he said, "is holding steady for the moment, but the upcoming election might be kinda delicate if the Jeffersonians come to power. New York commenced voting in April, but others won't vote till October, and things is bound to be a little tense till the votes get counted next February." He took a deep swig off his brew. "But if Old Tom *do* get in, ye can be damn sure he'll cut costs by reducing the navy and making peace with France, which leaves Toussaint in the lurch. Your Yankee merchant don't give a hoop who's in charge in the island as long as he can trade for coffee and sugar."

Merchants be blowed, I thought; a fellow had to think about his employment.

"But that just plain wouldn't be right," Gaswell continued. "Imagine what the world would think of us, was we to lead a man on by false promises and then stand by while his life and freedom are snatched away! The planters in Jamaica and the Bahamas don't cotton to the idea of a sovereign black nation anywhere nearby. It gets 'em in a pucker. But right is right, and I'll say so, too."

"I don't guess they're any too fond of a black republic in Washington, neither," I said.

He snubbed up short on his hawser and give me a stare. "You know, I forgot you're part something or other," he said. "But don't you fret, son. We row in the same boat, you and me. Things is delicate, that's all I'm saying. Delicate." He recommenced his pacing. "We're at peace on paper, anyway, us and King George. But there ain't no love lost between us and the Royal Navy—*I'll* say not. They just can't get their heads around the idea that Yorktown and the Treaty of Paris all went in our favor. Unfortunately for you and me, they got the means to make their unhappiness be known. So you're required to assist and cooperate with 'em whenever possible, but you'll *associate* with 'em at your peril. That dog bites, y'understand me, son?"

"Yes, sir."

He was hardly even looking at me anymore, so I scratched at my skeeter bites while he tromped back and forth across the light. How the blame things could find their way across several miles of ocean I didn't know, but we'd fetched a cloud of them aboard the *Tomahawk* near about the moment we raised the island. I'd have to try smoking them out with sulfur and gunpowder and anything else that come to hand and was noxious enough. It probably wouldn't help with the skeeters, and nothing helped with roaches, but it might at least amuse the rats. I finished my calibogus and waited for the commodore to fetch his moorings.

"I am going to tell ye something now that ye must keep under your hat, Mr. Graves," he said, with a stiffness that was so unlike him that I sat up and gave him both ears. "Say ye'll keep this under your hat."

"I'll keep this under my hat, sir."

"Well, then . . . All that stuff I was saying, that ain't my primary concern at all. I mean, it is, but it ain't to be *your* primary concern."

"Yes, sir."

"Hearken ye well now, for this is the third joy I told ye about, though it may not seem like it at first." He held up a warning hand. "Asa Malloy has the *Constellation* now, as I guess you know, and is bucking for commodore. To mollify him more'n anything else, he is to get the *Tomahawk* as his tender."

"Him! You're right it don't seem like a joy, sir. We near about got a blood feud going."

"Now, now, now, you just hang on. He ain't going to get her just yet. That's just a story me and the Secretary come up with, and we'll figure how to get ye out of it when the time comes. There's . . . there's a little something needs doing, first."

"Aye aye, sir," I said, hoping he didn't hear the query in my voice. Last time he had a little something needed doing, I'd ended up to my neck in a sewer.

"Well, sir," he continued, "I guess I'll just have to come at it direct and hang the maneuvers. There's an American pirate that's begun to assert himself among the islands." He waved his hand at the table like he'd just set his magnum opus on it, plain as day, and expected me to pick it up and admire the detail. "There it is out in the open, and no way around it now." He gave me a significant look.

"Yes, sir?"

"Why, don't you catch it? It's like to be a great embarrassment to the United States in general and to the navy in particular if he ain't caught soon. Do ye know what I mean to say, son?"

"No, sir. Is he anybody in particular?"

"Is he anybody—" He looked at me all squinchy-eyed. "Calls himself Captain Mesh. Pretends to be a French privateer. That's M-E-C-H-E, by the way. Got one of them little backwards marks over the first E. God knows why he calls himself such a thing."

If God knew why, then I guessed Gaswell would know it also in the fullness of time; but it was his business if he wanted me to figure it out too. "*Mèche* is a French word with several meanings, sir. It can mean a lock of hair. It can mean a match fuse, or a candlewick. It can refer to a secret."

He raised an eyebrow. "Say, that's not bad. A secret, hey?"

"Yes, sir," I said, wondering what he was up to. "*Éventer la mèche* means to discover a secret, and *vendre la mèche* means to let one out."

"He's stole an 8-gun Bermuda sloop, which he calls *Suffisant*. We want her back."

"Stole her, sir? You mean he captured a privateer and, what, didn't have her condemned proper?"

"No, hang it! I mean he absconded with a navy vessel." He looked around like someone might be listening—which they probably were, knowing what officers' servants are like, but I didn't guess his man would talk even if he dared to. "He's reported to be a very tall chap, with a long nose and a pointed chin. Wears a bandana low on his brow."

Low on his brow . . . "He calls the sloop *Suffisant,* you say, sir? As in 'Breezy'?"

"Ye got the weather gauge on it, son. Now close in and grapple."

He looked so grim I almost laughed; only I didn't, because he looked so grim.

"Tell me, sir, are her bulwarks scarred on the starboard side, and does her gaff mains'l bear a patch like a yellow cross?"

"Just so." He tapped the side of his nose, and then flung up a warning hand as I brought my lips together to form the letter P. "Avast! *Don't* say his true name. Don't. Get that into your head. Ye must never say the name you knew him by, for reasons that will come to ye if they ain't already. One more thing—and I stress again the need for a tight jaw in this matter, you hear *me*—he has made himself a loan of eight barrels of Spanish dollars meant for General L'Ouverture's use."

"How many dollars, sir?"

"Sixty thousand, give or take. That much coin goes by weight rather than per piece, but you can figure there's seven or eight thousand to a barrel. New milled dollars, probably all of the same date."

"What's 'milled,' sir?"

"It's them ridges along the edge."

"Yes, sir. And all the same date, which is what?"

"Seventeen seventy-six."

"Well, sir . . ." I scratched my ear till I realized I was doing it. I put my hand down. "If they're new, why ain't they dated eighteen hundred?"

"Because the Dons ain't too particular about the dates on their American coins, I guess. Dies are expensive. I don't know. But that don't signify. All ye need to know is if ye come across a heap of shiny dollars all of that date, minted in Mexico City, with Carlos the Third on the front—and yes, Charles the Fourth has been King of Spain since about twelve years now—you're probably on the right road. We don't think Mèche's people know about the silver, else why would they be pirating instead of spending? He's lately been in the Virgin Islands, we believe, and was run off by the Dons at Saint John's in Porto Rico. Ye must ferret him out. Do that, and the president will sign your commission as lieutenant. No more temporary position, but a permanent rank, yours to keep as long as you care to. Fail, and ye will answer for it, et cetera, et cetera, and so on."

And there was my third joy at last, unfolded like a bad hand at cards and almost entirely marred by its incumbent burden. I didn't know whether to be elated that Peter was still alive, dismayed at his dishonor, or insulted that Gaswell supposed I would even consider the job of hunting him down.

But of course the old sea dog knew I would take the job. My only concern was how to get it done.

ELEVEN

The beginnings of a hot dry *carbine* blew from the north. The same "shotgun" had nearly wrecked a French fleet twenty years back, when the *Intrépide* had caught fire and blown up. If that fleet hadn't gotten out of the bay and arrived off Yorktown before the British fleet come back from New York, the Battle of the Virginia Capes would never have took place, Cornwallis wouldn't have surrendered, and the Continentals would probably have lost the war. Not nearly so much depended on my getting *Tomahawk* out to sea, but it was grinding my bones to be embayed with a blow coming on and the wind veering east of north. It would be coming dead foul if I didn't get out soon.

I glanced at Horne, but whatever he was thinking, he wasn't showing it.

"Near as she'll lie, Gundy," I said.

"Near as she'll lie, aye aye, me cabbun."

He said it a bit short, and I thought about bracing him up, but I put the thought away. He was steering as small as he could, and I needn't have said anything in the first place.

I leaned back against the weather rail, staring through the heat haze to the east. We were heeled over so far that the rail was near about leaning against *me*. I stepped down the deck to the binnacle and checked the compass, looking across it at the morro peak of Monte Cristi, where the Spanish territory of Santo Domingo began. I ran aloft with a glass and peered at the sea creaming white over the rocks and reefs around the point. I looked out to sea, and at Cape Français in the west. I checked the apparent wind direction with a glance at the cork-and-feather dog-vanes flapping on the quarters, and checked its true course by noting the paths it made across the surface of the sea. Then I stared hard at the reefs again. Satisfied, I swung back down to the deck.

"We got some room. Let's see can we weather the point on this tack."

Columbus had lost the *Santa Maria* on a reef just a league or two down the coast when the officer of the watch had gone to sleep. I didn't guess I'd be taking a nap anytime soon, but you never knew when something might carry away. I glanced up at the furled topsails and at the trim of the fore-and-aft sails.

So did Horne. He'd taken off his stocking cap, and his wild braids whipped around his shoulders as he craned his head back. He glanced at me and smiled, and I smiled back, and then his white teeth and pink gums gleamed in his black face as he laughed.

Peebles, though—he paled as *Tomahawk* swooped over the Atlantic rollers. The boy seemed to have lost his sea legs in the short time we had been playing bo-peep with Gaswell off Le Cap. I tried to gaze imperturbably into the wind as a good captain should, but the day was so glorious I couldn't help throwing my arms back and hollering.

Half the people stopped and stared at me, only to hop back to business when Horne stepped to the break of the quarterdeck and scowled at them. I'd've been scared of him too, was I in their place; his skin was so dark that his face turned all teeth and eyes when he wanted to look ferocious. Some of the hands still snuck looks, though, as soon as he turned away. Simpson and Hawkins—two enormous waisters I'd gotten from the flagship, such powerful men that they might not have needed the winch to get our fore-and-aft sails aloft—turned around to gawp at me, and Yancy, a white-haired, spectacled sailmaker's mate that the commodore had loaned me, popped his head out of the fore-hatch to see what the excitement was. In fact, every man who looked around for more than a second was wearing a red-checked shirt of the sort favored in the *Columbia*.

"Mr. Horne, as soon as it's convenient, let each new man be issued a couple of shirts from the slop chest."

"Aye aye, sir." There was nothing else he could say, but he hung a question on the end of it.

"Put 'em in blue checks like the rest of the people," I said. "Take their old shirts away, show 'em they're all Tomahawks now. Oh—and remind me to go over the watch bill. I want the Columbias divided evenly between the la'board and sta'board watches."

"Ah," he said, rubbing his hands together. "Aye aye, sir."

I was glad he approved, but of course it wouldn't do to say so. And here was Peebles, who'd been grinning like a scared monkey ever since I hollered.

"Grand day for sailing, ain't it?" I said.

"Y-yes, sir."

"I got a reputation as a lunatic, you know."

"Yes, sir."

"Worried?"

"Yes sir! I mean, no sir! It's just that—" He gulped wetly.

"To loo'ard," I said, and then had to grab his ankles to keep him from going by the board.

We rounded Cape Samanà on the eastern end of Hispaniola, and loitered across the mouth of the long and narrow bay to the south. We saw plenty of small craft in there—a lot of them French, too, for sure, but the Spanish fort on the north side of the bay and a battery on the south side put them out of our reach. What was more important, though, was that I could see straight down the bay, and no *Suffisant* in sight. Rather than buck the awkward winds and twisting currents of the Mona Passage just yet, I settled for beating along the northern coast of Porto Rico.

A Spanish *guarda-costa* came out to meet us as we approached Saint John's. She was schooner-rigged and pierced for ten guns.

"Looks to be held together with spunyarn and prayers," I said, examining her through my glass. I handed it to Horne.

"We could give her tops'ls and t'gallants," he said, looking her over, "and still sail her under in an hour or two."

"Sure, but that wouldn't be right."

"Oh, sir!" said Peebles, as a jet of white smoke spurted from her away side. "He wants us to—"

"Heave-to, if you please, Mr. Horne," I said, but Peebles looked so disappointed that I had to laugh. "He has every right to find out who we are, Mr. Peebles. We're in his yard, after all."

Turned out the *guarda-costa*'s artillery consisted of eight swivels—little half-pounders at that, hardly bigger than a blunderbuss—and no carriage guns at all, despite her ports. Her captain came aboard of us by hauling alongside and swinging across on a line seized to his mainyard, to save the trouble of launching a boat.

"I am Capitán de Corbeta Zamora y Ramos of the *San Buenaventura,* at the gentleman's pleasure," he said in English, straightening up after a deep bow and a pretty flourish of the most immense cocked hat I ever seen. His long jaw needed a shave, and his blue uniform was stained at the elbows and knees as if he'd tried to disguise the worn places with ink, and the red of the lapels and cuffs was faded to nearly pink, but he had a solemn kindness about him that I liked. We exchanged a few pleasantries that were too elaborate for me to keep up with easily, but I just bowed him along until we'd fetched the cabin. I waved him into a chair and called for coffee.

After a lot of jawing it transpired that yes, *el capitán de corbeta* Zamora y Ramos would take some coffee if I no have the chocolate, and no, this Mèche fellow was no in San Juan.

"Five days," he said, sitting with one knee crossed over the other in my cabin and spooning sugar into his cup. "Then he sail east." He waved his spoon in a direction that might have included anything between the Virgin Islands and Africa.

"You seen him yourself, sir? You watched him leave?"

"Oh, *sí, sí.*" He nodded a while, his lips pursed and his bristly chin sticking out. "Yes. Yes, I follow him myself for half a day. We no want him back. A most unsavory character—he is a *norteamericano,* you know," he said, as if that explained a host of ills. He slurped from his cup. "Brandy might improve this coffee."

"I got some whiskey, or tafia if you druther." I opened a locker and hauled a couple of square case bottles out. "Did you talk to him personally, sir?"

"Tafia? Bah. I try the whiskey, if it please. No, *señor,* to answer your question, but I see this Mèche in port. Is most illegal, you know. He bring in coffee and sugar." He slapped himself on the forehead. "*Stupido,* selling coffee and sugar in this island." He curled his lip and waggled his fingers alongside his head. "*We* sell coffee and sugar."

"But it's illegal for non-Spanish merchants . . ."

He rubbed his thumb against his first two fingers. "*La mordita,* the how-you-say—"

"The bribe?"

He raised his hands in mock horror and clucked his tongue. "Ai-yi-yi, such a harsh word! The 'little bite,' always please to say—is alive in this island, and I, the vigilant Capitán Zamora, cannot be in all places at once."

"Yes, sir. And no doubt Mèche had his reasons for selling here."

He shrugged, smiled. "No doubt. He sell his ship along with the cargo. A nice little *bergantín*—a brig, two masts—with a hole in the side."

"A hole?"

"Such as a round shot would make. They patch it and paint it, but one could see it all the same. One learns what to look for."

"He was *in* a brig?"

"No, *señor,* he has a brig *with* him, which is what he sell. He himself is in what you *norteamericanos* call a sloop. One mast, eight guns, and a patch like a yellow cross on the *como se dice,* how-you-say, the mainsail. *¡Sacrilegio!*" He crossed himself.

"Was the brig armed?"

"Oh, *sí.*"

"So she might've been a lawful capture. A letter of marque, maybe."

He shrugged. "Then he must to take her to the prize court in your country to be condemned, no?"

"Well, there's a prize court in Le Cap now, but yes, a capture needs to be condemned legal so the owners can have their say if they want it. They usually don't. But you said you saw him. What does he look like?"

"A tall unpleasant man, thin and bitter. He has the scar on his cheek. His nose is long and his chin is like the crescent moon. It is said he has the mark on his forehead, so." He traced a comma on his brow. "But he wear his hat low, and I do not see this."

"He was here five days, sir, or he left five days ago?"

"He leaved yesterday morning, *señor.* I return only last night."

"Then I must leave immediately, sir, while the wind serves. You will forgive me?"

"As we have finished the coffee, *señor,* yes, by all means, go find this bad fellow. But allow me to send some chocolate aboard—if the young *capitán* is to entertain more of my countrymen, he will be thankful for it. It will take but a moment."

"I'm most grateful, sir. In exchange, will the captain accept some American whiskey?"

Zamora smiled with more politeness than enthusiasm. "An acquired taste, but one that might be amusing to acquire."

With the *guarda-costa* receding in our wake, I called Horne down from the masthead.

"Couldn't see behind the morro fort, of course, sir," he said, "but other than that I could see down the whole length of the harbor, and *Breeze* ain't there."

"You mean, *Suffisant* ain't there."

"Yes, sir, that's what I meant."

We nosed around to windward of Porto Rico to no effect, rolling around on the Atlantic mostly because I was too stubborn to admit I didn't know where to look and too proud to ask Horne or Gundy for ideas. I had pretty near made up my mind to drop down to Saint Thomas in the Virgin Islands, on a bright afternoon with Isla Cagada lying three leagues to the southwest across the sparkling sea, when we sighted a grubby brig coming up toward us from the Danish islands. She looked to me like she was trying to edge away from us, like she weren't too sure if we were salvation or doom. Well, I guessed I could answer that for her pretty quick.

"Mr. Peebles, run up our colors and see if she salutes."

As soon as those fifteen glorious red and white stripes commenced to snapping in the breeze, the brig threw her helm over and tried to waddle off among the thousand or so cays to the south. I would've bet we drew less water than she did, but her captain could lead us a long chase if he knew the shoals at all.

"Mr. Horne, what do you make of her?"

"Yankee, sir."

"Then why's she running?"

"I don't know, sir."

I took another long look at her through my glass. Even from a mile off she just about oozed shabbiness and neglect. I wanted to take a bucket and brush to her.

"Me, I'm just busting to find out. Gundy, lay a course to bring us alongside of her. Mr. Peebles, here is the key to the magazine. You may have a dozen three-pounder cartridges—you, Eriksson, go with him and make sure he don't blow us to hell."

The two came back with the first cartridge properly stowed in a wooden cartridge box. Eriksson looked expectant, but Peebles looked positively cheerful.

"Now then, Mr. Peebles. Clear away the forward gun on the sta'board side."

"Aye aye, sir! Eriksson, O'Lynn, to me!" He picked four more men and set them in position around the gun. "Take heed! Silence! Cast off the tackles and breechings." He got the tampion out of the muzzle and the lead apron off the vent. "Unstop the touch-hole. Handle the priming wire. Prick the cartridge." Eventually he got to "Handle your crows and handspikes—point the gun to the object," at which point I stepped in.

"Belay that, Mr. Peebles. We don't need to sink her just yet."

The men laughed at the notion that our three-pound shot would sink the brig, but not unkindly. Peebles got a little red, crouched down behind the gun and sighting along its length, but he swallowed his embarrassment readily enough.

He got to his feet and touched his hat. "Gun ready for firing, sir."

"Very well. Let's show her some smoke."

"Take your match and blow it—fire!"

Eriksson blew on his smoldering slowmatch and pressed it to the touch-hole. The priming flared, the gun shot backwards, the iron ball and fiery wad flew off into the wild blue yonder, Eriksson stuck a leather-covered thumb over the vent, and the brig continued on her course like we weren't there at all.

"Give her another."

"Aye aye, sir."

The closer I let Peebles get to her, the more she ignored us—or it seemed that way, at least. I was starting to get vexed. We had a steady breeze on our starboard quarter, and I didn't have to resort to sextant and cosines to see we'd overtake her unless the ocean opened up and swallowed us. Which could happen. Or a sudden hurricane could spring up, or we could get hit by a waterspout or a white squall, or we could hit a whale, or the nails might fall out of our hull and sink us in the low and lonesome sea, which would be much the same thing as the ocean swallowing us, which is what got me started on that line of thought in the first place—any number of things might impede us, from the possible but not very likely to the damn near impossible; but they were only worth acknowledging as a way of warding off the Furies. I touched wood.

We were closing the distance without even having to crack on sail. The sea was calm, nothing on it but a long, gentle swell. It was about as pleasant a day for sailing as ever there was, but I wasn't enjoying it too much. I let Peebles have another dozen cartridges. At long musket shot I had him train his three-pounder as far forward as it would go.

"Now then, Mr. Peebles, see how close can you get without you hit her."

The shot must have passed over her deck, for her helmsman

throwed a glance over his shoulder, and a head or two popped over the rail before ducking down again, but we got nothing else out of her for it. Three more times we fired as we closed the distance, all three of them close enough to put a buzz in their bonnets over there; but they declined to come up to the wind, and I began to think that if Peebles accidentally put a shot through her, I would be obliged to cuss him out but my heart wouldn't be in it. When a naval vessel shows you her colors and gives you a gun, you're supposed to heave-to and satisfy her curiosity, damn it.

At pistol shot I said, "Gundy, put us across her stern." I snatched the speaking trumpet out of the beckets—I wanted to make sure everyone aboard her heard me—and called across, "This is the United States armed schooner *Tomahawk.* Heave-to!"

"Nay! Nay! I'll not," cried the helmsman.

"Heave-to or I'll blow your cabin to flinders! I'll rake you stern to stem, by tarnal thunder, see if I don't! You, sir, will be the first to go!"

At that he threw up his arms and she flew up into the wind. Her sails flapped confusingly for several minutes, and then her yards got braced round properly and she rode easily with her fore-topsail against the mast. We stood off her to windward.

I called across, "What brig is that?"

"*Horseneck,* Cap'n Browbury," said her helmsman. Without prompting he added, "We were four days out from Antigua, laden with sugar and coffee, nothin' but light airs all the way, when we got jumped by a ding-dang son-of-a-caterwampus flying American colors. Cleaned us out and took every nigger in my crew as well. Nay, nay," he said, apparently alarmed at the cheerful industry with which Horne and the boys were hoisting out our boat. "Ye needn't bother comin' aboard. I bein't in need of assistance."

"It's no bother."

"Nay, nay!"

"Yes, yes! Here I come," I called.

"Oh—hang it."

With pistols and cutlasses all around, I went across with Horne and four Tomahawks. Browbury—he and the helmsman were one and the same—offered no resistance, and his crew merely stood around staring cow-eyed till we herded them all together on the fo'c's'le. They were a hungry-looking lot, and every bit as dirty as the brig, but Browbury had them beat. He was a big shaggy man, squalid and moldered, as if the clothes was rotting off his body. His petticoat trousers was more rags than legs, he was missing his left sock, and it was hard to tell what color his shirt was, or even if it was checked or plain. The lower half of his face was hidden beneath a wild black beard, and his nose and cheeks were smeared with tar or grease—I couldn't tell what, and I didn't particularly want to know. He wore an enormous slouch hat with a brim that looked like he chewed on it in his spare time, and his hair hung in mats around his shoulders. Peeking out from behind his saggy trousers was a girl of six or seven, with scraggly black ringlets poking out every which way from under her bonnet, and a grubby but expensive-looking doll clutched to her bosom.

"That rover I told ye about," said Browbury. His eyes kept wandering uneasily to Horne beside me. "He got himself within pistol shot, all man-o'-war fashion and strictly by the book, just like you done. And then he raised the Jolly Roger with a horrible shout and was aboard afore we could so much as raise a musketoon. Er, not that we have any arms at all, no sir. Long as we go unarmed, we ain't legal prey for French privateers, you know. Which don't stop 'em, blast their hide. Anyways, that's why we was leery an' dinnit heave-to at first—thought ye might be another pirate."

"Don't worry, Captain," I said. "You'll pay the shot. I'll see to it."

"Oh, bill me for the ball and powder ye fired again' us, will ye! Ay-yuh, you do that, sonny, you go ahead." He spat tobacco on the deck. "I'm about cleaned out, so what do I care? Anyway, we'd a-had 'em, if he hadn't been a sneaky snake." He put his antique tricorn over his heart. "Imagine, profaning the Stars and Stripes thataway. Ay-yuh, he were a bad 'un."

"Ay-yuh, mate, he were a bad 'un, all right!" said the girl. Except for bonnet and beard, she and Browbury were the spirit and image of each other. It was hard to tell them apart by smell, too. They reminded me of the neighbors when I was a boy.

I doffed my hat. "Hello, Miss." I waved my hat at Browbury. "Do you know this chap?"

"Sure, I'd know him anywhere! He's my old man."

I drew her out from behind her father's legs. She would've been pretty if someone had bothered to wash her face and comb the nits out of her ringlets.

"What makes you say he was a bad 'un?"

"He almost stole my dolly!" She wrapped both arms around it.

"Whatever did you do?"

"I did like this," she said, and kicked me in the shins.

Browbury doubled over. "Oh, ha ha ha! A real fighter, she! Ay-yuh!"

The girl had her hand over her mouth, her eyes shining with the effort of not laughing.

"Oh, oh, oh!" I cried, hobbling around the deck and rolling my eyes. "Sweet jumping Jehoshaphat—carve me a peg-leg and call me Gimpy, for I am lame, sure!"

The girl dropped her hand and giggled.

Putting my hands on my hips and frowning with mock severity, I said, "Now that's no way to treat an officer, is it, Miss Browbury? Kicking him, and then laughing in his face!"

"I'm sorry, mister," she said, all contrition. She held the doll up toward me. "Yvette says she's sorry, too. See?"

"Yes, I see. Is Yvette your dolly's name?"

"Martha," said Browbury, "less said, soonest mended."

Her eyes flicked toward him and then back to me. "Ay-yuh. She's from France, you know."

"Enchanté de vous voir, ma'm'selle," I said, bowing low over the doll's tiny hand. *"Exquisite,"* I said to Martha. "The best hand-painted porcelain. And dressed in the height of fashion, too. She must be very rich, to dress in silk."

"Oh, ay-yuh. She's a com . . . comtuss . . ."

"Comtesse?"

"Ay-yuh, that's it—what you said. That's what the pirate captain said she were. Do you know him? I had called her Eve, but that's not so very grand as Yvette. He were real nice and spoke French as good as you. I'm sorry I kicked him. He weren't really going to take my dolly, you know."

"Martha," said Browbury, his voice low with fury.

She scowled but didn't look at him.

"Your father must think pretty high of you, to give you such a doll."

"He dinnit give it to me. I took it." She looked pretty pleased with herself about that. "We had lots of them, but the pirate stole 'em all, along with the clothes."

"Clothes? You mean the dresses the dolls were wearing?"

"Ay-yuh . . . nay. Nice silk clothes. Not *clothes,*" she corrected herself. "*Cloths.* Big bundles of it, and lots and lots and lots of dollies all wrapped up in paper."

"Martha!"

"Well, we did so have them!" She stamped her foot. Then she gestured me closer so that I knelt down. Jerking a grubby thumb at her father, she confided in a stage whisper, "He tried to take Yvette away when he seen you coming. It were him I kicked, not the pirate."

I grinned. "You don't say! Well, you know what? I've got heaps of chocolate on board, given to me by the Viceroy of Porto Rico himself. Would you like some?"

Wide-eyed, she nodded, then took me by the hand and led me away from her father, who stood there twisting his hands together and looking at us a-lopsided. I knelt beside her.

"I had chocolate once," she said. "The pirate give it to me while he were taking the clothes away. I mean, cloths. And it were very nice, but you know what?"

"What?"

"It wants sugar."

"But don't you got lots of sugar?"

"Nay, hardly never. Just 'lasses sometimes, but they don't hardly ever gimme any."

"But your father says you had a cargo of sugar."

"Him!" She beckoned me close again. "He tells fibs."

"Well," said I, standing up, "I have sugar, too. Would you like some of that as well?"

"Ay-yuh, if you please."

We shared a warm little smile as we walked hand in hand back to her father. He stood apart from his crew, or they stood apart from him; whichever it was, they were mighty uncomfortable associating with each other. That weren't entirely unusual, as merchant captains are pretty tough with their crews as a rule. They don't feed them enough and will put them on the beach with or without pay, if the mood strikes them and they can get away with it, but usually a ship's company will stick with their skipper. It's only natural to prefer the devil you know. But these men shrank away from him like he had the fever on him, which alarmed me till I looked again and saw that what might've been a flush was just dirt, and the rheum in his eyes was just from rum.

Horne came up from the hold. "She's in ballast, sir. Some ship's stores, not much, and most of it rotten or wormy. It smells of spirits, but I didn't see any. I found a few muskets and such, but no more than what he might need for defense."

"Or shooting pigs." The Spaniards had left pigs and goats on islands all around the Main, as a way of supplying themselves with meat that kept itself fresh. "What kind of ballast?"

"Local rock."

"Any sign of coffee or sugar?"

He shook his head. "Would've smelled the coffee. Didn't see no sugar, just black strap in hogsheads, and none too much of it."

"Captain Browbury, let's have a look at your papers."

Browbury's cabin was a close and nasty place where even the air felt moldy, but at least it was away from other ears. I sat in the single chair and looked through his books. They were scratched out and scribbled over, but a few minute's study made the pattern clear.

"You've been a naughty fellow, Captain Browbury."

"You're a hard-hearted young sprout, ain't ye?"

"So I been told. But I ain't concerned with what happened in the long ago, you may be glad to hear. It's the recent past that interests me."

He squinted. "Like for instance?"

"Like for instance you were running a load of silk out of Guadeloupe, weren't you?"

"Nay, mate, I dinnit never! Silk comes from China. Now I ask ye, do I look like I been in China?"

"It went to France first, obviously—the dolls. Your end of the deal was to run it to where, Charleston? Baltimore? No, not Baltimore. Too many chances of getting boarded by a revenue cutter on the way up the Chesapeake. Course, with all them creeks in the Eastern Shore to hide in . . ."

"I never in life been to Guadeloupe!"

"All right then, Martinico. And you been carrying a powerful lot of brandy, too, by the smell of it."

"Ah, ye wrong me!"

"The hell you say. Yvette is a fashion doll, out of Paris. The ladies use 'em to see what the latest mode is. Your daughter said you had lots of 'em and a cargo of silk cloth besides. But I guess it don't matter now where you were bound. Fact is, tell you true, I don't care one way or another." I tapped the book in my lap. "But you'll have to tell your owner something, and I got to tell the commodore something. I think you were in ballast already, looking to pick up a load of something somewhere, to be bought with a draft that was waiting for you at wherever it was you was bound for, and this so-called pirate couldn't be bothered with you."

"Sugar and coffee, it was—the finest quality!"

"Don't insult me. I don't see a manifest here, no bills of sale, nothing to prove you're who you say you are. I could seize your brig and arrest you all."

His mouth made a little *o*. "Now, mate, ye wouldn't. Think of the lass."

"*You* think of her. I'm too busy thinking of *me*." He got a calculating look, and I guessed I was hitting the right notes. "The naval agent in Le Cap is a mate of mine. Nathan Levy—tight with a dollar, but he's a man for business and we get along. He'd make sure this here brig was condemned in court, all above board and proper. She'd fetch about two thousand dollars after me and my boys cleaned her up, I bet. We'd keep half the proceeds, and half of that would be mine, free and clear. You and Martha on the beach, Mr. Browbury, and me with five hundred dollars in my pocket." I pretended to calculate. "Base pay, with cash value of rations and various allowances . . . Say, that's better than six months' pay for me."

Now that my eyes had gotten used to the dimness, I could see piles of filthy clothing on the deck, and decayed remnants of dinners long past, and broken pieces of machinery that might've been pieces of pistols or lamps or tackle.

"Not to mention whatever you got paid for your contraband," I added. "We'll confiscate any cash you got and lump it in with the profits, unless of course it happens to find its way into someone's pocket between now and then."

"Well, you tell me what to do, then," he said, pretty severe considering the bind he was in. "This rover I told ye about was real enough, an' he were an American."

"I thought you said he spoke French."

"He did when he were aboard of us, aye, but it seems to me, now that I look back on it, that there were a good deal o' play-actin' about him. Always with big gestures and broad looks to convey his meanin', and except for the handsome one, the others just grunted when they said anything a-tall. An' speakin' of his crew, I been wonderin' what it was that struck me so strange about 'em, an' watchin' your boys, it finally come to me. They had navy discipline."

"What makes you say that?"

"Well . . . there weren't no sir's or salutes or none o' that, but they knowed what they was about, and no bickerin', and no question about who was in charge. And no molly-maukin' around or any o' that, like you get with your inferior quality of freebooter."

"Oh ho," I said, thinking I smelled triumph. "So you know about pirating?"

"And who don't who spends any time in Charlotte Amalie?" He waved a dismissive hand. "The Danes don't care what goes on there, and couldn't do nothin' about it if they did."

Charlotte Amalie on Saint Thomas was the main Danish settlement in the Virgin Islands. It had been declared a free city a while back.

"Browbury, tell me true. When the pirates boarded you, it was all dumb-show, right?"

"Ay-yuh, a little bit of a show for the boys to tell about when we get back home. I wanted to make it look good." He tried a wink on me. "*You* know."

"That's taking a hell of a chance. What if one of your people had fought back?"

He grinned, revealing yellow gums and black stubs of teeth. "That lot? Not likely. The only ones with any spunk was the niggers, and they all jumped ship and j'ined the pirates."

"So you met him in Charlotte Amalie and proposed to sell him your silks?"

The grin disappeared. "I struck up an acquaintance with him, ay-yuh."

"An easy man to get to know, hey?"

He brought his eyebrows together so fierce I thought he was going to wring them right off his face. "Him! He must've been titted on vinegar and weaned on lemons. I thought he might kill me with a look."

"Then why do business with him?"

"Struck me as honest. Most chaps in Charlotte Amalie will cut your throat as soon as look at ye, but he looked like he'd at least want a reason. He stood out."

"But weren't you afraid someone might do for him and make off with the whole caboodle, yours and his alike?"

"*Hell,* no. Pardon me for speakin' an oath, but even them renegadoes and villains steered clear of him. They was a-feared of him, and that was my protection."

He'd lost his low cunning look, as well as his bluster, and he seemed smaller without them. He didn't look any cleaner, though.

"Describe him."

"Oh, he were a beanpole. Had a phyz on him ye could use to cut cheese." He passed his hand over his face, like he might pull it into the shape he was trying to describe. "He was all nose and chin. Wore his hat low over his brow, like he had a secret he were hiding. I mean, every man in Charlotte Amalie got a secret, but they usually don't make no bones about 'em. Maybe he just weren't accustomed to the trade, I dunno."

"Anything else?"

"Ay-yuh, he had a scar on his la'board cheek." He touched his face, considering. "Nay, I tell a lie—it were on the sta'board. Kinda pinkish and puckered, like it were recent but not too recent."

"Did he call himself Mèche?"

He shrugged. "Could be. Somethin' French. He spoke his English with an accent, but it were a little unwieldy on him."

"His English was unwieldy?"

"Nay, mate, it were the accent he had trouble with."

"Did he say where he was bound?"

He shook his head. "If he did, I wouldn't put no stock in it anyway."

"I guess not." I handed him back the brig's papers. "It's too bad there ain't nothing in there to say what he took from you."

"Well, he didn't just steal the stink out o' the bilges."

I looked out the stern lights to hide my smile. "Molasses, then," I said. "Black strap, fair to middling quality. Thirty tons of it, I expect."

"It were rum. Ay-yuh, rum." He nodded his head wisely. "Decent stuff. Not the finest quality, perhaps, but none of that foul tafia."

I shook my head. "Shipping rum to New England? That's daft. Molasses, definitely. Not so very good molasses, neither. Sulfurous, thin—about twenty-five tons, I'd say."

"Forty ton—good molasses. Or not bad, I should say," he said, catching my look. "And it were took by a short, one-eyed Johnny Crappo operating outside his proper sphere—one of them half-nigger renegadoes from San Domingo gone on the account, eh?"

"I am astonished and mortified to hear it, sir, and I'll report it to the commodore the very moment I see him. Them French pirates is everywhere, and we're determined to root 'em out and destroy 'em. Why, that is my very mission. Now, this pirate of yours—I don't care if he was short or tall, and I don't care how many eyes he had. But it would be convenient for him to be French."

"Ay-yuh, he were French. Most fatuously."

"Fatuously . . . you mean emphatically?"

"Ay-yuh. What you said."

I got up to go, but then I thought of something that had been bothering me. "How many men did he have?"

He looked at me blank, and then scowled something fierce. "Say, now that ye mention it, I dinnit see but half a dozen niggers an' the two white men he palled around with. Sometimes he had one with him an' sometimes the other, but never the three of 'em ashore at once. He had a one-legged nigger cook aboard, too, a squinty-eyed cuss with a temper on him, but they dinnit pay him no mind. A slave, I expect."

"How do you know he was a cook?"

"Well, who else dumps tater peelin's an' beef bones over the side an' threatens to whomp his shipmates over the noggin with a skillet?"

"He spoke English?"

"I dinnit say he did. He shook a fryin' pan at 'em and scowled, but all's he said for sure was, 'Sacker blue.'"

"'Sacker blue'?"

"Ay-yuh, 'sacker blue.' Frenchies say it all the time."

So did Doc, our old one-eyed and peg-legged cook in the *Rattle-Snake* and most recently of the *Breeze,* when he was trying to talk to a Frenchman—or pretending to be French.

"Mèche's two mates, the white ones," I said, "what did they look like?"

"One was a ugly squirt, an' the other was excessively handsome."

"Excessively handsome?"

"Ay-yuh. Like in a painting or something. Like a angel, maybe. He pretended to be rough-hewn and low, but he were a gentleman, no doubt of it."

"Did either of them talk?"

"The handsome chap did. Spoke French." He stopped to pick his ear while he thought. "The other fellow was near as dirty as me. Face like a rat. He grimaced an' grunted an' gestured . . ." He pulled his finger out and looked at it. "But now you mention it, I don't guess he spoke one word, except in the cap'n's ear."

I got up from the chair and commenced to shoving things around with my foot while he pretended he didn't know what I was up to. I turned up an ancient beef bone here, some sticky britches there, a tin plate planted with a crop of mold, a broken jackknife, a hat with a busted crown . . . all sorts of antediluvian rubbish, but, thing was, it was in heaps instead of layers. That kind of filth takes years to accumulate, unless it's dumped down all at once. I kicked a last greasy hat aside and exposed a hatch secured by an iron bar and padlock.

"What's this?"

"Oh, just my glory hole." He laughed weakly. "Ye know, where I'd keep my treasure, *if* I had any."

I poked the lock with the toe of my boot. "Open it."

"Well, now, son—"

"You can open it quiet, or I can open it noisy."

"Oh—hang it." He hauled a big iron key out of his britches pocket and undid the padlock.

I hauled the hatch open. The compartment it covered was filled with a canvas sack, and the canvas sack was filled with something that clinked. The blame thing wouldn't budge, though I seized it in both fists and hauled away. I slashed it open with my jackknife and reached inside. The stern lights was so grimed over that I could barely see what I'd grabbed—but I know money when I feel it. I stepped to the better light in the companionway and opened my fist.

"Goodness me, Captain Browbury," I said. "Look at what I found."

He clutched his shirtfront like he was about to tear it off, and his eyes were fixed on my hand, but he didn't come any closer. "What is it?" he said.

"As if you didn't know." I held it out so he could see. It shone even in that light, and its milled rim was rough beneath my fingertips. "You seem to have a bag full of Spanish dollars."

"What of it? There must be millions of 'em in circulation all over the world. The Chinese won't take nothin' else in trade. An' that there dollar is legal tender from Peru to Penobscot."

It was a little larger and a little heftier in the hand than a U.S. dollar, and bore a profile of a chubby man with a large nose and an odd smirk, looking off to the right. His hair was tied at the nape with a ribbon, same as any gent, but he seemed to be wearing a laurel wreath and a Roman toga as well. Below him was the date, 1776. In a semicircle around his head ran the legend CAROLUS III DEI GRATIA.

"Says here, 'Charles the Third, by the grace of God,'" I said. "But what is he by the grace of God, I wonder. Captain Browbury, what do you think?"

He worked his mouth, but he shook his head without saying anything.

I turned the coin over. It had a quartered shield on the back bearing the castles and lions of Spain on it, supported by a pillar on either hand and with a crown above it. The legend on that side read HISPAN ET IND REX.

"Oh, here's the rest of it," I said. "See there? It's short for *'Hispaniarum et Indiarum Rex.'* That's Latin for 'King of Spain and the Indies.'" I pointed at the other letters. "The M is for Mexico City, where it was minted, and the numeral eight and the letter R is for *ocho reales.*"

"So it looks like a million other pieces of eight. What of it?"

"What of it, indeed. What if I was to pull out a few handfuls at random—how many of 'em would have the same date?"

He shrugged. "How the hoo-roar would I know?"

"Let's have a look, then." I grabbed another fistful of coins. "This one on top is from seventeen seventy-six." I flang it at him; he snatched it out of the air like a dog snapping at a fly. "And this one is . . . seventeen seventy-six. What about this one? Hey, seventeen seventy-six. See where this is going?"

I threw the coins on the deck and admired the way they rang. Say what you will about the Dons, they know their silver. Browbury knew his silver, too, and he scooped them up quick as lightning.

"These here coins are all twenty-four years old," I said. "By the date on 'em, anyway. But look how they shine! Like they're just minted. And you know why? Because they just been minted. Mèche stole some barrels of coins just like this." I flipped a last coin in the air and caught it. "This here is the money you got in payment from him."

He squinched his eyes at me. He was already on his knees, but he didn't look scared at all. He just looked sad.

"It were a good piece of actin' all around," he said. "An' I guess I'd of gotten away with it if ye hadn't poked your nose in where it weren't wanted."

I put my boot on his shoulder and shoved him back on his rump. Without his legs under him he wouldn't be tempted to jump up on me.

"Tell you what," I said. "Count me out a hundred of them dollars so I got something to show the commodore, and I'm gone. You remember now—he was French."

"Oh, ay-yuh, that he were. Short and fat, he was. An' he stank like Old Harry's outhouse, too."

"Don't be making up anything your people didn't see. Just keep saying he was French, and I'm satisfied. I'll be sending over some chocolate and sugar, and some milk from my goat as well. Be sure Martha gets it." I rubbed my shin. "She'll be expecting it, you know."

"Oh, ay-yuh," he said, also rubbing his shin.

"Good-bye, good-bye," Martha called as we pulled away from the *Horseneck.*

"Good-bye, dearie, good-bye," the Tomahawks called in return, waving their hats and missing their stroke.

"Eyes in the boat," growled Horne. "Give way, dearies!"

TWELVE

As I lay in the stuffy darkness of my cabin that night, waiting for daylight before making the run down the West Channel through the Virgin Islands, my eyes kept springing open. It wasn't just worry that kept me from sleeping, and it wasn't just being bent double in a hammock instead of swaying gently in a hanging cot, neither. It was Greybar, rumbling on my chest like a Watt steam engine. The vibration was comforting, but a hot fur plaster ain't what you want in the tropics.

It hadn't sat right with me, coercing Browbury into lying about Peter. I thrashed around in my hammock till Greybar dug his claws into me and I lay still again.

Browbury had it coming, but I hadn't gave it to him. What I had gave him was a bagful of silver for dealing in smuggled goods. I told myself it was just on account of his daughter that I'd let him keep the money; but it weren't my money to give, which meant I'd as good as stole it.

And I couldn't believe that Commodore Gaswell was conducting this charade willingly, but conducting it he was, and I had to follow his lead wherever it went. And that fool cat kept a-digging his claws into me every time I fidgeted. I hauled him up by the scruff, dropped him on the deck, threw my legs over the edge of the hammock to follow him—but if I did that then the watch on deck would know I couldn't sleep. I flopped back into the hammock.

"Shit and perdition," I whispered in the dark, but a whisper don't carry the comfort that a full-gale bellow does. I trailed my hand, letting Greybar bat at my fingers.

I didn't want anybody but me going after Peter. Anybody else would kill him or die trying. It was like trying to get a badger out of a steel trap. I just wanted him out and gone. "But I want to keep my fingers, too," I said to Greybar, withdrawing my hand, and he thumpered off somewhere in the dark.

I sat up again and swung my feet. So, what was justice? Peter had a fine sense of it, or at least he'd showed himself highly sensible of *in*-justice—if it was even Peter I was looking for. Maybe the commodore hadn't come at it direct because he wasn't entirely sold on the notion that Peter and Captain Mèche were the same man. But his cook sure sounded like Doc, and the handsome fellow and the dirty one sounded an awful lot like Corbeau and Ben Crouch.

Whoever it was I was looking for, he had two days' head start on me, according to Browbury. They'd sailed south-southwest with a load of silk and dressmaker's dolls. The direction made the Dutch islands of Saba and Saint Eustatia unlikely, and they were too near the British naval base in Saint Kitts, anyway. Mèche might be making for a port to sell his cargo, or heading for a depot of some sort. He was short-handed, else he wouldn't be taking men every time he detained a ship; and from what I'd gathered from Browbury, the raree-show had occurred with Saba in sight about ten leagues north-northeast.

And almost as clearly as if he stood before me in the flickering shade of a paw-paw tree, with a wicker basket dangling from his hand and the Atlantic stretching out at his back, I heard Peter back in San Domingo saying, "I shall go where the birds dwell." And with that memory to spark it, my mind's eye conjured up the map of the Caribbean that I'd been looking at day and night.

I leaned my head and give a yell: "Ahoy on deck! On deck there, fetch me a light!"

When it didn't magically appear right at that very second, I grabbed a candle, ran up the ladder, and stuck my head through the hatchway. In the dim glow of the binnacle light I saw O'Lynn at the tiller and Horne at the conn beside him, both of them looking at me like I had horns on my head.

"Here!" I held out my candle. "You got nothing quicker then light it off the stern lantern."

Burning candle in hand, I hopped back down the ladder and into the alcove that served as the *Tomahawk*'s chartroom, yanking out drawers and pawing through charts till I found one that showed the whole West Indies.

Considering his cargo and his poverty of documentation, Browbury would have kept Saint Kitts and its cruisers at a respectful distance, but long habit and a natural desire to make good time would have held him within a reasonable distance of the Leeward Islands. If I was to run contraband into the United States I would have stood out into the Atlantic, to keep all islands and shipping lanes as far away as possible, but more than likely Browbury's deep-water navigation left something to be desired, and he poked along from landfall to landfall. He wouldn't be the first ship's master to be bested by sines and cosines. But a man like Peter, a man with mathematics and an understanding of old-fashioned saltwater sailing, the kind you did with taste and smell and a feeling in the gut—

Somewhere . . . for the life of me, I had no idea what—there! A tiny footprint out in the middle of nowhere, south-southeast of Saint Croix and a hundred-something miles west of Guadeloupe. It was about as far from land as you could get in the eastern Caribbean, and probably so low it was near about invisible till you rode right up onto it. I smacked my hand on the chart table.

Blinking in the light of the single candle, the big man edged beside me into the alcove under the ladder. Drops of spray on his peacoat filled the tiny space with the smell of damp wool.

"Mr. Horne, how is your navigation?"

He looked at me kind of sideways. "That's Gundy's department, ain't it, sir?"

"It ain't like you to shirk, Mr. Horne. He's a rating, you're a warrant officer."

"I'm not—yes, sir." He rubbed a knuckle against his nose. "Well, I can box the compass."

"You say it like pulling teeth out of your own head. Can you read and figure?"

"Yes, sir. A bosun has to be able to keep a log."

"I guess we should have Mr. Peebles here. Is he on deck?"

"No, sir, the child's asleep. Want me to roust him out?"

"Not yet. Now, this is important." I pointed at an X I'd penciled on the chart and a line I'd drawn away from it. "There's our position. Where are we, what course is that, and where will it take us?"

"Looks like seventeen degrees, forty-five minutes north by forty-five degrees, forty-five minutes west. That can't be right. Oh, I see—it says here, 'Longitude west from Ferro,' which is the northwest tip of Spain. We're using Washington City as zero degrees now, ain't we?"

"Them charts is a mish-mash of American and French and Spanish and British. The British use their observatory at Greenwich as zero degrees, and considering how many ships call at London, that's good enough for me. I've wrote the differences in the margin."

"Yes, sir, I see it now." He picked up a pair of dividers.

"This here chart's six years old," I said, "but I don't imagine the islands have moved much in that time. Now, how do we get from here to there?" I tapped my finger on *here* and *there.*

He adjusted the dividers against the scale in the chart's margin. "After we round East End on Santa Cruz, we head southeast by south for . . ." He walked off the distance with the dividers. "About forty-five leagues, looks like, till we get to fifteen degrees forty minutes north. Then we start looking for this Birds Island, it says here." He ignored the Spanish name in capital letters, ISLA DE AVES, in favor of the English name below it in italic.

"Don't forget about leeway and the prevailing current."

"No, sir, I haven't. That's why I figured on sou'east by south instead of sou'-sou'east. Let's see now." He took up a pencil and made some calculations. "I go with that," he said, showing his numbers. "Then when I got about here I'd start heaving the lead. No need to break out the deep-sea line—anything less than twenty fathoms puts us on the Aves Bank. I've sailed across the north end of it, up by Saba, same as near about everybody else in the schooner, though I never heard of this island before. I'd charge the lead, too—muddy bottom puts us to the west of the middle ground, and sand puts us east. Rock puts us in the middle. Once I've found those rocks, then I know where I'm at on the bank, and once I know that, it's just a matter of walking down south and a little west till we fetch up against it." He pointed at a dotted line and a mess of crosses around the north side of the island. "Hopefully not at night, though, because of this reef here."

"Very good. Any questions?"

"Yes, sir. What's at Birds Island?"

"Dunno yet. Now rouse out our young gentleman. I want a word with him."

Our young gentleman was eager but unequal to the task of figuring out where *Tomahawk* was, much less where she was to go. His guess that we fetch Birds Island by sailing southeast along a line penciled on the chart was accurate in that the island lay in that general direction, but by his method we might fetch bang-up against Trinidad before we knew we'd missed our mark. I couldn't remember the last time my head didn't hurt, and a dreary sense of responsibility began to temper my enthusiasm for command—a notion I recoiled from as soon as I thought it.

I made myself look around my cabin—*my* cabin!—while Peebles labored over his figures. I still had to sleep in a hammock, true, but that was because I hadn't bothered to get someone to knock a cot together for me. Same with a table—I could've had at least Peebles and Horne in to share my salt pork and beans. If I was lonely it was my own dang fault.

I had to guide Peebles into useful subordination, not force him. Of course he was near useless, it being the natural state of boys, as I well knew from my own self, but it was my responsibility to make him useful; and if I did it right, it might be well worth the effort in years to come. But right now I had to find some way for him to pay his own freight.

Despite myself I was feeling a bit of appreciation for my old captain in the *Aztec,* Asa Malloy, who'd promoted me over Dick and the other fellows. He'd rarely had me beaten—just that one time, really. He'd gave me all the responsibility I could handle and then some, which naturally rendered me capable of more responsibility. I'd misliked it at the time, wanting to skylark in the rigging by day with Dick and the other reefers, playing follow-my-leader through the rigging or running along the yard with arms thrust out for balance, praying I reached the topping lift before I lost my balance and ran off into the void. I wanted to pull pranks again, like the time half a dozen of us ran through the gunroom at four bells in the middle watch, cutting down the warrant officers' hammocks and then scampering for our lives up the rigging as the gunner roared and the sea officers like to died laughing. I'd wanted to sleep the night away like the others. Instead I climbed out of the fuggy warmth of the midshipmen's den to stand watch in the middle of the night, and got my ears boxed by the sailing master when I was stupid about answering questions, and tended to the schoolmaster and his perdition trigonometry in the forenoon, and learned my knots and splices from my sea daddy in the dogwatches. It was only that Malloy had knocked me down with his bare hand instead of dealing out proper ship's discipline that had brought on our falling out. And Peter had put up with a good deal of inconvenience on my behalf as well. It must've been a burden to him that I was the captain's cousin when we were in the *Rattle-Snake,* and a raving looby half the time before the end, but he'd managed to terrify me into obedience at the same time he helped me build a belief in my own abilities as navigator, sailor, and leader.

I'd been lax with Peebles. I didn't guess he'd respond too well to terror, but he was so tarnal inoffensive that I wanted to thump him sometimes.

I gave him an impromptu lesson in basic seamanship, coaxing him through the thirty-two points of the compass and then showing them to him on the compass rose, printed right there on the chart, and then making him box the compass again.

"Here," I said, showing him the chart once more. "That mark is where we are, and that island is where we want to get. And the chart has some remarks on the island, see?"

He peered at the faint script, his lips working as he read.

"Says there's a couple trees, or were at one time, and those marks around the"—he broke off to consult the compass rose again—"around the northeast, that's a reef, or rocks, I expect."

"So then what's the correct course? Listen," I said, when he mumbled another wrong answer, "you got to learn your trigonometry, Mr. Peebles. Someday it might keep you off a lee shore or close you more readily with an enemy. You can use it to find your position, or tell if a chase is closing the distance or pulling away from you. You can use it to discover the exact distance of an object of known height, like a mountain or a lighthouse or, say, the *Columbia*'s maintop."

"Aye aye, sir."

"Trigonometry ain't an arcane and frightening science. It's just triangles, is all it is, and the compass points are just another way of expressing the number of degrees in an angle."

"Yes, sir."

"If you know one side of a triangle—say, a lighthouse that rises eighty feet above sea level—and two of the angles—in this case a right angle, because the lighthouse is perpendicular to the sea, and whatever angle you get when you shoot the lighthouse with your sextant, or octant, or whatever you happen to have—why then, you can calculate any of the other sides or angles."

"Aye aye, sir." He stifled a yawn, opening his eyes a little wider to keep looking like he was interested.

"Triangles are the simplest of shapes," I said, "and a pleasure once you get used to 'em. That might seem pretty strange to you now, but when you're a post-captain booming along in your very own forty-four-gun frigate, I guess you'll see what I mean." I felt like an idiot as soon as I said it. What did I know about booming along in my very own forty-four? But the boy wanted perking up. He was droopy. "And who knows," I said, "maybe you'll even be a commodore someday, with a line of frigates at your beck and call!"

"Aye aye, sir. I mean, yes, sir."

"Now then, mister, to brass tacks. In a frigate there'd be a schoolmaster to learn you your numbers, and learn you your grammar and make you write a fair hand, and learn you drawing and watercolors for making maps, but in a little old schooner like *Tomahawk* we'll have to toss you in and see can you swim. But I know you can keep your head above water until you find your stroke."

"Yes, sir. Aye aye, sir."

"We are in a delicate situation, Mr. Peebles. You've heard rumors of this man Mèche we're seeking?"

"Yes, sir. Real name's Peter Wickett and he's gone a-pirating, sir."

"Oh. Yes." I cleared my throat. "It looks that way. Well, we're to bring him to heel. There'll be no margin for error. There are certain extraordinary steps I got to take to make sure of our success." I reached over and knocked on the wooden bulkhead to ward off hubris. "I got to make the most of every advantage that presents itself."

"Yes, sir. You want Mr. Horne as mate instead of pretending like I'm second in command."

Out of the mouths of babes! "What makes you say that, Mr. Peebles?"

"Stands to reason, sir. He's your only warrant officer besides me, and he's a man-o'-war man through and through, which I'm not yet, and the people like him. He occupies himself taking sightings when it's his watch. He's been trying to teach me but without much success. I think I'm getting close. It makes sense when we're talking about gun trajectories—which, now that I think of it, is much the same thing."

"Horne takes sightings when he's on watch?"

"Yes, sir. He plots our dead reckoning, but always sort of on the quiet, as if it's a hobby or something. And he shoots the sun at noon, and he takes at least two star sightings at morning and evening twilight both. I think he's got the star almanac memorized."

"Well, I doubt that—"

"Besides, sir, it's the guns I love," he continued, unmindful that he'd interrupted his captain. "Mr. Horne's amazing quick when it comes to elevations and ranges, but I think I've begun to headreach on him. I don't have to work out the calculations, though he makes me do it, and lord how tedious that is, I don't mind telling you, sir. I can *feel* the trajectories—I *know* when a gun is laid right. Don't know how else to describe it, sir."

"But that's exactly how navigation is, Mr. Peebles. The difference is that with navigation, you don't have to deal with trajectories—it's as if the shot didn't drop but kept going in a straight line after you fired it, and at a constant speed, too. Except that the wind varies, sure, but that's analogous to the sea's currents. There's no gravity to skew the results, is what I mean. It's much simpler than gunnery."

"Oh, no, sir, I *beg* your pardon. You're quite correct, I'm sure, but laying a long gun's hardly the same as plotting a course on a dismal old chart. And as for that big lovely carronade, oh! You haven't let me touch her yet, you haven't let me fire her at all, but if you would—!"

"I'll see that you supervise the firing of it next time, Mr. Peebles." I wondered if I'd just been blackmailed. "I noticed you'd took a shine to our armament, but I hadn't appreciated the depth of your interest. I guess it won't hurt anybody if you was our gunnery officer." And especially it wouldn't hurt anybody if Horne didn't have to pretend to defer to the boy, and the boy didn't write to his father the congressman to tell him I'd put a black man over him. "Now, get on back to your hammock. I'll need all your attention when we fire off that carronade tomorrow in the afternoon watch."

You pompous ass, I laughed at myself as I went topside to let the breeze into my shirt and trousers; a captain should speak in monosyllables, not blabber away like a pedagogue.

"Mr. Horne," I said, examining the traverse board in the light of the binnacle. "Take a star sighting for me, please. I need to know our exact position. You'll find the celestial tables and Maskelayne's almanac in the chartroom."

I went forward while Horne fussed with the sextant. The sky shone like a jar full of lightning bugs, yet it was powerful dark out; the moon had been in the last quarter two days ago, and would be a new moon in, let's see, six days. Make it Thursday. Birds Island lay about two hundred and sixty-five nautical miles to the south-southeast, which gave us plenty of time to get there, barring accidents and hidden disasters. I knocked on the rail to hold disaster at bay, and then clasped my hands behind my back when I realized what I was doing. Every time I turned around I was knocking on wood.

Horne called out, "Going below, sir."

"Who's at the conn?"

"Gundy's come up from below, sir."

"Very well."

I went and fetched the binnacle sextant and shot Formalhaut, a hand's-breadth high in the southeast, and Arcturus in Boötes, an hour from setting at west by north, and then joined Horne in the chartroom.

He glanced up from a scrap of paper he'd covered with figures. "I'm sorry, sir," he said. He held his back as upright as the low deckbeams would allow, and his brow and upper lip were sweaty. "I just can't seem to make it come out right."

The man was embarrassed. It wouldn't do to patronize him, but I had to be able to rely on him. Privately I was as happy as a clam at high tide that he'd gotten this far.

I looked up Formalhaut and Arcturus in the almanac and then glanced at his scribbles and cross-outs. "Did you allow for the magnetic variation?"

"No, sir." He rubbed the bridge of his nose, cleared his throat and began again. "Here you are, sir."

I compared his new result with my own and drew it out on the chart. "That's well. We'll clear Carvel Rock with room to spare. The western Carvel Rock, not the eastern one." There was another Carvel Rock over in the British line of cays and scrubby humps that stretched eastward from Saint John in the Virgin Islands. "Lay our course, then all hands to make sail."

It wasn't darkness that had prevented me from heading down the West Channel earlier, but indecision. If I couldn't turn up any sign of Peter at Birds Island, I'd look foolisher than an old man at a kissing bee. It's a rare commander whose crew don't think he's a fool, but I had to do *something.*

Little Passage Island slipped by to larboard, a looming presence that I felt more than saw. No, that wasn't quite right, I thought, smiling in the dark. I could smell the land, and I could hear the ocean thrusting past it. The wind blew light and steady from the northeast, easing *Tomahawk* at a constant three knots down the channel.

At four o'clock the watch changed, and I stood at the windward rail, taking comfort in the matter-of-factness with which the blurred shapes of the men went to their stations. There was no moon or planets abroad, and without them the sky seemed as featureless as a face without lashes or brows, but by the stars in the sky and their reflections on the water I could see for some distance: low shrubby islands all around, Mount Sage on Tortola clipping off a segment of starry sky to the east, and under the keel an eerie green phosphorescence shooting through the sea as a pack of barracudas tore apart a drift of squid. Someone on the fo'c's'le laughed, followed by a voice that seemed to say, "Hewdie hewdie hewdie," and then more laughter. Erne Eriksson was amusing his mates by saying things in Swedish. The great pale band of the Milky Way stretched overhead. I breathed in slowly, steadily, deeply, like I could inhale the whole world into my chest.

"Ease up on the sheets," I said. The cheer would not last if I piled up on something in the dark.

A while later Gundy coughed discreetly. "Wind's backing against the sun, zur."

He meant it was going widdershins, veering around counterclockwise, but the words were strange to hear at night. It was coming up gusty and pulling clouds in with it, too: low, loomy piles of them that blurred the horizon and blotted out the stars.

"Very well. All hands to shorten sail." The cry ran along the deck, and then rigging creaked and the hull vibrated as the men scampered along to their stations. "Mr. Horne, get a man for'ard with the lead, if you please."

And then the rain came in blinding bursts that filled the air like drownding. We rode it out under a double-reefed maincourse and a prayer we weren't whirling away alee, and then the rain dropped off to a nagging drizzle and the wind fell away to a light air from the northeast; not the true trades, but steady and reassuring as a handrail on a darkened stair. The ceiling remained low and the air stayed wet, but a band around the horizon glimmered and twinkled, and a faint streak of false dawn grew in the east.

"Excuse me, sir," said O'Lynn, doffing his sodden hat as he stepped onto the quarterdeck. "But 'tis a light I think I've seen."

"That's just the zodiacal light. It's the atmosphere of the sun."

"Oh, no, beggin' your honor's pardon, sir, but 'tis a true light from a lantern."

I hadn't thought I could be any more awake, but of a sudden I was. "Where away?"

"A point off the la'board bow, sir."

I took the brass and mahogany night glass out of its leather case and peered forward. A tiny smear of light shone from beyond the larboard cathead, sure enough, diffused by the rain but plain to see now that I knew to look for it.

"Mr. Horne, send the lookouts aloft, if you please, and let the soundings be passed from man to man instead of sung out."

"Aye aye, sir." He went forward to give his orders quietly.

The leadsman sang, "By the mark—" before Horne had a chance to get to him, and then left off in mid-chant. A man touched his hat to me before swarming up the windward shrouds. Gundy turned the glass in the binnacle and started forward to strike the bell.

"Belay that till further orders," I said. I checked the traverse board. "Let her fall off a little."

"Let her fall off a little, aye aye, zur," he murmured, echoed by the man at the tiller.

Not too far, now, I thought as her head came a little to leeward—I couldn't see the shoal of coral heads that I knew lay in wait there, but I could just about feel it in my gut.

"That's very well thus," I said. "Brace up. That's well your braces. Quietly, now." The *Tomahawk*'s little quarterdeck was already too crowded, but something was missing. "Did anybody rouse out Peebles?"

He popped his head out from around the other side of the mainmast. "Here I am, sir."

"Good. Clear away your guns."

I could hear the smile in his voice. "Aye aye, sir!"

"Quietly." No need for more words than that. I'd have plenty of time to strangle him later.

Not seeing for myself was more than I could bear, and I took the night glass up to the fore crosstrees. The lookout silently pointed at a faint patch to windward.

A ship lay there, all right, a long, sleek ghost in the gloom. She was an inverted ghost, as a lens to correct for that would also lessen the light in the glass, and she seemed to be wearing topgallants. Topgallants at night made her a man-of-war, probably, and the loft of her masts compared with the lowness of her hull made her a frigate, more than likely. Behind me, *Tomahawk*'s long commission pendant flopped soggily at the main. What breeze there was—two, three knots maybe—was just enough to give us steerageway.

I tapped the lookout on the arm. "Go alow and tell Gundy to come a point to sta'board, then come back here."

Gundy had more sense than to reply, but the swaying of my perch changed as *Tomahawk* altered course. We'd be past the coral heads by now, but Carvel Rock lurked somewhere to starboard. I ducked my head to peer between the forecourse and topsail, and saw it looming; or, more accurately, I heard a difference in the sound the sea made as it lapped against its steep sides. I'd have to come about soon. That would take us toward the unidentified ship. The schooner's advantage, being able to sail closer to the wind than a square-rigger, was unavailable to me; my only choice was to slip across the ship's stern and hope that when morning busted out on our heads we'd be in the shallows on the other side of the channel, where no frigate could follow us. And I'd want to be at least a mile away—farther, if she carried anything larger than twelve-pounders.

I squinted through my glass at the ship's mastheads, dark against the first gray hint of the rising sun. She looked more French than English, but there was something comforting about her appearance. The rain was lifting and the rising wind continued to back. I would need speed soon, not stealth.

"Come four points to la'board," I hissed. The command ran softly down to the quarterdeck, relayed in a whisper from man to man.

The stranger altered course as well, bearing up and heading north, and I guess I wasn't the only Tomahawk who sighed with relief. We'd cross the ship's wake with room and to spare. Once we'd cleared the channel, we could fly northeast and scrape off any pursuer by darting in among the cays.

The clouds began to break up. *Tomahawk* passed nakedly into a patch of sea bare of rain, and I squinted as a shaft of rising sun caught us. The bare patch was wide enough to include the ship: a frigate for sure, and at quarters, of course, as any man-o'-war would be at first light; and the sight of her run-out guns and the man at her masthead pointing at us caused my scalp to crawl. I was about to holler down at Gundy to come about and damn the paint, but something in the back of my mind made me look at her again. Then a gust billowed out the red and white stripes of her commission pendant, and I recognized her.

"Ahoy the *Choptank!*" I called.

"Well, well, well, Mr. Graves," said Captain Oxford, pumping my hand in the broad, many-windowed after-cabin of the *Choptank*. She was only a 28—that was her rating, anyway; she carried twenty-four 12-pounders on her maindeck and eight 9-pounders on her quarter-deck and fo'c's'le, same as her sister ship, the *General Greene*—but the

Choptank was not new-built and had some comfort in her. I returned Oxford's handshake firmly, though I didn't like touching the hand that had signed the death warrant of François Villon Deloges. A pirate Villon had been, caught with blood on his hands and my watch in his pocket, but he'd saved my life once, which was more than I'd done for him. "*Lieutenant* Graves," Oxford added, reaching out to tap me on the epaulet. "Let's wet the swab, shall we?"

I looked him in the eye. Peter was wanted dead, I knew, and I knew that it would be hushed up afterward, and I'd be a private embarrassment to the gentlemen of the navy, an irritating reminder of a fellow officer's indiscretion. Peter was a plague sore, a festering bubo, which as soon as I lanced it would cover me with its contagion. My brother officers would despise me like a bloody-handed surgeon in a parlorful of physicians. But I'd have my epaulet and Gaswell's backing, and they could all go hang. It was that or go home. I needed to keep my head clear.

"That's good of you, sir, thank'ee. But I'll just take coffee."

He looked at me oddly, like I'd said something beyond his ken, but then he said, "Nonsense! It's wine you want on this beautiful morning. The rain has lifted, and the sky stands as clear as thought."

"Really, sir—"

He cut me off with a shout. "Steward, there! Break out a couple of bottles of the yellow label, and pass the word for Mr. Brownstone and anyone else who's off duty!" He muttered a few more well-well-wells and looked at me sternly, like he was going to give me some advice that he didn't want to give me any more'n I wanted to hear it.

I held my head high, though it took all my strength. I knew what he was going to say—not the exact words, maybe, but the thrust of it—and he could stow his gob, as far as I was concerned. I would do Commodore Gaswell's filthy work, but bugger me sideways if I'd have an audience. Even Tom Turdman got privacy when he cleaned out a shit-hole.

Then there came a knock at the door, and Brownstone, the first lieutenant, stuck his head in.

"Come in, Tommy," said Oxford. "Come in, and see who I have here!"

Brownstone drifted in, brown-eyed, handsome, and looking at me like he was a happy bachelor and I was someone's doughy daughter being pushed on him. At his heels came Halliwell, who was the second lieutenant, and Mr. Smiley, a lanky, redheaded midshipman. They all of them looked so much the same as last I'd seen them—when Billy and Peter and I were dining in her and the *Harold* had brought word to Billy to surrender his command—that I might've just stepped out for five months and come back an instant after I'd left.

"Mr. Graves, what joy," said Brownstone, without joy. "I saw you come aboard. So, you've made lieutenant. We'll see what comes of it."

Halliwell offered a chubby hand and cheerful delight that was as pleasant as it was honest. Smiley, who'd been a peer to me last time I'd seen him, smiled at me with an odd mix of deference and envy.

"She's a fine little thing," said Oxford, gazing out the stern windows at *Tomahawk*. "Fast enough to windward, I bet, ain't she?"

I didn't guess he was being anything more than polite—I was acutely aware of her shabby paint, and the stains along her scuppers, and a long splice in a main topsail clewline that weren't Horne's best work ever—but I felt a surge of pride anyway.

"We made over nine knots for a watch and a half on the way down from Hampton Roads." I smiled despite my caution. "And my quartermaster swears she topped eleven knots once. I own it's hard to swallow," I said when they looked doubtful. "Her hull ain't long enough to crack along like that, I guess. But she's fast to windward, as you say, sir."

The steward had been opening a bottle of Madeira as I spoke, and when he handed me a glass I took it without thinking.

"Old, isn't she?" said Brownstone.

"Yes," I said, "about your age, I think."

He let that one go. "And is that a traverse-mounted gun amidships?"

"Yes, a twelve-pounder carronade."

"And how does that serve you?" He looked at me sideways, first one way and then the other, like a lizard hunting flies.

"I rig a hose to the pump to use as a fire engine. I wet the sails and pray the good Lord willing the flaming wads don't set our canvas afire." I grinned at Halliwell and made him laugh. "Other than that, it's a fine piece of ordnance."

"Oh, I don't doubt it," said Oxford, like he'd just come back from far away and hadn't heard the beginning of the conversation. He pulled his whiskers and drank off his Madeira, and muttered, "Well, well, well" again.

The four of them exchanged glances. Oxford coughed into his fist. Then, "Say, I figured you might pass through here. The commodore—how's that wine, by the by?"

"It's a good bottle, sir. No, no more—well, thank you, sir. The commodore . . . ?"

"Yes. Well. That is . . . The commodore asked me to cruise these grounds in hopes of intercepting you." He shook his head. "Those Danes. Uppity fellows. Keep asking me what I'm doing here, and I keep telling 'em it's none of their never-you-mind, but they persist."

I was getting a cold feeling up my backside, the way he was skipping around without engaging his subject. But he was a post-captain and he'd spill it when he was ready.

He looked again out the stern windows. "Ugly business you're engaged in. No offence, Mr. Graves—far from it. I admire a man who can do a dirty job and keep his hands clean. Oh, damme, that's not what I meant to say at all. Look at me," he said, swabbing his chin with his handkerchief. "I'm all flummoxed. Now, see here, Mr. Graves, I'm trying to soften the blow, but I have to admit I'm doing a damned poor job of it, pardon my French. But easing up on a blow that must be delivered only makes it hurt the worse when it finally is delivered. Do you know what I mean?"

My head had sunk. I lifted it. "That a certain lieutenant truly is dead, sir?"

He choked on his wine. "Oh, good God, no. Him!" He hauled out his handkerchief again and dabbed at his chin with it; Brownstone took it from him and mopped his cravat for him. "Not yet he isn't, the son of a you-know-what. There are some things we dasn't discuss, but if you was to come across a certain 'Captain Mèche' and bring him to me I'd be beholden to you, as I'd like to put the noose around his neck myself." In his agitation, he stuffed his wet handkerchief back up his sleeve. "No, sir, no, it's *bad* news I have for you. Mr. Towson of the *Insurgent* was a friend of yours, I take it?"

"*Was* is right, sir."

"Oh, you've already heard, have you?"

"Heard what, sir?" My heart commenced to thumping, his face was so long.

He tugged on his side-whiskers. He was going to snatch himself bald if he kept that up. "Why, that he's been lost."

"Taken prisoner, sir?" I didn't guess jail would do Dick much harm, and probably some good. I'd heard the one in Guadeloupe wasn't so bad. It sure couldn't hold a candle to the one Juge and I had been in last spring in Jacmel. "Well, the French'll return the officers soon enough. They always do, sir."

"No, son, I'm afraid he wasn't captured. Stewart in the *Experiment* spoke the *Insurgent* off Barbuda. Seems Towson was aloft, leading the mids in some kind of capers, when a white squall came up of a sudden, as they will, and when it had passed over, he was gone. Vanished—swept away. Stewart and Fletcher spent the better part of the afternoon looking for him, but they never found him."

"Stewart?" says I, my mind gone blank. "I thought Maley had *Experiment*."

"So he did. But he got caught sending a shipload of niggers into the Havana instead of sending 'em back to Africa, if you can believe it. Damned paperwork. I'd've set 'em adrift . . ."

His voice droned on, not needing me to listen to it. I was aware that I should've felt a great loss, but I didn't. I'd gone empty in the heart, like an essential part of me had jumped ship. It felt the way I imagined it might feel to have a hand chopped off. I'd adapt in time, but in the meanwhile it was going to be damned awkward.

"If you'll excuse me, sir," I said. I stood up, and went lightheaded. I was cold despite the heat. "I got to be going. I got an idea Mèche's base is to the south, and I mean to cut him off from his supplies." The leg of my chair caught my ankle. I sat down again.

"Damme, but I'm a lummox," said Oxford. "This has struck you harder than I thought. You have an understanding with Towson's sister, I recall."

"No, sir, a *mis*understanding with his sister." I laughed outright when Oxford looked shocked. It was like I was watching myself from a distance.

"Shall I call the surgeon?" says Brownstone.

"No. I'm all right."

"I insist," said Oxford. "No doubt he'll want to bleed you. I've entirely bungled this—I didn't realize you were high strung."

"I ain't high strung, sir. Just give me a little whiskey. Yes, rum'll do, thank'ee." I poured the spirits down my throat, reveling in the heat fanning out across my chest and up my spine to the cavern of my skull. An old pine tree in a forest fire weren't in it. My head blazed like glory, and I held out my glass for a refill. "I'm entirely well, honest I am. Just a little upset. If I can just sit quiet here for a minute, I'll get over it." I'd be giggling pretty soon, but I knew the cure for that. I kept my mouth busy by pouring liquor into it.

"There's some mail," Oxford said at some point. "The commodore put it aboard of us in case we should meet. I've already had it put in your boat." Later on he said, "Are you sure you won't take some broth? The surgeon—"

I found myself in my stuffy closet of a cabin, swaying in my hammock and watching a matched pair of Choptanks disappear and reappear in the swell. They got smaller each time we crested a wave; and each time we did that, about a pint of rum sloshed around in my bilge, first away off to larboard, and then roaring through the middle and off to starboard and back again. My arms were swinging around in the air, and I kept busting out into snatches of "Hark, hark, 'tis a voice from the tomb! 'Come, Lucy,' it cries, 'come awa-a-ay,'" but that was tarnal gloomy, and I switched to the one about how if Neptune had been wise, "Instead of his brine, he'd have fill'd the vast ocean with ge-enerous wi-hi-hi-hi-hi-hi-yine," till my head felt like it'd been cleft in twain with a rusty axe.

I calculated if I could stay in my hammock without hanging on, I weren't near as drunk as I was going to be. All I had to do was open my mouth, and my steward would bring me all the whiskey I wanted. But every time I opened my mouth I started singing again, and I figured if anybody else aboard hated to hear me sing as much as I hated to hear me sing, I might not survive the night. It was a dilemma. I wanted whiskey, and I wanted to sing.

Two letters from Dick lay unopened on my chest. They were the only personal letters for me that had come across in the locked canvas bag from the *Choptank,* and one had been stuffed inside the other.

While I watched the clouds crawling past the little stern windows, I chanted, "What Cato advises most certainly wise is . . . we pass the long evenings in pleasure away," but I couldn't remember the middle part, and I sang the beginning and end of it over and over till I thought my brains might leak out my eyeballs. At long blessed last, just at six bells in the afternoon watch, *Tomahawk* skimmed past Round Island and I fell silent. I listened to O'Lynn's Irish lilt as he sang "fifteen fathom . . . sixteen fathom . . . fourteen fathom . . . no-o-o-o bottom! No bottom with this *li-i-i-ine*" as the island came into view on my right and sank in our wake.

Horne left me alone as the watches changed, but shortly into the first watch we rounded Saint Croix, and I was required on deck to supervise the change of course. "South by east," I croaked, clutching one-handed at the weather rail. A storm was blowing up in the north, announcing itself with spindrift and gusty showers. "Put a reef in the gaff mains'l. Set the square course and tops'l on the fore. Call me if there's any change."

The closest land afore us now was a good forty leagues away. Unless something carried away or an enemy hove over the horizon, I could wallow in whiskey for twenty hours or more, and maybe for as much as four days if the wind dropped.

But as it happened I left the bottle alone, and when I read Dick's letters I did so with a mix of dread and hope. If I was drunk at all it was on sorrow, not spirits.

Thurs., Augst. 6, 1800
White Oak Plantation, M^{d}.

Dear Matty,
Good news, just rec'd word Captin Fletcher has asked for me in the Ensurgint frigate. A good Word from Father is to blame I'm sure, no doubt my Alowance has as much to do with it as Fathers influence in Congress. I will put in my pennys worth to get you as my Bunky, if Fletcher is lunk head enogh to take me, sure he'll take you ha ha!

The boat awaits. will mail soonest.
Your friend,
Dick

P.S. *Wasn't Arabella mad when you upped Anchor and sailed away. Vexation ain't in it, as you would say.*

P.P.S. *Mrs. Towson sends her love.*

The next had been scribbled in pencil and sealed with a wafer instead of wax:

Ensurgint
Friday, Septr. 4, 1800
at Sea, near Barbuda

Dear Matty,
We are hove-to next the Experiment schooner. Liu^{t} Stewart has her now, did you know that? He continues to play merry Hell with the French, taking Deuce Amis of 8 guns Tuesday last. He says he is to rendazvou with the Choptank or her tender, and will take our mail.

Just found my previous unsent in my other coat pocket, which I will send with this (the letter I mean, not my pocket!) Hope you are not still mad I got this birth. Fletcher sailed on short notice, I had barely slung my hammok when we put to sea and did not see the inside of it for two days. I wish you had come aboard with me, my jaw is sore yet, but I am not.

Continued fair weather, and dull if you ask me . . .

I came on deck, not sure of the reception I'd get. Horne moved to leeward, to give me the weather rail. Gundy stood unusually straight by O'Lynn at the tiller. All three of them looked a little saggy under the eyes.

"Good morning, Mr. Horne," I said after digesting the information on the traverse board and the slate, and glancing over the rough log. "You all will want your beds, I expect."

"Not on such a beautiful day, sir," he said. I couldn't read him at all.

"As you will, then," I said.

But here was Greybar, taking the air on the quarterdeck. I bent down to pet him. He scooted away and stopped just out of reach, looking around at me and twitching his tail.

I got down on one knee. I held out my hand and made kissy noises, the way O'Lynn and the others called him. And dog me if the little chap didn't come to me. He rubbed his cheek against my outstretched fingers, and I tried scratching him behind the head where the fur was thick. He hunkered down and commenced to purr.

I snuck a peek at Horne and Gundy. Horne was examining something in the maintop and Gundy was shading his eyes and staring at something on the horizon.

Greybar twisted around to rub against my shin. The tip of his erect tail tickled my chin. And then, as I knelt there, he put his paws on my knee. His purring got louder, and he hopped up on my thigh. His claws were like little needles as he kneaded my flesh.

Well, I couldn't kneel there all day with a cat tearing holes in my britches. So I tucked him under one arm and put my other hand under his hind legs and stood up. My chest rumbled from his purrs. He had his eyes squinted shut against the sun. I bent my head to see was he all right, and he touched his nose against mine.

He opened his eyes like he was as surprised as I was. But then he closed his eyes again, and purred like cannons going off. That's how it felt in my heart, anyway. I stood there trying to decide if I was going to weep or something.

And then a flying fish soared in over the rail and hit me in the face. Greybar hopped down at once, all business with the flopping fish, and Horne and Gundy had lost their unnatural preoccupation and all was as it should be on a quarterdeck of a man-of-war.

Horne looked at the scales and fish guts that Greybar was flinging around the deck.

"Nothing a bucket of water won't cure," I said.

Horne didn't smile much, but when he did it was like sunshine in February. I near went blind from the brightness. "Yes, sir," he said.

THIRTEEN

Even half a hundred miles west of the arc of the Leeward Islands there was any number of island traders, some of them probably even legal, that slapped on canvas and melted away from us like butter in August. We took the opportunity for a little gun drill, running out the three-pounders and using up some of the powder supplied by the goodness of Congress for the preservation of free trade and sailors' rights. Two of the ships we managed to overhaul threw all aback and awaited our pleasure after a single shot, which disappointed Peebles tremendously; but I didn't trouble myself to look too close at either of them, as it wasn't in my orders, they spoke English, and we didn't have any people to spare for prize crews even if they'd turned out to be sailing on the account—which if they were, they wouldn't have heaved-to in the first place. That was my thinking on it, anyway. Three times in one forenoon watch we heaved shot into ships in earnest, or at least in their general direction, which all in all it was just as well they gave us the air, us being shorthanded as we were. We whiled away the afternoon watch by blasting the great blue empty with the carronade just to make some noise. It had a boom that got you deep down in the oysters and set your blood a-boiling in a way that a pop from a three-pounder never could.

At four bells the next morning, though, with the sun's disk just clear of the eastern horizon and gleaming like gold on the untroubled sea, we found ourselves in chase of a large cutter. She was pierced for fourteen guns and flying British colors. Now Johnny Crappo had a few cutters, some very large ones in fact, but I'd never seen a French one in West Indian waters. But there was something odd about her that I couldn't quite figure out.

I offered Horne my glass. He took a long squint and handed it back.

"Just your ordinary royal scout and dispatch boat, sir."

"Gundy?"

He shrugged his shoulders and pulled a long face while he took his turn with the glass.

"Not sure, me cabbun. Cutter rig's as English as chasse-marée is Vrench—but if English, why do 'ee run vrom us?"

"If he's carrying dispatches he'll be under orders not to sit around jawing with admirals nor anyone else."

"But he'd fly a signal to say so, sir," said Horne. "And he's not exactly cracking on sail."

"Odd place to find 'un," said Gundy.

I glanced at the compass. "Nor'-nor'east on the sta'board tack. Could be coming up from Jamaica, bound for Spanish Town or even England."

"He'll be a while if he doesn't jank 'ee along an' zcoot away," said Gundy.

I looked at Horne. "He means if he doesn't hurry up," he said.

"Is't an echo, Mr. Horne?" said Gundy. "Didn't I just zay—"

Peebles had wandered over. "Why doesn't he stop and say hello?" he said to no one in particular.

"Maybe he just doesn't believe our colors," I said. "Hoist the challenge of the day."

"Aye aye, sir." He had to look it up in the codebook, which took him several minutes to find, and the answer was several more minutes in coming. Then three pieces of bright bunting broke out at the cutter's peak. Peebles ran his finger along the lines of text and the hand-colored drawings. "She hoists the right reply, sir."

She also fired a gun on her away side to indicate a peaceful intent. I might have been forgiven for thinking all was well with her; but the name on her transom was missing, as if it had been blacked out, and she looked like she had more speed in her than she was showing; but we were at quarters with our slow match smoking, and I was curious.

She rolled along on a bowline to windward and sunward of us on the starboard tack. Except for having come about to follow her, we kept the relative position we'd had at sunup, which was about half a mile to leeward of her on her larboard quarter. Gundy and Horne shaded their eyes with their hands against the sun.

"There, she done it again," I said, lowering my glass. "Didn't she just luff up?"

"No, zur. I didn't—"

"She does too spill her wind," said Horne, opening his fingers and squinting. "Just a tiny—there! She's doing it again."

"Nay, me luvver," said Gundy. "'Ee art bedwaddled."

"Oh, I'm be-what-led, am I? Don't deny what I can see with my own eyes. Now I ask you plain, does she luff up or doesn't she?"

"I'll not argy again' 'ee, Mr. Horne. She luffs up, aye, but not by scuddin' 'ee wind."

"Well, how then?"

"By doggin' a zee-anchor, is how."

"Oh, a sea-anchor, you say?"

"Iss, zur, a zee-anchor, zes I."

"What in tarnation Harry are you two on about?" I said, pretending like I hadn't been listening with every ear in my body. I raised the glass to my eye again. She was dragging a line, sure enough, but I didn't see any spars or canvas or anything else in the water that might slow her down.

Gundy pointed with a gnarled finger. "There, me cabbun. Like a shadow under the zurface, just abaft 'ee rudder-post."

"I see it, sir," said Horne. "It's awkward for her on the weather side like that. It snubs her short, which is why she luffs."

"I expect so." I said it sharp—Horne could admit to being wrong all he wanted, but I couldn't have him include me among the ignorant. Besides, I could see it for myself now, showing as a paler patch of sea off the cutter's starboard quarter. The line leading to it tautened as I watched, faint as a spider's thread at that distance, and I followed the progress of its effect with my glass. Her bow gave a little jog to windward, her great gaff mainsail shivered just for an instant, and the way came off her just a touch.

"We're not buying today," muttered Horne.

"If you please, sir," said Peebles, "what's happening?"

"I don't know," I said. But that didn't seem like the right thing for a captain to say, so I added, "Either he's French or he thinks we're flying false colors. Either way, he's trying to lure us close enough that he can put on a sudden burst of speed and snatch us up."

"Iss, zur," said Gundy. "But he'll have to ease 'ee along more 'an'some than that to fool we."

"Any fish'll bite if you got good bait." I glanced up at our commission pendant and then at the compass. The breeze was holding steady in the northeast.

"But if he's British, sir," said Peebles, "won't he just let us go afterwards?"

"It's an insult to have to show every British skiff, yawl, and bumboat our papers," I snapped. "That's what our flag is for. Besides, we let 'em on board who knows how many people we'll have left afterwards. They'd take Gundy and O'Lynn and every other British seaman, claiming they're King's subjects or deserters."

There'd be no escaping to windward, even if the cutter didn't have the weather gauge on us already. Just as I was about to tell Gundy to put us about and run like Jiminy to leeward, the lookout hollered, "Sail ho!"

"Where away?"

"Two points on the sta'board bow." He pointed. "A frigate, sir, about three-quarter-mile yonder of the cutter."

The frigate had placed herself well, or taken the utmost advantage of her luck at first light, swooping down from windward with the sun at her back and all her cloth abroad. But the cutter is a nimble rig, and this one had teeth as well. She let her head fall off the wind, bringing her starboard broadside to bear against the frigate. She stood out in sudden silhouette against a bank of white smoke.

Gundy stiffened like a hunting hound. "Areeah! Raked 'un!"

I had counted past two and not quite to three when the low rumble of gunfire reached us. That put the cutter at just about exactly half a mile, which is what my eye had told me, and as I was congratulating myself on my fine eye for distance, she let fly with her larboard battery as well—the one facing us.

"Well, that's just pure meanness," Horne said.

"Sure, 'tis a wicked waste of the Dear's good powder, tryin' to hit us at such a distance," said O'Lynn at the tiller.

Horne laughed, and Gundy told O'Lynn to hush 'eeself and mind 'ee luff, and then a line of splashes rose about halfway between us and the cutter. Naturally I was pleased to see her shot land far away and no harm done, but I doubted she was armed with anything larger than a four-pounder, not if she wanted to keep her speed. She could hit us in theory but not too likely in fact.

The splashes melted back into the sea. We sailed along in company to enjoy the view. The frigate yawed to starboard, and a sudden bank of smoke hid her. More low thunder rumbled across the water, a nation louder than the cutter's broadside. *No sense sticking my nose in where it might get bit,* I thought, but as I opened my mouth to say, "'Bout ship," a weird groaning came out of the sky. A forest of geysers shot up around us.

My mouth was still open. I sang out, "Four points to la'board."

"Four points to la'board, aye aye, zur."

I glanced along the deck and up aloft. "They hit anything?"

"Nobody's screaming, sir," said Horne. "That's always a good sign."

"Very well."

Pointing our bow north by west brought the wind onto our starboard beam, buying us a little speed. The spray had been close enough to drift aboard of us, but no more than that. The frigate was still a good half-mile away and wasn't trying to hit us.

I took a couple of turns up and down the deck. A Frenchman's usual tactic was to fire high, to disable his enemy, and then attack or run, depending, while the Royal Navy fought the same way we did—shooting to kill and dismay. The frigate must've aimed at the cutter's rigging, and the shot had either passed overhead without hitting anything vital or had passed astern of her. The latter was likely; the cutter must've cast off her sea anchor, for she was headreaching on us already.

The frigate had to be French. I took another look at her, and my brain kept jibing between what experience told me and what my eyes were seeing. She sure looked like a king's thirty-two. But the cutter looked British, too, and she was climbing hand-over-fist to windward.

The frigate had come about to close the angle between herself and the cutter. The white ensign streamed from her mizzen peak, and the sturdy elegance of her lines said she was the British cruiser that she proclaimed herself to be. In fact, I could swear I knew her.

I studied her some more, and then I had to laugh. I handed my glass to Horne. "Tell me what you see."

"*Clytemnestra,* sir. My, how that man gets around."

"Plot me a new course for Birds Island from our present position. Gundy, 'bout ship and dismiss the watch below."

I like to died from wanting to know why Captain Sir Horace Tinsdale was in deadly chase of a British cutter in the middle of nowhere, but there are some things in this world we ain't privileged to know. Not till their proper time, anyway.

FOURTEEN

On the evening of the autumnal equinox, below a golden crescent moon drifting toward the blue horizon in the southwest, we worked *Tomahawk* down the Aves Bank toward Birds Island. I put double lookouts aloft and promised an extra tot of grog to the man who first sighted land; but the island was supposed to be so low that I didn't guess I'd have any takers. True to the chart, however, the tallow plug in the end of the lead brought up mud on the western side of the bank, and then showed the indentations of rocky ground as the bank rose to its apex, with the piece of leather with a hole in it that marked ten fathoms just topping the swell before the leadsman hauled the line back in. A squeaking and squalling cloud of seabirds reeled overhead, a sign that the island was close; but with the last of the twilight suddenly gone, I judged it was time to work our way back up to windward and try again in the morning. And then a sudden flash of phosphorescence revealed the northeastern barrier reef in a fleeting crown of green fire.

"Land ho, zur!" came the cry from aloft, followed closely by a shout from Eriksson and a surprising number of others. A dozen Tomahawks were clinging to the rigging with one hand and pointing with the other, and hooting like baboons. Any more of them up there and we'd like to keel over.

"Gundy," I called, "what're you doing up there? You ain't on watch."

"Just keeping a good lookout, me cabbun."

"Well, we all seen it at once, I guess, so come down here where you'll be some use." There was a sort of dissatisfied silence all around, so I added, "Which means we'll all splice the mainbrace once we're squared away," and the mood brightened considerable. "And douse the lights, damn it."

"Douse the lights, damn it, aye aye, sir," said Horne.

Surf hissed on coral, shooting the sea with pale light as we eased down toward the low island. The chart had indicated an anchorage of three and a half fathoms off its southwestern tip.

"Ahoy der deck," called Eriksson from aloft. "Dere's a light, sir."

"A ship's lantern?"

"No, sir, on der shore. Looks to be a fire, sure it do."

I tried not to breathe too deeply as we crept up on the land. The air stank of bird dung, and the Tomahawks gave voice to their disgust.

"Silence!" I hissed.

"Put a stopper in it," Horne added.

"Mr. Horne, d'you see the fire?"

"Aye, sir. And another yonder. A little one, sir, to larboard."

The fire on the main island was low to the ground, where you'd expect to find a fire, with shadows moving across it as I watched through my glass—a cooking fire, maybe. Sparks rose into the night sky as someone tossed a chunk of wood onto the coals. The other fire, which looked to be burning on the southernmost of the two guardian islets west of the anchorage, was small and barely showing, like it was hooded or dying. It faded from sight as we nosed up into the natural harbor.

"By the mark, three," came a mutter from the leadsman. Then, "And a half, twain!"

Fifteen feet of water where there should have been twenty-one. Still, it was plenty enough to float us.

"Steady," I said.

"By the mark, twain!"

Two fathoms—twelve feet. We drew eight-foot-ten forward and eleven foot aft. I took a lump of tallow forward and charged the lead. It came up coral sand. No sense in dropping the hook; it wouldn't hold well in that bottom anyway, and we could kedge off the soft sand easy enough if we went aground. And it wouldn't be any use getting into trouble we didn't have to. We came to the wind with the warm stink pressing against us like a blanket in the dark. The current, split by the island, came endlessly back together with a steady sucking whisper.

"Keep her so."

I went aloft but could see nothing in the dark anchorage. I climbed down again.

"Let's work our way around to windward of the island again."

With the wind coming across the island toward me, and the ground dropping away aft to bottomless black water, I could hold my position without fear as long as the wind stayed steady. But if Peter was holed up there to windward, he wouldn't have to come down to *Tomahawk* and give battle in the morning. He could just dance away and leave us in his wake.

But, drag my Aunt Fannie through a house afire if Horne wasn't looking at me in the dark; I could feel it.

"Yes, Mr. Horne?"

"I don't guess this here island is likely to haul its wind and escape, sir."

Uncertainty shot through me. "Are you being sarcastic, Mr. Horne?"

"I don't know what sarcastic is, sir. I mean no disrespect."

"Then what *do* you mean?"

"It'd be a shame to work up around this here island in the dark just to lose it again by morning, sir."

"Go on."

"Well, sir, we'll have to feel our way pretty far up to be sure not to run up on the reef during the night. And the island's so low we might not be able to see it even with the sun up. We'd have to go around the lee side to make sure we don't run aground, and without knowing the speed of the current and our speed over the bottom, who knows where we'd end—"

"All right, all right. I see your point. Keep her thus, like I said." The uncertainty still hung between us. It would grow if I wasn't careful. I took a turn around the deck. And suddenly I laughed. "I wonder how long it'll take to get used to the smell."

Sunup found us half a mile offshore. On either side and aft as far as I could see, the sea sloped away as pale blue as a summer sky. The shadows of little fish darted around the shadow of the beard of weed on our bottom. We took in all our square sails, ran out our guns, and eased upwind.

A pink ruff of flamingos edged the island at the shoreline, and gray-capped noddies and sword-billed terns wheeled in the sky in the tens of thousands. Through my glass I could see a great cauldron sitting in a pile of ashes and charred log-ends among the dunes, with boxes, barrels, and a few sailcloth tents scattered around it. On the islet where a low fire had burned last night stood a wooden platform, and sitting on the platform was a pair of—

"Carronades, sir," said Horne.

"Got 'em." There was nobody around them, which was some mighty lax watch-keeping ashore and I was grateful for it. I looked aloft. "Mr. Peebles there, d'ye see anybody moving?"

"No, sir."

I swept my glass across the dunes. Everything in sight—boxes, barrels, tents, guns—glistened with a white rime, and seemed to be getting more so as I watched, like it was raining bird shit over there.

The anchorage held any number of blue angelfish and yellow-tailed snappers as we glided into it, but no trim little eight-gun sloop with a cross-shaped patch on her course. On the white sandy bottom lay a small anchor with a few fathoms of cable still attached to it, cut clean, as if its owner had left in a hurry.

"Mr. Peebles! What d'ye see?"

"Birds, sir." From forty feet up, he could easily see over the top of the island. "Some more tents. A couple men sleeping."

"Sleeping?"

"Yes, sir. Dead to the world—haven't moved a hand or foot since I've been watching."

"Since you been watching? You mean to tell me you seen somebody and didn't tell me about it?"

"You asked if I saw anybody *moving.*"

"Don't be a danged idiot, Mr. Peebles. Just for that, you can stay where you are till I tell you otherwise."

Leaving him with the best view in the schooner wasn't much of a punishment, but mastheading was a time-honored punishment for youngsters and at least it gave the appearance that I was doing something. I looked at the gun platform again.

"You don't see anybody watching, Mr. Peebles? Nobody walking around?"

"No, sir."

"Very well. Mr. Horne, get the boat in the water and secure those carronades." He already had his boat's crew told off, half a dozen likely lads with weapons bristling in their belts. "See they keep them pistols at half-cock," I said, "lest they blow their balls off."

The men laughed, and Horne allowed himself a smile. I kept throwing glances at the island despite the lookouts aloft and alow, but I couldn't see any sign of the fellows we'd seen moving around the fire the night before. Then Peebles sang out shrill enough to shame a Sunday school choir:

"Hey! There's a boat putting off."

"Where away?"

"Far end of the island, sir. They're heaving it through the reef and having a hard time of it. They're upset—no, they're all right now. Now they're heading away from us."

"What course?"

"Dunno, sir. East?" He pointed. "They're hoisting a sail."

Horne was already lowering away. The boat touched water and the crew cast off.

"Mr. Horne," I called, "I'm taking the schooner to go fetch that sail. You take them guns yonder. If anybody tries to stop you, arrest 'em. If they defy you, knock 'em down. If they shoot at you, shoot back."

"Aye aye, sir."

"Gundy, let her fall off. Take us around the lee side."

"There, sir!" called Peebles. "A lugs'l yawl!"

As we came around south of the island, I saw the yawl with her odd, trapezoidal sails running free on the larboard tack to the southeast. She would cross us if she kept her course. Three white men were sailing her; there was something moving beneath their feet, and as we drew near I saw it was two things; and as we drew nearer still I saw the things weren't things at all, but another white man and a black man. The scoundrels didn't have a chance of escaping, but that didn't stop them from trying. Twice they crossed our wake as we tried to cut them off, and once they crossed our hawse and near got themselves run under. A musket ball across their course didn't stop them, and neither did another over their heads. Only when the *Tomahawk* grazed the boat's side, and I shouted as we passed that the next time I would run them under, did they drop their lugsail. There was a commotion in the boat as we hove-to: two men in chains struggling as the other three tried to dump them overboard.

O'Lynn was closest. I said, "Come with me," and jumped over the rail.

The three men in the boat were none too friendly. O'Lynn had thought to bring a belaying pin with him, though, and he entertained them with it while I grabbed the end of the chain and near about went overboard with it. I braced a boot against the side, hauling and straining, but each time I gained a few feet I had to let go with one hand to haul in the next few feet, and I lost what I had gained. Finally Gundy hopped down and gave me a tail, hanging on to what I'd hauled in while I reached down to grab a few more feet.

Then suddenly it got lighter, as if someone was helping from below, and up came a white man and a black man, chained together, gasping. We grabbed them by their kerchiefs and laid them out in the bottom of the boat. It's amazing how much seawater a man can hold, I thought, as the brine come a-spewing out of their gullets. The black man, who was missing his left leg, finally rolled over and looked at me accusingly through his one good eye. He had a ferocious squint on him, and the whiskers were black and silver across his cheeks and throat. His head was shaved close, but he would've been nearly bald regardless. A long scar ran from his forehead to his chin, passing over the empty eye socket on the starboard side.

"Why, Doc," I said. "Why ain't you in the *Breeze?"*

"You sho' took yo' time, Mr. Graves," he said severely. "Good thing I got a peg-leg, or I mighta sunk. Time pass mighty slow when yo' drownin', you hear you *me."*

"But what are you *doing* here?"

"Why, looking out for Mr. Wickett, sah." He reached out his manacled hands for me to help him sit up. "He da troublest man I know."

"None of your gob, now, Doc. What're you doing here?"

"Dat's a long story, suh, best told over a pint o' grog wif dry clothes on."

We got the three would-be murderers into the *Tomahawk* and put their own irons on them as we made our way back to the island. O'Lynn stood over them with his belaying pin, just itching to pound them some more if they so much as spit. The white man that Doc had been shackled to was a little fellow, near about my size; without a word he held out his wrists for me to examine. His wrists were raw where the shackles had been.

"Dey done me da same way," said Doc, "an' my ankle is some messed up, too, sah, if you cares to look." He pointed at the three men who'd tried to teach him to swim. "These here son of a bitches was tryin' to run away from dat hangnail and sell us fo' slaves in Guadeloupe. We all woulda drownded fo' sho' if you hadn't showed up when you did."

"Wait, wait, wait. You were running away from a hangnail?"

"Mr. *Agnell,* sah. Ain't no hangnail."

"All right, then, *Agnell.* Who is Agnell?"

"He da debbil, sah. He da debbil in hisself. I done tole Mr. Wickett he too bad."

"You seen Peter Wickett?"

"I sho' did, sah, same as I done told you. He da most sorrowfullest man you ever laid eyes on, now, 'cause he think he lost. He even readin' da Good Book, lookin' fo' answers. But I done tole him: I said, 'God don't need no Scripture. God don't need no translatin',' I says to him. 'An' you don't need to read no book to be washed in da blood ob da lamb. You just need to do good works and stop yo' wickedness.' I tole him, but I don't guess he believe me, 'cause he off bein' wickeder'n ever, now." He shook his head.

"Where's he gone to? What's he up to?"

"I don't know, sah. I don't listen to dem white men talk."

I gave him my coldest stare. "I can hang you right now as a pirate, Doc."

He stopped grinning, but if he was scared he didn't show it. "I follows orders just like I s'pose to, Mr. Graves. Mr. Wickett, he say, 'Go here,' I goes dere, same as if he give any other order. Mr. Wickett, he say, 'Stay here till I knows what to do wit' you.' And dat's what I aimed to do, till dem white trash decide to sell me off or wo'se."

"You mean to say them three decided to sail a hundred miles upwind in an open boat just to sell a one-eyed, one-legged, cantankerous, shifty, flea-bit sea cook like you?"

"Well . . ." He glanced at the three men sitting in irons on the fo'c's'le. "Not just me. Dey's also gonna sell dat half-pint Irishman I was chained to, I expect."

"I don't think they meant to *sell* you, Doc. I think they meant to drown you so's you wouldn't tell me something."

"Dem three? Dem three couldn't drown turds in a shithouse. No, sah, dey was gonna sell us befo' da *other* British so-an'-sos was going to sell us."

"What other British?"

"Dat's what I'se tryin' to *tell* you, sah. It was da English bastards in da *Shearwater* cutter was goin' to sell us. Dem French sugar plantations is desperate for slaves, what wif da Royal Navy got all dey ships bottled up at Brest or someplace."

"They must be desperate to waste their money on you."

He looked insulted. "I can cook, sah. I'se better'n some no-count field nigger."

"Course you are, Doc. Course you are. But listen now, does this *Shearwater* got a black hull, with her name painted out?"

"Name painted out? How you speck me to know dat, sah? You think I spends my time gaping around the stern? 'Oh, excuse me, Mr. Englishman, does you mind if I walks around on yo' quarterdeck fo' a while?' No, sah, it don't work dat way fo' a nigger."

I was itching to hear about this *Shearwater* cutter and what it had to do with Peter Wickett, but I didn't guess Doc would tell me the truth unless he wanted to. If he really thought I was going to hang him, he'd just blab any old thing he guessed I wanted to hear. All in good time, then, so long as it was a short time.

"Well, I will let you off the hook for the time being," I said, "on account of we been taking turns cooking and I am sick of salt-junk and boiled turnips."

He chuckled. "I knows you gonna do right by me, Mr. Graves."

"Your neck ain't out of the noose yet."

He kept smiling. It looked a little strained, but it was a smile. "I knows you gonna do right by me, sah."

Greybar had come up on deck to see what was going on, and Doc scrunched down, his peg-leg sticking out in front of him. He held out a finger. Greybar stared at him, half-arching his back, and then he trotted over, squeaking with each step.

"Dat's a boy," said Doc, rubbing his forehead. "I guess dere's *someone* around here dat appreciate ol' Doc's cookin'. See dat, Mr. Graves?" he said. "Dis here cat remember me. It all dat fine fish I give him on da way up to Warshington last June, I expect."

"He just wants to sharpen his claws on your peg-leg, I expect."

Greybar tilted his head back so Doc could scratch his throat.

"Don't pay no 'tention to dat awful man," said Doc. "C'mon, you cat, an' he'p me find da galley an' I fix you up a treat." He stumped off forward with Greybar dancing along behind him.

• • •

I turned to the man that Doc had been chained to. His face was scabbed and peeling, as if it had gotten burned and burned again without healing, and his black hair hung low over his dark blue eyes. He refused all speech until O'Lynn talked to him, and then he became a torrent of Gaelic.

"Says his name is Kennedy, sor," said O'Lynn. "Says there were Americans here, but they've been gone t'ree days, and Agnell left soon after. He's got them t'ree fellas turrified, there. They suspect to get their toongues cut out for 'em, whether we're here or no. Ah, they're morderin' slyboots in their own right, but they're afra'd of Agnell."

"Not Mèche?"

"He says he seems a just man, sor, if it's the American you're meanin'." He listened to Kennedy a moment more, then added, "He was short-tempered and sarcastic, he says, and pretended to be French at first, but his men called him Peter Wicked an' that gave the game away. An' for all his pretendin' to be a hard man, sor, he crewed his sloop with runaway slaves, them that was unwillin' foremast jacks in the ships he took, an' they had a great admiration for him. But Agnell is cruel."

"Thanum an Dhul," said Kennedy. He touched his sunburnt forehead, his heart, his breast on either side.

"Name o' the devil," said O'Lynn, and crossed himself as he listened to Kennedy. "The Stinkard's own man for the lash, that Agnell, sor, and all were mortal afra'd of the cargo."

"What's he mean, afeared of the cargo?"

"Africans, sor. Wild men from the interior, the most ferocious craytures to be imagined, and captured in some war or another as is none of our affair. The Shearwaters stole 'em out of a slaver they came across as it was sinkin', and all her people dead, there. The men guessed Mr. Martin—himself as was captain of the cutter—he meant to sell them wild men, sor, and they decided among themselves they would have a piece of that money. So they mutinied."

"Sell them where? In Guadeloupe?"

"No, sor, never in life, he says, for the French would impound the cutter. An' they cannot go to Havana or some such place for the same raison, even if 'twas legal to trade in a Spanish port. The American is to find a buyer and meet with Agnell, there."

"Meet where?"

"Dunno, sor."

"Mèche met the Englishman here to buy slaves?"

"No, your honor, he says. He says the meeting was happenstance."

"Did Mèche abet the mutiny? Did he aid 'em at all?"

"Dunno what *abet* is, sor, but he raised not a hand to stop it."

There would've been little that Peter could've done, him with a few dozen men against the cutter's sixty and more. And why should he interfere? The mutiny was King George's problem, and he was welcome to it.

"Tell me one other thing. Did they paint over the cutter's name?"

"Aye, sor, an' so they did. No names an' no colors. Agnell said 'twasn't piracy that way."

I gazed hard at Kennedy; he stared at my feet, but from the looks of him he was just a clodhopper from some boggy hole in Ireland.

"I guess you must be an honest man to believe such a lie," I said. "Tell him that, O'Lynn. And tell him he'll be hanged in chains if a King's ship takes him."

Kennedy mumbled a few words in Irish. He gave his former captors a contemptuous look, sitting side by side in chains on the deck and sneering at him, and then he smiled at me.

"He says he'll put his hand to any work your honor cares to give him, sor, an' be glad of it," said O'Lynn, "but he'll meet his fate in the Dear's good time."

"Very well. We'll sign him on."

Kennedy crossed himself when O'Lynn told him the news. If he was grateful it was to God, not me.

"Now as for you three," I said, turning to the others, "suppose you tell me your story."

They were as speechless as if this Agnell really had cut their tongues out. They transferred their sneers from Kennedy to me.

"You're hard fellows, ain't you," I said.

"Aye, that we are," said the largest one. "Harder than the likes of you, an' we'll say no more than that." He hawked and spat, but his aim was off and he gobbed up his britches.

"Very well. If you can spit on yourself, you can shit on yourself. Simpson and Hawkins," I said to our two largest men, "put 'em in the hold to stew till they get tender."

Horne had found two men on the island. They were remarkably filthy even for seamen gone ashore and left to their own devices, not least because of the steady drizzle of guano. They'd had a fight before we got there, too, but whether with each other or someone else wasn't immediately clear. One's head was leaking bright blood into the white sand. He breathed, but didn't respond to questions or poking. The other was curled up around himself, writhing like a snake on a pitchfork, but he wasn't going anywhere. Not with Horne standing over him with his foot on his neck.

"To stop him running off again, sir," he said before I could ask.

"Again?"

"Again, sir. Not that he'd get very far, but I thought you'd want to talk to him before he slips his hawser. He's got a knife in the belly."

"You can take your foot off him now, thanks." I knelt down and tipped my hat back on my head. "What's your name? Here, let me see that."

"Leave it be! God . . . fuck your . . . eyes," he hissed, clutching the handle of the knife. "If the blasted thing could be fetched out . . . I'd have done so . . . wouldn't I? It's stuck . . . in me spine."

I had to get down on all fours to hear him. He could barely whisper, and the shrieking and whistling of the birds near deafened me.

"Keep a civil tongue in your head," I said. "I could hang you out of hand as a pirate."

He sneered. "You've a brave little . . . tongue in your head . . . haven't you? You and your 'I could hang you . . . out of hand.'"

His breath came in ragged gasps. "I'd regard it as . . . a kindness . . . truly . . . and so would you . . . was you . . . in poor Isaiah B. Harrison's place." He waved a hand at himself to indicate he was the poor Isaiah B. Harrison in question, and then jerked his head toward Horne. "First order o' business—get this nappy-headed barstid . . . out o' me sight."

"Why would I do that?"

He bared his teeth in a hideous grin. "On account of . . . you want to know . . . what's been going on here."

"Mr. Horne, there's a pile of goods over yonder. I'd like an inventory of them."

He reached in his pocket. "Aye aye, sir. Got a list right here."

"Double check it, please."

"Aye aye, sir." If he'd stepped on Harrison again as he left, accidents will happen; and if Harrison hated him a little more for it, he hated him already. But Horne just walked away.

Harrison watched him go. He chuckled. It was a mistake. He clutched at his belly. When he'd gotten his breath back down to a steady pant he said, "You're a sorry barstid."

"Why's that?"

"Why's that? Because you've been . . . presumed upon, mate. They've foisted . . . a nigger bosun . . . on you."

It was like he'd smacked me on the back of the head. I looked at Horne, moving purposefully about the pointless task I'd given him. It'd be easy to use Horne to get to Harrison. All I had to do was go along. I looked at Harrison, with his eyes bugging out as he grinned at me.

"He bleeds red," I said. "Now suppose you tell me what happened."

"What you think happened?"

"I think you participated in a mutiny, threw in your lot with a man I'm looking for, and got in a fight over how best to dispose of the goods once he left."

"'How best to . . . dispose o' the goods.' I like that, mate . . . An' you're not too wrong, neither. But if leading you . . . to your quarry . . . gets a rope around that barstid Agnell's neck . . . I'd be happy to provide." He worked his lips. "Providing you provide."

"And what do you think I should provide?"

"And what ought . . . the gent'man provide? Why, a drop o' rum . . . would be a good . . . beginning."

"Rum? Man, in your condition it might kill you."

He giggled, a nasty, wet sound. "I'm a dead man already, mate . . . don't think I don't . . . know it. If you want your man . . . you'll want Agnell . . . an' if you want Agnell . . . you'll give us . . . a tipple." After whiskey mixed with a little lemon juice and three parts water had been brought, and he had drunk it and complained that it wasn't rum, he said, "Make for the Virgin Islands. Drop your hook . . . in Deadman Bay . . . an' I'll tell you more."

"If you live so long."

"That's right, mate." The bones of his skull were prominent beneath the skin. He grinned.

I found Horne up in the dunes that ran along the crest of the little island—not that I had to look too far to find him. You could pretty much see the whole place from there. Chests and crates and barrels surrounded him—ship's stores, mostly, from the look of it—and the sand all around had been dug up. Not recently, though, as it was dry. In his fist, dangling by an ankle, was a doll like the kid had in the *Horseneck.*

"What did you find?"

He held up the doll. "Bunch of these, sir. No silk cloth, though, except what the dolls are dressed in." He referred to a scrap of paper in his hand. "Ten barrels of gunpowder of various grains, a large quantity of shot in mixed calibers, and two dozen cartridges for the shore battery down at the cove. But what the people are more interested in is these two casks of rum and that hogshead of wine over there. I got Wright standing guard on it."

Wright touched his hat at the mention of his name. He was a little fellow with a long nose, a water-only man from Boston, a religious bigot but steady otherwise. He could be trusted to relish the job of denying drink to his shipmates.

"Good," I said. "What else?"

Horne rattled off a list of pretty much everything you might need for a sea voyage—bedding, hardtack, salt junk, dried peas, lemons. Twenty water butts: ten of them full, one of them half-full, and the rest empty. Firewood. Cordage, pitch, turpentine, and other ship's stores.

"Seventy-five gallons of blue paint, ten of yellow, five of black, and one pot each of white and red," he finished. "What were they doing with so much blue paint, I wonder?"

"I guess they captured a cargo of blue paint. Did you find any money?"

"No, sir."

I took his list and looked it up and down. I turned the paper over and read some more. Even without the eight barrels of silver it was quite a haul, and all of it mine. Well, a quarter of it, anyway, after the government and the commodore and everybody else took their shares. Assuming they ever saw it, of course . . . It would be wrong to load *Tomahawk* up with what she could carry and make for a free port, with no questions asked or answered and no duty paid but a few bribes. Captains better regarded than I was had abandoned their missions to take prizes and sell the proceeds, with no harm to their careers. They'd retired as rich men who snapped their fingers at Congress. That would be something to bear in mind if I couldn't bring Peter to heel.

Which it wasn't worth thinking about just yet. I looked over at the *Tomahawk,* with her hasty black coat of man-of-war paint looking sad over the old blue and yellow. Then I went down to the cove to take a closer look at the shore battery.

On the southernmost of the two islets that guarded the anchorage, on a raised platform about eight foot square, a pair of twenty-four-pounder carronades squatted like big-mouthed gargoyles on their sliding carriages. Above them hung a lantern on a mast, clearly meant to guide a friend into harbor at night—or to lure an enemy. I got a mild case of the South Carolina quick-trots at what might've happened to *Tomahawk* if the battery had been manned the night before.

Beside me, Peebles stared at the carronades like it was free candy day in Candy Land.

I looked over at the *Tomahawk,* at Horne already telling off a detail with scrapers to get the loose paint off her sides and rails, and then back at the boy beside me.

"Doing Tom Cox's traverse, Mr. Peebles?"

"Oh, no, sir. I don't even know him."

"He's the fellow that's up one hatchway and down another."

"Pardon me, sir?"

"Then he's three times around the mainmast and has a pull at the scuttle."

He still looked blank. I sighed.

"Tom Cox is what sailors call a man who makes himself look busy without actual doing anything. In everyone's mess and no one's watch."

He'd gone back to staring at the carronades. "Yes, sir."

"Ain't anybody give you something to do, Mr. Peebles?"

"No, sir."

"I told Mr. Horne he could paint the schooner. Why don't—"

He'd lifted a hand to point at the guns. "Oh, sir! Can't we—"

"No."

"We could—"

"No."

"But—"

I held up a finger.

With my hands clasped again behind my back, the way Peter had taught me, I rocked on my heels and cogitated on the logistics of replacing our twelve-pounder with one of them monsters. It would weigh in at about fifteen hundred pounds with all its tackle, not quite twice what the twelve-pounder weighed, but only about three hundred more than a long three. A long gun used a third as much powder as the shot weighed.

"Mr. Peebles, what's the powder-to-projectile ratio of a carronade?"

"One to eight, sir."

"Three pounds of powder for each shot, then. I don't calculate her timbers'll stand the firing of it."

Now he looked like a boy with a toothache on free candy day, but it was a small misfortune, as misfortunes go. I climbed up on the wooden platform, which was about waist-high in the front, and looked around.

There was no other anchorage. Birds Island was little more than a crust of sand and guano over a footprint-shaped lump of rock, reaching at its highest about thirty feet above the surface of the sea. It was perhaps two miles long and a thousand yards wide, running from east by north to west by south. No trees grew on it, but, down at the north end, a couple of ancient stumps scraggling against the sky showed that some had grown there once upon a time. The crest was carpeted with survival weed, a tough-looking type of purslane that if you chewed it you could get enough moisture to stay alive a while. An outwork of coral reef on the windward side, the northeast, kept the surf from washing the island away, but hurricanes probably swamped the dunes several times a year. In addition to the wetter aspects of the island's atmosphere, the trade winds kept up a steady precipitation of sand. It was one of the miserablest places I'd ever hoped to see.

Far up the beach, near the reef's southern end, a flurry of gulls seemed to be mobbing something crawling in the sand.

"Mr. Peebles, come up here. What do you make of that?"

"Looks like a naked fat man, sir."

I jumped down from the platform. "Mr. Horne," I called across the cove. "Come with me."

Half an hour later, we discovered that our naked fat man was in fact a large pink pig rooting in a pit. Several seamen who had escaped the painting detail had followed us up the beach.

O'Lynn clutched his head in horror and pointed at the pit. "Oh, the cannibal! The devil swallow him sideways!"

Showing through the sand were human legs, arms, heads with the faces chewed or pecked away. The flies and gulls that had scattered at our approach resettled on the corpses, covering up the hideous grins with a living shroud.

An older sailor put his hands over Peebles's eyes. Peebles struggled free of the hands and stared into the pit.

"Get him out of here," I said. "And fill that pit in. No, belay that—Mr. Horne, take Simpson and Hawkins, here." Simpson and Hawkins were ex of the Royal Navy, strong as oxen and twice as smart, but they were lambs when it came to following orders. "Look for papers, diaries, clothing, anything that will identify these men. When you're done with that, bury them proper. You others, drive that pig down to the cove and kill it."

I stalked back down the beach. The pig trotted beside me, jostled along by the men and rolling its eyes with worry. I had the men bury the powder and shot and the rest of the stores. Peebles I put in charge of marking the sites, to help him not think about the pit.

A man came to cut the pig's throat. The pig broke away, screaming in fright, but another man snatched up a barrel stave and whomped it on the head while his mate stuck it in the throat.

"Hang him up to bleed, Bob Wilson!" cried the man with the barrel stave. "And fetch a basin—you'll want his blood for pudding."

"Hang him up to what?" asked Bob. "They ain't nothin' to hang him *to.*"

"Fetch a basin, I tell you!"

"*You* fetch a basin."

And so it went while the pig wasted its blood in the sand.

Simpson took off his hat and tugged his forelock, British man-o'-war fashion. He was soaked from head to toe, as if he'd tried to wash off the stinking gore that still clung to him. "Beggin' your pardon, sir," he said, "but Mr. Horne sent me to say as we have finished searching and burying the dead."

"Thank you. Go aboard the schooner and shift your clothes."

"If it's all the same, sir, I'd like to come with you. Be a shame not to see 'em off proper."

"You didn't know them."

"They was someone's mates, sir."

"Very well."

I walked back up the beach with *Tomahawk*'s prayer book and read over the grave. The men stopped what they were doing to gather around—most of them to catch their breath as much as to show respect for the dead, probably, but they stood properly silent with their heads bared. It was more of a sendoff than some tars got.

The wind had fallen into confused airs, and the smell of the fresh pork that Doc was roasting down the beach distracted somewhat from the ceremony.

The pig's last meal put no one off, fresh meat being fresh meat. After all had eaten, I took Horne, Simpson, and Hawkins aside to look over what they had gleaned from the bodies.

"There wasn't much on them, sir," said Horne. "They were stripped down to their smalls. But look at this." He held out a length of tarred rope. "Their hands were tied with it."

"Yes?" I examined the rope. It was tarred hemp, same as in any ship I ever been in, except for the blood.

"Tell him, Simpson," said Horne.

"See the white yarn, sir, wove amongst the tarred stuff? Well, it's red with blood now, aye, but it was white when it was fresh. That's rogue's yarn. White rope has a strand of tarred stuff in it, likewise. The Royal Navy uses it to tell who's been stealing of H.M.'s cordage. They does up their canvas with a colored yarn for the same reason."

"Could they have gotten it out of a Royal dockyard or a British merchantman?"

"No, sir. Paint, spars, anything you want, even guns for the right price. But sail-yard dockers—them's the buyers of swag stole out of dockyards—they don't traffic in cordage or sails. That's nobbut a way to get nicked. And it didn't come from no merchantman. Strictly Royal Navy stuff, that is."

"Mr. Horne, you say they were wearing smallclothes?"

"Yes, sir. Knee-britches and white vests, most of them. Five of them were rougher looking and wore trousers."

"The ones in britches were King's officers, and the others were foremast jacks, and the cutter is Royal Navy. I bet she was the same one we saw the *Clytemnestra* in chase of."

"Is it our business, sir?"

"Aside from being piracy? Piracy is every navy's business. But it's got plenty to do with our man Mèche, I guess." Lord, I hoped not. "You get back to your painting and have O'Lynn and Kennedy come to me."

Bob Wilson and his mate set up an awning for me on the carronade platform. I listened with half an ear while they discussed the relative merits of the different ways of getting their task done. "That's no way to stretch an awning!" said Bob. "Gwan if it ain't!" said his mate helpfully; "throw a hitch over that there bollard!" "What bollard?" "*That* bollard." "If you ain't the ignorantest thing ever," said Bob, shaking his head; "I pity you, truly I do. That's a bitt, not a bollard!" "It ain't!" "Is!" That was the high point of it, but they got it done at last, and at last I was out of the reach of the bird bombs. It was shady and breezy, pleasant except for the smell, and I would've been happy if I could've gotten one of Uncle Jupe's whiskey juleps.

Horne and his crew had gotten the *Tomahawk*'s hull above the waterline painted a brilliant blue and were starting in on the yellow trim. When I squinted a bit I could see her as a merchantman. If we struck her topgallant masts and let a line hang over the side here and there, we could look like some decent bait.

O'Lynn and Kennedy waded through the shallows toward me. Kennedy stared at me like I was a Protestant at High Mass or something, pale beneath his sunburn, but O'Lynn spoke in his ear and urged him along. They stopped at the base of the platform with their hats in their hands and squinted up at me.

"Come on up here," I said. "Sit down in the shade and talk to me."

"What shall we be talkin' of, then, sor?" said O'Lynn when they'd sat down. They didn't look near as comfortable as they might've, sitting in the shade while their shipmates labored in the sun.

"Ask Kennedy what ship he was in when he got pressed."

They gabbled at each other, all throat-hawking grunts and rolling R's. "He don't know what you mean, sor," said O'Lynn.

"Yes he does—tell him to look at me. Now ask him again."

"*Wilhelmina,* he says, sor, a Dutch fly-boat out of Bonaire, carrying salt to Rotterdam."

"Ask him what he knows about this." I held up the bloody strand of rope.

Kennedy jerked away from it, babbling.

"He says he don't know a t'ing, sor."

"I think he's a deserter from a British man-o'-war cutter. Tell him I think he helped kill his officers and bury them in that pit."

Kennedy wept, shaking his head no, no, no. He spoke urgently in Gaelic.

"Himself was pressed out of the *Wilhelmina* last year," O'Lynn translated, "and became a foretopman in the *Shearwater* cutter, sor, of fourteen guns and a crew of seventy. That's a guess, sir, of how many was left after . . ."

"Right. Go on."

"He says they were bound from Barbados to Jamaica, sor, when they saw a sail here in the cove, which was presently discovered to be the *Sofie's Aunt.* Can that be right, sor?"

"*Suffisant.* Go on."

He listened to Kennedy some more. "They'd seen her before, on the Dutch side of Saint Vincent. Martin, the master—her skipper, he means—sent Agnell aboard of her there to check her papers and spake with her captain—"

More musical Irish gabbling. It was like watching a man singing as his world tumbled down around his ears. Then: "Captain Martin there had been suspicious of the American before but hadn't been able to prove anythin', he says, but when they saw her again at such an out-of-the-way place as this, they stood in to see what was about. Martin guessed she was a freebooter, and so it was he had the arms chest opened as they went in. A grand mistake, that was. It was for some time the people had been discontent, and they fell into an evil mutiny right here in the offing. The American captain was unhappy about it. But Agnell said they had struck a bargain, and he would hold him to it."

Mutiny was one thing. But murder on such a scale was something else again. My heart dropped, and I wondered what to do.

"What was the bargain?"

"It wasn't our man's place to know, sor, but he says them's Agnell's very words, sor: *You've struck a bargain, and I'll hold you to it.* Kennedy thought there would be a fight."

"They killed their officers over a couple of buckets of paint?"

"No, sor. Besides the Negroes, sor, there was gold, too, a great chest of it."

I looked at Kennedy. "O'Lynn, did he see this gold himself?"

Kennedy listened to the translation and then shook his head.

"Scuttlebutt was there was a chest in *Shearwater*'s glory-hole, sor. Agnell had the officers carry it up the island, there. He made them bury it, and then he and his mates killed them."

"The gold is under the grave we just consecrated?"

"You mean read the words over? Aye, sor." Kennedy talked some more, and O'Lynn said, "The American had hove her cable short, an' cut an' run when the killin' begun. As soon as Agnell was done, he followed after."

"Where did they go?"

"He don't know, sor. I think 'tis the truth, for he's after swearing it on a Babble."

"And his mother's grave, too, I expect."

"Oh, no, sor, just a wee Babble will do."

"There were maybe two dozen men in that pit, most of them gentlemen. More of the crew had to've stayed loyal than that. So where are they?"

"They bargained to be taken someplace where a ship might call. Agnell left Kennedy and Jeffers here—Jeffers it was whose head was bashed in—he left 'em here to 'guard the stores,' as they said, sor, meanin' they might never be found, or perhaps later killed at leisure if they didn't care to take a chance in the yawl. The killin' fit had passed on the crew, and no doubt they'd not take a hand in more morders—but Harrison an' them others might oblige. The blackamoor cook was ashore when the horror begun, which is how he came to be left behind."

"He helped in the killing?"

"Oh, no, your honor."

"What happened to Jeffers?"

"Harrison did that because he refused to swear his loyalty to Agnell, and Kennedy here stabbed Harrison."

"Why?"

"Because Harrison thought they ought to bloody their own hands or die with the others."

"Why didn't anyone stop him?"

"Harrison was not a well-liked man, sor."

Which didn't answer the question of why they didn't stop Agnell, but some questions just got no answers. I got up to stretch my legs and try to straighten out the truth from the lies. "That's enough for now, then," I said. "Tell the new cook I want him."

Doc arrived, looking like a man trying to look like he wasn't up to anything—but that was how he always looked.

"You weren't entirely honest with me, Doc."

"Oh, no sah," he said to my question, "I dint kill nobody, no sah!"

"But you knew about it."

"I'se jus' a cook, Mr. Graves, you know dat. Oh, I crewed a gun or two in my time, sho' I did—I'se a navy man, ain't I? But I ain't no killer, no sah. I just kep' my head down, like dis here." He got a sleepy, stupid look on his face. "And dey marched dem po' gennlemen away. Dey was a argument, 'cause Kennedy and dat other fella wif da busted head whose name I dint get, dey dint wanna do it. Well, dey done it anyway."

"Kennedy and the other one, they took part in the killing?"

"No, sah. Ain't dat what I been tellin' you? Dem *other* ones is who done it. Den dey come back and dey was gonna do fo' me, too, but I went like dis here." He rolled his eyes around in his head, his teeth chattering, and threw himself at my feet. "An' I goes, 'Lawsa mighty, massa, please don' do it, I'se jus a po' nigga cook what don't want no trouble, no sah!' And dey believe me, too. Sho dey did." He got to his feet again and laughed. "Shucks. An' den I told dem other three fools dey could get good cash money for me and Kennedy if dey was to sell us 'steada shootin' us. But if I'd a-knowed dey was gonna take us to market in a open boat, I woulda thought of sumpthin' else. Yes, sah."

"What were you doing ashore?"

"Huntin' turkle eggs, sah. Same as ever mornin'."

"Where are all the Breezes? How did Peter Wickett get 'em all to join him?"

"Oh, he didn't, sah. Da new fellas called her da *Sofie's Aunt.* Dem ol' ones, what call her da *Breeze* like befo', dey all around on islands and in old schooners and such what we come across. Arter a while dey's all Sofie's Aunts an' no mo' Breezes. But dey's all safe, yes sah. First he got one or two away at a time on some excuse or 'nother, and marked 'em R for *run* in the book, and took on new hands out of dem ships he stopped. Den arter a while he just say, 'Get gone on dis here island,' or skiff or whatever, 'or you can walk home.' Dat done it. Didn't nobody want to take him up on dat offer."

"But *why?*"

Doc screwed up his face in a scowl and said, "I expects you better ax Ben Crouch about dat. He act like he know somethin' ol' Cap'n Wickett don't want nobody else to know. An' dat's all I know, suh."

"You were born to be hanged, Doc."

"No, sah, I very respectfully declines da honor." He thumped his chest. "Dis chile gone die in bed. Now if you'll excuse me, I'm gonna catch us a mess o' turkle eggs. Turkles been comin' ashore at night." He picked up a piece of planking for a shovel and headed toward the high-water mark, saying to himself, "Is dey good eggs? Oh, yes, dey is."

FIFTEEN

Harrison lived longer than he wanted to. He like to talked his head off in his fever, too, as we sailed north for the Virgin Islands. "Tortola," he said one afternoon, or "Tortuga," or maybe it was "turtle," which is what *tortuga* means in Spanish; and "one week after the new moon. Blue Peter . . . four guns . . . windward. Freebooter's treasure, that's the point." With eyes that were clear but saw far beyond the cabin, he looked at Horne, who sat beside him on a stool at the chart table, and said distinctly, "We'll know you by that."

"By what?" said Horne. He rubbed sweat off his lip.

Harrison's mouth worked, but no words came out. His eyes followed something that wasn't in the cabin.

"The Blue Peter," I said. "Then four guns to windward. Is that the challenge?"

"Aye." Even the single word caused him to struggle for breath.

"What's the reply?"

"Rise and fall . . ." He didn't seem to notice the sweat running down his face. "Spanish . . . main."

"The Spanish mainland? You mean New Granada?"

"No, you— Spanish . . ." He gathered strength. "The *main.* Then show the black dog."

"Show what?"

"Your true colors, you black-hearted dog!"

Horne had risen from the stool and crouched over Harrison's hammock. I touched Horne's sleeve and shook my head.

"Harrison," I said, "is this a rendezvous?"

"Rondyvoo? My, that's a fine word," he said. He reached out, and Horne took his hand. "I'll chalk it—" He gulped air and tried again. "Chalk it up . . . on the binnacle."

"I mean, is it a secret meeting."

"Aye. 'Nice and cozy. Just the three of us,' he says. 'Three's a crowd,' says I." He ran the back of his hand across his forehead.

"Just the three of you?"

"Aye. Peter Wicked will have the other one." He fell quiet. I thought his wits had wandered. Then he said, "Him and Agnell worked it out, like, when first they met."

"Peter Wicked will have the other one what?"

He clutched at the kerchief around his throat. It was knotted loose enough, but Horne untied it for him anyway.

"The Yankee Doodle's off to . . . to snatch a schooner or summat." His body jerked. He shrieked like to stop my heart.

Horne cradled his head with one hand, shushing him like a baby and mopping his face with his kerchief. "Maybe he ought to have some water, sir. I never felt a man's skin so hot."

"No, the book says not to." All my surgical knowledge was contained in a pamphlet I'd found in the schooner's medicine chest. There were diagrams showing how to take a man's arms and legs off, but nothing about getting a knife out of his spine.

"It's good, that," said Harrison. He blinked at Horne. "What gives, mate?"

I leaned closer. "Is Agnell expecting anyone in particular?"

His head turned toward me. His eyes were glassy. "No. Turtle to the hat . . . freebooter's treasure. That's the *point,* I tell you."

"How will he know what ship he's to meet?"

His eyes widened, and his head wobbled as he looked around, like he'd just then noticed me and Horne and the cabin itself. He strained against the ropes that bound him in his hammock. He thrust Horne's hand away.

"What place is this?" He clasped the handle of the knife that still protruded from his belly. "Oh, Lord Jesus," he whispered. "I'm a dead man."

I never did get the knife out of him. He never lost consciousness, neither, till he slipped his hawser ten leagues east of Saint Croix.

The three fish I'd been ripening in the hold stood blinking in the afternoon sun. Four days in the dark had left them weak and filthy. Only one of them bothered to look farther than the rail, but if he recognized the bay in which we sheltered and the islands that lay all around, he didn't show it. They all three wore shirts and sailcloth trousers of the kind that sailors make for themselves at sea, and which had been white once upon a time. They were barefoot, of course, it being the tropics, and were shock-headed and bearded.

One had several more teeth than the others. "Now then, Handsome Jack," I said to him. "Suppose you tell me your name."

"It's Morris," he said. "That's Manson and that's Jakes, and that's all what you'll get out of any of us till we gets summat to eat besides your filthy bread and water."

"Fair enough. If you want your dinner, strip down and throw them rags overboard. Mr. Horne, rig the fire engine and get these men hosed off. Then issue them something from the slop chest and see they get fed."

Morris exchanged evil looks with Kennedy, who stood with his hands hanging at his sides and his feet apart, like a wrestler waiting to grapple. Manson and Jakes looked at his feet, not his face.

The Tomahawks gathered on deck and in the rigging and silently watched them rotate under a jet of warm seawater from the fire pump. When their grime had been sluiced away with the help of a lump of lye soap—an article they seemed unaccustomed to and suspicious of—and they were newly clothed in white duck trousers and blue-checked shirts, and with the grease of their salt pork still shining in the stubble on their cheeks and chins, Horne marched them one-by-one to my cabin. Sequestering myself with them was purely for show, as the helmsman stood not four feet away in a straight line and no doubt could hear perfectly well through the open stern windows. Secrets were problematic things in a vessel barely twenty paces long on deck. Peebles sat at my desk with pen and paper before him. I kept my feet.

"Have a seat," I said to the first one—Manson or Jakes, one or the other. He looked around for a chair. "On the deck," I said. "You may lean your back against the bulkhead. Now then." I folded my arms and looked down at him. "Mr. Peebles here will write down what we say. It's for your benefit as well as my own. State your name, first of all."

"For why should I answer?"

"So you can be entered on the ship's books."

"I ain't enlistin', so bugger off."

"I can't issue you rations without you're entered, you know."

"Me name's Edward Teach, an' I'm cap'n of the *Queen Anne's Revenge*. Stick that in your pipe an' smoke it, mate." He gave me a leer.

I counted his teeth—all seven of them. "Very well, Mr. Blackbeard," says I. "Since you been dead near about a century, I don't calculate you'll be needing any rations." I raised my voice. "Mr. Horne! Put this man back in the hold and bring me one of the others."

"No, wait, mate—me name's Wat Manson. No need for haste, aye?"

"Write that down, Mr. Peebles. Now then, Manson, begin at the beginning and tell me what happened."

"I was born when I was little, and me muvva nevva loved me."

"And my mother's dead. Life's hard. Let's skip your personal life and get to the recent events at Birds Island. The men in the pit—who were they?"

"Dunno."

"Where did they come from?"

"Dunno."

"Manson, would you rather be hanged, or flogged around the fleet?"

"Oh, really, I don't know what yer mean. Hanged? Flogged? For what, if I may make so bold as to ax?"

"Hanged for piracy and murder, flogged for desertion. Either'll kill you, but I guess one would be more painful than the other."

"Pish. I'm a Yankee deep-water man what was pressed by pirates."

"Yankee, my granny! Your accent is closer to Hampshire than New Hampshire."

Manson grinned. "So I'm a immigrant. I bet half your crew spent time in one of His Majesty's ships. That don't prove nuffink."

"I don't have to prove anything. I just have to turn you over to the Royal Navy." I pointed out the stern window at a small island with a wide earthen scar across its face. "That's Dead Chest over there. We're lying in Deadman's Bay, off Peter's Island in the Virgins. It's an easy run down to Tortola from here. Whether I hunt up a King's frigate tomorrow depends on what you and your mates tell me today. Do you understand?"

"Can I talk it over wiv me mates?"

"No."

"Then I got nuffink to say, mate."

"I'm sure your mates will be impressed with your loyalty. Maybe they'll even drink your health when you're swinging in a gibbet. Mr. Horne, take this man away and bring in the next."

Morris proved no more pliable than Manson, but Jakes was already quavering when he entered the cabin. "Please, sir," he said when we had dispensed with the preliminaries, "I'm a deserter, true enough, but not from your navy. And I ain't no pirate, sir, and I didn't kill nobody."

"That's not up to me to decide, Jakes," I said. "But since you mention it, who are the dead men in the pit?"

"Why, the *Shearwater*'s orficers. Capting Martin and Mr. Ducker, who was the first lieutenant, and the master, bosun, carpenter—all the orficers right down to the reefers, sir. Billy Thomas was on'y nine year old, but Mr. Agnell cut him down as if he was a grown man. The poor little nipper took it like a man, though. Looked Agnell right in the eye, but he struck him down all the same, so he did, sir, God blast him! He said we was on'y to maroon 'em, sir."

He spoke all in a rush, as if once he started he couldn't hold back. He told a sordid story of butchery, claiming that he had hacked at the bodies for fear the mutineers would turn on him, but that he had killed no one himself. Some of the foremast hands had repented themselves when it was too late, and they, too, now lay in the pit—which explained why some of the bodies were wearing well-tarred slop trousers.

I said, "Were the Americans involved?"

"Oh, no, sir. And what could they have done even if they had knowed what was afoot? Them was on'y fifteen or twenty, but we was forty and more. Nearer seventy, counting them as stayed loyal. There was a ruckus, I'll tell you that. Brother Jonathan must've seen what we done, for he cut his cable an' run for it. Left his hook on the bottom of the cove, I expect."

I pictured it in my mind's eye—the British mutineers marching their captives up the beach, a bored lookout aloft in the *Suffisant* watching with growing interest and then alarm, the sunlight glinting on slashing blades, the hasty recall, and then the cutting of the cable in their frenzy to leave that place. Poor Doc with his peg-leg would've had a hard time running in the sand—assuming he even noticed the commotion. If he'd been off hunting turtle eggs like he said, the squawking of the birds could've kept him from hearing anything till it was too late.

"No blame to Brother Jonathan, neither," Jakes was saying. "Who among us wouldn't have done what he done, eh?"

I hauled my mind back to the present. "Who's to say what's right, you mean?"

"That's right, sir, who's to say. Agnell said the Brother Jonathans would hang anyway for stealin' the sloop, was they to squeak."

He stared at me a long minute, and then put his head in his hands.

Despite my threats, I didn't want to have any dealings with British cruisers—partly because I couldn't have explained Peter's presence, and partly because I wasn't sure if my three fish were still of any use to me or not. We took a roundabout course north through Drake's Bay and into the Atlantic between the Camanoes and the Dogs, and west past Guana Island with the strange saurian outcropping that gave it its name. There we turned south inside Vandyke's Island, through the sound west of Saint John, and kept west along the coast of Saint

Thomas and its lush sugar plantations until by and by we arrived at the mouth of Long Bay, where there was a busy harbor. The island was Danish, but no questions were asked and no explanations were offered in the free port of Charlotte Amalie. Which didn't mean I couldn't see what I could see, just that I should be careful where I look, lest someone poke me in the eye.

So much small craft had crowded into the bay that it looked like a basket full of chickens on market day. There was a dispirited-looking naval brig with the white on red of Denmark drooping from her peak, and a few island schooners that had a dangerous air about them, but no *Suffisant* and nary a cutter answering *Shearwater*'s description lay among them. It was a pleasant day, mild as ever in the Caribbean except when it tries to blow you halfway to Peru. We came to an anchor in eighteen fathoms, with the star fort bearing north and Skytsborg Tower, the castle where Blackbeard was said to have scanned the sea for victims, on its hill above the point bearing north-northeast.

I sighted our bearings again to be sure the anchor was holding, and checked Mr. Peebles's figures to see if he was coming along any in his sextant work, and checked Horne's figures just to make Peebles feel better, and wrote up the result on the slate so there'd be no mistake, and said, "Let's hoist out the boat, Mr. Horne. I'm going ashore."

"I'll come with you, sir."

"No, you won't neither. You'll stay here with Mr. Peebles." I nodded at the swarm of bumboats that was pulling for us, laden with fruit and monkeys and parrots and sure-as-shootin' enough rum to get every man aboard drunker as a bag of judges before the day was out. "Pass out small arms and rig the boarding nets. The men may buy fruit and other foodstuffs, but no liquor and no pets. Cash only—no trading away their clothes. And no women nor anybody else aboard that don't belong aboard."

"Aye aye, sir."

"You needn't look so sour, Mr. Horne, I ain't going ashore because I like it. Where's Gundy?" I buttonholed him as he trotted by in the cheerful rush of Tomahawks getting ready for market. "Gundy, do you have any experience with smuggling? I mean, with smugglers?"

He grinned in his beard. "Either way, zur, might be I do."

"Good. Mr. Horne, if we're not back by first light . . ."

"Please don't say I mustn't come and look for you, sir."

"How you talk. I was going to say come and fetch us off."

Charlotte Amalie by day was a sullen hole, but it came alive as the sun went down—alive like a dead dog is alive with maggots. It gave me a strange and lonely feeling to see the boat's crew heading back to the *Tomahawk* without me and Gundy. She looked fine in her blue paint and yellow trim, and across the water I could hear Horne roaring at the bumboat women to mind the paint, damn their poxy whatevers.

Dressed in white slop trousers and plain blue jackets, Gundy and I walked up and down the narrow strip of streets and alleys along the waterfront till we come to a tavern that spilled out a little light and a lot of noise. It wasn't the only such place, but it was the first one I was willing to set foot in. On the signboard over the door were the words DRIE LUS and a painting of a trio of lice on a blue background.

"On a field azure, three gray ladies, rampant," I said. "What's 'Drie Lus' mean?"

"Three lice, zur."

"What I thought."

"Just like home," he said, and I wondered if he was kidding. The shutters of the Drie Lus stood open, and enough candles were burning in there that you could see a knife coming. I looked at Gundy.

He shrugged. "Good a place as any, zur. Us probably won't get our throats cut if us don't get drunk." He patted the cutlass in his belt as if to reassure himself, which didn't reassure me much at all. I touched the hilt of my own sword, just to remind myself that it was there.

A wave of liquor fumes and tobacco smoke rolled over us as we stepped through the door. There was customers just about everywhere, seamen mostly, but a few swelled-up merchants and sugar planters sat among them as they took their ease on chairs, benches, or overturned barrels, or slouched against the whitewashed walls. Every man I could see clutched pewter tankards and clay pipes in every hand, babbling away in as many languages as were spoke in the West Indies. There was even some Chinee, though most of the rascals seemed to be Danish or French from their language. Over by the bar I saw a couple of Danish sea officers, and I pulled my hat low. I didn't guess they'd care about us one way or another, but I'd hate to have them ask me any awkward questions about pratique and quarantine. In the darker recesses, men turned away from my glance or dipped their heads as if to hide their faces. Way in the back I thought I saw the red britches and vest of a French officer, but he'd pulled his hat low, too, and it was plenty dark back there, and I was willing to ignore him if he ignored me.

From the number of heads that came together and the glances that came our way, though, I guessed the coins in our pockets were already being counted against the possible quickness of our blades. I put my hand on the hilt of my sword and marched over to a table by a side door, trying to catch a phrase or two as I went. I'd think I'd caught a thread of English or French, only to find it led off into something else entire. We sat down, trying to see everything at once without looking like we were looking.

I leaned my head close to the old quartermaster's. "What're they talking, Gundy, some kind of creole?"

"Negerhollands, zur, or Hoch Kreol, as some calls 'un. 'Ee's mostly Dutch and Danish, with a vair measure of English and Vrench, and a bit of Spanish thrown in gratis and vree."

"Do you speak it?"

"Nay, zur, but I can understand 'un well enough." He took off his neckerchief and swabbed his face. "The day gets no cooler by night, dos't?"

"No, but at least the sun ain't burning our eyes out. How do we go about finding someone who'll talk to us?"

"Us don't, zur. Order a bottle of rum and several glasses, if 'ee be zo kind, zur, and us'll zee what is to zee."

I ordered from a passing black man in a grimy apron and got us a couple of tobacco pipes as well. We'd barely had time to pack and light them before two colored men approached us.

"Pardoon, manier," said the smaller one. He wore a red silk vest but no shirt.

"'Pardon me, sir,' say my friend," said the other. His eyes were black, and his hair was black, and his teeth were black, but his skin was no darker than my own. He wore a yellow scarf on his head, and he jingled when he moved on account of all the gold rings in his ears.

"My name is Graves. This is Gundy."

"Every man is called something. I am called Cocro. This one is called Kakerlak."

"Cocro no bang kakerlak, kakerlak no bang cocro," said Kakerlak.

"He say, 'The crocodile is not afraid of the cocker-roach, and the cocker-roach is not afraid of the crocodile.' He always say this. Is not true. Fear is the great friend of the little man, yes?"

I puffed smoke.

"You are United States American, from the schooner, yes?"

"Yes. What do you want?"

"This is direct. I like it. What I want? I want rum."

"That's easily solved." I sloshed out two generous portions, and they sloshed them down.

Cocro smacked his lips and sighed. "A better question, what is *you* want?"

"Een man dod', een ander man brod," said Kakerlak.

"'One man's death, another man's bread,' he say. You want someone kill, maybe?"

"No, I don't want someone kill, maybe. I want to find someone, though."

"Kapitan Mèche."

"How'd you know?"

Cocro shrugged. "He is not French. He is United States American, I think. You are United States American." He smacked his hands together.

"How often does he come to this port?"

He shrugged. "He is *mumbo-jumbi,* a ghost. He is here, he is not here."

"Is he here now?"

He looked over his shoulder while Kakerlak stared at me. "Yes. No."

"Have another drink." I followed his glance. The man in the red vest and britches had put on a blue coat—definitely a French naval officer—and was working his way along the wall toward the side door behind our two friends. As I looked, he bent his head and said something to a fellow sitting at a table. They both laughed.

"Water kok fo fes, fes no weet," said Kakerlak, watching as Cocro filled our glasses. They both drank, but Gundy had touched my arm under the table and I let mine sit.

"You don't drink?" said Cocro.

"Poor tender worm," said Gundy, "dost 'ee think us a paar o' country louts?" He shifted just a little, but his legs were under his weight now, and I tensed as well. He jerked his beard at Kakerlak. "Wilt tell what Jack-o'-Lent just said?"

"It is nothing," said Cocro. "A saying only."

"Iss, it's a sayin': 'The water's boilin' for the fish but the fish doesn't know it.' Do 'ee take we for a paar of anticks?"

"Oh, no, sir," said Cocro, putting up his hands and wrenching his lips in a grin. "Truly it's—"

The French officer was stepping lively toward the door. He passed under a swaying lamp. His eyes met mine.

I started to stand, started to call out his name, when something—the monkey grin on Cocro's face, an eagerness in Kakerlak's, a rush of air—made me twist out of the way as a heavy blade smashed into the table where I'd been leaning. And there was Ben Crouch on the other end of the cutlass, trying to shake a hunk of splintered wood off his blade.

Gundy went one direction and I went the other. No time to draw steel. I tried to roll away, but Cocro wrapped his arms around my ankles. I tried to brain him with a chair and missed. Shrieking, he clawed his way up my leg. Beyond him I saw Crouch had cleared his blade. His arm swung up. Cocro's grubby fingers were on my face, in my mouth, searching for my neck. I bit down. I'd amputate his damn fingers with my teeth if I could. He screamed, but a stiletto glittered in his other hand. He raised his fist, grinning in triumph. I punched him in the throat. I hit him again and his head snapped back. And a cutlass swept down and split his skull.

"Oh, God fuck me!" cried Crouch. He yanked his blade out of the bone, but the French officer grabbed his arm and hissed, "Stop it, you peasant!"

I spat out a mouthful of Cocro's blood. "Corbeau!"

Corbeau smiled beautifully and swept off his hat. *"Bonsoir, monsieur!"*

I kicked out from under Cocro's body. "Stand where you are!"

"I choose not to. *Au revoir!*" And with that he pushed Crouch through the door and followed him out.

Our little confab hadn't gone unnoticed, of course, not even in that den. Money was changing hands, and there weren't just a few disappointed looks thrown our way—disappointed that we'd survived, I guess, and they'd lost their bets. But more important than that, the Danish officers had swords in their fists and were trying to make their way through the milling crowd.

Kakerlak was rolling on the floor, clutching his walnuts. Gundy drew his foot back and kicked him again.

"No time for that!" I grabbed the back of Gundy's shirt, and then we were through the door and hooking along down an alley.

Gundy was sprier than he looked. Maybe it was just on account of my short legs, but I couldn't hardly keep up with him at first. We tore up one street and down the next, looking for a dark doorway that didn't have a thief or a drunk or a whore in it, but the town was full up. By the third or fourth time down an alley that was getting mighty familiar, he began to flag at last. I pulled him into the shadow of a dray wagon.

"Who were they fellows?" he puffed.

"Fugitives from the *Suffisant.* But where is she? She wasn't in the harbor."

"No—" His chest was heaving. He fetched up against a wheel to catch his breath. "No, me cabbun, but could be she's in Magen's Bay, on the var zide of the island." He stopped to listen for sounds of pursuit. Glass broke somewhere, followed by a burst of drunken laughter. "It's not more than a few mile, maybe, though a bit up and down. A younger maan than I could make it in a short while."

"Then let's go," I said, starting off, but he stopped me short with his hand on my collar.

"No, no, me cabbun. Beg your pardon for pullin' on 'ee, zur, but what art us to do on our own? I'm werry to the bone, and us don't even know the way."

"But it'll take days to get the *Tomahawk* around there."

He laughed gently. "Don't be so grainy as to think us can taak they alone, me 'an'some. 'Ee bist a boy and I bin an ould maan."

I was about to snap that he was half right, but I stopped myself. I poked my head out from the stern of the dray. "Looks like there's a riot going on down at the Drie Lus, but it's calm as clams between here and the waterfront. Let's steal us a skiff and get back aboard the schooner."

"Dos't mean 'borrow' a skiff, zur?"

"Why, yes, ain't that what I said?"

"Art learnin', me luvver. My faith in 'ee grows by the minute."

The bay was a lovely bay, with water the color of my coat when it was new, and palms swaying in the breeze along the shore, and a sandy beach as bright and pure as the finest sugar. The way I'd figured it, Peter'd had two choices: fight the northeasterly wind and the Atlantic swell all along the line of the Virgins before working his way south again through the cays around Anegada, or else drop down the wind to Hispaniola, Cuba, the Gulf of Mexico—anywhere in a wide arc from Bonaire to the Bahamas. That was the easy way, and that's what I would've done; but if that's what he done, I'd missed him. The bay was empty.

"Magen's Bay, zur," Gundy was saying, "where Zur Fraancis Draake whiled away the time between plunders. A West Country man and a vair bet 'ee was a brother in the coastin' trade, like all of we a-times . . ."

"A brother!" I slapped Gundy on the shoulder and laughed. "You are a wonder to me, Gundy. Mr. Horne, there! Let's bear up for Guana. I got a brother there."

Assembly Pleasance's head was like a boulder in the sea, with his bald dome being the top of the boulder, and his beard and the long curls that tumbled from the nape of his neck being the fringe of weed that surrounds it. We sat drinking under-sweetened chocolate on the veranda of his rambling, airy house, which sat between two peaks and faced north toward the Atlantic. He wasn't a brother but a Brother, whose grandfather had established a colony of the Pacific Brotherhood on Guana Island some fifty years before. They'd lapsed into celibacy for some reason, which made recruitment hard, and eventually they'd died out; Brother Assembly was the last congregant and sole heir. He knew Phillip well, by bills of lading at least. He also knew that Phillip was overextended and having trouble getting insured.

"He is in danger of disownment from the Brotherhood," Assembly said, "should he lose another hull." He said it with complacent disinterest, as if commenting on the weather. "It helps him not that he has a warmonger for a brother," he added. "However, I am situated in such a place as to observe commerce in action rather than seeing only its happy profitability. It upsets Providence none at all should a friendly man-of-war be sailing nearby when pirates heave into view."

"Have you seen anything of an American pirate in a Bermuda sloop?"

"Probably. The Indies are full of Americans in Bermuda sloops."

"This'd be a tall man, with a recent scar on his cheek and a port-wine stain on his forehead. Might be calling himself Mèche and pretending to be French."

"French? Not with that accent. Maybe Canadian. I bought a load of silk from him in Magen's Bay these few days ago."

"That's a bad business, dealing with pirates."

He sipped his chocolate with a sort of triumphant distaste, like he was taking medicine. "I have already traded the silk for sugar. And thou hast no jurisdiction here, regardless."

I went to the railing and looked out over the sea. It had been fussing earlier in the day, but now it lay greasy and hushed. "You got you a tremendous prospect from up here, Brother Assembly."

"Aye. Two evenings hence, for instance, I noted thy schooner passing westward. I also saw a cutter at the same time, a low and black-hulled cutter, British from the look of her, beating eastward beyond Vandyke's. She kept the island betwixt herself and thee, and sailed on into yon flat ugly yellow clouds." He nodded to the east.

I got a crawly feeling between my shoulders, like I'd been hunting a panther and discovered it had been hunting me. "Well then," I said, "I guess I'd best be shoving off."

"Tomorrow is the first of October. There have been no hurricanes yet this season worth mentioning, but a noteworthy one approaches now, thou mustn't doubt. Do not cling too tightly to ephemeral notions and worldly things, Brother, lest thou lose what thou most values." He whistled an old Shaker hymn that was popular among the Brethren:

> *'Tis a gift to be simple,*
> *'Tis a gift to be free,*
> *'Tis a gift to come down*
> *Where we ought to be . . .*

I knocked on the railing, annoyed with myself for my superstitiousness but angrier with Assembly for baiting me. "Of all the infernal meanness," I said. "Don't whistle for a wind in hurricane season!"

"Oh, as for that," he said, the corners of his naked lip turning up just a little bit, "God watches out for sailors and the wicked, is't not what sailors say? And the wicked, too, I doubt not."

I picked up my hat. "Good day to you, Brother Assembly. I'm obliged for the scuttlebutt."

"Thou leavest already? As thou wilt." He raised a hand. "But one thing more—that same cutter was at Charlotte Amalie. She had slaves aboard of her, but human chattels is one thing that cannot be bought or sold there, not openly. She was to meet 'the turtles at the hat,' or she was the turtle who would wear a hat, or something like it. Her people were very droll about it. Kept putting their dirty fingers beside their great red snouts when they said it, before dumping them back into their rum. Said it so often that even the dullest intemperant in Saint Thomas could have divined the answer. Dost glean anything by it?"

"Was the cutter called *Shearwater?*"

"She was called nothing that I know of. The name had been blacked off the transom."

I consulted the chart in my head. "Much obliged to you again, Brother," I said. "I'll mention your kindness next time I'm at Baltimore meeting."

"I thank thee not, Brother." He set his mug aside and dabbed his lips on a plain cotton wipe. "I would not be associated with thy name. But thou mayest shelter here from the storm."

"Thank'ee, but I mean to catch that slaver."

"Is running slaves illegal now?"

"No. But they're murderers too. I mean to do 'em a hurt."

"Will that stop them from having murdered?"

"No, hang it. But they might know where to find a man I'm looking for."

"Why dost thou seek him?"

"I aim to save him from temptation."

"He must do that for himself. Thou wouldst best run for shelter with that little schooner of thine whilst thou mayest. The breath of God is soon upon us."

We worked *Tomahawk* upwind through an ugly, tossing sea. I called a council of war with Peebles, Horne, and Gundy over dinner in my cabin. Dinner was cut-and-come-again of cold beans and cornbread with molasses, which I thought was bully fare, having grown up on it, but Peebles looked like his stomach ailed him.

Gundy waved his fork at him. "What 'ee need, zur, is a piece of fulsome pork to sit on your dinner and hold 'un down."

"But it's a banyan day," said Peebles, white-faced. "No meat today."

He put two fingers to his lips. His shoulders heaved, and his cheeks puffed out.

"There's a bucket abaft your chair, sir," said Horne.

Peebles shook his head no, but I edged my plate out of range anyway.

"Now, like I was saying," I cut in, "I want to figure out what Harrison was on about." I looked at my personal log, which was open on the table between us. "He mentioned a freebooter's treasure, which I'm guessing has something to do with pirates."

"And he said, 'That's the point' afterward, sir," said Horne. "I remember he stressed that word: 'Freebooter's treasure, that's the *point.*'"

"Treasure's always the point with such as him," said Gundy.

"Yes, but he was so close to dying, he was choosing his words tarnation careful. I don't think he was just being cranky."

"Point," said Horne. "Indicate, index, finger, fingertip, arrow . . ."

"Point of a compass, the reason why—neaps and nattlings," said Gundy, looking at Doc, who'd just come in with the rest of yesterday's pudding.

Horne looked cross. "What are neaps and nattlings?"

"Turnips and pig guts, of course, Mr. Horne. 'Ee bake 'un in a pie."

"What's that got to do with anything?"

"I'm wanting belly-tember—I'm leary with hunger!"

"Hunger? Hmmph," said Doc, plocking the platter onto the table. "Man get better'n some, an' da man what get da least complain da least."

"Not the *point,*" said Peebles, sitting upright and with color coming into his face. "But *a* point!"

We all looked at him. "What?" I said, it being the first thing that come to mind.

"Freebooter's *Point,*" said Peebles. "He meant a cape, a peninsula—"

"Freebooter's Point," said Horne. "Treasure Point—"

"Anegada got both," said Doc.

"And Sombrero Island—" I started.

"Hat Island," said Doc. "Dat's about sebben leagues east of Anegada, or I'm my Auntie Greselda come back to life." He clomped out.

The English renegades confirmed all, once I'd made them a certain swear. I made sure of my wording.

"That's a promise I'm holding you to," said Manson.

"On my honor as a gentleman, I promise I won't turn you over to the Royal Navy," I repeated.

"Nor to any other," said Morris.

"Nor to any other. I swear it."

Morris grinned at Manson. "Let him club-haul his way out o' that one."

Tomahawk behaved with her customary sweetness in Anegada's meager shelter—shelter from the seas, not the wind, it being an uncommonly flat island—but as we rounded the long reef that reached to the southeast, she took the wild Atlantic rollers on her port bow and didn't like it. We braced up and settled in for the ride.

"Mr. Horne," I said, "keep them two islands in sight—I don't have to remind you of the dangers of a lee shore."

"That's true, sir," he said cheerfully.

I scowled. "Call me immediately if the wind shifts."

"Aye aye, sir." He laughed outright, and then so did I. The schooner was rocking and bucking like a mule with a briar up its funnel, but the groaning of her timbers and the creaking of her rigging was settling down to a steady chorus. The sun shone through the spray, and sun and wind and spray all felt good on my face. But I had business below.

I found our white-haired sailmaker working with a palm and needle in the light of a purser's glim, which is to say near dark. His eyelids were constantly puffy, and he peered at me like a mole in a hole.

"Yancy," I said, "do we have any black cloth?"

"Yes, sir. The men make going-ashore kerchiefs from it."

"I need you to make me an ensign."

"Well . . ." He looked at me over his little round spectacles. "It is silk after all, sir."

With no purser aboard, each petty officer was assured of his own little fiefdom of graft, releasing the materials entrusted to him at a small but reliable profit. If I pressed him, he might have difficulty locating the desired material, which would result in bad feelings on both sides.

"A little 'un, then," I said. "I'll pay whatever's fair."

"I think I can find enough for a little one, sir. Maybe even bigger than little."

"I'm glad to hear it. Now, here's what I want you to do." I handed him a design I had sketched on a piece of paper.

A large, low, black-hulled man-of-war cutter sat in the darkening east, hove-to with whitecaps running past her hull. At her peak she flew the Blue Peter, a white rectangle on a blue field. She looked to be the same cutter that had run from the *Clytemnestra.*

We'd struck our topgallant masts and the fore-topmast, and slung a painted canvas screen across the open rail where the three-pounders hunched; that and our gaudy blue and yellow should make us look like something entirely other than what they'd seen not so many days before. I hoped.

I looked at Gundy, standing at the conn with his petticoat trousers snapping like Mother Hubbard's laundry in the breeze, and O'Lynn and Eriksson double-manning the tiller.

"Are you sure you're well with this rig?"

Gundy took the tiller in his own hands. He let it press against his thigh while he stared up at the new leg-of-mutton topsail on the main. He pushed her head off the wind, but she came right up again.

He grinned. "She's honey-sweet no matter what 'ee does to 'er, zur."

I looked down at Jakes, sitting spraddle-legged in the lee of the rail. His ankles sported a nice pair of darbies, with an iron bar spreading his legs apart.

I went over to him. "That the *Shearwater?*"

He squinted through a gap in the hammock netting. "Aye."

"Put us on the sta'board tack, Gundy. Let's see how close we can get to her. And Mr. Horne, ready that signal."

When we had thrashed to within a mile, fighting the wind and waves all the way, the cutter fired four guns to windward.

Rise and fall the Spanish Main, Harrison had said.

"Hoist away." The red and yellow ensign of Spain rose to where our commission pendant should have been. I counted slowly to sixty. "Take it in again."

A red flag of mutiny adorned with a skull and crossbones rose to *Shearwater*'s peak.

"Show 'em our colors."

Peebles had already bent our temporary ensign on, and I watched it rise: a black banner with three white tombstones on it. Captain Graves was an excellent name for a pirate, and it would be a shame to have to change it.

I calculated I knew how a black widow's husband must feel as we crawled upwind toward the cutter's waiting guns. Assuming I was right in believing she carried four-pounders, her throw-weight of twenty-eight pounds a side was exactly seven pounds more than what *Tomahawk* could muster—and she had seven chances to hit compared with our four, and twelve pounds of our broadside was taken up by our short-range carronade. And I had no way of knowing exactly how many men she carried, but it was a good bet she outnumbered us by two to one.

We closed to within a few hundred yards, trying to get to windward or at least abreast of her, but she surged up to cut us off. A squat man in a monkey jacket called across from her quarterdeck, "Come into my lee! Damn your impudence."

"That's Mr. Agnell," said Jakes. He shrank down, even though he was out of sight behind the bulwark.

I waved my hat gaily. Horne and Peebles and I had removed our uniform coats and gaudied ourselves up with ribbons and lace that had mysteriously turned up among the men after we'd been at Birds Island, and I reckon we made a sight. Having decided to be French as well as a pirate, I waved my hankie at the cutter and called, "'Allo, 'allo, Mistair Englishman!"

Before anyone could laugh, I muttered, "Ready about. Stations for stays. I'll stop the grog of the first man who talks."

The wind sent the stench of sweat and excrement roiling down upon us as we came into the cutter's lee, but, barring a retch or two, the sail-handlers ran to their positions with their yaps shut. Gundy ran the *Tomahawk* through the tossing water, with the sails just on the edge of shivering but no closer.

"Ready . . . ready . . . ease down your helm." We eased off the jib sheets and hauled the booms amidships. I glanced aloft; I felt the wind on my cheek; I glanced at Gundy. "Helm's alee." I caught the cutter out of the corner of my eye, closer than I liked, and I sang out the command in French for their benefit, *"Adieu-va! Envoyez!"* as Gundy swung the bow neatly through the eye of the wind. "Let go," I added in a lower voice. "Of all, *haul.*" It was near about doing me a hurt not to bellow the commands, but the Tomahawks knew how to sail her, and we skipped along on the new tack as pretty as a Sunday bonnet on a summer brook. A summer brook with a thunderstorm brewing, I thought as the image come to me—the clouds were low overhead and the sea churned like a millrace.

I could get me a good look at the cutter now. I could see the small smokes rising from her gunner's linstocks, and a knot of petty officers staring at us from her quarterdeck. I didn't see any commissioned officers anywhere. I turned and strolled past Gundy. "Edge us around astern of her, if she'll let us."

"Wee wee, monsoor," he said, startling me into a sputtering laugh.

"Ahoy," Agnell called. "What schooner is that?"

I picked up the speaking trumpet and raised it to my lips. *"La Tromperie.* Capitaine Matthieu Tombe eez my names. An' what sheep are yew?"

"Never you mind what 'ship' I am. You tell me what you're doing at my rendezvous."

"Air frien' Capitaine Mèche 'ave send me."

There was a long pause. I watched the smoke from the linstocks while I waited, and breathed the stench of captive humanity, and felt the hatred rising in my chest. The pause grew from uncomfortable to scary, and I wanted to kill.

Then, at blessed last: "Are you ready to buy?"

"*Mais oui,* if zey air in zee good condition."

"In course they are. Twice what we'd bargained for and ten times as ugly. Can you handle fifty?"

"Off cairse, zat an' mare," I said. "Jig over," I muttered to Gundy as we crept astern of the cutter. *"Non, non,"* I said to Peebles at the guns, and then quieter, "Hold your fire unless I give the word. They got a human cargo, don't forget."

I near about dropped my speaking trumpet when Bob Wilson and his mate, both of them up on the main-topmast yard, sang out together, "Sail ho!"

"Par où?" says I, hoping the exaggerated way I pretended to look around the horizon would make my meaning clear and remind him we were supposed to be French.

"Zee wind-waird," said Bob.

"More like two points off the wind," said his mate, low but insistent.

"Yer s'posed to be French, you damn fool," said Bob in a hoarse whisper, but before I could shoot them both they fell silent, having clapped their hands over each other's mouths—and then the *Shearwater*'s lookout distracted everyone by shouting, "Deck, there! A Bermuda sloop. It's that Brother Jonathan."

"Don't get excited, Monseer le Frog or whatever you are," called Agnell. "That'll be our mutual friend Captain Mèche. Come alongside and mind the paint."

Horne had run halfway up the windward shrouds. *"Suffisant,"* he called, pronouncing it more or less in the French fashion. In a stage whisper he added, "She's being chased."

"Here, what's that big nigger about?" cried Agnell. "Stand off or I'll fire into you!"

"Not when I am astride your stairn, you silly fellow," I said. I shook my head at Peebles, who was looking at me pleadingly. We could've sent every shot we had right through the length of her, and not a gun would we get in reply.

Shearwater's lookout bellowed, "There's a man-o'-war in chase of her, sir! A frigate—it's the fucking *Clytemnestra*!"

Oh, lordy. "I know thees *Clytemnestra,*" I shouted. I shook my fist. "You 'ave betray me, dim your eye! I run away!" I glanced at Gundy. "Keep her thus."

"Betrayed you, is it?" called Agnell. "Not I, you frog-eating bastard! Bear off, or you'll get a bellyful, I swear it!"

Her mainsail began to come around—too late, ha ha! Her sternmost gun fired, spurting its load into the wide blue never.

"Drop them colors and raise our own! Mr. Peebles, cast off the canvas screens!" I held up my hand lest he fire too soon. The Stars and Stripes snapped open in the breeze. "Now! Fire!"

We gave them a "bellyful" of our own—four of them. The canister on top of grape on top of round shot from the three long guns on the larboard side knocked a shower of splinters off the *Shearwater*'s taffrail, and the carronade's load of chain tore a wonderful big hole in her gaff mainsail. But even before the smoke cleared, a group of men was popping off at me with muskets from her stern.

A ball buzzed past my head. Out of the corner of my eye I saw Bob and his mate swinging down from aloft. The cutter's side was coming around toward us.

"Mr. Peebles, clear his quarterdeck! Leave her hull be, damn it!"

Bob and his mate lit on the deck with a slap of bare feet. "Beat you!" said Bob. "Didn't," said his mate. And then the muskets fired again, and Bob's head splattered like a dropped pumpkin.

The carronade roared and the musketeers vanished. Somebody aboard the *Shearwater* was tarnal concerned about something—even through the ringing in my ears, I could hear 'em hollering. Then the three-pounders popped off at once and I couldn't hear again.

"Hold your fire! Gundy, what're they saying?"

He shrugged his shoulders up to his ears. "Blaamed if I know, zur."

The *Shearwater* fell off to leeward, her sails flapping. Her rudder wandered back and forth.

"Follow her around," I said, and Gundy kept us turning in a slow circle to larboard. We had to come over onto the starboard tack and gather a little more way to keep on her stern, but no one aboard her seemed to be paying us any mind.

Our gun captains stood with their fists in the air to show that their pieces were ready for firing. "Shall I give 'em another, sir?" said Peebles.

"No."

Whatever the Shearwaters were doing, it wasn't minding her sails. A weird roaring rose from her. There was something so all-fired unholy about it that I jumped up on the rail to have a look. Sailors ran around her upper deck, not trying to brace around to bring their guns to bear on us or get out from under our guns, but pointing down into the hold at a horde of black men swarming up from below. A couple of sailors lay slumped beside her wheel; it turned idly as the passing swells played against her rudder.

Before I could think about it, I said, "Bring us alongside, Gundy! Touch and hold her!" I ran forward, calling, "Boarders to me! To me, Mr. Horne! Boarders away!"

Tomahawk's bow scraped across the cutter's starboard quarter. I scrambled up onto her quarterdeck with my boys behind me, Horne with his broadax, and Bob's mate with blood and tears on his face and a cutlass in either hand, and all of us shrieking like Pawnees . . . And we all stopped at once, amazed by what we saw. There weren't just black men but women, too, most of them naked, and all of them beating the Shearwaters with fists, buckets, the loose chains on their manacles—whatever weapons lay at hand.

"Mr. Horne, secure the wheel. You others, clear the quarterdeck."

In a sudden weird quiet, the Africans laid off throwing Englishmen overboard and looked at us. I wondered what John Paul Jones would've done; and then, like the voice of tarnal salvation rumbling out of the heavens, it come to me:

"Run like hell, boys!"

The Tomahawks flooded back over the rail into the schooner, but Horne was too far away, too close to the mob. As he turned to run they knocked him down. There was nothing for it—I raised my death's-head sword and ran screaming into the crowd. With a rasping shriek, Bob's mate ran in beside me. The mass of people parted like a single being, and then engulfed us.

Hands grabbed at my hair, my clothes. Hands closed on my blade. I yanked it free, and there was gore on the blade. I saw a bloody black hand waving a blue jacket. The crowd surged, taking me with it like the tide. I saw a naked white man. I guessed him to be Bob's mate, but his head was gone. And then a powerful arm hooked around my waist and flung me toward the stern rail. I rolled on the deck and there was Horne, grabbing me again, hauling me to my feet, and the mob melted away foreward, running down more of Agnell's men.

Horne and I goggled at each other, astonished to be alive, and then vaulted over the rail together.

As the cutter fell away to leeward, men and women, black and white, living and dead, dropped into the sea or fell fist and tooth on each other. The wind had kicked up considerable, and we thrashed along to windward; and then the *Breeze*—which I am ashamed to say I had forgotten about—tore by at long pistol-shot off our starboard bow. She had her guns run out, and we didn't have so much as a peashooter ready on that side. On her quarterdeck, Peter stood with his arm raised as if about to give the command to fire. He stared at me.

"You! Peter Wickett!" I shouted.

He swept off his hat, and his face twisted in the grimace that passed as his smile. "Hello, Matty! Fancy meeting you here!"

"Heave-to, Peter!"

He laughed. "In this blow? I dare not." He glanced over his shoulder at the *Clytemnestra*, tearing along toward us with her twelve-pounders showing. "My work here is done. You'll forgive me if I don't stop to chat, but I have urgent business elsewhere."

"I've been sent to bring you back, Peter."

"'Always catch a man before you hang him,'" he called, quoting Whipple. "Perhaps some other time. I do believe that cutter needs—" And with that he was out of shouting range.

But he wasn't out of shooting range. "Permission to run out and fire, sir?" said Peebles.

The *Clytemnestra* was taking in sail and heading to close with the *Shearwater*.

"No. Run the guns in and secure them. Gundy, bring us alongside the cutter again."

The *Shearwater* fell helplessly down toward Anegada. The setting sun cast a golden light on her untended canvas beating itself apart in the blustering wind. The fighting had stopped, but no one moved to check her course toward the reefs of Anegada; white caps broke over the sunken rocks and coral ahead, but I didn't guess there was anyone left alive on board that knew how to sail her.

Three times we crept close enough for Horne to heave a line, and three times it fell into the sea. On the fourth try a man caught it, but a surge tore it from his hands. Soaked with spray, his face twisted with fury or tears, Horne hauled the dripping line in and coiled it for another heave.

The *Clytemnestra* loomed up on the far side of the cutter, riding far more steadily in the seas than we could. A shirtless ape of a man in her larboard mainchains swung the belaying pin on the end of his line in a slowly widening circle and then heaved it across. A black man in the *Shearwater* caught it—but instead of hauling it in, he tied it around the rail. A midshipman in the frigate shouted from an after gunport, pointing behind him where men would be waiting on the gun deck with the other end of the hauling-line made fast to the large towing-cable, ready to pay it out like lightning when the order came; but the black men in the cutter didn't understand what they needed to do. Or maybe they couldn't understand each other—some were trying to haul the line in, while others pushed them away, pointing at the knot. The

Clytemnestras heaved the end of the cable overboard and pantomimed hauling the line in, but the seas sent the frigate one way and the cutter the other. The heaving-line snapped.

"Close her, Gundy," I said. "I'm going to jump."

"Zur!" He pointed downwind toward Anegada, where surf climbed the reef in booming white towers.

Horne shouldered Gundy aside. His coat was torn, and he was missing a shoe, and his face was a welter of scratches. "Please, sir, let me go."

We were on the verge of arguing about it when the *Clytemnestra* fired a gun across us. On her quarterdeck, Captain Sir Horace Tinsdale, in his workaday coat, looked strangely small without gold braid and epaulets. He lifted a speaking trumpet.

"Stand clear! That cutter, sir, and all in her, is His Majesty's property."

And he was welcome to her. "All hands, Mr. Horne," I said. "'Bout ship."

"But—but you can't just leave her, sir!" He looked across at the Africans in the cutter.

I looked at them, and I looked at Horne with his skin as black as a coal bin, and I looked down at my brown hands; and I looked across at Sir Horace, standing with one pale hand on his hip and never doubting he would be obeyed.

My hatred for Agnell and the murderers was gone. I didn't know why I'd come. I turned away. "All hands, ready about," I said again, and the Tomahawks ran to their stations. I heard the cutter hit the reef, but the cries were lost in the wind.

Once we were clear of Anegada, I took a few minutes for an unpleasant task that still needed doing. I hove us to and pointed to the yawl we'd taken aboard off Birds Island. "Mr. Horne," I said, "get that boat in the water."

Horne gave me a ferocious look, his head jutting forward, his wild braids snaking around his shoulders in the wind. No land or ship lay close enough to be fetched safely by boat, and the men who made whatever trip I had in mind would have a wild time of it.

Before he could defy me, I said, "Did I mumble, Mr. Horne? Get the yawl in the water."

"Sir—"

"You got a better idea, Mr. Horne?"

"No, sir." With a troubled look he turned away, cupping his hands around his mouth and shouting, "All idle hands! Man the stays. Walk away with the stays—so! Lower away of all!" The yawl jounced as it touched water.

"Now," I said, "fetch me Morris and Manson."

"Aye?" said Manson, eyeing the boat as it bobbed and skipped in the waves.

"That yawl belongs to you. You're going to get in it."

"Here now! Yer wouldn't give up a good pair of sailormen. Yer promised us safety!"

"I promised I wouldn't turn you over to the Royal Navy nor anyone else, and I aim to keep that promise. Now get in."

He looked up at the clouds rolling down the wind, and looked over the side at the roiling sea. "We won't do it—we'll drown!"

"Not if you're the sailormen you say you are. I ain't of a mind to drop you ashore with dry shoes. Now, ups-a-daisy. In you go."

"Sweet Christ, yer wouldn't," cried Morris. "I'll sign the articles. Yer can use two good topmen, sure!"

The wind moaned in the shrouds. The air was wet with spray or rain. The Tomahawks began to edge in closer, but whether to stop me or help me, I didn't know. Either way, I couldn't give them time to commit themselves. Once they acted in concert without me, they'd be beyond my control.

"I won't have skulking dogs in my crew!" I pointed to windward. The wreck of the *Shearwater* hung on the reefs of Anegada. I could see people moving on her, jumping into the surf and not coming up again. Beyond the island the frigate labored. "Look, the *Clytemnestra*'s bearing up. She'll be heading this way. Make up your mind, man—the boat or a hanging."

"What about Jakes?"

"He stays. You don't have much time."

The yawl strained at its tackle, skipping off the top of the waves and slamming against the *Tomahawk*'s side. Another moment and its wales might get stove in.

"But it's murder, sir," said Morris.

A mutter ran through the crowd.

Manson raised his hands. "Lads," he cried, "will yer stand dumb whilst we are assassinated by a bloody tyrant?"

Jakes hobbled forward, the clanking of his irons filling the sudden silence. "Down with the bloody tyrant!" he shouted, to my horror. But then he continued, "Three cheers for *liberty,* and bugger King George!"

Huzzahs all around, except for Manson and Morris.

The last I saw of them, they were pulling at their oars for all they were worth. Manson spared a moment to shake his fist at me before a wall of rain hid him from sight.

SIXTEEN

It was too late to take refuge in Drake's Bay, the sheltered pool encircled by the eastern group of the Virgin Islands. Closehauled on the port tack, we clawed off the line of islands that lay to leeward till we had passed safely south of Saint Croix. Then we lay to under the close-reefed gaff mainsail and steadied her with a goose-winged topsail—made up snug on the windward side and with the lee clew set—taking the seas on the larboard bow. We drifted downwind that way, but now we had a good six hundred miles of open water under our lee.

Horne rigged the tiller with relieving tackles, and the Tomahawks stowed every bit of equipment below that could be gotten below and lashed it all down taut. We ran the long guns out—if we needed them in this weather it would be on short notice—and lashed them fast with canvas covers over their tompions and touch-holes, and double-lashed the carronade to the deck. We roused out a spare lantern to read the compass card by. We rigged lubber lines to give the watch on deck something to hang on to and as a guide for the helmsmen when they couldn't see aught else to steer by, and we spread tarpaulins in the lower weather rigging to give the watch on deck some shelter from the wind and wet. Wooden wedges lay ready by the chocks to secure the rudder in case the tiller broke or the relieving tackles snapped, and Horne roused out a spare tiller bar and placed it by the helm. We unshipped the anchor cables and got the ends inboard, and packed the hawsepipes with greased oakum and pounded wooden plugs into the ends. We stretched canvas covers over the hatch gratings, and nailed wooden battens over all to hold them shut, leaving an after corner of the main hatch open for ventilation and so the watches could come and go. The topmen labored aloft, sending down whatever wasn't necessary—having our topgallants and fore-topmast aboard was a good head start—and rigging preventers on the weather side of the yards, and doubling any gear that might be carried away, and making sure all loose ends of line and sail were tucked in tight against the wind. Then I sent the watch below to their hammocks, there to lie in the shrieking darkness and wonder if I'd drown us all.

In a rare moment when I found time to snatch a few minutes below, I drifted in a kind of waking sleep, staring back at Greybar staring down at me from on top of my clothes rack. The storm wouldn't last long, I thought. But it lasted three days, and on its heels followed another blow worse than the first, and then another worse than that. During the brief lulls between them we worked to windward, hoping to make Saint Kitts or Dominica or any of the other British islands open to us. After two weeks of battering and our water running low, I even considered Guadeloupe, the big island where the French stowed captured Americans, but the gales came howling across from Africa again and *Tomahawk* swirled across the sea like a rat in a millrace.

The wind dropped away on the Ides of October and left us tossing in the middle of the Caribbean. Occasional gaps appeared in the writhing clouds, showing the sun by day and the stars by night. That was the natural order of things, and my sextant told me our position between the poles—fifteen degrees and some minutes north—but I had no way of knowing what our precise rate of drift had been. We might be far away at sea or about to fetch up on the swampy shores of the Yucatán.

Despite the tempest and the misery, life and routine continued in their course. We even found time for punishment.

"It's hardly a flogging offense, Mr. Peebles," I said. The wind had dropped but the sea still sloshed and slapped against the hull.

"But sir! He was smoking below decks!"

"Well, what of it? It's been tarnation wet out, you know. No harm done, was there?"

His lip quivered. "No, sir. But you said you'd flog any man that smoked below decks and break his pipe, too."

"I did? I never."

"You did, sir. Back when Mr. Horne first showed you where the powder is stored."

"Oh, that's right. Well, didn't he put his pipe out when you told him?"

"Yes, sir. But he laughed when he did it."

I felt sick to my stomach. "So you said you'd see him flogged, I expect."

"Yes, sir."

I took a turn up and down the weather rail, hands clasped behind me. I'd never ordered a flogging before, but I guessed it was something I'd have to experience sooner or later. I didn't see how I could get out of it, anyhow. Peebles was firm, and discipline required that I back him up.

"I said he'd have a dozen, sir."

"Very well, Mr. Peebles. Call the hands to witness punishment. But just so you know—" I leaned close so only he could hear me. "I'm not flogging him for smoking. I'm flogging him because you said he'd be flogged."

With the Tomahawks toeing the line along the starboard rail, Horne led Hawkins to the upended grating and lashed his wrists to it. The big bosun, so recently a bosun's mate and used to being his captain's whip hand, took the cat out of the bag and ran his fingers through the white whipcord strands. He held his hand out, palm up, to show me that he hadn't concealed any red ochre or anything else that might look like blood. I knew he wouldn't show mercy on any man he was required to punish, but tradition must be observed.

"Off hats! Carry on, Mr. Horne."

Horne slowly reared back his powerful arm and brought it round in a smooth arc. The strands cracked against Hawkins's broad shoulders and left a red swath of closely spaced welts.

I nodded at Peebles, standing an arm's length away from Hawkins and Horne.

"One," he said.

Horne swung again, laying a fresh line of welts alongside the first. The cords in Hawkins's neck stood out as he strained to keep his mouth shut.

"Two," said Peebles.

Again Horne swung his arm, and this time little dots of blood welled up in the streaks.

"Three," said Peebles, a little less crisply this time.

Hawkins stood spraddle-legged, his head hanging. His broad shoulders twitched, the way a horse's withers do while it's waiting for the switch. Horne reared back and laid another stripe across his back.

"Four," gulped Peebles.

Horne laid in the fifth stroke sidearm. The whistling strands scattered a mist of blood across Peebles's face. "Fi— five," he said, like his stomach was galloping. He took a step back.

"As you were," I roared. Pale beneath the spatter, he resumed his position.

Horne combed out the wet strands with his fingers and laid in again. He did it with the full strength of his arm, as duty required.

Peebles's eyes bulged as he lunged for the rail. He hung there, his legs twitching as he puked. I felt like joining him.

Hawkins had raised his head to stare dully at him.

"Punishment completed, I think, Mr. Horne," I said. "On hats and dismissed."

The morning after the flogging, Simpson threw a bucket of rotten turnip ends into the wind. It was a lubberly mistake and might've been laughed off if he'd born the brunt of it, but Horne and I happened to be walking by; the wind caught the mess and splattered it against our legs. It had to have been an accident. I was tempted to shrug it off with a rebuke, but I hated turnips. The watch on deck stopped their work to see what I would do about it. A few of the ex-Columbias nudged each other and grinned.

I contemplated my spattered boots. My stomach churned at the thought of ordering up another flogging so soon.

Horne coughed quietly into his fist. I raised an eyebrow at him.

"Flogging the man will do no good," he muttered.

"He's a nation old enough to know better," I shot back.

He nodded unhappily. "But if the people need an example, sir, there's Hawkins still in his hammock."

I spun on my heel. "For shame, Simpson," says I. "That's a sojer's trick, and a sojer you shall be. Mr. Horne, give this man Marine duty."

American Marines did no work at sea beyond standing sentry. A sailor who'd never seen Marines in action might be forgiven for thinking they were shirkers, "in everyone's mess and no one's watch," as is said. Howsomever it may be, custom had made *sojer* one of the worst insults that could be heaped on a sailor. Horne set Simpson to marching up and down the rolling deck with a handspike on his shoulder for a musket. The ex-Columbias continued to grin, but now they grinned at him, not me. The ugly mood disappeared, as if blown away by the wind.

At last the clouds broke up and the steady trades returned. Our longitude no longer mattered much. Finding hospitable land was simply a matter of putting us on the known latitude of any number of English islands to the east until I sighted land. But I had other plans.

Morning four days later found us off Birds Island. It was a tidy piece of navigating, if I say it myself, but I allow we would've arrived sooner if the topgallants of a frigate away off in the northern distance hadn't forced us to detour south before making our offing. She'd had a French look about her that I misliked.

After a circumnavigation of the low heap of sand convinced me that it had remained uninhabited in our absence, we dropped anchors fore and aft in the little cove. The stores had not been touched, but best of all was a big feed of turtle eggs that Doc slung up for us. Water was still short, but there was a good deal of it in the disinterred casks, stinking and soupy with algae though it was. Allowing it to be mixed with the vinegary wine disguised the disagreeable flavor of both somewhat, and the men pronounced the "punch" more wholesome and beneficial than its constituent ingredients taken alone. And then, while digging up some of the cached stores, a party discovered a wooden shaft in the sand—the remains of a well. Once Horne had repaired it, it yielded a small but regular quantity of drinkable water. I raised the ration to three-quarters and had the excess put into casks.

Once I'd had Horne set a couple of barrels of water aboard, he and Gundy had things so well in hand that there really wasn't much for me to do except keep Peebles out of mischief; but I hated to ruin the men's fun and his education, and I let him run loose. Our little hump of weed and sand was small enough that I could walk across it, and up and down it, and best of all around it, bathing my bare feet in the waves, and still be close enough to keep an eye on things and answer questions. Sticking to the shoreline also got me out from under the birds, mostly.

If sand is what you're looking for, Birds Island has a leg up on most places. As I walked around the leeward tip I felt like every windward inch of me was getting scrubbed with a wire brush. By the time I'd gained the weather gauge, I was surprised to have any hide left.

But it was a glorious day. The Caribbean melded from sugary white to pale green to a piercing blue to deepest lapis as it stretched away to the unbroken horizon. Despite its loneliness, or maybe because of it, the island was a busy place. Birds, crabs, and who knew what all had left their thousands of tracks where the waves hadn't reached yet. And here were some tracks that reminded me that I'd forgotten to eat my dinner: the digs and drags left by a turtle's flippers and shell as it returned from burying its eggs before dawn. The marks disappeared at the water's edge, and a while later I saw a leopard-spotted three-footer not a dozen yards offshore, flapping solemnly along with its armored fins. I thought of turtle soup, rich with Madeira and gooey with that stuff from under the shell, and proper turtle steaks and roast—a Chesapeake terrapin will give it a run for its money, but a sea turtle has got your snapper beat to hell and back, as far as I was concerned, and is a much more agreeable beast as well. You won't find a more harmless and obliging fellow as a sea turtle. Set on his back and doused regularly with seawater, he'll keep himself fresh for weeks. I made a note to myself to have the night watch catch us a couple.

But I guessed maybe I was enjoying my laziness too much. Here we were, blessed with both the opportunity and the necessity for hard work, and it wouldn't be right to waste it. I rubbed my hands and laughed at the pleasant thought of rousing out all the *Tomahawk*'s stores and guns, laying her on her side on the beach, and cutting and scraping and burning away the weeds from her hull.

I looked to the sun. The day was getting old, but there was always tomorrow. Horne would be pleased. Bosuns and first lieutenants were demons for making men work. I could just see his face. "Let's scrape her clean and bream her," I'd say, and he'd reply, "Aye aye, sir," and my work would be done. Command was a joy.

A little sweat wouldn't do Gundy any harm, neither. He'd been getting a little too full of himself and could benefit from some healthful exercise. I glanced around to see where he'd gone and was surprised to see the old rascal astride the *Tomahawk*'s main topsail yard, gone aloft to bathe his beard in the light of the evening sun, for all I could guess. I walked back down the beach and had myself taken aboard.

"Mr. Horne!" says I, climbing over the rail. "Are you in? You there," I said to Kennedy, knowing full well he wouldn't understand me at all, "tell Mr. Horne I've come a-calling. Pray let me present my card, ha ha!" He looked at me like a mouse that had gone looking for cheese and found a cat instead. But then here was Horne, stuffing his long, matted braids into his stocking cap as he came rolling aft and saving the little wild Irishman the embarrassment of a reply. "Mr. Horne," I said, and then Gundy sang out, "Sail ho! Ahoy the deck! Sail ho!"

"Where away and what is she?"

"A point avore the staabard beam, me cabbun." He pointed somewhat north of east. "Looks to be that vrigate us zaw yesterday."

Shit and perdition! If an enemy frigate knew we were here we wouldn't have a chance, except to run away. My heart thumped in my chest, and I forced myself to think. Even if they did know about the island—whoever *they* were—it didn't necessarily follow that they'd be able to find it. Or even that they were French, I thought, getting ahold of myself.

I looked to the west. The sun was orange and already reaching down for the horizon. I'd wanted to load as much of the stores and sellable goods as we could carry, but working after dark was out of the question now. I dasn't risk showing a light.

"Douse all fires, Mr. Horne," I said, as an unformed thought itched in the back of my mind. I grabbed a glass and ran aloft. "Shove over, Gundy."

He scrunched out a short way, and then stopped with the yard clutched between his thighs.

"I said shove over, Gundy. You look as clenched up as a virgin on her wedding night."

He came all over shamefaced. "Wast said as I'd get to like it aloft, zur, but I never did. That's the why of how I've made myself zo useful on deck."

"Then what the tarnal damnation are you doing up here in the first place?"

"Ooh, there be too much blaam work alow, zur."

I turned to stare at him, but he just grinned. He raised his arm and pointed. "There, zur, about handsbreadth to la'board of that babby-rag of cloud."

Once I had it fixed in my glass, I could make out what looked like the topgallants and topsails of the same frigate as we'd seen the day before—and something ahead of her, smaller and hard to make out in the gathering sea-twilight.

"She seems to have a friend." I handed the glass to Gundy.

"I wasn't sure avore, zur," he said, after he'd had a squint. He gave me back my glass. "But small 'un appaars to be a Bermuda sloop."

The sloop's mainsail gleamed suddenly against the darkening sky as she wore around onto the larboard tack.

"She heads zou'east, zur."

"Mmm."

Peter Wickett, leading the French to his island hideaway? But there was any number of similar sloops in the Caribbean, and her present leg would let her fetch Guadeloupe without touching a rope. And yet she could be the *Breeze*'s twin.

And maybe I was being a daisy-pants. For all I knew they were strangers bound for Guiana from New Orleans, with nary a thought that there was an island or a Yankee man-o'-war anywhere around. Or they could have been blown off course by the storms, the same as us. Or maybe they were a British frigate and a prize.

None of which meant the sloop wasn't the *Breeze*. Pirates were fair game for all nations, and maybe Peter's luck had run out.

Something on the sloop caught my eye. There it was again.

"Gundy," I said, handing him the glass, "is the sloop flying colors?"

"Iss, me cabbun. Johnny Crappo over Yankee Doodle."

That answered two questions at once: the frigate was French and had captured the sloop. And now I could make out the cross-shaped repair to the sloop's mainsail. She was the *Breeze* for sure, and that her captors were flying our colors under their own meant they'd taken her as a prize of war, not as a pirate. At least they wouldn't hang Peter; I surprised myself by being grateful for that. But that made my job just a little more difficult. Somehow I must separate the sloop from her escort.

Resting my eyes before peering at the sloop again, I was distracted by a wobbling light on the now dark beach. Before I could say anything, however, Horne had bellowed, "You, douse that light!" and the guilty seaman had hastily blown out the candle in his lantern. And suddenly I had the solution to the problem.

"Gundy," I said, "you're a Cornishman originally, ain't you?"

"Iss, zur, there and abouts."

"And you already told me you know a thing or two about the smuggling trade."

"About matters of moonshine? Aye, zur."

"Know what *jibber the kibber* means?"

He bared the stumps of his teeth in a wide grin. "Ooh arr, zur, 'deed I do!"

From offshore the bobbing lantern looked very much like a ship's lantern—like *Tomahawk*'s own little stern lamp, I thought, as I sat in the jolly boat a few hundred yards offshore. But the motion was still wrong. I put my speaking trumpet to my mouth.

"Handsomely!" The light slowed. "Stea-eady! That's *well* your light! Let it sway!"

Proper jibbering—or kibbering, whatever the right word was—required a horse with one of its forelegs tied up and the lantern dangling around its neck, but Doc with his peg-leg unshipped and another man, carrying the lantern on a line between them, might do.

"That be the right way, zur," said Gundy.

I squinted at the wobbling glow on the dark beach, convinced at last that it might actually deceive someone, as for instance a French frigate captain tearing down on what he mistook for another American prize. The moon wouldn't be up for hours yet. Even then it would be only a sliver; and with the cloud cover, the surf and sand did not shine too much.

"Give way." Kennedy and O'Lynn rowed us over to the *Tomahawk,* and I sent them back to the beach. "Make sail," I called as I climbed over the rail. "All hands to make sail! D'you hear the news, there? We're off to hunt Johnny Crappo."

Most of the Tomahawks were ashore with Horne, floating the twenty-four-pounder carronades on water-cask rafts around to the weather side, the reef side, of the island. In addition to Peebles, I took with me Eriksson the Swede and Wright the Boston water-only man for working aloft, the waisters Simpson and Hawkins for hauling the halyards and manning the braces, and old Gundy for steering. They were all I'd need to be successful. If I failed . . . well, that was about as far as my head would let me think.

I regretted my comment about hunting as soon as my lips had stopped flapping. It began to rain, and the island soon lost itself in the gloom, but I had embarked on this course of action and had to back up my mouth with results. Figuring that the sloop and frigate had miscalculated how far west they had come and were hauling to windward along the island's line of latitude, I stood to the east and as north as we could point the schooner, climbing up the wind toward Guadeloupe.

We saw no lights that night. We didn't see anything at sunup, neither, and I was toying with the idea of giving it up, when we come across a Yankee bark that'd lost her main-topmast and smashed her compass during the last storm. When her skipper come aboard with his papers, I gave him his present position and a glass of whiskey.

"Eighteen days—I say, eighteen days out of British Honduras with a load of mahogany," he boomed in a voice you probably could've heard halfway to Jamaica. "Y'ever deal with them pirates? That's what them woodcutters are on that coast, y'know. Pirates." He drained his glass and set it hopefully on my desk. "Name's Lamb. Don't take me for a *sheep*, though—that'd be *shear folly*. That's a joke, son. Say, you're a little young, ain't ye?"

"There's a French frigate prowling hereabouts, Captain Lamb," I said, pouring him another dose. "She got an eight-gun sloop with her. Seen 'em?"

"No, sonny, I aren't seen 'em," he retorted. "I wouldn't be here by myself if I had, now would I? And I don't intend to wait around for 'em, neither." He wiped the tobacco juice off his beard with his sleeve and shook his head. "You're sorrowful ignorant to be looking for unnecessary trouble. Damn ye for a dog, why don't ye escort me to a safe harbor?"

I looked at him wasting my good corn. He had more men and guns than I did. "I mean to catch that frigate."

"And when ye go fishing—" He stopped to laugh. "And when ye go fishing, do ye use yourself as bait?"

I laughed along with him. "Pretty much. What's it to you?"

A calculating look came into his eye. "Ye'll not be needing your provisions for much longer."

"I wouldn't be doing this if I thought I was going to fail, Cap." I drank off a dram while I thought. It was in my orders to protect American commerce and treat the vessels and people of all nations with civility and friendship. I was pretty sure that was a direct quote from the Secretary. "What do you need?"

"Why, I—" Suddenly he put his hand on my arm. "Look, sonny, I aren't so low as to do ye that way. I was only fooling."

"*I* ain't," I said. "I calculate I can give you a barrel of pork and another of water. Want 'em or not?"

"Well, now, the water'd be grateful. And a little pork, flour, anything ye can spare. But don't do yourself short, son."

Eriksson ran a whip up to the mainyard, and Simpson and Hawkins pulled up their britches and spit on their hands by way of getting ready to hoist the barrels aboard the bark. I watched the first barrel settle on her deck and listened to the earnest voices—*handsome does it, lads, handsome does it*—and suddenly I wanted to take my jackknife and slash the hoist and stave the bark's deck in, because they could go home and be safe while we had to go see someone get dead. At last the second barrel stood on Lamb's deck, his crew cast off the tackle, and we got it in.

"All hands to make sail," I said. "Sheer off, Gundy." We got our courses and topsails abroad, and as we dropped down the wind, Lamb gathered his little flock together at the rail. Their voices came along the waves in Paine's "Adams and Liberty," the burden of which runs:

> *And ne'er may the sons of Columbia be sla-aves,*
> *While the ea-earth bears a pl-a-a-a-ant,*
> *or the sea*
> *ro-o-olls*
> *its waves.*

Its tune was stolen from "To Anacreon in Heav'n," which somebody must've left lying around, as it is a miserably unsingable air, and using the tune of an English drinking song for a patriotic hymn is just plain simple anyway. Worse, it reminded me of Peter in Le Cap. I was about to shout across that Lamb could stow his song and be damned, but then I saw Gundy and Eriksson and even Wright the water-only man were standing unnaturally straight, like it was an anthem or something, and I could swear I saw tears in their eyes. My eyes stung, too, but maybe it was just the wind.

"Mr. Peebles," I said. "Let's give 'em a salute."

He grinned all over. Puppies weren't in it. "Please, sir, may I use the carronade?"

"Why not. Simpson and Hawkins, rig the fire engine."

The merchant sailors must've gotten their hats cheap, they way they throwed them in the sky and cheered their heads off when the carronade flashed and boomed. I got to say, though, I was glad for all the smoke, elsewise I'd have had to find some other excuse to put my handkerchief to my eye.

"Come abaat an' fetch the island, zur?" said Gundy.

"With a sendoff like that? How you talk. Put her on the la'board tack and steer sou'east."

Maybe the frigate and the sloop were bound for Guadeloupe. Maybe they weren't looking for Birds Island. Maybe they were there already, and the Tomahawks all taken prisoner. *Maybe you're an idiot,* I told myself in disgust. *And maybe we should go back and see,* I shot back. My head hurt.

We wore around to the southwest at noon, put ourselves on a pleasant beam reach to the northwest at four bells, and bore southwest again at the beginning of the first dogwatch, making a series of long, two-hour legs on the way back to the island. I had give up expecting to find the frigate anymore, and the more I thought about it, the less I wanted to find her. *Let them be heroes as want to,* I thought; *that's my motto.* We made better time with the wind abaft the beam, and I shot the sun each time to fix our position, chalked up the result on the slate, and marked our movements with the pegs and spunyarn on the traverse board.

At the beginning of the second dogwatch I again turned to the northwest, intending to make one last leg till the ocean twilight had faded into full dark; then I would bear away westward, making for the island and so admit defeat. I was wearing Juge's hat, with its curled brim and jaunty red-and-white plume, and I toyed with it while I thought, tipping it to the back of my head like I was cheerful about something and then shoving it forward, low on my brow to shade my eyes from the sun and maybe even make me look ferocious. Juge never gave up while he lived; but what could I do? It was a good joke that Peter had saved himself by getting captured—assuming he was still alive, of course. And it was a good thing he spoke French, too, as he'd have to avoid English-speaking countries once hostilities ceased.

And then I had a pleasant thought. Maybe my job was done after all, and the enemy had unwittingly saved me an ocean of trouble. All I had to do now was pick up the rest of the Tomahawks and head for home with the more valuable goods from the island. Mr. Campbell, the naval agent in Baltimore, would be pleased to see what I'd brung him. I'd have to question Doc more closely before I left, too. If Peter had hidden the barrels of silver coin on the island, the one-legged cook might know more than he'd been telling. I wondered what eight barrels of dollars would look like, poured out in a big shiny heap on the floor in the front parlor of my very own house. A man could live pretty comfortable on that much money. And that wasn't even counting the gold that was supposed to be buried under the British grave. And then I touched Juge's hat again and realized those things didn't bear thinking about. Wrong is wrong, and no two ways about it.

Eriksson at the masthead saved me from finding a way around that by singing out, "Sail ho! Deck dere, two sail!"

"Where away?"

"T'ree points off sta'board bow, sir. It's dot frigate and a friend."

Shit and perdition! I ran aloft to see for myself. There she was, sure enough, bearing maybe just a point west of north, with the sloop ranging before her as they reached southeast on the larboard tack. And then, to a signal that I couldn't see, they both turned west—away from us, but on a course that kept the weather gauge for themselves and intersected our own.

"We been spotted, sir," said Eriksson, astride the yard beside me.

I rebuked his familiarity by not bothering to reply. I was thinking, anyway, and not liking what I was thinking. With the wind on her quarter and enough sea room, the frigate would inevitably sail us under; her loftier sails, deeper keel, and longer hull would all conspire to see to it. *But I ain't a-gonna* give *you enough sea room, Johnny Crappo.*

"All hands ahoy," I called. "Ready about!" I let myself down the windward backstay and looked at the compass and traverse board. "Come four points to larboard, Gundy. Steer due west. Mr. Peebles, give 'em a hand at the braces."

I hauled out the sextant. While I shot the sun, burning low in the west, I said, "Gundy, how much daylight you reckon we got left?" I knew the time of sunset to the second, according to the tables, but sunset and darkness are different things.

He chewed his teeth for a moment before deciding. "An hour, zur. Maybe a little maar avore the daark of evenen."

The wind veered south. It didn't help nor hinder the frigate any, her with her lofty square sails, but with the wind astern of us we had to get in our fore-and-aft sails and shake out the square foresail. She rode easier that way, with less danger of driving herself into the back of a sea. The wind picked up, too, and we bore away with both sheets aft.

"Eriksson," I called aloft, "how do they lie?"

"Dey gather on us, sir."

I carried a sextant up with me, but even before I took my sightings I could see Eriksson's eye had told him true. The frigate and sloop were forereaching on us; more importantly, they were edging in with us, too. I noted the angles of their masts to their heading, which would tell me their exact course, and their positions and headings relative to our own. I went down the backstay again. It would need retarring soon, the way I was mistreating it.

I took another look at the traverse board and slate. "Call me if anything interesting happens," I said, and went below to strap on my sword with its steel *memento mori* on the hilt. "Remember you must die," I whispered. Not that I expected to stick anybody with it, but a sword's handy for pointing at things.

All fires were out, and I squinted at the charts in the dimness of the cabin. I was sure as certain about our position, and my sightings told me theirs. If the frigate continued on her present course, she would pass harmlessly by the island. I needed to get her farther north. But we couldn't hope to fight her by ourselves, and tangling with the sloop at the same time was right out. My duty was simple, then, and so was my plan: catch-as-catch-can and no holds barred. It's always the bigger man that insists on a clean fight, anyway.

It was getting tarnal gloomy out by the time I went on deck again, but there would be enough light to see by for a little while yet. The sloop was near, but still under the frigate's lee, like a dog that couldn't be trusted to run free. They were both still out of gunshot, but too close for comfort. There was an orange flash and then a distant pop as the frigate fired a gun on the near side.

"He wants us to heave-to, sir," said Peebles.

"Oh, say it ain't so."

He thought about that. "Any reply, sir?"

"Yes," I said. "Hoist *X-Y-Z*. Let 'em stick it in their pipes and smoke it if they can."

I hopped up on the weather rail and hooked an elbow through the main shrouds. *"Shipmates,"* I called, and then I stopped, surprised by the power of my own voice. Brass trumpets weren't in it; and here I'd expected it to come out a squeak. But everyone was looking at me.

"Shipmates, I aim to close the sloop. They'll think we mean to board 'em with our mighty horde, but you'll be sad to hear we ain't a-going to oblige 'em." They gratified me with a laugh. It weren't much of a laugh, as laughs go, but all six of them joined in. "Instead we're going to give 'em a bellyful of iron."

A mutter ran through the little crew. "We'll pay 'em in full," said Simpson.

"Nah, mate," said Hawkins, giving him an elbow in the ribs. "Let's give it 'em free, gratis, and wi'out charge."

"Aye, that's the right price," said Wright.

"An' wif in'rest, too," said Hawkins.

"*Compound* in'rest," said Simpson.

"Nay, mate," said Wright. "Compound interest is usury."

"An' what if it is?"

"Iss," said Gundy. "Us'll make they drink it to the dripshams."

"Dot's easy for you to say," said Eriksson. "Speaks anyone English here?"

"Oh, *please* be quiet," said Peebles, putting his hands to his head.

I waited till they minded me again. "And while they're stowing it"—I swept Juge's hat dramatically toward the enemy—"we're going to put a finger in that frigate's eye." Gundy led them in a cheer while I hopped down from the rail and settled my hat firmly on my head.

"Mr. Peebles," I said over the hoo-roar, "load chain on top of round shot and run the guns out. Let's show 'em how Yankee Doodle do. Er, does." I hoisted the colors myself.

The frigate proceeded calmly under battle sails beyond the sloop, disdaining to reinforce her stays and slings with chain, screened by her escort but imperturbably lethal nonetheless. As if by clockwork her larboard gun deck ports opened, and a dozen large guns poked their snouts out. Four lighter guns, nine-pounders maybe, appeared along her fo'c's'le and quarterdeck bulwarks.

We shook out our fore-and-aft sails, braced the topsails right around, and hauled our way up on the larboard tack toward the sloop as she edged down to meet us. She was *Breeze,* without a doubt—she that had been the pirate sloop *La Brise* when the *Rattle-Snake* took her in the Windward Passage last spring, and lately the *Suffisant*—with Frenchmen manning her once again.

"Fall not off," I said as our topsails come a-shiver.

Gundy touched her to the wind, pointing her as close as never-no-mind.

The *Breeze* yawed to bring the four guns of her larboard broadside to bear. I could've sworn I seen the handsome Monsieur Corbeau on her quarterdeck, tipping his hat to us in the formal salute, but I was a tad busy right about then and couldn't return the favor.

"Gundy, let her fall off a couple points and show her our teeth. When your guns bear, Mr. Peebles," I said as we came around, "you may—"

"Fire!" he yelled.

The *Breeze* fired at the same time, and the air filled with smoke.

"Stop your vents," Peebles called. "Sponge your guns!" He strutted down the line like a banty rooster, making sure the guns were swabbed clean of any burning residue. "Load your guns!" It was slow going with only four men and him to work three guns and a carronade. *Breeze* put two holes in our mainsail before Peebles could get to "Prime your guns!"

"Mr. Peebles," I called. "When you're finished loading, run 'em out and secure 'em."

"Aye aye—"

His voice was lost in the banging as the *Breeze* fired again. The mainsail jerked as they shot another hole in it. I ran my eyes across the rigging. Nothing important had carried away yet.

"Gundy, I'm going to put her on the starboard tack and give 'em what for. Mr. Peebles, is the carronade ready?"

"Canister on round shot, sir!"

"Good! I'll want you to paste 'em with it in a minute. Ready about! Stations for stays!"

Eriksson and Wright ran forward to ease the jib sheets, and Simpson and Hawkins got ready to haul the fore-and-aft booms amidships.

"Keep her full for stays, Gundy. Ready! Rea-eady! Ease down your helm! Helm's alee!"

Simpson and Hawkins hauled the booms across, keeping the sails full for as long as possible; the fore-topsail came a-shiver and then flattened as the bow swung through the wind.

"Haul taut! Main topsail haul!" We paid off to larboard. "Let go and haul! Haul of all—get it all, there!" Eriksson and Wright braced the fore-topsail around; we filled and drew, and gathered way on the starboard tack.

"Stand by the carronade!"

Peebles was already there with the others, squinting along its short barrel as Eriksson and Wright trained it around. He said something to them, they stood back, and he looked at me with his fist in the air. "Ready, sir!"

"Go it, little man!"

The *Breeze* had turned with us, and we stood broadside to broadside. I had time to note that it really was Corbeau on her quarterdeck waving at me like a ninny in a yacht. And then he fired sixteen pounds of iron into us, and we gave him twelve in change.

Something gave way in the *Breeze*. She flew up into the wind.

"Caught her flat aback, ha ha!" said Wright.

"Stop your vent!" called Peebles. "Sponge! Here, Wright, ply that sponge."

"Gundy, come up a point. Meet her! Simpson, Hawkins, man them braces!"

"Handle your cartridge! Put it into the gun!"

The *Breeze* hauled out her jib to pull herself around on the larboard tack and keep us from raking her.

"Wad to your cartridge," Peebles called. "Dog gone it, handle the rammer—" He looked up at me, his eyes bright in his powder-streaked face. "Sir, I can't traverse enough—"

"Gundy, meet her there!"

I heard Corbeau calling orders in his rich and fruity voice, and then all at once her topsail yard sagged in the slings, her sails commenced to flapping like a loaded clothesline on a windy day, and the air was filled with the horrible groaning of round shot and grape. Our hull shook as something slammed into it, and a horrid shriek rose over the din. One ball ricocheted off the water and bounded up in an arc so lazy that I had time to wonder if it was a twelve-pound ball or an eighteen.

The frigate had fired through the *Breeze.* With her headsails shot away, and no longer balancing her, the sloop rounded on the frigate and lodged herself in her fore shrouds. Axmen in the frigate began hacking *Breeze*'s jib boom away in their eagerness to be at our throats.

The light was nearly gone.

"Gundy, has anything carried away?" First things first.

"Nay, me cabbun."

"We took a hit. I felt it."

"Below, zur."

"Very well. Bring us around—" I looked at the compass in the failing light and glanced at the fluttering dog-vanes. "West by south a half south. Hands to the braces."

We settled safely on our new course, and I could ease up a little. Time to deal with the killed and wounded. "Mr. Peebles, is anyone hurt?"

"No, sir."

"Someone screamed. Who screamed?"

"Dunno, sir. Sounded like it came from below."

"Then get below and look."

I counted noses. All seven of us were accounted for, and all of us standing. Standing around like loobies, that is.

"You, Simpson, light the stern lamp for me. Don't you let too much light show, now. When you're done with that, light that dark-lantern and give it to Wright in the bows."

Peebles ran back up on deck. "We're pierced through and through, sir!"

"Where?"

"Your cabin, sir."

"Are we taking on water?"

"No, sir, but your furniture's all ruined."

"Furniture! You mean my hammock and thunder mug? Glory, what'll I do!"

While they laughed I looked astern. The frigate had disentangled herself from the sloop and was bracing her yards around. And here she came, with the wind on her quarter and whitewater at her forefoot, abandoning her prize in pursuit of us. I stood in the weather shrouds to give them a good look at me. "You'll have sand in your ears before morning, m'sieur!" I shook my fist and patted my rump, and then thumbed my nose for good measure.

"That ain't entirely genteel," I said to Peebles, "but I want to make sure he chases us."

"I have no doubt he will, sir," he said, looking up at me with gleeful terror.

It was full dark now. Lanterns rose to the Frenchman's mastheads, lighting up the several Tricolors flying there—an awful sight, a majestic sight, that was about as cheerful as a damp shroud. Then she sent an iron ball our way with her bow chaser.

"Hey now, time her, Mr. Peebles."

"Aye aye, sir." He stared at his watch in the light of the binnacle until the Frenchman fired again. "Three minutes exactly, sir."

"Very well." She wasn't in range yet, anyway, but she was closing.

She fired again. I watched the white winks on the dark water as the ball skipped along toward us and then sank in the sea.

"Two minutes fifty-six seconds, sir."

I found myself staring at the Frenchman, waiting for the next little spurt of flame. That wasn't the way to do.

"Here, let's have a song," I said. "How about 'The Yankee Man-o'-war'? C'mon, Mr. Peebles, d'ye know that 'un?"

"Yes, sir," he said, and sang in a sweet soprano of John Paul Jones in the long ago:

> *'Tis a song of a gallant ship that flew the stripes and stars,*
> *And the whistling wind from the west-nor'west blew*
> *through the pitch-pine spars,*
> *With her sta'board tacks aboard, my boys, she hung upon*
> *the gale,*
> *On the autumn night we raised the light on the old head*
> *of Kinsale.*

He was interrupted by Wright crying, "There it is, sir, there it is! The island, fine on the starboard bow."

I ran forward to see. There—a hint of a green glow, less than half a mile away, and just above it the orange spark of a lantern. It winked out and then shone again, as Horne closed and opened the shutter of his lantern. Wright flashed back at him and Horne's light went out.

Not time yet to turn away. I went back to the quarterdeck. A ball from the frigate's bow chaser skimmed the sea, near enough to sting the back of my hand with spray. I leaned out over the starboard rail, peering forward. Five hundred yards . . . two hundred . . . I thought I could hear the hiss of the reef.

Another ball came across. With a shriek and a clang it knocked the stern lamp clean away, leaving behind it a tang of hot metal and a ringing in my ears.

That's fine, that's fine. I pressed the heel of my hand against the ripped skin of my cheek. But I wasn't fine. Something was lodged in my face: a smoking shard of brass from the lantern. My mouth was filled with gobbets of seared blood and bits of broken tooth. It didn't hurt yet.

"In the bow, there," I called to Wright. "Show the light again!"

The words came out wrong as ejecta spilled down my chin and throat, but an intermittent glow forward showed that Wright was working the door of his lantern open and shut, open and shut, projecting its beam toward the island and cutting it off again. Two flashes, a pause, two more. Onshore, a bobbing lantern dawned bright.

No need to dowse our stern lantern, it being blown away and all. The frigate would bite at the bait, or she wouldn't. Another ball rumbled overhead, and I clenched my neck and shoulders lest I shame myself by ducking.

"Hard over!"

Tomahawk swung to larboard. I looked over the rail. Great golla mighty, I'd cut it so fine that our wake rebounded from the reef and broke against our side. I looked over my shoulder.

The frigate continued on her course, continued, continued . . . then came shouts and consternation as her crew realized our deception. She threw her rudder over, coming about to larboard. Heartsick, I realized she might make it.

Then Horne fired the carronades in his island battery. For an instant, orange flames lit the beach, the guns, and the men on shore.

The frigate wavered. Her spanker spilled its wind and her headsails hauled her head back toward the reef.

She struck.

Like a pair of dancers in unison, her fore and main-topmasts sagged in the middle, bowing forward, held aloft at first by her rigging and then toppling as inertia carried them along, her topgallant and royal masts still upright but sinking serenely at first before plummeting like huge javelins to her deck, all cascading in a shower of soaring canvas and whipping cordage and sparks from her proud masthead lanterns. Her bow rose, oak and copper shrieking against coral as she crested the reef; then she came to rest, cockeyed and askew, with little pieces of her floating around in the firelight.

Even the wind fell silent.

And then came a great crack that I felt through the sea, through the deck beneath me, as the frigate's back broke under its own weight. Her bow nosed down over the jagged reef and the rest of her slid sternward toward the sea. There was another silence then, a grim, determined silence, as what was left of her crew settled into the business of making their way ashore, backlit by the fires set by her fallen lanterns. In the glow, I saw Tomahawks helping the French matelots across the lagoon between the coral and the sand, hauling in lines from the men still aboard, and setting the dejected survivors down beneath the twin maws of the carronades.

The hump of the island came between us, but I saw the flames rush up the frigate's tarry shrouds, rising into the sky and silhouetting the low island in a halo of fire. Peebles and Gundy were looking to me for orders, but I found myself unable to speak. My mouth hung open and bloody drool slobbered down my shirtfront. The world was turning upside down. How peaceful it would be to sprawl on the sanded white deck, the smooth deck gleaming in the starlight, as the blood oozed out of my face and spread around my head like a gory crown.

"Do 'ee ail, zur?" shouted Gundy. He was hollering like I was away off on a mountain someplace.

"I'm bully!" It came out *Eye boo ee.* I sounded like a monkey. I probably looked like one, too, the way he stared at me.

He pointed toward the beach. "Us got bettermost of the Vrenchmen, zur. I reckon they'll be wantin' to come aboard, an' not for a dish of tay."

We had rounded the reef. Close on the starboard side lay the dark dunes, with the frigate's burning rigging towering up behind. Over the low ridge came Horne and the rest of the Tomahawks, backing up with their muskets at the ready as a mob of Johnny Crappos advanced warily on them. I could even see Doc, hopping along on one leg.

"Edge in."

I couldn't hear my own voice properly, and streaks of pain from the effort of talking clearly dazzled my eyes.

"Tend . . . your guns, Mr. Peebles," I called. "Carronade . . . canister . . . train it around—" I made a circular motion with my hand. "Sta'board."

I went to the rail. "Mr. Horne!" I found if I held my jaw in place I could make it work right. "We're com' for you!"

He turned toward me in the flickering light and waved his cap. Below him, in the cove, the jolly boat shoved off. It was too crowded for rowing, and the men paddled with their hands or pieces of planking. The rest of the Tomahawks bunched up behind Horne on the beach—sailors as a rule don't know how to swim—till he began grabbing them by the scruffs and heaving them into the sea. That set off a splashing stampede in the wake of the jolly boat. A couple of foremast jacks stayed with him, holding the enemy at bay with their muskets, but as the beach emptied of Americans it began to fill with Frenchmen—which it didn't take them long to discover that the retreating Tomahawks had left their muskets in the sand.

A wave of shouts and screams washed over me as my full hearing returned. I heard the whoosh of years-dry wood going up in flames and the squealing groan of the frigate's hull still slipping slowly down the reef. I heard the cries of the dying and the doomed.

Tomahawk's keel shushed along the sandy bottom. "Come la'board a point!" She slithered free. I looked to my lads in the water. Someone heaved them a line and someone caught it, and at last they come pouring over the side.

A shot from the beach buzzed by.

Horne and his last two Tomahawks were in the water, swimming steadily toward us. Then a hand reached up: Horne, climbing into the mainchains. He reached back and pulled the other two men out of the sea.

A musket fired on the beach: first the flash in the pan, then the orange blossom at the muzzle. Another ball flicked past.

"They've found the muskets, sir," called Peebles. He stood at the carronade.

"Thank you, Mr. Peebles."

"Look at the enemy, sir, milling around like lambs in a pen—oh, what a target! Any reply, sir?"

They still had fight in them. It was my duty to destroy them. "No."

"Me cabbun, zur," said Gundy, "what course shull I staar?"

"Any course, I don't care." No, that wouldn't do. I looked at the stars, felt the wind and the loom of the land. "Keep her thus."

Gundy steered us away from the island. I heard another musket shot, but who knows where the ball went. And here was Horne, with his long braids hanging heavy with seawater.

I returned his salute. "Good job, Mr. Horne," I said. *Though you might've saved the tarnal muskets and powder, or throwed 'em in the sea before abandoning them,* I was thinking, when the frigate's magazine exploded with a flash so bright and prolonged that I could see the *Breeze* in its glare, thrashing up from the south toward us with her guns run out. Then came a deep roar that swallowed sound, as if a pair of mighty hands had clapped me over the ears. The hump of the island protected us from most of the shock, but chunks of flaming timber rained down on us.

"Put out them fires! Mr. Peebles, look alive on the sta'board side!"

The *Breeze* had the advantage of us, what with the flames lighting us up from behind, but the clouds had parted and the slender crescent moon had risen. I couldn't see *her,* but . . . *there!*

"Two points to la'board." I could see her bow wave. Good enough.

"Two points la'board, aye aye, zur."

That brought the guns to bear, but the Tomahawks didn't know teacups from pisspots after their unaccustomed bath, and the *Breeze* fired first. The four sparks of her starboard broadside seemed like fairy lights compared with the blazing wreck astern, but the iron they fed us was real enough. Someone forward howled as the shots hit home.

I raised my speaking trumpet. "Mr. Peebles, I could use them guns."

He waved his hat, and I could hear his piping voice: "The long guns, fire!" The thin *crack-crack-crack* of our starboard three-pounders answered the sloop.

I didn't see where the shots went. All that mattered was that the French knew we were shooting back. Maybe some of them would keep their heads down instead of tending to their work.

"You—Simpson and Hawkins—grab them grapnels and get ready to heave 'em. Boarders, now! Boarders, grab you a tomahawk and a cutlass, for we're fixin' to pay a call. Gundy, bring us alongside!" I jammed Juge's hat down firmly on my head. Then I drew my death's-head blade and wrapped the sword knot around my wrist.

We crashed starboard bow to starboard bow, scraping along side by side till we fetched up nose-to-tail. The Frenchmen tried to boom us off with their sweeps, long oars that were too slender for the task. They began to snap as our two hulls surged together. Simpson and Hawkins swung their arms, and our grapnels soared aloft. They fetched their lines in taut and bound us together.

"The carronade—*fire!*" yelled Peebles. Twelve pounds of lead on top of a twelve-pound ball of iron slapped the Frenchmen away from the *Breeze*'s rail.

I set Juge's hat on the deck for safekeeping. Then I was balancing on our own rail, feeling the send of the sea between the schooner and the sloop, listening to the hulls grinding together. I raised my sword. My nostrils filled with the salt of the sea and bitter gun smoke. And then the moment was right—leap now or live in shame—and I was down in the sloop's waist and the Tomahawks poured across behind me.

The short blade of a cutlass came at me out of the dark. My sword arm was up without my thinking about it. The blade ran down mine on the outside. I stepped in and drove my head up into the Frenchman's chin. He fell. Simpson and Hawkins loomed reassuringly on either side of me. I looked for Horne. There—scything his way through the Frenchmen with his broadax and heading for the *Breeze*'s quarterdeck.

"Follow me!" I couldn't hear my own voice in the din. I grabbed Simpson's sleeve, but he sagged to his knees. The Frenchman who'd killed him looked up in terror as Hawkins sprang in front of me and grabbed him by the throat. Hawkins's cutlass swept down, and came up and swept down again, flinging a spray of hot blood through the air. On my right I saw Wright plant his tomahawk in a man's head and then the heaving crowd swallowed him up. I saw Peebles with his dirk in his hand, trying to get past Gundy's restraining arm.

I flailed away in front of me till a space cleared and I ran up to the quarterdeck. There was Corbeau up on the binnacle, waving his sword around, and nobody paying attention but me. I slipped around behind him. He was hollering in French, I didn't hear what. I brandished my sword at the man at the tiller and he ran away. And there I was, all alone with Corbeau, and him with his back to me. I grabbed him by the waistband and yanked.

His britches come right down, which got his attention in a hurry. He shot me a startled look, reached for his britches, and tried to leap away from me all at once, but he got all tangled up in himself and fell smack into Horne's arms. It was a tossup about which was more surprised. They both jerked their faces away from each other, staring.

"Just hold him!"

I jumped to the rail, trying to sort through the halyards in the uncertain light; and then I said the hell with it and swept my sword through them all. The *Breeze*'s colors came tumbling down.

The Tomahawks roared, overwhelming the French crew and herding them forward, and then Frenchmen were dropping their weapons and throwing up their hands. There were a lot fewer of them left than I expected. The Tomahawks ranged through the little crowd, kicking weapons aside and pushing the prisoners into the bows.

Then I heard a squalling, the crowd parted, and O'Lynn emerged from it with a roaring bundle in his arms. "Found the wee nipper behind the windlass, sor," he said, and there with his arms wrapped around the Irishman's neck was little Freddy Billings, the *Breeze*'s smallest boy, hollering that he wasn't a pirate and blubbering fit to drown us all.

And there I was, with my sword in my hand and no one to stick it into. I leaned against the mast, trying not to breathe through my broken teeth. Just the touch of the air on them hurt like sweet bejeebers. O'Lynn clucked over Freddy in Irish and lifted him over the rail into the *Tomahawk* and took him below. Horne handed me a sword.

"Mr. Corbeau's, sir."

"I don't want the blame thing." Horne looked hurt, and I wished I hadn't said it. I slipped my own blade into its scabbard. The bodies along the deck seemed to writhe in the flickering light of the frigate burning over yonder. The faces stared at nothing. I took Corbeau's sword from Horne and threw it overboard.

Corbeau averted his eyes from my oozing jaw and gazed around at his lost command. "Ah, well," he said, playing the philosopher, "such is the way of war, *n'est-ce pas?*"

"I wouldn't know," I said. "We ain't at war. Are the Americans below?"

"This is the question I dread." He squared his shoulders. "I am sorry to say that when we regained possession of our sloop, we transferred our American guests to *La Flamme*—that frigate which you lately have so unceremoniously blown up. Such an unfortunate name." His jaw trembled as he glanced toward the fire in the distance. He swabbed his face with a powder-stained handkerchief, and said, "Your pardon, *monsieur.* I have the grain of gunpowder, perhaps, in my eye."

"You ought to watch where you look then," I said.

Freddy's voice rose up from the *Tomahawk*'s 'tween-decks, wailing that he didn't *want* to get into any durned old hammock, and I nearly ordered him up a spanking till I realized I was just sore at him for being the last of the Breezes. Breezes, Suffisants—whatever Peter had done with which, they were all muddled in my mind. There was a sickening emptiness in my chest. All the fellows—friends, strangers, enemies—all gone in a puff of smoke. At least their families would be spared the shame and expense of a trial, and small comfort that would be. But maybe it *was* a comfort. I'd just as rather not have to watch Peter hang, which is what he might've ended up doing if I had arrested him.

"But what am I saying?" Corbeau tucked his handkerchief into his sleeve. "There are two Americans still in board. I am surprised they have not come up on deck. The last I see him, M'sieur Crouch is on his way to the magazine—"

We stared at each other for a second till we could get our feet going, and then we were both running for the forward hatch. A flash lit up the companionway as we jumped down it—I near about swallowed my heart, expecting to be launched into the forever—followed immediately by a bang, and after a pause a shriek, and then a billow of smoke rising from the narrow passage that led to the sloop's store of gunpowder. Out of the smoke a man staggered. His face was a blackened mess and his hands were gone. His charred tongue worked in the bloody hole of his face, and then he fell to the deck.

He still moved, waving a stump as if to beckon me closer. His breath came out of him in a bubbling squeak as I knelt beside him.

"Peter Wicked," he rasped, so hoarse and faint I could barely hear. He mumbled something else. I bent my head close, but he was dead.

I followed Corbeau back up the ladder and across the deck and down the after hatch into the *Breeze*'s cramped stern cabin. A lone candle flickered on the desk; and at the desk, with a battered calico cat growling by his side and with a pistol in his hand, sat a tall, gaunt man in his shirtsleeves.

Corbeau went to him. "You are well, my friend?"

Peter nodded, looking at me.

"Yes? I will leave you then to the privacy," said Corbeau. "Do not worry if I am to escape," he called as he mounted the ladder. "I consider myself to be once more under the arrest. You will note I never once left M'sieur Wickett's company, even after I am returned to my countrymen."

The right side of Peter's face was stained—with burnt gunpowder, I realized as I leaned forward to look—and blood oozed from a blackened crease in his forehead. Dark speckles surrounded a splintered place in the bulkhead to his left.

"I don't suppose you'd lend me a pistol," he said. He glanced down at the one in his hand and set it on the desk. "There was a great lurching, and I seem to have missed."

He pulled his kerchief out of his sleeve and pressed it against his forehead.

SEVENTEEN

The *Tomahawk* and the *Breeze* lay hove-to abreast of each other along the golden streak cast by the rising sun on the sea. Fine on the larboard bow, the limestone cliffs of Cape Rojo, the southwestern tip of Porto Rico, showed as white patches through the haze. The cape bore northeast by north, distant four leagues, which I'd written down on a piece of paper along with the rest of my instructions.

"The Mona Passage ain't as bad as its reputation, Mr. Peebles," I said. "Just you keep in our wake and no harm'll come to you."

"Aye aye, sir."

I never seen a kid look so small as he did there on the *Breeze*'s quarterdeck. "The weather should be fine for most of the day," I said, "with maybe some rain and a blow commencing along about the second dogwatch." I hadn't tried the Mona Passage before, neither, not on my own, and my only practical knowledge of it was a single memory and what the sailing directions said to expect—namely, light airs in the morning, squalls in the afternoon, and a blow at night. "You don't want to run all the way down to loo'ard of Hispaniola and then have to beat back up through the Windward Passage, do you?"

"I guess not, sir. I expect I hadn't thought of it that way."

"Good man. I've written down your course for you, and Mr. Horne here won't let you come to grief. Ain't that so, Mr. Horne?"

"That's so, sir." If Horne resented being used as a dry nurse for the boy, he had the sense to keep it to himself. Well, tough if he didn't like it, I thought—Peebles's father the congressman would have a word or two with Secretary Stoddert if I missed the chance to let his boy come home with a prize beneath his feet.

"You remember your instructions, Mr. Horne?"

"Yes, sir. Follow you through the passage and rendezvous at Samanà if we get separated."

If they could find it, anyway. "Just follow the coast of Hispaniola nor'west till you come to a long, narrow bay with a fort on the northern headland," I said. "That'll be Samanà."

"Aye aye, sir," said Horne, with just a hint of exaggerated patience, and I remembered too late that we'd sailed past the bay before meeting the Spanish *guarda-costa* off St. John's.

Hispaniola's east coast was all lee shore, but I had to credit even Mr. Peebles with enough sense to stay clear of it. The trick to being a good commander, I was beginning to realize, is knowing when to keep your damn mouth shut; but knowing something and actually doing it ain't always the same thing. "And watch yourself around Hourglass Shoal," I said. "It might get rough there. I marked it on your chart."

Even Peebles had gotten an indulgent look. "We'll be fine, sir," he said. "Don't you worry. And if we meet anyone I'll just stand along, like you said, and not heave-to unless fired upon."

"Unless it's one of our own," I said. No point in getting anyone mad at the kid.

I looked across the way at Corbeau and Peter pacing the leeward side of *Tomahawk*'s quarterdeck. Peter's head hunched between his bony shoulders and his beak poked this way and that as he stalked along with his hands clasped behind his back. Malloy in the *Constellation* was supposed to be cruising somewhere along the north coast of Hispaniola. I hoped to pass him in the dark sometime in the next few days, so I could honestly say I'd been in his neighborhood but hadn't seen him. He might be legally entitled to take possession of the *Tomahawk*, but I didn't aim to give him Peter as well.

I was nearly right on all counts. The light airs and long seas of morning gave way to black squalls and lightning in the afternoon, which in turn gave way to wild blows that night, through which we boomed along under jib and double-reefed fore-topsail, looking lively on deck when it gusted; and morning found us with light airs again, and so on through the cycle till we were well past Samanà—but if we snuck by the *Constellation* on any of those nights, nobody told me about it. We did run right spang into her a couple days later, though, south of the Silver Bank with Old Cape Français bearing south by west through the haze. By the time O'Lynn sang out from the crosstrees that the *Connie* was flying down on us from windward with bunting flanging every which way, and clouds of smoke spurting from her fo'c's'le as she banged away with her bow chaser in case we hadn't got the message, there wasn't nothing for it but to heave-to on the starboard tack. She come plenty fast, too, wearing just about every stitch of cloth she possessed as she swooped down on us.

"What's she flying above her main royal?" I said to Gundy. "The gunner's hanky?"

He squinted at it. "Old woman's smicket, I be thinkin', zur."

"Smicket? Is that the Cornish word for skys'l? Oh, there it goes. And there go her stuns'ls, too." The Connies were tucking and furling faster than a woman with ten kids getting in her laundry in a rainstorm. I looked at Gundy, but he was studiously watching our backed topsail and not meeting my eye. "C'mon," I said, "what's an 'old woman's smicket'?"

He hung his head. "Ah spoke out o' turn, zur."

"No, tell me."

"Smicket be a woman's shift, zur. On account of Cabbun Malloy be called Old Woman behind he back. Ooh look, zur, she be zendin' a boat."

I bet I could travel the world over without finding a man so all-fired sure of my ignorance as Asa Malloy was. I'd've guessed he was at least forty-five, but with the powder he wore in his hair and the flat-faced spaniel he wore tucked under his arm as he paced around the chair he'd plonked me down in, he might've been even older, like a leftover from Revolutionary times—which he was, if truth be told. They'd been his best days, when he'd groveled his way up the staff of one of the Maryland regiments until an exploding gun at Guilford Court House had left him half deaf. He would've saved the world some trouble if he'd chosen to be a schoolmaster instead of a naval officer.

I'd never been in the *Constellation*'s great cabin before, but I didn't guess those lace curtains had been draped across the stern windows last February when old Tom Truxtun had whupped *La Vengeance* in a running battle that only ended when Truxtun got his mainmast shot away, allowing Johnny Crappo to bugger off in the dark after having struck his colors twice. My pal Jemmy Jarvis had been aloft in that mainmast, too, when the whole thing fell in the sea and drowned him. Malloy hadn't had anything to do with it, but—entirely ornery though it was—I still disliked him for having been given the *Constellation*. She was above him. Yes, and I bet that damask carpet hadn't been underfoot neither, when Tom Truxtun had her, all spangled with milkmaids and stinking of dog piss.

"I mislike that sword you are wearing, Mr. Graves," said Malloy.

"Yes, sir. I don't much care for it myself."

He put his hand behind his right ear. "Hey? What's that you say?"

"I said I'm entirely in agreement with you, sir."

"Then what do you mean by wearing it?"

"I'm required to wear a sword, sir, and it's the one I have."

"Well, I mislike it. Is that a *memento mori* on the pommel?"

The sword knot had slipped, revealing the grinning death's-head. "Yes, sir. It's uglier as homemade shit." I wondered how he'd like the arcane Latin mottos engraved on the blade, and the bylaws of the blood cult I'd stolen it from.

He stuck his ear in my face. "Hey? What?"

"I said I don't know what to make of it! Sir!"

"Do not," he said, his finger quivering in my face, "wear that while you are in my ship."

"It's my only sword, sir, and I'll wear it if I want to."

"Say that again?"

"I said I have another one, sir, but I don't know where it's gone to."

"Then you will wear no sword at all. Take it off right this moment, sir, and do not put it on again in my sight, ever."

"I'll take it off for now, sir."

"Eh?"

"I don't want a row, sir." I unslung my belt and scabbard, and laid them across my lap. He had no right to ask it of me, but he could put me under close arrest for so much as sneezing if he wanted. I'd be absolved as soon as I could complain about it to the commodore, but it might be a long several months before that happened, and I dasn't just think of myself. There was still that tarnation Peter Wickett to think of.

Malloy finally stopped pacing and lit on the yellow satin settee, with one knee crossed over the other and the dog in his lap. "You took your time in getting the *Tomahawk* to me."

"Yes, sir." I nodded vigorously. The spaniel wagged his tail at me.

"Why?"

"Commodore Gaswell sent me out to arrest Peter Wickett, sir." I saw his hand coming up to his ear again, and I repeated it louder. The story would be all over the lower decks before long, if the Tomahawks hadn't spread it around already. "He told me to steer clear of you till I'd done that."

He drew back, his fingers to his lips. "He told you to—? Why—I shall write a letter to the Secretary of the Navy about this."

It'd make a change from his usual letters, I thought, in which he was ever careful to point out how much money he was saving the Republic by never firing his guns. His letters were often reprinted for the public, though I doubted it was because he was admired; even newspaper editors have a sense of humor.

"Why ever was Wickett not in irons?" he added.

"I wouldn't slap a pair of darbies on a brother officer, sir. It don't look right."

"Hey?"

"I said, because he's an officer, sir."

Malloy give me a look like he'd been eating lemons soaked in lye. "An officer? He stole a vessel belonging to the United States Navy.

That's hardly the action of a gentleman."

"I didn't say he was a gentleman, sir. I said he was an officer."

"And you also let a Frenchman run around loose! Why ever for, Mr. Graves? How could you countenance it?"

"He's an officer as well, sir, and as he'd given his parole—"

"Parole! He is a prisoner of war who absconded from custody."

"Well, now, I reckon not, sir. He was in the custody of a navy officer, whose movements and actions were not his to question, till the *Breeze* was took by *La Flamme,* at which point he was released from his parole. Mr. Corbeau ain't done nothing wrong, sir."

"Which officer is now safely locked up, no thanks to you," said Malloy. "I shall send him home with that charming young chap, what's his name—Peebles. Won't his father be proud! A congressman or something, isn't he?"

As if he didn't know. The way I calculated it, Old Woman Malloy aimed to get himself in the man's good graces by letting the boy show up not just with the recaptured sloop, but with a traitor under his heel as well. It was a nice little one-up on me. I had to give him that, but I didn't have to like it.

"I don't mean to question your judgment, sir," I said, "but you might want to run it by Commodore Gaswell first."

He gave me another sour look—rotten vinegar weren't in it. "Hey? What's that? Do you presume to offer me advice?"

"No, sir."

"I think you mean to offend, Mr. Graves, despite your backing and filling, pretending innocence while shooting your barbs, but I won't rise to it. You were a promising young navigator, I allow, but never a gentleman. You might still make a good sailing master, was you to learn how to hold your tongue, but you should never have been let to set your foot on the ladder of promotion. Your father is a shopkeeper, isn't he?"

"Distiller and farmer, sir. A congressman once, too."

"*Once* isn't *is.* And now he is parasite, sucking the blood of the common man by selling him cheap liquor."

"Graves & Son Genuine Patent Old Monongahela Rye ain't cheap, Captain Malloy. It goes for a premium."

"You haven't the *ton,* Mr. Graves," he said, as if I hadn't spoke, "however skillful a sailor you may be. I'll have you out of my navy."

"That's well with me, sir," I said. "I was on my way home anyway."

"I remember that sad day you sauced me on my own quarterdeck. I knocked you down for it, and I ought . . . What was that? You say you're on your way home?"

"I'm done with the navy, sir. I calculate to try my luck running goods down the Ohio and Mississippi. I was all set to cut on out, too, when Commodore Gaswell sent word he wanted me to track Peter down on the sly. I only done it as a favor to the old gentleman. He's been kind to me." Malloy was of an age with the "old gentleman," and he gratified me by setting his jowls all a-quiver. Even the dog couldn't stand it; he hopped down and whizzed on a leg of the settee.

"Good boy," I said. I held out a finger, and he came over to lick it.

"Is that how you resolve yourself, sir?" said Malloy. "You ease yourself by flying from your troubles? The service is better off without you, Mr. Graves." He got up and pulled his handkerchief out of his sleeve. "Yes, do you abscond to the frontier. You will find it easier to lose yourself among the savages than to stay where the eyes of your betters are on you." He got down on his knees and mopped up the puddle. The dog went over to him and wagged his tail. Malloy scrunched down to let him lick his face.

"I'd a-larruped him a good one for slicking up the deck like that," I said.

"You are not I," said Malloy. He'd gotten tarnal quiet for no reason I could fathom. It was almost eerie, the calm he had on him.

"The commodore wanted to keep it quiet what Peter done, I guess," I said. "But if you want to wave it around and call attention to it, you go right ahead. I ain't a-goin' to stop you."

He stared at me like a chicken eyes a bug. There was a power of dignity in the Old Woman, even on his knees with a piss-rag in his hand. "Stop me? You, *stop* me?"

"No, I said I *ain't* a-goin' to stop you. I'm throwing over my commission. Then you won't be my superior officer anymore, and I'll be able to call you out. What d'ye think of that, Captain Malloy?"

He sat back on his heels. "I think you haven't a commission to 'throw over.' You still resent me for knocking you down. Surely it was a year ago by now. It will eat you up if you let it." He took the wet handkerchief into his quarter galley. "I repent of it," he called from behind the door, "if that mollifies you." There was a muffled splashing as he wrung the cloth into the head. He came out without it, and rinsed his hands at a ewer and basin in the corner, watching me over his shoulder. "No, don't get that sneering look in your eye, young man. My repentance is not born of fear, any more than is my contempt for dueling. Tell me, have you ordered any floggings since you've had your little command?"

"Maybe."

"I can't hear you—you have your head down. How many?"

I squared my shoulders and looked him in the eye. "I disremember, sir." That was a lie. I'd never forget the look of dumb patience on Hawkins's face as Horne tore his back open.

Malloy settled into the settee again. The spaniel stood on his lap and licked his chin. "I'll wager you flogged at least one man and found you didn't like it."

"No, sir, I don't guess I did like it."

"Do you know why that is?"

He toyed with the dog's ears. The dog stared at him with melting eyes, and I got an unsettled feeling as I realized that something loved Asa Malloy.

"I'll tell you why it is, Mr. Graves. When you flog a man, it's because you have failed. Failed to keep order, failed to hold the men's respect, failed to lead. I myself have not had a man beaten since . . . well, since that incident that first drove you and me apart. We got on well before that, I do believe."

"Yes, sir, I remember. You learned me my sines and cosines so's I could keep 'em in my head. You told me about Al-Jayyani the Moor, too, but I never could grasp spherical trigonometry. I like a triangle to have a hundred and eighty degrees and no more."

He smiled fondly, the indulgent schoolmarm. "You and Dick Towson were both charmed by the Indian maiden, Princess Sohcahtoa, as I recall. A lovely mnemonic, that."

"I guess it's a bit more genteel than *Oh hell, another hour of algebra.*"

He laughed. "I hadn't heard that one."

"Sure, sir: O-H-A-H-O-A, for *opposite, hypotenuse; adjacent, hypotenuse;* and *opposite, adjacent*—"

"With *sine, cosine,* and *tangent* understood," he finished for me. "That isn't bad. I tell you, Mr. Graves, I had a mind to—well, never mind what I had a mind to. Now that I've seen the *Tomahawk,* I find she's really not what I had in mind."

That stung. "She's a good sea boat, sir. Sags to leeward a bit, I allow, but she's nimble as a cat with eight lives gone. I sank a frigate and captured a sloop in her."

He laughed again. It was the kind of indulgent chuckle that usually gets my pelt up, and it near about irked me into telling him so. But then he said, "Don't allow your indignation to become more important than getting what you want, Mr. Graves. I relinquish the *Tomahawk* to you. You may console yourself that it be not the milk of human kindness that motivates me, but a desire that the *Breeze* and young Mr. Peebles not disappear on my watch. I turn over responsibility for them to you."

"That's easily dealt with, sir. I have a good bosun's mate and quartermaster that will carry her home safe."

"Oh, nay, for shame," said he, "to deny the young gentleman his chance. Mr. Peebles will sail her, or I withdraw my offer."

"You said, sir, that you repented of your ill-will toward me."

"Repentance is for the benefit of the trespasser, Mr. Graves, not the trespassed against."

He looked like as if he'd given me the key to his house when he said it. I went away smirking knowingly, with no idea what he meant.

EIGHTEEN

Gundy was a dark shape against the water tier down in the hold. The air was close in there, and I resisted the urge to climb out and direct him from the lower deck. I held the lantern in front of me, the deck above my head being too low to allow me to hold the light up. My shoes were soaked. The keelson was awash, and I could hear water lapping below the floor planks.

"What do you mean it's all run out?" I said. "Looks more like it's coming *in.*"

"Nay, that all be sweet water, zur." He held up a dripping hand. "Give 'un a taste."

"No, I'll take your word for it." The barrels were laid on their sides, of course, and slow fat drops dripped from their middles. I held the lantern close to the barrel tops. "They've been started. Look at the pry marks."

"That be traison!" he said.

"Not if it weren't one of our own, it ain't."

"Ooh arr. Then I reckon Manson or Jakes did it, zur. One of the mutineers."

I shook my head. "No, we'd've noticed it in the trim afore now."

He clucked his tongue against his teeth. "I reckon 'ee art right, zur, but it were zo gradual I never noticed."

"Was that Frenchman ever down here?"

"Perhaps 'ee were, zur, but 'un means nothing now. What us'n got topsides idden enough vor gettin' home with."

Which wouldn't have mattered at all if I'd remembered to rewater before we left Birds Island.

With the sun in the east behind a twist of silver clouds and a damp wind spitting down from the north, we dropped anchor in three fathoms water a quarter mile off the western shore of Salt Key in the Turks Islands.

"There bein't a drop of water here except as can be bought, zur," said Gundy. "And they salt-rakers get begrumpled if 'ee even ax 'un to sell."

"I don't aim to ask 'em." I took my glass and ran aloft.

I didn't dare come any closer yet, with coral all around and the morning sun in my eyes. Salt Key is an inverted right triangle, about three miles long on the southeastern hypotenuse, with an additional mile or so of thick coral reefs thrusting out from the southern and northeastern tips. The land is low and rocky, with a scurfy thicket of pines topping a cluster of limestone bluffs in the northwest corner, and a stretch of mangroves showing as a dull green ribbon along the sheltered southeastern shore.

From up in the fore shrouds I could see a smaller island to the northeast and a larger one to the north. The smaller was named Cotton on the chart and didn't look to have much on it but birds and rocks. The larger, Grand Turk, held an on-again, off-again settlement called Cockburn Town, several saltpans, and a huddle of stone huts for the salt gatherers, or "rakers." The islands stood on a shoal that rose suddenly out of the dark blue deep, about seven miles across from east to west and about twenty miles from the northern tip of Grand Turk to the jumble of rocks and coral that made up Sand Key in the south. The shoal wasn't but nine or ten fathom in the lowest parts, rising up to within a few feet of the surface in places along the eastern edge, where there were three more small islands; but the sea over it was so transparent and the sand of its bottom so white and fine that I couldn't have guessed its depth at a glance—where it was free of rocks and reefs, anyway. A particularly long reef ran along the south side of Grand Turk, extending down almost to the north shore of Salt Key, the near island.

I hadn't given Salt Key much more than a squint to make sure there wasn't anyone home, but now I ran my glass across it a bit more carefully. In the great stinking saltpan that filled its southern angle, a bunch of persimmon-headed flamingos moved back and forth amid a shifting gray mist of brine flies. On the near shore of the island stood a few limestone huts. No smoke came from them, no movement except for a haunted-looking cat slinking along the roofs. The huts were deader than last week's salt cod.

The bluff at the northwestern corner of the island hid us from any eyes on Grand Turk as we made our approach. The salt-rakers habitually cleared out for Bermuda by that time of year, and there weren't any salt boats or whalers on hand, neither; but you never knew who might be sneaking around.

"Watch for any ships," I said to O'Lynn, perched above me on the topsail yard. "And keep an eye on Cockburn Town over yonder, too. Give a holler if a boat puts out."

I took the dignified route down the ratlines rather than slide down the forestay. My trousers were getting to be as tarred as any foremast jack's.

"Gundy," I said, stepping onto the quarterdeck, "hoist out the boat and put the barrels in her."

The barrels would weigh a good two hundred and fifty pounds apiece when they were full. A bosun would know how to deal with that.

The *Breeze* had hove-to in the deep water offshore, about half a cable's length off our larboard quarter. I stepped to the rail with my speaking trumpet. "Ahoy, Mr. Peebles!"

The boy waved his hat. "Sir!" His voice was thin from distance, and the wind whipped it away almost before I could hear it.

"Come to an anchor and send over Mr. Horne!"

"Aye aye, sir."

Peter and Corbeau stood behind him, as if they'd stopped in the middle of jawing about something. Probably talking French, too, they being the only men in the *Breeze* that understood it. Peter had his hands clasped together in front, which wasn't a usual posture for him.

"Here, Mr. Peebles," I called, "what're them two doing on deck?"

"Taking the air, sir."

"Is Mr. Wickett in handcuffs?"

"Yes, sir, I dasn't take them off. He says he'd have a word with you, if you're willing, sir."

"Then let him come to me," I said, as half a thought tickled the back of my mind. "Send him and Corbeau to the beach with Mr. Horne. And take off the irons—I don't want him falling overboard and drowning."

The salt-rakers had hacked or more probably blown a channel through the coral, the better to ferry their salt out to the schooners that came down from the New England fishing towns. Without Turks Islands salt there wouldn't be any salt cod, I guess—which the Spaniards call *bacalao,* which we got boiled on Fridays, and which the Spaniards are welcome to it.

The Tomahawks ran the boat up on the sand with a crunch, I stepped ashore dry shod, and Eriksson got Simpson and Kennedy and the others busy trundling the empty barrels up toward the stone huts.

The *Breeze*'s boat delivered Horne, Peter, and Corbeau to the beach, along with the seamen who rowed it. It also brought Peebles, sitting in the stern sheets with a pair of pistols in his belt.

"Mr. Peebles," I said, "what are you doing here?"

"These are important prisoners, sir," he said, sitting very straight. "Captain Malloy said that I should be particularly careful to keep my eye on them."

"Very well, then, you can sit here in the wet while you keep an eye on Mr. Corbeau and the boats."

It wasn't exactly raining yet, but the sky was boiling up, and the gusts were already plenty damp. I expected we'd all be soaked before the day was out.

"Oh, but sir!"

"It's a small island, Mr. Peebles. I doubt either one of 'em'll go anywhere without us. Now, Mr. Horne," I said, pointing my thumb over my shoulder, "get along with the Svensker and them, and see they don't drop the barrels down a privy by accident. If you need to rig a tackle, you can fetch what you need from the *Tomahawk.* No breaking into houses."

"Aye aye, sir." He set off up the path with the cheerful look a man gets when his job is mostly telling other fellows what to do.

"Mr. Wickett, a word with you, if you please. This way—there's better footing away from the beach."

"And fewer ears, too," he said, but he had sense enough to say it in French.

Peter shook his hands and rubbed the raw places on his wrists as we climbed up a low limestone embankment. A stiff breeze hit us hard enough to make the scattered raindrops sting. When we were out of earshot of the beach, he said, "So, what happens now?"

"Same as what has been happening."

"Shall we continue to speak in French?"

"Is there any point to it?"

He glanced around at the limestone barrens and pine thickets. "I suppose not."

I turned to look behind us. Peebles had gotten the boats drawn up on the sand and had moved with Corbeau into the lee of some rocks, which was well enough; and he'd let his men wander all up and down the cove, which might also be well enough. The *Breeze*'s boat carried a mast, which was unstepped at the moment. I'd have used its sail as a rain shelter, but Peebles could figure that out for himself, or not. The *Breeze* and the *Tomahawk* tugged at their anchors against the wind and waves. I trusted Gundy to see to my schooner; the *Breeze* I didn't know about, but Malloy had stocked her with some of his Constellations, and I guessed they could sail her without my help.

I said, "I'm taking you to Commodore Gaswell."

"Young Mr. Peebles seems to be of the opinion that we are going to Washington City."

"Mr. Adams and the Congress ain't due back till November," I said, thinking of how Peebles would preen in front of the quality. Then I realized it would be at least November by the time we got home again, anyway.

I looked at Peter out of the corner of my eye. He had gone from thin to downright scrawny, but there was still strength in the set of his jaw and the look in his eyes.

"Gaswell's been tarnal tight-mouthed about this whole thing," I said. "Way I figure it, he *wants* to keep it quiet. And since I doubt he could keep it quiet was he to hang you, I guess your best chance is with him."

We walked in silence a while, and then he said, "I notice that you do not wear a sword."

"All I have is that assassin's sword. Captain Malloy asked me to take it off, and I ain't been able to put it on again since."

"I thought you despised Malloy."

"That don't mean he can't be right about anything."

We found a sandy path leading inland. Low, twiggy pines lined it. They tossed and moaned in the wind. Peter tugged his hat down tighter.

"You are not, I suppose," he said, "trying in some clumsy way to do an old shipmate a favor, are you?"

My heart thumped. "Not this child."

We crested a hill overlooking the far side of the island. Below us lay a long inlet overgrown with mangroves. A crick emptied into it, but there didn't look to be enough water to wash your socks in. Loose rocks shifted under our feet. A small cascade of chalky pebbles clattered down the slope.

"The whalers'll start showing up pretty soon," I said. "Couple weeks, a man might have his choice of berths."

I turned my back to him. Down among the stone huts, Horne had found a cistern with a winch and bucket built over it, and had the men employed in filling the barrels. As I watched, they hammered the lid down on one of the barrels, rolled it aside, and dragged another into place. I couldn't see how Peebles was faring down in the cove, but all seemed well with the sloop and the schooner.

"Can you imagine me in a whaler?" said Peter, stepping up beside me. "Flensing the leviathan, boiling the blubber, lingering aloft in a crow's nest filled with straw to keep my feet from freezing . . . I would do all that if I had to. But I cannot picture myself crying out, 'Thar she blows,' can you?"

"You could be a mate, or even a captain."

He stared off toward Horne and his men, his eyes clenching against the breeze. "I believe those jobs are in short supply."

"It'd get you off this here island."

"I know nothing about catching whales." He looked down at me. "What are you up to?"

"Trying to save your neck."

"Why?"

"I feel responsible. I let the *Rattle-Snake* sink out from under us."

"You give yourself too much credit. Now, with your permission, I wish to be alone with my thoughts." He put his hands behind his back and walked away.

I took a step after him and then stopped. "Well, then, you tell me: How do I make it right?"

"You cannot," he said over his shoulder. "You cannot leave me here, because you could not explain it later, and regardless, there is simply no place for me to go. I shall take my chances with the commodore, thank you very much." He started off toward the mangroves.

"Consarn it, Peter, come back here."

"Leave me be."

"Why'd you do it?"

He stopped and spread his hands, his back to me. "I was crippled with uncertainty and melancholy. You saw how Ben Crouch presumed upon me, speaking at my own table without speaking to me first. It was not the limit of his presumption. I was too preoccupied with my own misery to realize how deeply I had sunk. I felt much as if I were slogging through a fetid swamp." He looked over his shoulder. His brows and lips twisted in a contemptuous scowl. "I proved to be shockingly weak. And then one day we had gone too far, and there was no turning back. I could slow it. I could save the good men. But I could not undo it."

"I think you're right it was shock. From losing the *Rattle-Snake*."

He took his handkerchief out and touched it to his nose and eyes.

I wanted to shake him. "Don't tell me you're suddenly going to get tender-hearted, Peter. You already told me it weren't my fault and I can't make it right anyway."

"You have hardened." He turned toward me and tucked his handkerchief back into his sleeve. "I felt a sneeze, but it seems to have passed. You may be interested to know that Captain Tingey's aide-de-camp, Mr. Crawley, tried to make me sign a confession of having mutinied against your cousin in the Bight of Léogâne. He was insufferable."

"So you shot him."

His old sneer was back. Deep creases lined his cheeks, and his nose and chin seemed to reach toward each other.

"He had the gall to attempt to brace me about it in public. I asked him to explain himself. He would not. He could not, I think, as it touched on matters that the navy finds too sensitive for the public stomach."

"So you got yourself in a snit and threw away your career by challenging him to a duel."

"I would not characterize it as a 'snit.' Regardless, it would have been my career had I *not* challenged him. No one speaks to a man who lets himself be spoken to that way."

His face had worked itself into a scowl so deep that the corners of his mouth dragged his face about halfway down his neck. He turned his back to me again.

"It was not petulance, Matty. Besides the monstrous lie of it, had I confessed to mutiny, I would have implicated you and Dick Towson and John Rogers as well. I had no choice but to refuse." He shrugged, an odd gesture for him. "Besides, it was in my nature to confront him. I cannot change that any more than you can change your skin—for which you might wish to wear gloves and a broadbrim hat, you know.

You are darker every time I see you."

I stared at a spot between his shoulder blades. "I thought that was safe with you."

"It is. Whether it is safe with *you* is another question entirely." He turned and gave me the old bleak smile. "I managed to keep the pillaging to a minimum. I realize that hardly counts, but there it is all the same. And I made sure to put the loyal Breezes in a safe place."

"Safe for them or safe for you?"

"Both. Whichever was convenient. I wished them no harm, for their sake as well as my own. I sent them on fool's errands in Washington and Norfolk. I stranded half a dozen on Tortola, and no doubt they found their way to one of the forts overlooking the roadstead. I left others here and there, replacing them with volunteers from the ships we detained. All volunteers, my band of fellows." He bent down and picked up a rock. He threw it down toward the crick. "And all dead now, too."

"Except for Freddy Billings."

"Except for Freddy. I despise children, I will have you know. But I could not chance that he would be mistreated, so I kept him on."

He started to step away again and I took his sleeve. "Crawley didn't have nothing to hold against you, nor us, neither. You should've demanded a court-martial to clear yourself."

"I saw Mr. P. Hoyden Blair at the navy office in Washington."

"Him! You talked to him?"

"I did not. I said I saw him. He was skulking out of Tingey's rooms. Scuttled away when he saw me coming."

"Talk about chickens coming home to roost." Blair the skulker, Blair the liar, Blair to whom all good things came in time.

"While he yet lives," said Peter, "he schemes to destroy us. To perjure himself would be nothing to him."

"We ought to go back and face him. Elsewise we'll never get out from under it."

He shook his head. "John Rogers is dead. Dick Towson is dead. I am destroyed."

"So why did you tell me where to find you?"

He looked at me as if from the bottom of a well. "I never did. Why should I?"

"When you brought Greybar to me at Mr. Quilty's hospital, I asked you where you'd go, and you said you'd go to live among the birds. Something like that, anyway. That's how I knew to look for you at Birds Island."

He shook his head. "No doubt I meant it flippantly, as when you ask directions of a clodhopper and he bids you, 'Ask mine arse.'"

I put out my hand again, but I might've been a feather falling on a mountain, for all the effect I had on him. He was already out of reach. I watched him striding down toward the mangroves on those long shanks of his, and I was tempted to let him alone. But I had one more question to ask. I trotted after him, and then I heard a distant pop, faint against the wind.

The shot came from down in the cove. The surrounding rise had muffled it, and I might've missed it entirely if Peter or I had been speaking at the moment; but as it was I charged down there with Peter on my heels. I expected another shot as I ran—Peebles had two pistols—but it never came. Then at last we clattered down the little bluff to the beach and I saw why. Peebles had dropped one pistol at his feet. The other he held cocked in his hand, but Corbeau had his fingers in the lock so it wouldn't fire, and the two were wrestling grimly for it. None of Peebles's men were anywhere around, and I was unarmed. It was a situation that demanded the utmost in subtlety and tact. So naturally I started blabbering the moment I saw them.

"Hold, hold, hold!"

I don't know how many times I said it, but they both looked up at my cry. Peebles had a face on him like he'd come to the edge of the world and didn't care for the view. Corbeau didn't seem any more cheerful, but he did have the presence of mind to get a new grip on the pistol. He twisted. Then he stood away from Peebles with the cocked piece in his hand. He waved it to include us all.

“We will thank you to lend us a little boat,” he said, speaking quick and low. “You have two and will not miss one for a little while.”

“You’ll have a time of it,” I said, “keeping your powder dry while you get a boat in the water.”

He hesitated, brightened. “You will do it for us!” He backed away, trying to point the pistol at me on one side and Peebles on the other, and Peter between us.

“We ain’t the only ones that heard the shot,” I said. I doubted it, but I had to say it for style. I took a step away from Peter and Peebles, off to my left. “There’s about thirty men that’s going to come down on your head in about a minute.”

“All the more reason to be quick, then.” Corbeau reached the boat, pressing the back of his leg against the gunwale. “Come, we are in the hurry.”

I kept sidling along to the left, my hands raised, palms to the fore. I didn’t know how quick or accurate he was, but I figured he could at least get his shot off before I could rush him. I eased in a little closer. “There’s that ‘we’ again,” I said. “Who’s ‘we’?”

Peter stepped forward with his hand out. “Give me that pistol.”

Corbeau smiled beautifully. The pistol pointed at Peter, but the barrel wavered and then drooped. “We should not wish the accident, eh, my friend? This Mr. Peebles has put the hole through my good coat already. I did not think he had it in him to shoot a fellow.”

“He wouldn’t stop, sir,” said Peebles.

Peter continued his advance, slowly, hand out.

Blood was seeping red on red down the front of Corbeau’s vest and britches even as the color drained from his face. He felt behind him. He found the gunwale and sat on it.

“But for why do you look so grim, my dear friend?” he said to Peter. “I have occasioned the means for our escape. We will continue our grand times, no?”

“There’s nowhere to go,” said Peter. “It’s over.” He came slowly up to Corbeau and put his hand on the lock. His fingers closed over Corbeau’s, and then he eased the pistol out of his hand.

"But I have let out the water," said Corbeau. His lips quavered. "Now is for when you say how clever I was, to get them to stop to rewater."

Peter had sat down beside him. He uncocked the pistol and put an arm around Corbeau's shoulders. "You are hurt. Let us attend to it."

Corbeau leaned into him. "You forgot to ask my parole, messieurs. I am the prisoner, whose duty it is to escape if he may."

"Of course, Iréné. Of course," said Peter, patting him awkwardly.

Peebles looked at Corbeau like he'd farted in church. "It isn't right, sir," he said.

I took the pistol from Peter and gave it back to Peebles. "Yes, well, here comes Mr. Horne and his party with plenty of fresh water, and your boat's crew wagging their tails behind them. It'd be a shame to waste this beautiful breeze. Let's go home."

NINETEEN

"Oh goodness no, madame," said Citoyen-Lieutenant de vaisseau Iréné Hubert Bontecu St. Jean-Baptiste Corbeau to Mrs. Ebeneezer Bunce of George Town. Corbeau's wound had turned out to be little more than a long streak of torn skin along his hip and side, and three weeks at sea and a fortnight in bed ashore had cured him as much as he'd ever be cured. The handsome Frenchman was in great demand in the Federal City as a cultured and exotic guest, a rare treat, a human hothouse vegetable, and was brightening up an otherwise bleak autumn day in the great oval reception room at the President's House.

"The pirates pitched their black colors into the sea when their capture was imminent, thinking they could escape prosecution that way," he continued to Mrs. Bunce. "And later the first mate, the presumptuous M'sieur Crouch, attempted to fire the magazine, but *La Flamme* had left us so little powder that when he discharged his pistol into the powder keg"—he spread his hands in a helpless gesture—"there was only enough remaining to separate the face from the head and the hands from the wrists." He gave her a little bow. "I beg Madame will pardon me if I am too descriptive."

"Oh! Oh dear! Such a life you sailors lead! How you thrill me," gasped Mrs. Bunce, fanning herself and leaning on Corbeau's right arm.

"Yes," said he. "And to think all this transpired long after the accords were signed at Mortefontaine. I am chagrined to discover we are at peace since the end of September." He transferred her with admirable skill into the care of a startled army ensign.

Captain Tingey's adjutant, Lieutenant Crawley, had found me behind one of the pillars meanwhile in the cross hall I'd been hiding in. He was gray-faced and remote, and seemed to sag though he carried himself stiffly upright, which I suppose happens when you have a pistol ball lodged in your chest. "Someone should have a word with him, Graves," he said. "We don't want him airing our dirty laundry."

"I don't have any dirty laundry, Crawley, but you go right ahead."

Though we were both lieutenants, he was far senior to me and had the ear of an influential captain; as he stared at me I began to think of how warm it was in the reception room, where a fire crackled on the hearth and the dignitaries was all crowded in together cheek to jowl, and how cold it was here in the hallway, with its uncarpeted floor and an icy draft from the unfinished big room down at the east end. But dog me if I would haul Crawley's freight for him, I was thinking, when a waiter come along with yet another glass of sherry for Corbeau. I stepped out of my haven with a sigh.

"Ahoy, waiter," I said. "Shove off." I gave him a ferocious look till he went away. I was about to haul my wind when Corbeau spotted me and held out his arms. *"Ah, bonjour, citoyen-lieutenant,"* I said, kind of pointing behind myself toward the hall. "I was just—"

"The hero of Isla de Aves," he announced, sweeping away my attempts to dodge his embrace. "I hear your commission is confirmed, and this beautiful shiny golden epaulet on your shoulder shall have a permanent home, perhaps one day to be joined by another on your other shoulder. Can it be I am the first to offer the congratulations? Such joy, then! Lieutenant Matthieu Graves: this is a name I will remember." The sweet wine perfumed his breath, but something rotten lurked beneath it. He leaned close to whisper in French. "I will remember it, for one day I shall kill you for what you have done to *La Flamme.*" He kissed me on either cheek before he let me go.

Mrs. Bunce was much too grand to acknowledge a mere lieutenant of the domestic variety, until the army ensign asked if I was *the* Lieutenant Graves, who had single-handedly destroyed a French 44 and a 22-gun ship-sloop with only a schooner and a handful of men.

"Oh, is it true?" she asked, clapping her hands in expectation.

"'Fraid not, ma'am," I said. "*La Flamme* was a 28, the smallest type of frigate. I lured her onto a reef, or she would've took us for sure. The sloop was just a single-master of eight small guns, and of less weight of metal than ourselves," but my protests were lost on her. She must have the pleasure, the privilege, of presenting the Hannibal of the Indies to her friends. Under a full press of bosom, she towed me around the crowded salon, pushing my acquaintance on Senator and Mrs. So-and-so and Major and Mrs. Something-or-other until the Hannibal of the Indies longed for a quiet room to lie in and a bottle of whiskey to press against his skull. I noticed she didn't haul me over to the low stage where President Adams and his lady wife were nodding at their guests and allowing their hands to be kissed. My guess was she didn't know them.

"Allow me to get the lady some refreshment," I said.

"Nothing so strong as your grog, mind," she said, smacking me coyly with her fan. "I know how you sailormen like to thrust an advantage, and here am I with my husband away."

I sent a waiter with a glass of sherry in her direction and slipped back into the hallway.

Crawley tilted his head toward Corbeau, who had formed another clump of first-water somebodies around him. "You didn't do such a good job of hushing him up," he said.

"I kind of liked what he was saying."

"Yes, well, just make sure he doesn't spout off about the *Breeze* and Captain Mèche and—good lord, here comes the Secretary." He slipped out to put a hand on Corbeau's elbow. They put their heads together a moment, and then Crawley escorted him into the room next door where the cloaks were kept.

Secretary of the Navy Benjamin Stoddert, in a rich blue velvet coat with silver buttons and a gleaming white neck-cloth that exactly matched the powder in his hair, strode across the entry hall, calling, "Mr. Graves! Mr. Graves, there." He accepted my bow with a nod and edged me behind a column. His eyes were black, unreadable. "Again, my congratulations on a difficult task well done. Wish the loss could have been less, though a high butcher's bill looks well in the papers. Can't make bread without grinding wheat, I guess. Was that Tingey's first I saw leaving just now with our French guest?" Before I could answer, he continued, "And if the chaff hasn't been winnowed out, then it must be plucked from the bread before somebody breaks a tooth. We found most of the marooned Breezes where a certain acquaintance of ours said they'd be, and some of them none too happy to be rescued." He allowed himself a brief smile. "Charlotte Amalie has its delights, I dare say. What do you think of the President's House?"

"Drafty and unfinished, sir. And the people got me flummoxed. I don't know what I'm allowed to say, so mostly I've just been keeping my mouth shut."

"Good. I was told you were intelligent." He pressed down on my shoulder with one hand, as if to impress me with the weight he could bring to bear, and swiveled his head around as if to see was anybody looking. In a lower voice he said, "Now, there is one more matter, another delicate matter. I refer to a certain commodity that our former comrade was said to have on board the, ah, the vessel in question. You made no mention of its whereabouts in your report."

"But I did, sir. I said I recovered some of it from Captain Browbury and the rest of it weren't in the *Breeze.* Does Corbeau know anything about it?"

"He claims not to. But we are not interested in where it isn't. Speculate on where it is, please."

"I'd guess it's buried in a certain island or got burned up in *La Flamme,* sir. Ain't no one asked the survivors?"

"If it had been transferred to *La Flamme,* I think he would have said so out of spite."

"Peter Wickett isn't a spiteful sort, sir. Cranky, yes, but hardly—"

"I was referring to Mr. Corbeau. In the meanwhile, *Columbia* will rescue what she can from the island." He let his eyes roam over the company. "Our man . . . well, this is very embarrassing, y'understand, but our man said nothing while he was in your care?"

"Mr. Wickett ain't exactly talkative, sir. We had a falling out after the *Rattle-Snake* sunk. He wrote some letters, though, which Peebles passed along to me."

"Where are these letters?"

"Probably in the *Columbia*'s mail bag, sir."

He raised an eyebrow. "You gave them to Commodore Gaswell?"

"First chance I got, yes sir."

"You made copies of these letters?"

"I sure didn't, sir. They were private letters."

"Yes, of course. Certainly a gentleman would not read another gentleman's letters, except maybe by accident."

"If he did, he wouldn't remember what he read."

"No, of course not. And he wouldn't notice to whom they were sent, either, I suppose?"

"I doubt he'd give it a second thought, sir, beyond noting that they were navy men of the first rate. One of 'em was you, as I recall."

"And one of them was you, I suspect. What did he say?"

"Nothing I didn't already know, sir. He laid out the events as they transpired. The fight in the Bight of Léogâne, I mean, sir. Mr. P. Hoyden Blair has got a wild burr up his—" The Secretary looked like he was about to be displeased with my language, and I finished, "He got a strong dislike for the both of us, sir. I imagine Mr. Wickett just wants as many officers to know the truth of it as possible."

He cocked an eye at me. "As many officers as possible?"

"I misspoke, sir. It's only a select few."

"But unless I know which are the select few, a fair and impartial trial is impossible. He's muddied the waters."

"I got faith that my fellow officers can tell humbuggery when they see it, sir. And honor, too."

"Honor, certainly. But will the public know it?" Stoddert was fast in stays. He tacked so fast I couldn't keep up with him. "We received word from Paris, as you may know by now, bringing news that accords have been signed. That will mean a reduction in the navy, of course. Congress reconvenes next Monday. I should like to remember you favorably."

"I'd like that too, sir."

"Then pray call on me. Monday would be good; tomorrow would be better. Good day, sir."

It wasn't only perhaps-not-so-friendless lieutenants who worried about their jobs, I realized as I bowed to him. The results of the presidential election couldn't be guessed at for weeks yet, and wouldn't be announced till February, but Stoddert, a staunch Federalist, might not survive a change in the Executive.

A Negro footman met the Secretary in the north entry hall, opposite the reception room, and helped him into his cloak. He saw Stoddert to the door, nodded at something he said, and glanced toward me. Then he came over to me with a look like he was about to do me a big favor.

"Mr. Graves, sir?" he said. "Come with me, please." He said something to an important-looking chap, who twitched my neck-cloth around and muttered in my ear, "Do not turn your back and do not linger."

The important-looking chap led me over to the low stage at the far end of the room where the Adamses were doling out bows. "Lieutenant Graves, who destroyed the French frigate *La Flamme,*" he intoned as I sidled past the platform. Mr. Adams's expression changed from fixed pleasantness to mild interest as I made my leg.

"Ah, Mr. Gray," said he, "I recall the action very well. It was a pleasure to sign your commission yesterday, Mr. Gray; I remember it distinctly. Good luck to you, sir." While I was thinking about what should accompany my "Thank you, your Excellency," and whether I should tell him he'd gotten my name wrong or I should just change it, I got nudged aside and Mr. Adams was inclining the presidential periwig to the next guest in line.

"Good on you, sir," said Lady Adams.

I had an impression of pink cheeks, though whether from paint or from vigorous pinching, I couldn't say, and iron hair, and eyes as dark and inscrutable as the Secretary's, and then I found myself ushered into the cloakroom. I took my beautiful new fore-and-aft hat out from under my arm and settled it onto my head, reclaimed my greatcoat, stepped grandly out the south door, and tripped over my sword on the way down the steps.

My progress was halted when I banged into a gentleman in mourning clothes, who was waiting while a footman handed his lady out of a carriage. "I beg pardon, sir," says I, picking the gentleman up. "No harm, I— Why, Mr. Towson, how d'ye do?"

"I was well a moment ago, Mr. Graves," he said, yanking his arm away from me.

"A right pleasure to see you, sir. And you, ma'am," I said, doffing my hat and making a deep leg to Mrs. Towson.

"We read of your exploits, sir," said she. By God, that woman could smile.

"And I'm terribly sorry about Dick," I said. "I didn't know until after he'd sailed that he'd tried to get me appointed to the *Insurgent.* I sent a note as soon as I heard they was sank. I hope you got it." I turned to Mr. Towson and gave him a more formal bow than what I'd gave him already. "The expediencies of the service, sir, kept me from sending a longer letter to express my sorrow at the time, and I dropped anchor at Alexandria just the other day. I beg you forgive me."

Towson stepped back like I'd smacked him. "Forgive you! After what you did to my daughter, I oughtn't even be speaking to you. On whom should my friend call, sir?"

"Whom—? Ah . . . wh-wh-what," I stuttered cleverly.

Mrs. Towson put her hand on his arm. "Now, Elver."

"'Now, Elver' nothing, woman. I'm calling him out, and I don't appreciate you—"

"See here, Mr. Towson," I cut in, "I don't know what Arabella told you. Well, I mean, it's obvious what she told—"

He shook his finger under my nose. "You'll never have the pleasure of hearing him call you 'papa.' I have said enough, you damned puppy. Allow me, madam, to pass," he said to his wife, and motioned for the footman to put the steps back beneath the carriage door.

"For shame, Elver," she said. "The gentleman had no doing in that matter. Look how the people stare." They weren't staring, her husband having had the sense to keep his voice down, but he took the hint and closed his mouth. "You know this noble boy would never shoot you," she continued, "much as you deserve it, and I'll not let you shoot him. It wasn't he who ruined Arabella. You can thank your despicable Roby Douglass for that."

"At least he'll marry her."

"They were destined for each other. Alight, sir—take the carriage—go. I have things to discuss with the gentleman."

After her husband had slammed the door and the carriage had splashed away through the mire, her expression softened. "He forgets what it is to be young. I will remind him, one of these evenings. How fine you look." She lifted the edge of my cloak to reveal my single epaulet, gleaming golden even in Washington's bleak light. "You have regained your lieutenancy. It hasn't turned to ash in your mouth, I hope?"

"No, ma'am, I like it fine."

"Oh, what dreadful ordeals you must have endured! That scar on your cheek is most heroic." She fluttered her fingers over the plaster hiding the raw stitches that pulled my lip askew. "But I am sure you are weary of ladies swooning over you. Will you take me someplace dry and tell me all about it?"

I'd been lucky enough to secure a room to myself in a pleasantly obscure frame building near the water in George Town. The neighborhood was safely unfashionable; but it was a good two miles away from the President's House, there was not a carriage to be had, and Mrs. Towson's skirts were soaked by the time we reached it.

The taproom was too crowded with gentlemen drinking toddies and cobblers for quiet company, and no place for a lady, anyway. Calling for a pot of coffee and a cake, I showed her into the upstairs parlor, deserted at this time of day and unlighted except for a low fire burning on the grate. I lingered in the doorway until the colored girl had brought a tray and a pot, and then I couldn't decide where to sit. I stood across the low table from Mrs. Towson as she poured two cups.

"Will you take sugar, Mr. Graves?"

"Yes'm."

She stirred the cups so gently that the spoon never clanked against the porcelain. She looked up as Greybar slipped into the room, hugging the wall but with his tail up. "Is that sticking plaster on his tail?"

"Yes'm. He caught a splinter sometime during the hoo-roar around Birds Island. I heard him yowl, but I didn't know till several days later it was him. He tends to make himself scarce during a fight, and for some time after as well."

"A wise beast."

He stood with his front paws on my knee and let me rub his head. "I felt some awful when I discovered he'd been wounded. I got half a mind to put him in for a Badge of Military Merit."

"What's that?"

"A little heart made out of purple silk. It says 'merit' on it. George Washington created it, but I don't think it's been awarded since the Revolution."

Greybar went to her and let her fuss over him. When I started around the low table, though, he thumpered through my legs and out of the room, the white plaster marking his progress down the gloomy hallway.

"He actually likes me," I said.

"Oh, yes, I can tell."

I held up the flask of whiskey that I'd taken to wearing in my coat pocket.

She gave a little nod and pushed her cup toward me.

"I truly am sorry about Dick, Mrs. Towson. He was a brother to me."

"I know, dear, I know." She stroked the damask of the sofa cushion beside her. "He was so happy to be called to the *Insurgent.* Said with you as master's mate, the two of you were bound for glory."

"He was one for glory, all right."

"You must alight sometime, sir." She patted the cushion again.

I picked it up and sat in its place. We drank our coffee and whiskey for a while.

"I will not pretend I was a mother to him," she said, "but . . . one *misses* people."

Her chin trembled and I offered my handkerchief. "They never go away," I said.

She took my hand and kissed my fingers, gazing at me from behind tear-dewed lashes. "Ah, me," she whispered. "My breast is filled with grief and longing, both. Whatever shall I do?"

"Well, I guess *I* don't know."

She continued to hold my hand, resting it in her lap. Her hands were smooth and soft and warm, and I could feel the heat of her thighs through the damp stuff of her dress. I examined the dregs in my cup.

"What about Arie?" I said at last.

"You don't mean you still love her?"

"I don't know as I ever did. I think after all that it may have had more to do with . . ."

"The compulsions of Venus?"

My heart was scampering around like Greybar out in the hallway. "Pretty much."

"It is no sin."

I looked at her, and she looked back at me with a frankness that I found more alarming than guns. I leaned toward her and pressed the backs of her fingers to my eyes. "Mrs. Towson, I don't know what to do."

"You have all afternoon to decide, Matty dear. Though I confess I am uncommonly damp." She withdrew her hands and rearranged her skirts. "What will happen to your friend Mr. Wickett?"

"How do you know about him?"

"Men assume women are stupid, and so they tell us the most interesting things. And I know many men. Will he be hanged?"

"Between you and me and the fireplace, I think they'll let him get away, so long as he leaves the country. It'd be pretty embarrassing to hang him after the way he saved the *Rattle-Snake* in the Bight of Léogâne and all. Despite what that son of a . . . what Blair said, ain't too many in the navy that believe him, I don't guess. Listen, I really oughtn't to be talking about it."

"Then don't, darling."

Darling. Two little syllables that I felt right down to my toes.

She'd been picking at her crumb cake, washing it down with sips of coffee. She brushed her fingers. "To go anywhere in public life, dear, a man needs enemies as well as friends. Perhaps your Peter Wickett aimed too low. You, however, you've made a good start of it. My husband knows many men in high places, which means they now know you too. I will not allow him to challenge you." She held up her hand to shush me. "Nor will I allow you to challenge him. He and I are useful to each other, and there is a great fondness between us. But discretion is the watchword. If no public insult is offered, no offense can be taken. Happily, for the moment you cannot offend him further. But you must always keep in the public eye, now, as your best defense. I am speaking of your career, of course, not your private life. Though I dare say one can be accommodating in both."

She glanced around the room, taking in the cracked paintings and scuffed gilt furniture from Colonial days. "Will you take up permanent residence in this house?"

"As permanent as a naval officer can hope for. Assuming I'm kept on, now the war's over. But if Congress decides to award head and gun money for *La Flamme,* I'll have enough for a little house in Washington. Maybe someplace well away from the government buildings. Lots can be had for as little as eighty dollars, I'm told. And there's also a passel of valuable cargo at a certain out of the way place, which I can claim a significant amount of—I've got a list. I thought of going back to Phillip's for a while, but . . ."

"But there is no freedom of movement under his watchful eye."

"Right." I took her hands again in mine, turning her soft, slender fingers under my calloused, flattened ones. I ached to kiss the tapered nails. "The way he thinks of it, the way his Pacific Brotherhood does, I'm free to do whatever I want so long as it don't hurt anybody and I'm prepared to accept the 'consequences of my actions.' He's big on consequences. Though the most painful consequence is usually having to listen to one of his lectures. I'm babbling. I'll shut up."

She laughed softly. Her breath ran over my skin like a caress. "I owe you a painting, darling. I promised I would give it to you once you had a home of your own."

"The one of the plums? I'd be honored to receive it."

"I also finished that portrait of you. It came out well, I think. Pity, because Elver is sure to throw it in the fire when we return to White Oak. So I should like to paint another—a proper portrait, in the heroic tradition." She had dimples busting out all over. "In the classical tradition."

"But Mrs. Towson, classical figures—"

"Are undraped, yes."

She was pretty as a wildwood flower when she smiled.

AUTHOR'S HISTORICAL NOTE

This isn't much of a historical note, as such notes go. I made up pretty near everything except John and Abigail Adams, and even them I stretched a bit. However, it will come as no surprise to the astute reader that they were real people. So was Benjamin Stoddert, now that I think of it, whom I know only through letters and a single portrait; Captain Thomas Tingey, late of the Royal Navy, about whom I know even less; and the unfortunate Mr. Brown, whose accident while carousing in Fell's Point allowed Dick Towson to take his place in the *Insurgent.* I'm nearly sure I manufactured everyone else, though it's possible I borrowed someone out of a history book and forgot to put him back again.

The locations in *Peter Wicked* are also real, including Isla de Aves or Birds Island, although it has changed drastically over the past several centuries. When I first began writing this book I had a beautiful map of the Caribbean, printed in London in 1797, with notes on it indicating that Birds Island was considerably larger than it is today. It mentions the scrubby vegetation that still covers parts of the island, and the stumps of trees that had become extinct on the island even then. It describes the Aves Bank and what the bottom is like and how deep it is. I wish I still had that map, but I moved twice while writing this book and a box of papers somehow went by the boards. At any rate, coral and sand have built up Birds Island again since Hurricane Allen reduced it to a pair of islets in 1980, but at less than four hundred yards long and fifty yards wide, it's still much smaller today than it was two hundred years ago. Taking an eighteenth-century mapmaker's word for anything is a dicey proposition, of course; but apparently the island was even larger when Père Labat accidentally spent a few weeks there in 1705, and he says it was dotted with guava and custard apple trees. Regardless, the Venezuelan scientists and military personnel who occupy the Simón Bolívar naval base at Isla de Aves today, to bolster claim to a broad exclusive economic zone surrounding the little blip of sand, have had to retreat to a platform raised on pilings. This may give some comfort to Dominica and other island countries that dispute Venezuela's sovereignty.

Some of the naval vessels in *Peter Wicked* were real, including the *Constellation,* the *Pickering,* and the *Insurgent.* (It was just as well that Dick Towson left the *Insurgent* when he did, as she vanished with all hands soon after.) The *Columbia* is a fabrication, but not a complete one; a forty-four by that name was commissioned in 1838 and saw action against Sumatran pirates the following January. The U.S. Navy had to wait till the twentieth century to get a *Tomahawk*—and a *Choptank,* too, for that matter—but the first was an oiler and the second was a tug. The *General Greene* served on the San Domingo station under Christopher Perry, with his son Oliver Hazard aboard as a midshipman; she was laid up in 1801 and burned by the British in 1814. There were two aircraft carriers named *Croatan* (CVE-14 and CVE-25) during World War II, but the *General Greene*'s sister ship *Croatoan,* named for the cryptic message left by the lost colony of Roanoke Island, is imaginary. The *Breeze* (or *La Brise* or *Suffisant*) never was, but the minelayer *Breese* helped sink a midget submarine during the attack on Pearl Harbor.

A number of people helped me in the writing of this book. Some of them I have never met, including Paul H. Silverstone, Christopher McKee, and John H. Harland, whose books are a continuing source of pleasure and illumination. I am particularly indebted once again to Jackie Swift for her insight, patience, and humor; and to Walter Mladina and Simon Brocas for their help with French idioms. The inevitable mistakes are my own.

B.C.
Ventura, Calif.

Glossary

aback, a sail is said to be aback when the wind presses it against the mast, driving the vessel sternward.

abaft, to the rear of a vessel.

abeam, toward or from the side of a vessel.

aft, after, toward, in, or from the stern.

alee, away from the wind.

amidships, toward or in the center of a vessel.

Anacreon, a Greek poet noted for his songs about loose living. "To Anacreon in Heav'n" was a British drinking song, written around 1770 and popular on both sides of the Atlantic; Francis Scott Key later used its tune for "The Star-Spangled Banner."

Anegada, a low island lying northeast of the VIRGIN ISLANDS and surrounded by numerous CAYS and REEFS.

astern, toward the rear of a vessel.

athwart, across.

avast, 'vast, given as a command to stop what one is doing.

bein't, be not.

belay, to make secure, as with a LINE TO A BELAYING PIN. Also given as a command to disregard a previous command.

belaying pin, a usually wooden dowel of about 18 inches long, fitted through a rail along the inboard side of a bulwark or at the base of a mast, and used to secure the RUNNING RIGGING.

battalion, under the French military system at the time, one of the three constituent units of a DEMI-BRIGADE, with a strength on paper of about 800 men, consisting of a GRENADIER company and eight FUSILIER companies.

bend, to attach securely but temporarily, as a sail to a SPAR.

binnacle, a cabinet that houses a ship's compass. It might also hold a lantern, a half-hour glass, a TRAVERSE BOARD, and a slate.

bit, an eighth of a REAL.

black vomit, YELLOW FEVER.

boarding ax, a tool resembling a hatchet with a spike opposite the blade, with a straight shaft from about a foot and a half to three feet long.

boarding net, a rope latticework meant to keep enemies from coming over the rail.

boarding pike, a short spear used by sailors.

boom, a SPAR to which the foot of a FORE-AND-AFT sail is attached. Also a pole used to push a hazard away.

bosun, or boatswain, a senior WARRANT OFFICER charged with the care of a ship's boats and RIGGING, and often with disciplining the enlisted men.

bosun's mate, a PETTY OFFICER who assists the BOSUN and flogs the men as required.

bow, or bows, the forward part of a vessel.

bowse, to lift or drag using ropes and pulleys.

bowsprit, a heavy SPAR to which the foremast STAYS and HEADSAIL gear are attached.

brace, a line attached to the end of a YARD and used to trim it fore or aft.

brail, a line used to haul the foot of a sail up or in.

brig, a two-masted square-rigger with a FORE-AND-AFT mainsail attached to the mast with hoops and extended by a GAFF and BOOM. See HERMAPHRODITE and SNOW.

broadside, a vessel's artillery considered as a whole, or the GUNS along one side, especially when fired simultaneously; also the side itself, above the waterline.

Brother Jonathan, British seamen's slang for an American sailor.

bulwark, the sides of a vessel above her WEATHER DECK.

cable, a heavy ROPE made up of several strands of HAWSER-laid rope, ten inches or more in circumference, used to anchor or MOOR a vessel. In the U.S. and British navies its length was calculated at 100 FATHOMS, which was conveniently close to a tenth of a nautical mile.

cable tier, the place in a vessel where a CABLE is stowed.

can, a tankard.

canister, a projectile made of small shot in a metal case.

Cap Français, also Le Cap, the principal city and capital of SAINT-DÓMINGUE: Cap-Haïtien (or Kapayisyen), Haïti.

capstan, a vertical WINCH, useful for moving heavy objects such as anchors.

captain, the top commissioned rank in the U.S. Navy, equivalent to an army or MARINE major, lieutenant-colonel, or colonel, depending on his seniority; by convention, the commander of any vessel. Also, the senior man at a given station, as captain of the foretop; also, an army or MARINE officer ranking between LIEUTENANT and major.

cartridge, a paper sleeve or cloth bag containing the amount of gunpowder needed for one discharge of a firearm, and, in the case of a musket cartridge, also containing a projectile.

cat, a heavy timber projecting from the bow and that keeps an anchor from damaging the vessel's side.

cat-o'-nine-tails, a whip of nine strands, each about 18 inches long and affixed to a hempen or wooden handle.

cay, or key, a low islet or shoal of sand, rock, or coral, usually with scrubby vegetation.

chains, the gear that secures the base of the SHROUDS.

chain shot, a ROUND SHOT cut in half and reconnected by a chain.

Charlotte Amalie, capital of the Danish VIRGIN ISLANDS. It is on the island of SAINT THOMAS.

clew, either of the lower corners of a SQUARE SAIL or the aftermost one of a FORE-AND-AFT sail.

close-hauled, sailing as near as possible to the direction of the wind, which in a SQUARE-RIGGED vessel is about six POINTS off. SCHOONERS and other FORE-AND-AFT rigs can point higher. Also called *on a wind.*

club-haul, to tack by using the lee anchor as a pivot; a risky maneuver that necessitates the loss of the anchor, used only in an emergency.

commissioned officer, an officer who held his rank by virtue of having been nominated and confirmed by the Senate. Commissioned officers were divided into LIEUTENANTS, MASTERS COMMANDANT, and CAPTAINS, who were on the LADDER OF PROMOTION, and SURGEONS and surgeon's mates, who were not.

commodore, a CAPTAIN appointed to command of a squadron, considered equal in rank to a brigadier general.

companion, companionway, a stairwell aboard ship.

conn, to steer or direct the steering of a vessel.

cook, the WARRANT OFFICER who supervised the cooking of the enlisted men's food. Officers usually had their own cooks.

corvette, a FLUSH-DECKED SHIP with a single row of usually less than 20 GUNS.

courses, the sails bent to the lower YARDS or STAYS; also the principal GAFF sails of BRIGS and SCHOONERS.

Creole, a French or Spanish colonial born in the Americas, sometimes but not always of mixed race; also a patois of various European and African languages, specifically the French Creole that evolved into Kreyòl, the language now spoken in Haïti.

cut-and-come-again, food left out for the convenience of the men on watch.

cutlass, a short heavy-bladed sword used by sailors.

cutter, a fast-sailing single-masted vessel, used to carry dispatches or for reconnaissance. Also, a broad ship's boat that could be rowed or sailed.

darbies, shackles.

dark-lantern, an enclosed lantern with a door for obscuring or showing the light.

deck, the flooring of a vessel.

demi-brigade, a French infantry unit consisting of three BATTALIONS and a small artillery train, with a strength of about 2,400 men.

Doc, nickname for a U.S. Navy COOK.

dogwatch, either of a pair of two-hour WATCHES, from 4 to 6 PM and 6 to 8 PM.

ensign, a large flag carried at a ship's stern to identify its nationality, and to distinguish the various squadrons of the Royal Navy. Also, an infantry SUBALTERN.

fathom, a unit of measure equal to six feet. To fathom something is to understand it.

flush-decked, lacking a raised FO'C'S'LE or QUARTERDECK.

fo'c's'le, loosely, the forward part of the WEATHER DECK. From *forecastle,* a fighting platform once carried on a warship's bow.

fore, forward, toward or associated with the front of a vessel.

fore-and-aft, trending along a vessel's centerline. Fore-and-aft hat: a bicorn worn with the points to the front and rear.

frigate, a fast SHIP of war usually armed with 28 to 50 GUNS that were carried, in theory, on a single deck, and which was meant to cruise alone as a scout or marauder.

furl, to STOW a sail by rolling it up and tying it to its YARD.

fusilier, in French armies, an ordinary infantryman.

gaff, a SPAR to which the HEAD of a FORE-AND-AFT sail is attached.

gig, a small ship's boat often reserved for the CAPTAIN's use.

grape shot, an artillery projectile made of small shot in a bag or wired around a dowel.

great gun, a piece of artillery firing shot of at least three pounds.

grenadiers, elite infantry, used to lead assaults.

grog, watered-down booze.

Guadeloupe, a French island in the Lesser Antilles.

gun, a cannon; GREAT GUN.

gunner, specifically, the senior WARRANT OFFICER charged with the maintenance of a ship's artillery and small arms.

gunroom, the cabin where the junior WARRANT OFFICERS ate.

gunwale, the topmost part of a vessel's side, so called because guns were once mounted there.

halyard, or halliard, a rope used to lower or hoist a sail on its YARD, GAFF, or STAY, or for raising and lowering a flag.

hand, reef, and steer, the minimum skills expected of an able seaman: to FURL the sails, to shorten sail, and to steer the ship.

handsomely, gently.

handspike, a wooden bar used to move a GUN laterally or turn the CAPSTAN.

hanger, a short curved sword designed to hang comfortably at the side of a man on foot; it was the edged weapon of choice among sea officers.

haul, to pull. To haul one's wind: to sail to WINDWARD, particularly to avoid an enemy to LEEWARD.

hawse, the place between a vessel's BOW and where its anchor CABLE enters the water. To cross someone's hawse: to provoke unwisely.

hawse-hole, a hole in the bow through which a mooring CABLE passes.

hawser, a three-strand rope of three-quarters to nine inches in circumference; hawser-laid rope is used in the RIGGING.

head, the foremost part of a vessel, and by extension a toilet, because sailors relieved themselves from the head. Also, the upper edge of a sail.

headsail, a sail set between the BOWSPRIT and the forward mast.

heave-to, to hold a ship in place by setting one or more of its sails ABACK; past tense is *hove-to.*

hermaphrodite, a two-master rigged as a BRIG on the FORE and a SCHOONER on the main.

Hispaniola, the large island lying between Cuba and Puerto Rico and containing the colonies of SAINT-DÓMINGUE and SANTO DOMINGO.

hogshead, a barrel holding about 63 U.S. gallons.

hoist, to raise aloft. In a flag, the part attached to the HALYARD.

jack, *Jack Tar:* a naval sailor. *Every man jack:* everyone present. *Foremast jack*: a navy enlisted man.

jackass, combining aspects of otherwise dissimilar things, as a jackass brig: HERMAPHRODITE.

jib, any of the outer FORE-AND-AFT HEADSAILS.

jib-boom, a moveable SPAR extending from the BOWSPRIT.

Johnny Crappo, U.S. Navy slang for a Frenchman. From *Jean Crapaud* ("John Toad").

jolly boat, a small rowboat with a wide stern, carried aboard a sailing vessel and used for light work.

keel, the main FORE-AND-AFT timber of a ship, to which the STEM, sternpost, and ribs are attached.

keelson, an internal KEEL to which the true keel and floor-timbers are bolted.

knot, an analogous measurement of a ship's speed, calculated by letting out a LINE knotted at certain intervals (usually 47 feet three inches) for a certain amount of time (usually 28 seconds).

ladder, a stairway aboard ship.

ladder of promotion, the theoretical route by which a COMMISSIONED OFFICER rose in rank.

larboard, to the left of a vessel's centerline when facing FORWARD; loosely, to the left.

lead, a lead weight attached to a LINE used for measuring depth; also the entire apparatus. Often it had a concave tip that could be loaded with tallow or clay for determining the composition of the sea floor.

Le Cap, CAP FRANÇAIS.

leeward, downwind.

leg, the distance sailed on a single TACK. To make a leg: to bow deeply with the forward leg extended.

letter of marque, a document authorizing a private armed vessel to seize the vessels and goods of an enemy in retaliation for alleged wrongs: a PRIVATEER. In full, *letter of marque and reprisal.*

lieutenant, in the U.S. Navy, a COMMISSIONED OFFICER ranking between a MASTER COMMANDANT and a MIDSHIPMAN. Also, a MARINE or army officer ranking immediately below a CAPTAIN.

lieutenant de vaisseau, a French grade of SEA LIEUTENANT.

line, a ROPE that is attached to something.

loo'ard, LEEWARD.

lubber, an ignorant or clumsy person.

magazine, a room where gunpowder was stowed and where CARTRIDGES were made.

main, the chief thing, as mainsail, MAINMAST. Also, SPANISH MAIN.

mainmast, the chief mast when there is more than one, or the second from the bows when there are more than two.

man-of-war, a ship belonging to a national navy and usually carrying more than 20 guns.

marine, a light infantryman belonging to a navy.

master, the commander of a MERCHANTMAN; also, SAILING MASTER.

master commandant, a sometime rank in the U.S. Navy between LIEUTENANT and CAPTAIN, akin to the British rank of commander.

master's mate, a senior MIDSHIPMAN or PETTY OFFICER, often but not necessarily an assistant to the SAILING MASTER.

mate, an officer's assistant, as a BOSUN'S MATE or a surgeon's mate; in the merchant service, an officer analogous to a LIEUTENANT. Also a shipmate, a pal.

mechanic, an artisan or machinist.

merchantman, a private trading vessel.

mess, a cabin where food was eaten, or a group that customarily ate together. The officers' messes often contributed a set amount toward making large purchases, as for livestock or liquor.

midshipman, a naval cadet. The typical American midshipman during the Quasi-War was 17 years old.

mizzen, of the sternmost mast in a SHIP.

mizzenmast, the one behind the MAINMAST.

monkey jacket, a short-tailed coat worn by junior officers.

moor, to fix a vessel in place by means of a ROPE or ropes.

mulatto, a person of mixed race, specifically half European and half African.

noncommissioned officer, an enlisted man, similar to a sergeant or corporal, appointed to his rank by the commander and charged with the regular execution of particular tasks.

paw-paw, a fruit native to eastern North America and related to the custard-apple and the soursop; also the unrelated papaya.

petty officer, a NONCOMMISSIONED OFFICER, such as a BOSUN'S MATE or QUARTERMASTER, akin to an army or MARINE sergeant and usually specializing in a particular type of task.

picaroon, a West Indian PRIVATEER of questionable legality, particularly one operating in French waters.

piece of eight, the Spanish silver dollar, or peso, which circulated widely in the Americas and was worth eight reales. In early colonial times it was commonly chopped into eight BITS, each in theory worth twelve and a half cents American (hence "two bits," a quarter dollar), but coins worth one-half to four reales were being minted by 1800.

point, the compass was divided into 32 points: north, north by east, north-northeast, northeast by north, northeast, northeast by east, east-northeast, east by north, east, and so on.

Port-Républicain, Port-au-Prince (or Pòtoprens), Haïti, during the French Revolution.

Porto Rico, the U.S. name for Puerto Rico.

post-captain, an officer holding the rank of CAPTAIN and entitled to command a SHIP of more than 20 GUNS.

privateer, a private armed vessel authorized by a government to commit certain acts that would otherwise be considered piracy; a LETTER OF MARQUE.

quarter, clemency, as in not killing a defeated opponent. Cry for quarters: beg for mercy. Also, either of the after quadrants of a vessel.

quarters, the place where a man sleeps or fights, depending.

quarterdeck, the after part of the WEATHER DECK, from which the CAPTAIN and his officers CONN the ship.

quartermaster, a senior PETTY OFFICER who helps to CONN a vessel.

quarter-gunner, a PETTY OFFICER who assists the GUNNER; in theory one was allowed for every four GUNS.

rate, status assigned to a man according to his skills.

ratlines, horizontal ropes strung between the shrouds and used as footholds for going aloft.

real, an eighth of a Spanish silver dollar. See PIECE OF EIGHT.

reef, a lower part of a sail that can be rolled up to reduce the area exposed to the wind; to shorten a sail by taking in a reef. *Close-reefed:* with all the TOPSAIL reefs taken in. Also, a chain of rocks or coral lying just beneath the ocean's surface.

reefer, a MIDSHIPMAN, whose duties included attending at the reefing of the TOPSAILS.

rigging, the general term for the ROPES used to hold the masts and SPARS up and to trim the sails; see STANDING RIGGING, RUNNING RIGGING.

rope, a LINE that isn't attached to anything.

round hat, a hat with a brim all around, rather than turned up as in a tricorne, which it began to replace around this time; it often looked like a low-crowned top hat.

round jacket, a short coat without tails.

round shot, a solid ball of iron used as a projectile.

royal, the mast, YARD, or sail immediately above the TOPGALLANT.

running rigging, ROPES used to control the sails and SPARS.

saber, a long and heavy cavalry sword, sometimes but not always curved.

sailing master, the WARRANT OFFICER charged with a vessel's navigation, equal in rank but subordinate to a LIEUTENANT.

sailmaker, the WARRANT OFFICER charged with the care of the ship's canvas.

Saint-Dómingue, the French colony on the island of HISPANIOLA. Now the Republic of Haïti.

Saint Croix, the southernmost of the Danish VIRGIN ISLANDS.

Saint John's, or Saint John, American names for San Juan, Puerto Rico. Saint John is also the name of one of the VIRGIN ISLANDS.

Saint Kitts, or Saint Christopher, a British island in the Lesser Antilles, where there was a large naval base.

Saint Thomas, the principal island of the Danish VIRGIN ISLANDS and containing the colonial capital of CHARLOTTE AMALIE.

San Domingo, American name for SAINT-DÓMINGUE.

Santa Cruz, SAINT CROIX.

Santo Domingo, the Spanish colony on HISPANIOLA. Now the Dominican Republic.

schooner, a FORE-AND-AFT-rigged vessel with a narrow hull and usually two masts, common to the North American coast and the Caribbean. Navy schooners usually carried a SQUARE SAIL on the foretopmast, and often on the maintopmast as well, to be handier before the wind.

scuttle, a porthole.

sea daddy, an experienced seaman who teaches a younger one the ropes and divulges to him a wealth of sea-lore, much of which is true.

sea lieutenant, "sea" to distinguish him from an army or MARINE lieutenant, whom he outranks.

servant, a seaman who cooked and served an officer's meals, cleaned his cabin, and tended to his clothes; also, a euphemism for "slave." MARINES might serve as MESS attendants on formal occasions.

sheet, a LINE attached to a CLEW and used to HAUL a sail taut.

ship, a SQUARE-RIGGED vessel with three masts; loosely, any vessel large enough to carry a boat.

shroud, a piece of STANDING RIGGING in lateral support of a mast.

sloop, a single-masted sailing vessel. Sloop-of-war: a warship of usually fewer than twenty guns.

snow, a sailing vessel similar to a brig except that the GAFF mainsail was hooped to a vertical spar or heavy rope, called a snow-mast or jack-mast, that was stepped immediately ABAFT the MAINMAST. The sail was usually set loose-footed.

sojer, soger, a derogatory word for a soldier, specifically a MARINE. To sojer: to perform a repetitive and often pointless task, as for punishment.

Spanish Main, the mainland of South America, and by extension the Caribbean Sea and its islands.

spar, a stout wooden pole such as a mast or a YARD.

splice the mainbrace, to have a TOT of GROG.

square-rigged, fitted primarily with SQUARE SAILS.

square sail, actually trapezoidal, but set "square" to a vessel's centerline.

standing rigging, LINES used to support masts and SPARS.

starboard, to the right of a vessel's centerline when facing forward; loosely, to the right.

stay, a FORE-AND-AFT piece of STANDING RIGGING in support of a mast.

staysail, stays'l, a FORE-AND-AFT sail set to a STAY.

stem, the upright timber at a vessel's BOW.

stern, the rear of a vessel.

stow, to lade a ship with cargo and make sure it is packed away in a manner that prevents its shifting; loosely, to put something in its proper place.

stuns'l, studding sail, a sail set outboard of a SQUARE SAIL in light weather.

subaltern, an army or MARINE officer below the rank of CAPTAIN.

surgeon, a ship's chief medical officer. Surgeons of the day were not usually physicians, who held a much higher social rank.

swivel gun, a small GUN mounted on a BULWARK and used to discourage boarders.

sword knot, a soft, braided rope wrapped around a sword's hand guard for decoration, and looped over the bearer's wrist in combat.

tack, to come about with the wind across the BOW. Also, the lower corner of a sail's leading edge. On a (STARBOARD or LARBOARD) tack: sailing with the wind on that side.

taffrail, the rail at a vessel's stern.

throw weight, the amount of metal that a gun could fire, or the amount that a vessel could fire from all of its guns in one go.

tomahawk, a narrow-bladed hatchet with a straight shaft, used as a sidearm; also, BOARDING AX.

topgallant, t'gallant, pertaining to the gear above the TOPMAST and below the ROYAL.

topmast, a mast's second section above the deck.

topsail, a square sail carried on a TOPMAST: *tops'l.* GAFF topsail: a FORE-AND-AFT topsail.

tot, a small serving of booze.

traverse board, a wooden disk pierced with holes set in concentric circles along each of eight points of the compass, and eight pegs attached to the center of the compass by twine; a peg is inserted in the board every half-hour to show the direction sailed.

Virgin Islands, a Danish colony composed of SAINT THOMAS, SAINT JOHN, and SAINT CROIX or SANTA CRUZ, and numerous smaller islands, lying east of Puerto Rico in the Leeward Islands. Also a British colony in the same group, consisting of Tortola, Virgin Gorda, ANEGADA, and other islands.

wardroom, the cabin where the senior officers ate.

warrant officer, an officer who held his rank by warrant rather than commission, meaning he was off the LADDER OF PROMOTION. Senior warrant officers included the SAILING MASTER, SURGEON, BOSUN, and GUNNER. Inferior warrant officers included the COOK and SAILMAKER.

watch, a stint on duty, usually four hours. See DOGWATCH.

watch below, the men off duty.

watch on deck, the men on duty.

wear, to come about with the wind across the STERN.

weather deck, a DECK exposed to the elements.

winch, a spindle set horizontally or vertically, used for hoisting or hauling, and stopped with clicks and pawls.

windlass, a large horizontal WINCH.

windward, in the direction of the wind.

Windward Passage, the channel between HISPANIOLA and Cuba.

yard, a SPAR used to spread the head of a sail.

yarn, a long and often intentionally preposterous story.

yellow fever, an acute infectious viral disease that occurs in the warm regions of Africa and the Americas and is spread by mosquitoes, so-called because of the jaundice that sometimes accompanies it.

McBooks Press is committed to preserving ancient forests and natural resources. We elected to print this title on 30% post consumer recycled paper, processed chlorine free. As a result, for this printing, we have saved:

8 Trees (40' tall and 6-8" diameter)
2,802 Gallons of Wastewater
5 million BTU's of Total Energy
360 Pounds of Solid Waste
675 Pounds of Greenhouse Gases

McBooks Press made this paper choice because our printer, Thomson-Shore, Inc., is a member of Green Press Initiative, a nonprofit program dedicated to supporting authors, publishers, and suppliers in their efforts to reduce their use of fiber obtained from endangered forests.

For more information, visit www.greenpressinitiative.org

Environmental impact estimates were made using the Environmental Defense Paper Calculator. For more information visit: www.papercalculator.org.